RACE TO MARATHON

The vast Persian Empire already dominates nearly half of the earth's entire population, but Persia's Great King now has his sights on Greece. *Race to Marathon* vividly imagines this key moment in history—the Battle of Marathon. The action unfolds through the stories of its participants—valiant women, fearsome warriors, and cunning leaders—woven into a fabric of intrigue and passion.

All logic is on the side of the Persians, and the fate of the Greeks seems clear: death or enslavement. But on the battlefield, shrewd intuition, a zeal for glory, and the breathtaking feats of long distance runners help the Greeks. At home in Athens, wives, mothers, and daughters wage a war of wiles against traitors who plan to help the Persians capture the city.

And the goddesses are watching.

Race to Marathon builds to a stunning end, which demonstrates that the story of Marathon is as relevant today as it was when men and women of fortitude struggled to preserve their freedom.

RACE TO MARATHON

A WORK OF FICTION
BY JAY GREENWOOD

NEW HICKORY PRESS

Published by: New Hickory Press
                Sacramento, California
                www.AncientGreecePersia.com

ISBN 978-0-692-11331-8 (hardcover)
ISBN 978-0-692-11033-1 (paperback)

Library of Congress Control Number: 2018903293

Illustrations by Ryan Scott Lewis

Book Design by Ann Amberg

Printed and Produced in the United States of America

For
Deb

CONTENTS

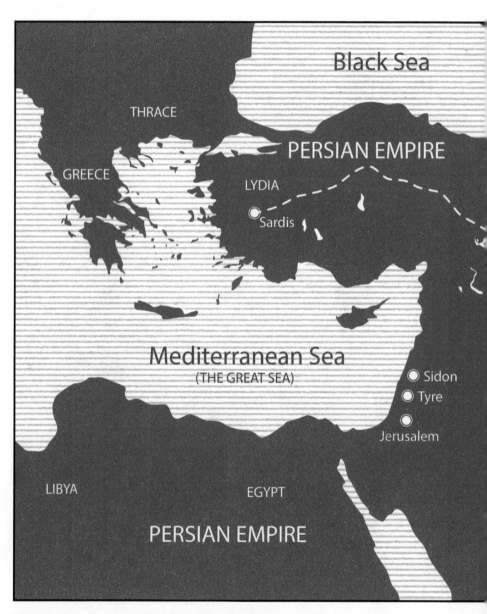

PERSIAN EMPIRE AND GREECE, 490 BC

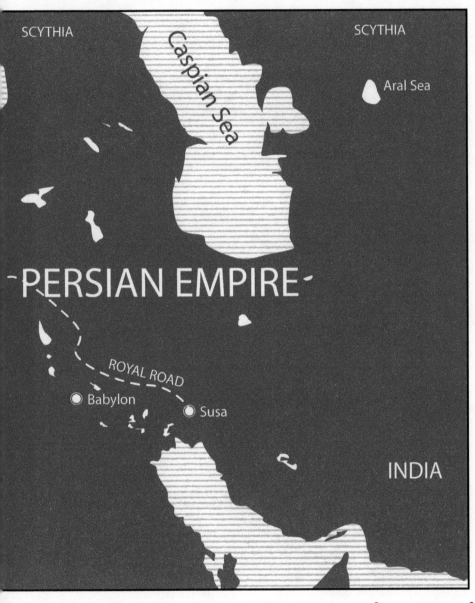

SCYTHIA

SCYTHIA

Caspian Sea

Aral Sea

PERSIAN EMPIRE

ROYAL ROAD

Babylon

Susa

INDIA

I----------------I
300 MILES

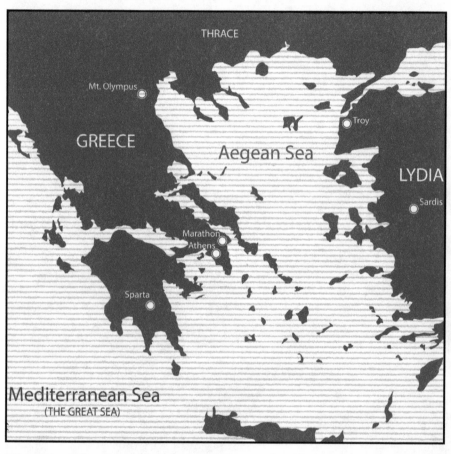

GREECE AND AEGEAN SEA, 490 BC

I--------------------I
100 MILES

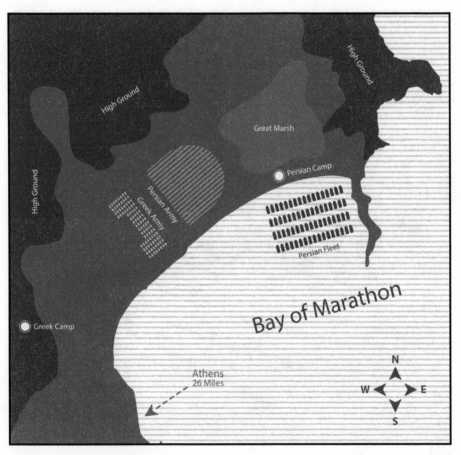

MARATHON, 490 BC

I--------------------I
2 MILES

GREEK PHALANX

IN THE BEGINNING

S he has never seen a meadow covered with so many flowers. Dashing away from her mother she goes romping across it, her hair the color of fresh corn, bouncing and waving as she runs. Every so often she stoops and picks a flower, gathering a little nosegay of yellow irises and white crocuses, pink hyacinths and purple larkspur. Her mother watches intently. She has deliberately brought her daughter to this place with the lovely name—Eleusis—with its multitude of flowers, lush, beautiful, and comforting under the spring sun despite the pool of darkness at its heart.

The little girl looks up from her flowers and catches sight of the shadowy circle in the center of the meadow. She walks toward it, stops, and stares.

From the surface, it looks like a deep puncture in the ground, created by some overwhelming force, as if a giant's fist had punched down through the flowers and deep into the earth. Curious but hesitant, she walks closer and tries to peer into it. She picks up a stone, tosses it into the emptiness, hears the rock striking the cave's walls, bouncing back and forth, down and down. There is no sound of it hitting bottom. She listens and wonders.

More cautious now, the girl inches forward to the brink of the opening. There is a strange attraction in the darkness deeper than night at her feet. She leans over to look for something—anything. Pressing her toes into the ground, she leans even farther over the gaping hole, then jumps back and drops her bouquet when someone grabs her arm. Wide-eyed, she looks up to see her mother smiling down at her.

The woman gently strokes her daughter's cheek and says, "This is the entrance to a cave of wonders. And the greatest wonders of all are at the bottom." She bends down to look deeply into her daughter's eyes. "Do you wish to go down there?"

The girl does not speak but slowly—very slowly—nods her head. Her mother envelops the girl in a gentle but firm embrace.

～◡

At the deep bottom of the cave, in utter blackness, she places her daughter on a large boulder and sits down right behind her. She raises her left hand and gracefully holds it above her daughter's head, then raises her right hand and rotates her wrist while strumming her fingers in the air. The cave fills with a dim light. When the girl looks up it seems that her mother is silently beckoning something, but what?

The rock walls around them begin to move downward, weaving and rippling like the surface of the sea. When the entwining undulations reach the cave floor, the ripples twist and coil until they all begin to move in the same direction—toward the girl. She watches, transfixed with fear; it is a gathering of dozens, of hundreds, of snakes.

The child is mesmerized as the snakes rhythmically sway and glide toward her. Then she hears her mother softly singing. It is a lullaby, a tender song sung in time to the snakes' movements. The mother is singing to the snakes, and they are dancing to her music. The girl's fear instantly vanishes; because of her mother's singing, she feels no terror even as the snakes begin to slither over her body.

They slide up the boulder in a gathering mass until the girl is entirely covered except for her face. Surprised that the snakes' skins are dry, she strokes them as they pass over her on their way to her mother. The girl looks up at her mother and is amazed; the woman is completely swathed in snakes. With her hands still uplifted, the woman's fingertips hold long stalks of grain now, which give off a golden glow. All over her hands and arms the snakes slither and writhe.

The girl looks at the snakes' eyes. Then she turns to her mother's eyes, which have become perfectly round, their eyelashes gone. Her black pupils are thin vertical slits surrounded by glossy green irises. The tip of her tongue flicks forward between her lips and then withdraws. All of the snakes' tongues do the same.

The woman lowers one hand as if in command and the snakes slide back to the floor, where they gather and slither back up the walls, stop abruptly, and freeze. After watching them go, the girl turns again to her mother, and gasps.

Her mother has become an enormous snake. As the huge snake's eyes slowly shut, the dim light fades until it is gone. The girl feels the wind rush past her as she is lifted up and out of the darkened cave.

◠

Her mother places the child down among a large cluster of bright red anemones. No longer a giant snake, she is, once again, Demeter, Goddess of Fertility and Snakes.

Demeter looks up to the sky and slowly shakes her head back and forth, making her long hair swirl and gleam in the sun. Her hair is a shade more golden than even young Persephone's. The goddess takes her daughter's hand and together they wander among the flowers until Demeter stops, lets go of Persephone, and begins a lilting dance. She sways her head in time to the music in her mind and dances in a circle around her daughter, then stops with a graceful skip, looking at Persephone with a meaningful smile.

The girl, quickly catching the idea, mimics her mother's movements, dancing in a circle around her, then stops with two skips and looks up at her mother. The goddess meets Persephone's eyes and waits for the questions she knows will come.

"Mother, when can I see the snakes in the cave again?"

"After the mortals arrive."

"Mortals? What are they? Where do they live?"

"For now, they are no more than a notion in the mind of your father. Later they'll live everywhere on earth. They'll be brave and craven, clever and foolish. They'll be born helpless and live their lives in confusion."

"Will mortals be down in the cave?"

"No. The snakes will be up here when you see them again. They'll rise to the earth's surface at my command."

"Why will mortals be created?"

"So they can worship the gods."

"Worship?"

"Persephone, you're young and need time to appreciate what I'm trying to say. But think about the times you want me near you and I'm not there. When that happens, what do you feel?"

"Sad, and sometimes confused, and sometimes afraid."

"Yes, and we call those jumbled emotions a feeling of longing. You want me near you; you long for me. That's part of what it means to worship. We gods long to be worshiped, and we want to instill in mortals a longing to worship us and therefore to be nearer to us."

Persephone pauses, looking doubtful. "But what about the snakes? Why must I wait to see the snakes again?"

"Because of your father's commands. The gods will be permitted to intervene in the lives of mortals, but not often, so I will wait until the mortals truly need me and my snakes. Zeus has said that when mortals are created, they must be granted the freedom to worship and act as they choose, and then the gods will judge them."

"What's freedom?"

Looking intently at her daughter, Demeter says, "Dear Persephone, your question is so profound that I cannot properly answer it, at least not now. Even later when you're a mature goddess the answer won't come easily. And for mortals the answer will be even more difficult. Many of them will neither understand nor appreciate what it really means to be free. And among those who do comprehend it, many will simply pretend that tending to their little lives counts more. The gods will dismiss such mortals as less worthy than even their ignorant brothers and sisters."

Demeter studies her daughter's bewilderment before lowering her voice and speaking more slowly. "Persephone, you must do your best to be patient. Think about the flowers you were picking. You were free to select which flower you wanted to keep and which to leave on its stem. You were free to choose. That is the essence of freedom—the ability to choose and the courage to act on your choice."

Demeter pauses again, uncertain whether her lesson is too difficult for Persephone. Then she says, "The ultimate test for mortals will be how they choose to live their lives, how they choose to treat one another, and how they choose to worship the gods. They'll make their own choices, and we divinities will judge them. I'll be allowed to give them gifts and sometimes affect how they behave, but only once will I use my snakes to interfere in their lives."

"When will you do that?"

"I don't know." She smiles at her daughter's innocence. "Gods and goddesses can see much of the future, but not everything. I want to use my snakes when mortals need them most. Perhaps when there is a great war."

"What is war?"

"You should put that question to your father. Long ago he led us in the war of dominion over the universe. We defeated the Titans who ruled before us."

"I almost never see Father." Persephone bends to touch a blossom of mignonette near her. "Sometimes I can't even remember what he looks like."

"Your father thinks of you often, I'm sure of that. And he—"

At a sound, Demeter looks north. The distant rumbling grows louder until the powerful pulsating noise booms directly overhead. Then the din abruptly stops. Wide-eyed, Persephone looks up to the sky.

"Your father," says Demeter, with a reassuring smile. "He sounds pleased. Always remember, Persephone, that whenever you see the sky, he is there. Zeus watches over you even when you don't feel his presence."

Persephone purses her lips in a defiant pout and says in a quavering voice that belies her words, "I'm not afraid of that noise! I want to see Father. And I don't want to wait so long for your snakes to come up here. I want to touch them again and hold them in my arms."

Demeter's smile is tinged with sadness. "You won't have long to wait. And while you wait, you'll grow from a child to a young goddess. Far more time will pass for the mortals. A single year for a god will be many millennia for them."

"I don't understand."

"I know. Just be happy you will never be a mortal. They'll be confused creations, and most of them will remain confused all their lives."

CHAPTER ONE

THE TYRANT RETURNS

Leaning on the ship's railing, the Tyrant of Athens works his jaw like a bad-tempered bull chewing its cud. His old-man teeth are loose, and his breath reeks like sodden compost. He watches the horizon that Helios, the sun, is about to sink below. Then he flares his nostrils so he can suck more air in and out until it makes him dizzy.

"After all these years," he mutters to no one, "I smell it again, the land of the Greeks." The air carries the sweet fragrance of mignonette.

Datis, the Persian commander, approaches him from the ship's stern. A gentle wind bellies out the rectangular sail above them. From below they hear the regular drumbeat setting pace for the oarsmen. Clusters of seamen and soldiers in gaudy uniforms stand around the deck. The ship rolls slowly from side to side as it moves ahead.

"So, Hippias, my good Greek guide." Datis is speaking in the workmanlike Greek he picked up as a boy in one of the Persian Empire's coastal cities. "I'll wager I know what you're thinking. It's been many long years since you were ruler of Athens, and in a few more days, you'll be back on your throne."

The two men are a study in contrasts. The Persian is half the Greek's age, in his forties to the older man's eighties. Datis' hair and beard are entirely black without even a hint of gray, whereas the old man's thinning hair is laced with silver. The Persian's beard is cut straight as a square across the bottom, and its tight curls glisten even in the sunset. The Greek's beard is a scramble of willful curls.

The Persian, with his protruding forehead and thick, dark eyebrows above a hooked nose, looks like he is brooding all the time. His loose shirt and pants are red, with wide blue and yellow vertical stripes from neck to ankle. His clothes are flamboyant compared to the Greek's simple white tunic.

"I didn't have a throne," says Hippias. "That's not the way in Athens."

"Ah. So many differences between Persians and Greeks."

Hippias gives the Persian commander a sharp look.

"Though yours was a harsh rule, I'm told," Datis continues.

Hippias sneers. "When the common people act like children with no discipline or respect, a ruler must be stern. They made me so. It was for their own good."

Both men pause. The rhythmic rowing of nearly ten-score oarsmen moves the ship through the twilit sea.

"Soon enough it will be as it was, with or without a throne," says Datis. "But this time you'll be more than the Tyrant of Athens. You'll be the Great King's satrap of all the lands of the Greeks—a reward for your submission."

Hippias scowls at this tactless reminder of his humiliation when he knelt before the Persian king with an offering of earth and water in return for the king's help in returning him to power.

"But right now, I wager you're thinking about vengeance," continues Datis. "Am I right?"

"Most of the time you'd be correct, Commander. But you'd lose this wager. Right now, I'm thinking about the men I'm going to reward. My old friends in Athens, men who will open the city's gates as if they're prying open an oyster, to let your soldiers in. My friends don't want chaos; they might end up on the wrong end of a spear. The sooner your men get into Athens, the better. Then we can pick and choose who we send to the Underworld. And how we send them."

"I can see the pleasure in your thoughts but we shouldn't get ahead of ourselves." Datis peers toward the west. "You said we should land at night.

You said you could guide us there blindfolded. Well, you'd better be right, Tyrant of Athens. Night's blindfold is about to cover the sky." Datis looks above them, past the sail, to where the dusk is furling into darkness. "Once we're ashore, we'll do what must be done, with or without friends opening Athens' gates."

"They'll open the gates."

"Your promises are about to be tested."

Hippias looks away for a moment, and then back at the commander.

"Last night I had a dream. I was lying in my mother's arms, like a newborn babe. The meaning is clear. Athens is my mother and now I'm returning."

"Is that the interpretation of the Magus?" Datis sounds skeptical.

"I'm in service to your king, but still a Greek," snorts Hippias. "I need no pious priest to explain dreams to me. Unlike you Persians, we Greeks don't run to priests ten times a day asking permission to blow our noses."

"But you have oracles."

"Ah, oracles help us understand the most difficult questions. But they don't run our lives. Greeks despise self-righteous finger-waggers."

"You're giving me a headache again, Greek."

Hippias shrugs and thinks: *Never argue with a fool, especially when he commands an army that will bring you back to power.*

A soldier steps out of the twilight. "Commander," he says in Persian, "the reconnaissance boats are ready to depart."

Datis and Hippias cross the deck and walk back to the stern, where three small boats are tied up, dancing in the mother ship's wake.

"You're sending the men with the best eyes?" Hippias asks, peering over the bulkhead at the scouts.

"They have eyes like a raptor's. When a killer-bird dives with its talons extended, men with normal eyes can't see the prey until the blast of feathers. My men can see it all from beginning to end."

Datis turns back to the boats, gives the order to depart, and waves them off. The boats then plunge away from the ship toward the dark line of shore.

Hippias and Datis have gone over this point many times: When the men in the reconnaissance boats get close to shore, they will need to watch for Greek signal fires in the hills. Those fires will be on the other side of the hills, invisible from shore, so the Persians with the best eyes will have to scan the sky just above the hills for any hint of dimming or flickering of the stars.

"Though I still worry about runners," Datis mutters as the boats fade into the dusk.

"Running to Athens is almost impossible in the dead of night," Hippias replies. "It would take at least five hours, on rocky trails over steep hills. And all the Greeks know a run like that is worse than dangerous with a good chance of a fall that will break a man's neck. Besides, they are spread thin; they know we're coming but they don't know where we'll land and they can't watch everywhere. By the time they figure out where we've come ashore, we'll be on them."

They are both silent for a while, contemplating the gathering darkness.

Datis finally says, "I think you should reconsider a throne; you will look good sitting there. I can see you on an ornate chair of solid gold, wearing a golden tunic, or maybe the tunic should be purple. That's an image to make sure the Greeks give you the respect you'll deserve. Don't you agree?"

Hippias does not answer. He does not even hear the question. He has lost himself once again in the thoughts that so often consume him. He catches another passing scent of mignonette.

He sees the scene so clearly in his mind. There will be chaos as the Persians slaughter the Athenians and any other Greeks who try to help them. But after that there will be order and calm. His subjects may not respect him, but they will fear him. And because of their fear, they will sing loud songs of praise. When fear and disrespect confront each other and fear wins, praise for the mighty ruler follows. As it should. As it must.

Hippias glares down his nose at the dark sea, blurred by the swirling in his head. His time has finally come again. The Tyrant of Athens has returned.

CHAPTER TWO

COUNTERPLOTS

Running over two hundred and twenty-five stadia—twenty-six miles—in the dark.* Running as if he is being chased by the God of the Underworld. Death breathes on Sicinnus' neck, pacing him step for step, waiting for a mistake—one stumble and fall and the runner's head will hit a rock hard enough to split his skull. His body will writhe for a few moments as Hades plucks away his soul.

His friend Phidippides, the supreme distance runner among the Greeks, calls him the finest runner in Athens—after himself, of course. No one can know for sure because Sicinnus is a slave and slaves do not compete in sports against free citizens.

Sicinnus has almost finished his run, with no mistakes. He can just make out torchlight atop the walls of the city ahead of him. He needs to be careful for just nine more stadia—barely more than a mile.

The moon rides pale in the eastern sky. Hades is still watching.

~～

Just outside the walls of Athens, northeast of the city, two lifelong friends in their mid-thirties stand close together. It's late at night. Aristides, tall and spare, is balding prematurely, which is why he keeps his dark brown beard and the sides of his hair long and shaggy. Many view him as the most honorable man in Athens—though some say the most self-righteous—and often refer to him as "Aristides the Just." His old friend Themistocles stands

* The ancient Greek measurement of a 'stade' is approximately 610 feet.

12

beside him, slightly shorter and more solidly built. His light brown hair and beard are cut short. Large, inquisitive eyes grace his round face. Most consider him handsome, with a deceptively calm and youthful expression.

"As you know, my fearless friend, I'm not easily impressed," Aristides is saying. "But I must say you were inordinately persuasive in front of that plethora of people in the Assembly this morning—helping convince a majority that when the fighting comes, we need to meet the Persians on the battlefield and not wait behind the city's walls. I'm sure Miltiades will praise your verbal acrobatics when he gets here."

"A plethora of people," repeats Themistocles, shaking his head.

Aristides chuckles. "I often forget a man who doesn't appreciate music tends not to savor the subtleties of alliteration."

"Aside from the fact you're a pompous ass, do you know how else we differ?"

"Interesting question. I'm good with numbers, but I don't think I can count that high."

"Then I'll tell you. Your fancy words with so many parts . . ."

"They're called syllables."

"I know what they're called . . ."

"Of course you do," Aristides interrupts again. "Perish the thought. My pardon. Proceed, please."

"Men listen to me because my words make sense and my meaning is clear. Not like your pretty words that make them glance at each other and wrinkle their lips."

"Perspicuity," says Aristides.

"*What?*"

"You're claiming to be perspicacious."

Themistocles snarls, beginning to lose patience, "I'll tell you what I claim!" But then he points toward the city walls. "Here comes Miltiades. Thank the gods, every one of them. I'm saved! If this conversation went on much longer, I'd start drinking my wine undiluted."

"An awful thought, given the rotgut you so dearly love."

"Now that's better. 'Rotgut' is my kind of word. You'll get the hang of it, someday, maybe."

With his typical swagger, Miltiades struts up and grasps Aristides and Themistocles by their arms to greet them. Second-in-command of the Athenian military, he is more than twenty years older than the two men. His short hair is flaming red, his long beard a mixture of rust red and iron gray.

Though an Athenian by birth, Miltiades had spent much of his adult life ruling a far-off Athenian colony in southern Thrace that bordered the Persian Empire. When the Persian King Darius the Great threatened the colony, Miltiades aligned himself with him. Later he demonstrated his capacity for duplicity by abandoning the Great King when it appeared Darius would be killed in combat. Darius survived, and when Miltiades found himself on the wrong end of the Great King's wrath, he promptly headed back to Athens and brought his knowledge of Persian military tactics with him.

"Well, you did it," Miltiades exclaims. "Congratulations! You both deserve a monument. If the Assembly had voted to keep the army behind the city's walls instead of going out to face the Persians head on, we'd have been doomed."

"Miltiades," says Aristides, "you know more about the Persians than any of us; the whole Assembly is well aware of that. I'm sure I speak for Themistocles too when I say we're proud to have supported your cause. But you would have handily won this morning's debate even without us."

"Maybe," Miltiades says with a shrug, "but you know how hard it is to deal with the Assembly. With citizens throughout Attica coming into the city for safety, the number of votes needed for a quorum, not to mention success, keeps growing. On top of that, there's the constant maneuvering for advantage among the tribes—and within them, too. But when it became clear that both of you and your tribes fully backed our plan to leave the city and fight in the open, the vote was guaranteed."

Aristides nods. "So we'll march with nine thousand hoplites as soon as we confirm when and where the Persians will land?"

"Yes, and Plataea will send another thousand. With the Plataeans, we'll be ten thousand strong."

"And how many Persians, do we guess?" asks Themistocles.

"Don't know," says Miltiades. "Yet."

Because they cannot answer this critical question, the men's silence stretches out until Miltiades and Aristides look up, startled, and gasp. A ghostly image has emerged from the darkness. The muscular figure of a huge man, naked except for a bronze helmet covering his head, face, and neck, starts marching in a circle around the three of them. The eye holes of the evil-looking helmet are glowing with a blazing light. The apparition's stomping abruptly halts and he turns to face the men. He clenches his fist, brandishing it at Themistocles, and shakes his head back and forth so his sinister helmet seems alive. Then the image evaporates.

Miltiades and Aristides look at each other, aghast, while a befuddled Themistocles looks back and forth between them.

Miltiades unconsciously takes a step backward and mutters, "The God of War, Ares."

"Why was he pointing at Themistocles?" Aristides sounds uncharacteristically worried.

"What in Hades are the two of you talking about?" asks Themistocles.

"You didn't see him?"

"Who? I saw nothing, and I don't want to spend time listening to the two of you losing your minds. We have life and death issues to deal with."

Aristides looks more closely at his friend. "If you'd seen what we just saw you wouldn't be so quick to dismiss this. There is an important message here—an omen—and it relates directly to you."

"Piss on your omen," growls Themistocles. "We're here tonight because the Persians are about to invade our land and kill our people. That's our priority, not some imaginary omen."

Aristides snorts back, "We just saw the God of War up close, and he was focused on us, mainly you. And your immediate response is 'forget it'? You're the one whose mind is going flaccid."

Themistocles opens his mouth to yell, but Miltiades intervenes. "Themistocles is right. Regardless of Ares' message, we don't have the time or ability to figure out its meaning. We must stay focused on the invading Persians and what we need to do."

"This is all too strange, but I'll abide by what you say, at least for now or until we understand what just happened," says Aristides. "Let's go back to how we deal with the Persians. What we need to know now is when and where we will fight."

"And *how*," says Themistocles. "We have no experience with anything like this. Our fathers had no experience like it either, or their fathers." Turning to Miltiades, he adds, "I don't see how we beat them."

"As usual you're thinking far in advance," says Miltiades. "Maybe too far. Besides, I asked the two of you to meet me here tonight to confer about a more immediate issue. Aristides, when Themistocles and I talked yesterday, he made a prediction I want you to know about so the three of us can think and act as one. Themistocles, tell him."

"I reminded Miltiades of a few things we all know," Themistocles says, turning to his old friend and rival. "The most important being that treachery is among us, as always." Aristides is tempted to look at Miltiades, the most accomplished betrayer among the three, but he resists the impulse and stays focused on his friend's face and voice. "Which is why the troops must leave Athens instead of waiting for some traitor to betray the city. We also know the old tyrant Hippias is guiding the Persians, and they'll think they have the advantage because we're not supposed to know where they'll invade. But then I told Miltiades something he didn't know—the exact beach where Hippias will guide the Persians."

"Really?" says Aristides. "Sounds like you've been seeking the advice of oracles, which you're not prone to do."

"Ask yourself the right questions and oracles aren't necessary. You remember the mind of Hippias, don't you?"

"Only too well. I'm amazed the gods still let the son of a whore live."

"Ah, 'son of a whore,' that's also my kind of talk."

"Pardon?" says Miltiades.

"Nothing, my mind wanders," says Themistocles. "As I was saying, the thinking of Hippias—do you remember, Aristides, his superstitions and fascination with prophecies?"

"He was always making odd connections with past events he thought could predict the future," says Aristides.

"Exactly," says Themistocles. "Now, my lifelong friend, I have two simple questions. First, who was the Tyrant of Athens before Hippias?"

"His father, of course."

"And his father struggled to maintain power; he was ousted and exiled twice," says Themistocles. "Then, when his father successfully invaded us a final time, his friends betrayed Athens by secretly opening the city's gates to him. My question—when Hippias' father made that last invasion to secure his power, where did he initially land on our shore?"

Aristides takes some time before responding, but the slow nodding of his head shows he knows the answer. Turning to Miltiades, Aristides points a thumb at Themistocles and says, "We're listening to a man with an adroit mind. Hippias will guide the Persians to where his father landed with such fruitful results. It will also give the Persians a perfect place for all their horses, a good harbor to disembark, and plenty of pasture and fresh water. As well as a route, though a bit off the beaten way, to Athens. A very clever choice and not one we would have naturally supposed." Then to Themistocles. "Am I correct? Do you mean Marathon?"

Themistocles smiles and nods.

"Their landing could be anytime now," says Miltiades. "When I realized the import and likelihood of Themistocles' prediction, I immediately sent more men to watch Marathon and . . ."

"Hold, look there," Aristides interrupts, his voice hushed.

The men look where Aristides is pointing and see the silhouette of a man running headlong toward them in the darkness.

"It's Sicinnus," says Themistocles. "Look how his legs kick out; I call him 'crazy legs.' Miltiades asked me to send him to Marathon and reinforce the runners already there. He just went up yesterday."

The three men trade glances.

Sicinnus slows to a stop just short of them, and his body heaves; this is the first time he has stopped since he began his dead run from the hills above Marathon.

Sicinnus is strikingly handsome. Thin and muscular, he is twenty-four but looks younger. His curly black hair is cut short and he is beardless. When women take a second look, they often widen their eyes and raise their eyebrows. Men tend to be less approving; how strange not to have a beard. But the opinions of others make little difference to Sicinnus. He cares about what his wife wants. Lela wants his face smooth.

"Sicinnus, your report," says Themistocles. "You can speak to the three of us as if you're talking to me alone."

"Persian reconnaissance boats—" Sicinnus gasps.

"How long have you been running?" asks Miltiades.

"About three hours."

"All the way from Marathon, at night?" says Aristides. "That's impossible."

Glaring at Aristides, Themistocles growls, "If he said his run was three hours, it was three hours." Looking back at Sicinnus, Themistocles says, "Come closer and stand with us."

Themistocles studies his slave for a moment and says, "You look worse than exhausted, Sicinnus. Are you all right?"

"I'm fine," wheezes Sicinnus.

"You don't look fine. Need anything? Water?"

"No, I still have water . . . I don't dare drink more yet."

"I understand. You're young and invincible and pigheaded."

Sicinnus, still wheezing, lowers his eyes and says nothing. *Like my master,* he thinks.

Miltiades leans toward the exhausted slave. "Did the boats land?"

"Yes . . . I waited for them to arrive . . . then started my run . . ."

"Don't speak more till you've caught your breath," Themistocles orders.

The three men wait impatiently until the runner, taking deep breaths, is finally able to speak easily. Sicinnus gives his master a grateful look.

"What about the main ships?" Miltiades finally asks.

"Before the sun went down," Sicinnus says, "I saw a very large number of warships and barges holding a distance offshore."

"A very large number," Themistocles repeats. "How large?"

"I can't be certain."

"I know how you hate to say anything that is not absolutely accurate, but I want you to guess. Tell me about the warships. Were there many triremes?"

"Yes."

"And roughly how many—dozens?"

"No. More like," Sicinnus pauses, out of fear of not being believed, "hundreds."

"Hundreds of triremes!" gasps Aristides.

Maintaining his focus on Sicinnus, Themistocles says, "How many hundreds? Their total number of warships—forget the barges for a moment—what is your estimate of all their triremes?"

Again Sicinnus pauses, looking intently into his master's eyes.

"Five hundred. Easily."

Themistocles jerks back at the same time Miltiades steps forward.

"How many barges?" asks Miltiades.

"As many as the triremes."

Shaking his head, Miltiades says, "Far more than they need for supplies. How well could you see them, the barges?"

"Not well, but I saw the reason you're shaking your head."

"Warhorses?" asks Miltiades.

"Yes—many hundreds. Beyond hundreds."

Shaking his head again, Miltiades mutters, "I knew they would come, but I hoped not so many."

"A moment ago you said I was ahead of myself wondering how we're going to fight the bastards," Themistocles growls at Miltiades. "Our valor may be superior, but it won't be enough. We'll figure out how to fight them, or we'll die and our people will be killed or enslaved."

"Yes, yes, you're right," says Miltiades. "But let me finish talking to your man. Sicinnus, you say the main ships had not landed before you started your run. Are there enough good runners to bring us word about the Persians' next moves?"

"Yes, the reinforcements you sent will ensure that."

"And you lit no fires while watching the Persians before you started your run?"

"Not one, just as you and Themistocles instructed."

The four men pause. Sicinnus takes a quick swig from his water pouch, now that it's safe for him to drink.

"So," says Aristides, "the invasion is happening as we speak."

"Sometimes the weather is very different at Marathon than here. How was it there?" Themistocles asks.

"There was a gentle breeze with no sign of change when I left."

"Perfect for an easy landing," says Themistocles.

"The gods aren't with us," Aristides adds.

Themistocles shakes his head. "One day without wind at Marathon tells us nothing about the gods. If they care anything about any of this, they'll wait to see what we do. And whatever we do now, with or without the gods, will determine whether we live in freedom or die fighting for it."

"I want to say you're wrong," says Miltiades. "But I can't."

CHAPTER THREE

FLIGHT OF PASSION

With a graceful leap from the mountaintop, she pirouettes and soars into the sky. Seemingly carefree, her pirouette tightens into a spin, slowly at first, then faster and faster, until soon she is almost a blur. The spinning slows again and finally stops; with her arms extended like wings she continues to soar.

Athena's emotions are complicated and conflicted, but that is nothing new for her, as the Goddess of both Wisdom and War. She is angry with her harsh father and conniving uncle, but now the winds are soothing her. Her thoughts go to the mortal man she loves. She is flying east, up high enough to be level with Mount Olympus, the home of the gods. She pierces the clouds one after the other as if playing a game, flying in and out of them, taking the moist air deep into her powerful lungs. She delights in the difference between the warm, dry air that brings up the earth's rich aromas, and the cloud mists that wash those odors away.

The scent of mignonette reaches her—her favorite flower, redolent of sweet honey, cherry blossoms, and raspberries. Its perfume is faint so high above the Aegean Sea and so far from the valleys where the flowers flourish. Still, she can almost taste the delicious fragrance, like a complex wine on lips ready to kiss or beguile. She is not after subtlety today. She dreams again and again of passionately making love in a meadow overflowing with wildflowers, but she will never live those dreams. To be and remain a virgin is her immortal destiny.

Her gray eyes shine even more intensely than usual. She turns her head and looks straight at the sun. She is hot, but not because of the glare of

Helios. Today, her heat comes from anger.

It has been seven mortal centuries since she felt this way. That was during the Trojan War, when she was infatuated with another Greek mortal, cunning Odysseus. Her father and uncle did not approve of that love either, and said she was obsessed. She despised their hypocrisy—the grand philanderers Zeus and Poseidon wagging their fingers at the virgin goddess.

Athena usually knows how to control her emotions. She has to, given her responsibilities. She is steady in the face of battle. But when a situation is personal, gods and goddesses can be just like mortals. When lust and love are involved, the rules of the game favor the impulsive and irrational.

Poseidon discovered her secret desire for Odysseus when he spied her wearing a short red dress—a chiton that revealed her thighs—instead of her usual full-length peplos, the white or golden tunic considered more appropriate for the perpetual virgin.

With tactless glee, Poseidon reported to Zeus that the Goddess of Wisdom was succumbing to the folly of love. A little brotherly goading turned Zeus' embarrassment into fury. Zeus confronted his daughter while Poseidon stood off to the side, chortling.

All the shouting accomplished nothing, of course. It did not take long for Zeus and Poseidon to forget the whole affair. But Athena never forgot—nor forgave them.

Today's confrontation with Zeus had taken her by surprise, but Athena's memory served her well. This time, she did not fight with him. Instead, she pretended to listen to his rants, while all the while she wondered how he knew about her new love. She certainly had not worn any short chitons lately. Her uncle Poseidon must be the conniving culprit, just as before, although how he could have learned her secret mystifies her.

But never mind, Athena tells herself. *It doesn't really matter—this time will be different.* She is confident Zeus and Poseidon will not pay attention much longer, if they are even watching. All this soaring and spinning—surely they are bored by now. Gods and men are much the same—no patience. Goddesses and women know how to wait; they've had lots of practice.

She told her father she would fly to Troy, the windswept ruin surrounded by plains that still ring, for her, with the echoes of long ago—clashing shields, spears, and swords. She yearns to feel again the bite of the high etesian winds whipping down from the north; they will help cool this anger.

She did not tell her father that after revisiting Troy she will fly to her new love, once again the most cunning man in the world. Her Odysseus has returned. But now his name is Themistocles.

CHAPTER FOUR

THE SECRET OMEN

The first Persian ship glides with a noise of heavy scraping onto the dark beach. Commander Datis stands alone at the prow. He feels his men's eyes on him even in the darkness, while everyone listens to the sounds of crunching as the ship grinds through the sand. Several men hold their breath when they hear three rapid thumps, like arrows hitting the side. Are they under attack? Have they struck rocks? The old hands smirk; they have seen this trick before. Datis turns to his men after silently laying down the long rod he used to pound the ship's deck three times. He takes pleasure in spooking his men a little, creating the sense that uncanny things happen when he is around. It makes them fear him, makes them easier to control.

The vessel plows to a dead stop. All is still except for the lapping of small waves against the hull. Not a sound, not a stir, not a Greek. *Good*, he thinks. *The scouts are right so far.*

More ships soon arrive, but he pays them no heed. Instead he studies the stars along the horizon. Nothing, no fading from the smoke or heat of signal fires, just as the scouts reported. Two thousand soldiers will disembark and set up defensive lines. Then the horse barges will arrive. The hordes of his army will follow at sunrise.

He jumps into the shadowy water and takes high, oversized strides inland. When he makes it to the dry beach he begins to run, disappearing into the night.

Back on the ship, Athens' former tyrant watches and wonders. Turning to a high-ranking Persian soldier, Hippias asks, "Your commander is gone—is that normal at such a critical time?"

"We have our orders," the soldier says. "As Datis serves the Great King, so we serve Datis. We don't need to be watched like children. Besides, we will see him again soon enough—perhaps when he performs his ritual."

"Ritual?"

A strange smile spreads across the soldier's face. "Our commander begins an invasion by consecrating fresh ground for the Great King."

"Consecrating?"

"You'll see, if you're lucky. And you'll probably hear it before you see it." The soldier snorts and stifles a laugh. "It's time to disembark."

After climbing into the water, Hippias wades to the beach and up onto dry sand. His vigorous stride belies his age. He has not felt this virile in twenty years. Pressing on until he is away from them all, he finally stops and turns around to survey the long beach before him, dark except for the glow of phosphorescence in the water, and the figures moving over it, vague against the starlight and faint moon. For a moment he is lost in thought.

Hippias remembers when he was a child playing on the shore. He would run back and forth between the safety of solid land and the unending sea, with its uneasy mystery stretching beyond the horizon. As a man, Hippias had chosen mystery and turbulence.

Now he bends over and scoops up a handful of sand. He holds out his fist with his thumb on top and slowly opens his fingers, one by one, from the bottom up. He feels the sand drift away. Hippias loves the beach, but he also fears it. He understands neither his love nor his fear, but he knows they are real. He also knows that other Greeks have the same feelings. The beach is transcendent—the in-between place where earth and sea merge, which imparts an inexplicable potency to Greeks. Hippias knows he and the Persians must get off the beach as soon as possible if they are to have any hope of conquering his countrymen.

He looks up and sees the stars disappearing one by one, like grains of sand in the sea of night. He turns his attention to the hundreds of laboring men, soon to be thousands. Their organization is something to behold as they move rapidly up and down the sand to guide the incoming ships. With silent gesticulations they direct each ship's commander, who relays instructions to rowers down in the ships' bowels—rowers who will later join the cohorts unloading cargo. The warships—triremes—come in first, with their three banks of rowers, almost two hundred sailors sweating below deck and thirty armed soldiers up top.

The long beach seems minuscule compared to the vast fleet. After the triremes quickly disgorge their soldiers, the rowers reverse stroke and take the ships back out to make room for more arrivals. Hippias watches the cargo ships move in. Huge numbers of soldiers begin to offload, and as the sky brightens with the rising of the sun, he studies the dress and arms of soldiers from different parts of the Great King's empire. He has seen them all before, but mostly as individuals crammed aboard the ships. Now he is watching them in an expansive, almost theatrical setting.

Because of their great number and bright adornment, the Medes from the heart of the empire are first to catch his attention. Gold glitters over their bodies and shiny, intertwined iron ringlets of armor make the men look like upright walking fish with vibrant scales. These fighting fish look fearsome carrying their short, stout spears, with daggers strapped to their legs. Their shields are thick wicker, and they carry bows and reed arrows in quivers down their backs.

The bows and arrows make Hippias shift his focus to a small contingent of Scythians now coming ashore—aggressive fighters from the northern edge of the empire, near the Caspian Sea. He remembers the thrill of seeing an army of Scythians shooting arrows from horseback at furious speeds. No surprise for the best archers in the world and the first people to domesticate horses. Scythian recurve bows pack far more power than longbows, and their bow tips curve away from the archer.

During his twenty years in Persia, Hippias had heard fascinating stories about the Scythians. His favorite is that Scythian women are like those ferocious female warriors—the Amazons—who live in a neighboring region. As the tale goes, Scythian women are required to kill a man before they can marry. When Hippias first heard that tantalizing detail, he knew Scythian women would be perfect for his bed, assuming they had already done their deadly deed. On the other hand, he had also heard that Amazons often cut off their right breasts to become better archers. He hopes Scythian women ignore that practice. He strains to see any women among the Scythian troops, but the distance is too far to be certain. His attention shifts to another exotic arrival.

The Ethiopians are also carrying bows and arrows, but of a very different type than the Scythians. Their giant longbows are more than six feet long, and their arrow tips are made of sharpened stone rather than iron. Even more striking is their dress—the skins of leopards and lions. Many of the Ethiopians also wear horse scalps on their heads, with upright ears and manes to make themselves look taller on the battlefield. Some of them are covered with bright red and white war paint.

More luxurious costumes appear as the Phoenicians of Palestine, the world's best sailors, disembark. They are descendants of the ancient and infamous Sea Peoples who ravaged lands and destroyed cultures throughout the Mediterranean during an age long-lost. Phoenician attire captivates Hippias, but not because it is ostentatious. In fact, the clothes are simple. It's the color that stands out—the celebrated Phoenician purple—unique and stunningly dramatic. Hippias knows their secret for creating such extraordinary dye.

During his exile in Persia, Hippias had traveled throughout much of the empire under the protection of the Great King. On his journeys he visited Palestine and the two major cities of Phoenicia—Sidon and Tyre— on the far eastern shore of the Great Sea north of Egypt. Hippias heard that Phoenicians are sometimes called the Little People because most of the men are barely five feet tall and the women are smaller. But more often they are called the Purple People.

Hippias had learned the purple dye in their garments comes from tiny sea snails that are crushed and squeezed to make the mollusk's gland, or bloom, yield a precious bit of fluid. At first the Phoenicians told Hippias the gland was near the creature's head—that story was one of many untruths they tell to ensure their monopoly on the dye's production. But later, during one of those drunken evenings when secrets get revealed, Hippias heard that the snail's gland is actually in its anus. He loved this revelation—such an esteemed and sophisticated offering to humans coming out of so many dainty defecating orifices.

Hippias had watched the Phoenicians squeeze countless numbers of the tiny mollusks. It was like seeing a multitude of miniature rainbows flowing through ever-changing spectrums, because the dye starts out clear when it squirts from its gland, and then, exposed to sun and air, undergoes a series of transitions from clear to white, then yellow, green, blue, and at last, purple.

Another secret Hippias had learned from his drunken Phoenician friends was the key ingredient for processing Tyrian purple: stale urine. Knowing about the anus gland secretions and aged urine, plus his friends' description of the mixing vats where men wade chest deep to mash the brew as if they are stomping grapes, Hippias sniffs now in disdain at the Purple People in their elegant outfits arriving on the Marathon beach.

Hippias sees the horse barges approaching. They are headed to a northern part of the beach, so he walks in that direction to get a better view. His eyes survey terrain he remembers well.

The entire seashore at Marathon is more than five miles long and curved to face mostly south. At the eastern edge of the bay, a thin peninsula juts out like a gnarled finger. The peninsula serves as a good windbreak, so the waters near it are the bay's calmest and best for the moored fleet. Close to where the peninsula joins the mainland is a freshwater lake, perfect for the thousand warhorses that will drink almost ten thousand gallons a day.

The Persian landing site stretches along the water for more than two miles. Inland from the beach in that area looms the Great Marsh, a delta for the river Charadra and the springs of Macaria. This stretch of beach is where the Persians will camp. If the Persians need to fight at Marathon instead of marching straight to Athens, they will move west off the beach and onto the level plain, and do battle with the Great Marsh to their rear.

Hippias' concentration on the landscape and the variety of soldiers from throughout the empire abruptly ends when he hears a peculiar noise. In a sense, the sound is recognizable, but he has never heard anything quite like it. It's a kind of singing, off-key but still a song of sorts, solo and high-pitched.

The song is loud and repetitive. The words are clear. "Oh, my joy. Oh, I am delighted and excited. Oh, my joy. Oh, I am delighted and excited." The refrain constantly repeats and the words steadily come faster and louder.

Walking around a large boulder, Hippias sees Datis in the distance. The Persian commander is dancing in a circle and pumping his left fist up in the air while he sings. The sight reminds Hippias of a big awkward bird trying to take flight with a broken wing, but he realizes there is more to Datis' antics than graceless dancing. This must be the ritual he was told about. Soldiers are bustling around and working in the vicinity. Hippias grabs one by the arm and, pointing, asks, "What is Datis doing over there?"

"Our commander is singing and dancing," replies the soldier, "and about to drop his seed to claim the new land for the empire."

"You mean masturbating?" asks Hippias.

"Our commander is good at it, isn't he?"

"What?"

"He's a good singer and dancer, don't you think?"

"Huh. Does he do this often?"

"Always, every time."

"Always? Tell me, does Great King Darius know about this . . . ritual?"

"Of course," says the soldier. "But the Great King cares about his ability to conquer lands for the empire, not about matters such as rituals."

Datis is singing now at full volume, "Oh, my joy. Oh, I am delighted and excited. Oh, my joy! Oh, I am delighted and excited!"

He circles more rapidly, flapping his left arm higher and faster. Hippias decides to skip the finale, turning instead to continue his walk toward where the horse barges are nearing shore.

He stops again. But this time the reason is internal. A strange, unpleasant feeling crowds into his head and chest. He begins to cough and thinks he might convulse. Then he sneezes, again and again. He can't seem to stop. After eight violent expulsions he is gasping and bent over with his hands on his knees.

Seeing his distress, two soldiers walk over and look at the dark red splashes on the sand below his head. Hippias kneels very slowly, glances up at the soldiers, and then stares down at the blood and says, "Look."

The soldiers step forward but Hippias yells, "Stop. Go back; don't step there. Look at the drops. Where is it? Help me find it!"

"What?" they ask.

"My mother," Hippias moans.

The soldiers look at each other, and one quietly says, "Get the commander. Now."

CHAPTER FIVE

A STRONG WOMAN CHALLENGED

After their late-night plotting against the Persians, Themistocles and Aristides walk together under the moonlight toward their homes. The runner, Themistocles' slave Sicinnus, walks a few paces behind them. When Aristides turns off to his own home with a grave farewell, Sicinnus moves up beside Themistocles. They walk the short final distance in silence.

The men's worried thoughts mirror each other. Both are certain that Marathon will mean an immense slaughter. Themistocles realizes this will be a battle unique for all Greeks; their ancestors have never experienced anything like what is to come, not even in the most savage battles in the long war against Troy.

Until now, Greek city-states had frequently fought one another. But their confrontations were almost always brief skirmishes to control terrain and seize arable land. Although deaths among hoplites—foot soldiers— were common, they seldom occurred on a massive scale and the cities had never been invaded by non-Greeks. Their struggles were primarily shoving matches, like large beasts taking each other's measure. Once supremacy on a battlefield was determined, often by the weight of numbers, the weaker group of soldiers usually retreated cautiously so they could fight another day.

But there would be no cautious retreat from Marathon. Themistocles knows that Marathon will determine the fate of Athens and all of the city's men, women, and children. What *will* happen there? Themistocles and Sicinnus both know the likely answer. They have tried to conceal that knowledge from their wives, and they both know they have failed. Reaching their homes, set side by side on a narrow path, Themistocles and Sicinnus stop but still say nothing.

The slave's feelings are even more complex than his master's. Sicinnus was born and raised in Persia before the Greeks captured him. However, for the last many years he has lived in Athens and absorbed its culture and appreciated the wonders of its free people, especially Themistocles, so Sicinnus fears for his adopted homeland as well as the safety of his wife and daughter. Still, he remembers his childhood home, his parents and brothers and sisters, his fellow Persians. His fear of the invaders arriving at Marathon is mixed with remorse at finding them his deadly enemies. But he will fight them with everything he has, and he knows that may include his life.

The two men stand together in the dark, and Sicinnus asks, "Do you need anything before we rise in a few hours?"

"Of course not," Themistocles says gruffly, doing a poor job of hiding his concern. "Try to rest. Don't expect you'll sleep much. Give little Alyssa a touch on the cheek for me." Themistocles turns and walks into his home.

Sicinnus stands alone outside his own home in the fragrant darkness of the late summer night. He knows the next few moments will be hard, perhaps as difficult as the battlefield. In a fight to the death, instincts take over. Sicinnus has superb instincts, but emotions are another matter. He takes a deep breath.

～כ

The Athenian Assembly has voted to allow slaves to fight in the hoplite ranks against the impending invasion. In return, the slaves who survive will be given their freedom. And Themistocles has promised him that he will fight directly behind Themistocles himself in his tribe's position within the phalanx. That will put him in the second row of the Athenian battle lines, a true honor for a slave. Also a true danger, because the first three rows of Greek battle lines do the killing. But, he reminds himself again, if he lives he will be free.

～つ

When he steps inside his home, Sicinnus hears Lela in the next room softly singing to soothe Alyssa. He pauses to listen. Although he often hears Lela sing, something is different tonight. He doesn't know if the difference is in Lela or in him, or perhaps in both.

He shuts his eyes and takes a few more slow deep breaths. Lela's music envelops him. It takes him far away. He does not know exactly where, but he is floating like a bird on spiraling updrafts.

Realizing he is dizzy, Sicinnus opens his eyes and puts his fingers on the wall to steady himself. He shuts his eyes again. In a few hours he will leave for Marathon where glory or death awaits him. Lela's music pulls him back.

His mind blurs as he feels pulled in two directions—the drive to march with the hoplites versus the urge to stay here in the warmth of his love for Lela and their daughter, holding them for as long as he can, protecting them. His fingers move along the wall and he opens his eyes just in time to keep from falling. Then a light smile spreads across his handsome young face at the thought of what he is about to see.

Lit by a small flame flickering in a dish of oil, Lela sits in a rocking chair holding their daughter, with the toddler's head resting on her shoulder. Just shy of her second birthday, Alyssa's face is continuing to subtly transform. When she was born, she looked more like her father, but gradually more of her mother's features are emerging. Sicinnus thinks Alyssa will have her mother's bottomless black eyes. Right now, the child's eyes are wide open, but a steady stare shows that sleep is near.

Sicinnus' entrance, quiet and slow as it is, breaks the child's trance and her eyes shift to her father. Her delight is clear. Sicinnus touches her cheek and she responds with a sleepy smile. Then her eyes close.

Sicinnus stands silently beside Lela as she continues to rock the baby. He softly says, "Tomorrow will be a new day, Alyssa, and you won't even remember my touch."

Lela's jaw tightens. Sicinnus reaches down and gently picks up the baby. After putting Alyssa in her crib, he leans over and, his mouth almost touching his daughter's ear, whispers slowly, "Persephone."

This is an everyday ritual for him; he always repeats the name several times while carefully pronouncing every syllable. Once, when Lela asked what he was doing, Sicinnus said it was a small secret between a father and his daughter, a secret of love. Lela believed the lie, perhaps because it was partly true. The whisper certainly is a secret, but small it is not. As only Sicinnus knows, this whisper is about more than love; it is about their survival.

After repeating his whisper to Alyssa three times, Sicinnus straightens up and turns around.

Lela is no longer in the rocking chair. She is standing in the moonlight by the window. Her back is to him, but he can tell she is wiping her eyes.

"You returned after just one day," says Lela. "Does that mean the Persians landed at Marathon?"

"Yes."

She sighs and Sicinnus says, "Please, Lela."

Lela turns around. She is no longer crying, but her face still glistens with tears.

"I promised myself I was not going to do this. I was not going to cry. And I've stopped; it's over. It won't happen again. I know it's hard for you, too. But today I wept for hours when Alyssa was sleeping."

She looks up at her husband. "Do you know why?" she asks.

Sicinnus does not answer. He feels an almost spiritual awe as he looks at this woman standing before him in the moonlight's glow. It has happened many times before. She enraptures him.

Lela is small, petite as a nymph, and twenty years old. She has lustrous black hair with long bangs down her forehead. Her midnight black eyes are strong and passionate. Up close, Lela's eyes are riveting. She is the most ravishing woman Sicinnus has ever seen.

He pulls himself out of his trance. He knows this is a time to listen. If Lela repeats her question he will try to answer, but he doubts she will ask it again, and she does not.

"I cried and cried because of Alyssa and you," she says softly. "It's not the fear—not the fear for me, not my fear for you, not even for Alyssa. Today I was overwhelmed with a thought I just couldn't bear. The sadness was too much."

Lela pauses and Sicinnus feels himself sinking into her bottomless black eyes.

"If you die, your daughter will not remember you. No matter what I tell her, she will have no memory of you. It will be to her as if she never had a father. Why must you to do this, why do you have to fight in the ranks with the hoplites?"

Sicinnus hesitates, uncertain whether he should try to answer, but Lela continues, "I know the answer. You say it will make you a free man and our slavery will end. And Alyssa might even marry a citizen of the city. Indeed. Themistocles promised you will be free. But not if you're dead."

Lela falls silent and lowers her head to hide the tears she cannot keep from gathering in her dark eyes.

No longer immobilized, Sicinnus steps forward to embrace her. They hold each other for a long time before he speaks.

"I have something to tell you. But first I have a question. The moonlight tonight, shining on your face when I walked into the room, that moonlight was just like two years ago when you were giving birth to Alyssa. And the jasmine and mint coming through the window tonight, just like when you were giving birth—a wonderful fragrance, but it also can be the sweet smell of death, like wilting flowers left behind after a burial. Do you remember that moonlight with the jasmine and mint when Alyssa was born and you were dying?"

"No. I don't understand."

"Please, Lela, I know I sound strange, but this is important. I'm going to tell you why our daughter will remember me. She will remember because I'm coming back from Marathon, and then we will make love again just as before."

"I told you I'm healed; I have been for months. I want you inside me. It's been almost two years."

"Please," Sicinnus says firmly. "I should have told you sooner but now listen, please. You were ripped wide open when Alyssa was born, and the midwives said, everyone said, you were going to die. They were certain you were going to die. But I prayed. How I prayed! I prayed to Hera, to Zeus, to all the Greek gods and goddesses I could think of. I even prayed to the one god of Persia, Ahura Mazda, the god you and I left long ago. Then I had a vision and I made an oath, and there was a miracle. You lived and recovered. No one could believe it, but it happened. Everyone said the gods intervened."

"What was your oath? Is that why you won't make love? You, of all people, the most passionate man in the whole world, my lover who now refuses me?"

"Lela, you are the smartest and bravest and most beautiful woman I have ever known—or imagined. You want answers, but you must trust me for a little while longer. Later I will tell you, but not now. My oath doesn't allow it."

Then, with a slight smile, Sicinnus leans back and says, "I'll tell you when I'm inside you—after Marathon."

Lela stares at him without an inkling of a smile.

Seeing his lighthearted effort fall flat, he quickly continues, "I can tell you this much. As I said, I had a vision and took an oath, and . . ."

"Was it a dream? Did Ahura Mazda appear in it?"

"No, it was not a dream, and it was not Ahura Mazda. I prayed to the god of Persia out of desperation; I didn't expect him to help, and he didn't. We are Greeks now, and I'm proud of it. Themistocles saved both of us years ago, and now the Greek gods and goddesses are saving us again. But please, don't ask any more questions. I don't dare say too much and violate my oath."

Sicinnus stops in silence and looks long and hard into Lela's eyes. He takes both of her hands in his and, in a soft but firm voice says, "One more thing. We have been waiting for Alyssa to say her first word. If she says it when I'm not here, be sure to listen carefully. See if she will repeat it. Make sure it is clear. And tell me as soon as you can. Will you do that?"

Lela stares at him curiously and says, "You are an intriguing man, Sicinnus. The smartest man I know. The most handsome. My friend. My lover. My husband. To me, you are the best of everything. And probably the strangest man on earth."

CHAPTER SIX

TIME ECHOES

Utter devastation.

Ages ago the massive walls around the city of Troy were yards thick and so tall that no one, not even the Trojans' greatest enemies, could hurl a spear over them. Now the mighty bulwarks are nothing more than crushed clumps buried in dirt and overgrown with weeds. The dusty air is almost as filthy as the ruins of the old edifices. Even the huge harbor is slowly disappearing. At the juncture of the Aegean Sea and the Hellespont, the once grand anchorage served seafaring commerce from afar as well as the enemies who moored there for the ten-year siege; now the harbor is silting up, and the abandoned city is gradually getting cut off from the sea.

However, there is still some life. A small hound walks by a collapsed arch. Barely more than a pup, it should be frisky. Instead, the dejected dog wanders lamely with its head lowered and ribs protruding. It is skittish but lacks the energy to shy away from danger, real or imagined.

And there are people, a few, who stay mostly out of sight. How terrible to be so weak, so vulnerable, knowing there are marauders who would show them no mercy. They are too desperate to realize that raiders seldom bother those who are too poor to have anything worth bothering about.

Athena ignores it all. As she walks among the ruins she focuses on her memories of the glory—the clashing of shield against shield ringing like echoes of the great city's destruction.

She stops and closes her eyes to listen to those memories: the sound of the Trojans' frenzy when they thought the Greeks had given up and abandoned the long war. And the Trojans' pounding drums as the people went mad with joy.

She begins to sway from side to side, keeping time with those drums. She throbs with each remembered beat, raising her arms, palms up. Her swaying changes to rocking as she begins to turn, looking up to the sky. The motion intensifies until, with silent but violent gesticulations, she thrusts her hips back and forth in orgasmic euphoria. With dilated pupils, her once-gray eyes turn black. She starts convulsing and they change again: pure white. A soft murmur grows to a loud moan until—her transformation nearly complete—she emits the deep-throated, guttural growl of a ravenous carnivore tearing its prey's throat. So it happens: Athena, Goddess of Wisdom, becomes again the Goddess of War.

~~⌇~~

Athena drifts back seven centuries in mortal time to when the Trojans attacked the Greek ships near the end of the long siege. Hector, the mightiest Trojan warrior, called for fire to burn the ships, but the Trojans' assault failed and the ships did not burn.

Later, at last, the Greeks disappeared from the plain around the city and their ships abandoned the beachhead. After ten years of the din of battle, silence fell over the city and across the land. All that remained on the beach was one massive towering shape.

Athena thinks of the huge wooden horse that stood glistening in the sun. The Trojans were astonished—a gift from the gods and a stunning memorial to their triumph. The dark grains of polished timbers flowed like waves along the horse's vast flanks and belly. Trojan sentries opened the main gate and wheeled the enormous beast inside the city, past the impregnable walls, and then shut and bolted the gate behind them. In the city center, the grand horse could be properly revered.

What revelry Athena witnessed! Everyone approached the horse and began to circle it. Soon, reverence turned into reckless ecstasy. Men screamed and beat their chests while women pierced the air with warbling cries. Wine flowed undiluted—now was no time for moderation—and drums beat louder and louder. The wine heated throats already raw from shouting, but with each swallow it went down more sweetly. Pandemonium took over. The adults spun themselves dizzy while the children ran about in wild confusion; none of the little ones could remember life before the siege and its constant fear. All praise to the horse, The Horse, their gift from the gods.

Ah, but how foolish the Trojans were, how misplaced their ecstasy. The horse was no gift. Like the Greeks who made it, it was a masterpiece of contradictions. The large eyes were blind, but the horse had another eye carefully hidden. And the horse's stillness hid subtle movements. It made sounds, though barely perceptibly. It breathed. It was alive.

After the Trojans pulled the horse into the city, after the pounding drums reached full volume, and after drunken shouting filled the air, a small part of the horse moved, ever so slightly. Inside the great belly, near a long front leg, a little hole appeared. In a flash, the hole became a watchful—very human—eye.

Athena's beloved Odysseus watched the wild, swirling scene below until after the sun went down, and longer still until the furious drums went silent. Then he opened the horse's hidden trapdoor from inside and thirty Greeks climbed down. They walked casually, slow and easy, staggering a bit, just in case someone was watching. They made it back to the main gate without resistance. As expected, it took several of them to lift the heavy timber and unbolt the massive gate. Slowly, silently, the structure opened.

Odysseus stepped a short distance outside the gate and looked toward where he knew the Greek ships were moored. The entire fleet had secretly returned in the dead of night, and the men had disembarked under the veil of darkness. He saw exactly what he had hoped to see—a slight movement in the distance. The open gate with Odysseus standing there was the signal the Greek scout had been waiting for. He was off and, soon enough, would tell the Greeks what they wanted to hear—their ruse had been blessed by the gods.

The ten-year war was about to end in decisive savagery. Athena watched as Odysseus, anticipating the pending slaughter, began to change. Standing just outside the open gate, he steadied his mind. He was the man of nimble wits, the most cunning man alive, but now he was absorbing an additional personality into his being—a monster brutal enough to do what this night would require.

The man of many wiles bared his teeth and curled his upper lip to expose his gums. His mouth filled with saliva and he let it run down his chin like a madman. Athena had taken the form of a golden owl to watch him in the dim moonlight. She loved this mortal man and she understood this preparation. She was the Goddess of War, and she knew he would do what he must. This would be the final battle, and he was making himself ready.

Odysseus felt the ground rumble. Then he saw movements in the distance. No shouts. A massive silent charge as the Greek fighters ran toward him and the open gate. And so far, no reaction from the Trojans. Perhaps the guards were drunk or asleep or, lulled into a false sense of safety, away from their posts. No matter; it was all over, except for the slaughter.

Odysseus stood still, watching the Greeks surge toward him. He knew exactly what was happening, but he did not want to move just yet, enraptured as he was by anticipation. Finally, just as he was about to be trampled, he turned and raised his sword and, with a bloodcurdling scream, led the destroyers into the doomed city.

The glorious devastation of hand-to-hand combat. From the bloody frenzy, glorious victory and glorious death. For the Goddess of War, it was delirious ecstasy to see her beloved lead her people to victory. By dawn the killing was nearly over. There was no mercy. The Trojan men were all dead except for the few who escaped, and the women were corralled like chattel.

All that remained were the children.

Those children of Troy had to be dealt with. If allowed to grow up, they would have only one desire—to avenge their dead.

Hecuba herself, Troy's widowed queen, clutched her little grandson, trying to soothe his fears. The young boy, barely more than a toddler, sensed that his father was gone, but he could not understand why. His grandmother held him now and her grip was too tight. The queen could not help herself; this was the last time she would ever see him.

A horror beyond imagining, sorrow beyond telling. Even the Goddess of War looked away. The boy would be taken to the high walls. When he saw and understood, a soldier would tighten his grip on the child's arm. No escape possible. The queen, tears streaming down her cheeks, knew that would be the worst moment. Not the fall through the air from such a terrifying height. Not the smashing on the rocks below. She knew the worst moment would be when the boy saw all the children ahead of him being thrown off the walls, and took his place in line.

And so it was. One after another. The children's cries, the falling, the thudding sounds below the walls, the little limbs bent wrong, and the wild dogs drawn by the sounds and smells.

The murders were more than vengeance. The Greeks wanted to end an entire people. They did not stop until the extermination was complete.

❧

Athena's gray eyes flash open. Images of those long-ago deaths and those children on the walls of Troy give way to a vision of the near future. It is blurred, perhaps because of its terror and perhaps because she cannot see everything. She focuses on the thought—the hope—that she might be wrong. But what if she is not?

Not Troy this time, but Athens, her namesake city. And the walls now are the cliffs of the acropolis—the high hill of rock at Athens' heart. The men standing atop those walls are Persians. And the children hurtling down—those poor babes are Greek.

In her vision, fires are burning everywhere in the city; the intense heat is all-consuming. The temples of the gods are being destroyed. Soon, everyone will be dead or enslaved. Utter devastation, an entire people wasted. Athens will be what Troy became. Her city and her people will cease to exist.

Athena's eyes blaze. The vision must not become real. She cannot save them all—only they can do that. But she can help.

CHAPTER SEVEN

ACROSS THE WINE-DARK SEA

Far from the land of the Greeks, across the wine-dark sea and deep inside the Persian Empire, a horse winces as its rider kicks harder. The sun is high overhead, and in the distance the rider sees Susa, the City of Lilies and one of the empire's capitals. He bears a message for Darius, the empire's Great King, and he is late. He must get to Susa before the King notices the delay, or else his fate will be, at best, uncertain.

This courier is one of dozens who ply the best road in the world—the Royal Road—which stretches nearly two thousand miles from the city of Sardis near the Aegean Sea, eastward to Susa near the empire's center.

Every day the Great King receives messages from riders of the Royal Road and from every other direction in the empire. As vast as his domain is, Darius learns about every action of consequence with remarkable speed. And with spies and informers everywhere, he often knows what will occur before it happens.

The empire has several grand capitals including Babylon, Persepolis, Ecbatana, and Pasargadae, where the first Great King, Cyrus, is entombed. Cyrus founded the empire three generations earlier, and under his rule it became the largest the world had known.

Darius is also devoted to expanding the empire and is renowned for building magnificent structures. In Susa, he built a monumental gateway with a huge statue of himself and inscriptions identifying his subject peoples, as well as an enormous palace with an imposing banquet hall.

It is midday when Darius walks through his grand palace toward the long banquet table awaiting him and his guests. At sixty, his tall and muscular physique could be that of a much younger man. His long thin nose makes a dramatic profile, and his face is wrinkled but still ruggedly handsome. His deeply tanned skin seems lightened by the blackness of his hair along with a flowing dark beard, thick eyebrows, and penetrating eyes.

The Great King is followed by an entourage of almost twenty men who are the envy of the guests—another hundred men who are powerful in their own right. Virtually all of them can make life and death decisions affecting millions of people throughout the empire.

Immediately behind Darius, two younger men walk side by side— the Great King's favored son, Xerxes, and today's guest of honor—a new emissary, Pharandates the Second, recently arrived from Egypt. Although they walk together, Xerxes and Pharandates do not speak to each other. As the guest, the young Egyptian emissary wants to follow protocol, so he is waiting for Xerxes to introduce himself. Xerxes ignores him.

Walking behind Xerxes and Pharandates is the royal court's chief official, the Master of a Thousand. He has the air of a prideful man, and with good reason. Within the palace, he is in charge of everything, including the safety of the king and his family. Everyone reports to him but he reports only to one man—Darius, his King.

Following the Master of a Thousand are several of the military's highest-ranking officers, including the Great King's spear carrier, his bow carrier, and his charioteer. The royal cupbearer is also in the entourage; he is one of Darius' most trusted officials because plots against kings often involve adding tasteless poisons to otherwise enticing drinks. The cupbearer's duty is to ensure that whatever the Great King drinks does no more than brighten the royal mood.

The banquet is laid out. For this meal, Darius commanded that the central dish be stewed humps of young camel in a rich sauce flavored with onions, ginger, and apples. On each side of the dishes of camel meat are plates of fawn, delicately roasted with pecans and pomegranates.

Farther along are piles of steaming goat brains stirred with artichokes and eggplant. Next are pheasants simmering with apricots and pistachios. The meat dishes continue in both directions along the vast table—beef, goat, lamb, mutton, pig, venison, chicken, geese, partridge, pigeon, and quail. Then the fish, both fresh and dried; trout is the Great King's favorite but he never tires of white sturgeon, which he slathers with its salty black eggs, or of salmon, shark, pike-perch, and carp. And then an abundance of strange little water creatures with shells and tails.

Each dish is individually seasoned with herbs and spices that also are in small bowls scattered along the table: basil, cardamom, caraway, cinnamon, cloves, coriander, cumin, dill, nutmeg, paprika, saffron, sumac, tarragon and turmeric. And there is a multitude of rice dishes and warm breads plus a host of nuts and seeds.

The vegetables arrayed for today's feast include asparagus, carrots, cress, cucumbers, garlic, onions, radishes and spinach. Finally, fresh and dried fruit: apples, cantaloupes, cherries, dates, grapes, lemons, limes, medlars, oranges, pears, plums, pomegranates, quinces, and raspberries. The mixture Darius uses to clear his palate between servings waits as well—a combination of crushed chickpeas, lentils, chestnuts, and walnuts, all stirred in a thick sauce of honey and yogurt touched with vinegar.

As is his habit, Darius strokes his beard when he sits down on the over-sized, ornately carved chair at the head of the table. The beard is a proud product of dye masters who color each hair individually, making sure every filament is completely and perfectly pigmented without ever touching the midnight dye to the Great King's skin.

Xerxes sits down to the right of Darius. Father and son have similar features, although Xerxes is even taller. Their beards are almost identical except that the blackness of Xerxes' beard is still natural—something likely to change soon enough, now that he has reached his mid-thirties.

The young Egyptian emissary sits to the left of the King. Pharandates, in his mid-twenties, is the only beardless man among the guests. He takes in the lavish display of food and is momentarily speechless. Just as he is about to express his compliments to Darius, a servant leans forward and whispers in the Great King's ear, "Remember the Greeks." The emissary hears the words and, out of the corner of his eye, sees Darius slowly nod his head with his eyes shut. The servant says again, "Remember the Greeks," and again Darius nods. A third time the whisper is repeated, and a third time Darius nods. The servant steps back and Darius opens his eyes. The emissary does not know what to make of this, so he sits there, staring straight ahead in silence.

Darius motions with his hand and servants immediately place a helping of camel hump on Darius' solid gold plate and similar portions on Xerxes' and Pharandates' plates of pure silver. The banquet begins, and food starts to move among all the participants as servants rush about.

"My Great King, this is truly spectacular," says Pharandates. "I have heard that your meals are marvelous, but I had no idea. This is beyond comprehension until one actually sees it."

Without responding, Darius takes a bite of camel and then flips the back of his hand so a servant immediately removes his plate.

Looking straight ahead but speaking to the emissary, Darius says, "You are named after your wise father, your Great King's satrap in Egypt. Your Great King often prefers shortened names for foreign elites. Henceforth, you shall be Phar."

"Great King, it is my honor for you to call me Phar."

"Now Phar, when are you going to ask me about the Greeks?"

"Great King, how perceptive, as if you can read a man's mind. Please, if you will, explain the meaning of the servant's words."

"It is true. Your Great King can read a man's mind, sometimes. And sometimes is enough, because a man never knows when the Great King might perceive the thoughts a man does not speak."

Darius makes another motion with his hand and a servant runs off. A moment later more than a dozen servants return carrying a table and an assortment of containers, which they arrange behind the king and the Egyptian. The servants lift Darius' ornate chair, turn it around, and do the same with the chair Phar sits in. On the table now in front of Phar are two place settings with bowls. Behind the place settings are two covered containers with small oil lamps under them.

Darius says, "Your Great King often desires the thoughts of foreign guests. Before you, on your left, is a Persian dish. On your right is a Greek dish. Taste carefully and render your opinion. Which do you prefer?"

A servant lifts the lid on the Persian dish to the left and, with a large ladle, empties a thick, chunky mixture into Phar's first bowl.

Phar's mind flashes as he remembers the guidance he received from his father before he left Egypt for Persia—beware the Great King's request for advice or an opinion; it will be a test.

Phar looks closely into his bowl. The concoction is dark brown, almost black. He puts his head over the bowl and slowly inhales the aroma. Pork. Then another slow, deep breath. Vinegar.

"Great King, what makes this Persian dish so dark?" asks Phar.

"Blood."

"So, Great King, blood is an ingredient in the sauce?"

"Not an ingredient. Blood is the sauce."

Phar raises his eyebrows but says nothing. He holds his breath and puts a spoonful of the sauce in his mouth. As he swallows he takes a slight breath, gags, coughs and quickly covers his mouth to prevent his spittle from flying across the table. He rapidly licks the inside of his hand in an effort to make his embarrassment go away, but he has to cough again. Keeping his hand over his mouth, he turns his head away from the Great King and makes two more hacking coughs, pauses, coughs one more time, and clears his throat.

"Is that your judgment of the Persian dish?" asks Darius.

"Oh, no, Great King. I swallowed wrong. I barely tasted the sauce."

Once again Phar takes a mouthful of the sauce and, stretching his neck up, swallows. This time there are no repercussions.

"So?" says Darius.

"I am ready to taste the Greek dish, Great King," replies Phar.

Darius nods to the servant who promptly opens the lid on the container to Phar's right and ladles a helping of the Greek dish into Phar's other bowl. The aroma immediately tells Phar this is a lamb entrée. He also knows that prunes and onions are integral to the sauce. A deep breath tells him the dish is complex with several spices and herbs, but there is something special he does not recognize—an ingredient that is intriguing and subtle but also mildly pungent.

"Great King, you just clarified that the Persian sauce was made of blood," says Phar. "Perhaps you will clarify what I detect in this Greek dish that I do not understand."

"Your father has an appreciation for fine food," says Darius. "He must have passed on the inclination to you."

"Great King, as far back as I can remember, both my parents obliged me to eat foods I resisted. Now I am happy about their demands. Today I know many herbs and spices, but there is an ingredient in this lamb dish I am not familiar with."

"Two important ingredients are onions and prunes."

"Yes, Great King, I recognize them, and I can tell there are other complements, but there is something I cannot put my finger on—something elusive with a fragrance that is tantalizing."

"Perhaps something like the whiff of distant garlic."

"That's it, Great King, exactly."

"Silphium," says Darius. "Giant fennel. It grows to a height of eight feet."

"Silphium," repeats Phar. "I have heard of it but I do not know the taste, Great King. I can't remember what I was told about silphium, but I think it is supposed to have a harsh flavor."

"Unpalatable if not prepared properly. Before silphium is added to a dish it must be cooked in hot oil. Otherwise, it is terrible," says the king with a subtle smile.

Phar swallows a mouthful of the lamb dish and controls his temptation to gobble more. He remembers more advice his father gave him: Darius is most uncommon as a man of power because he rejects sycophants and wants advisors to tell him what they really believe rather than what they think he wants to hear.

Phar almost speaks but stops himself. Wanting to think about what he will say, he returns to the Persian pork and takes a small taste, then back to the Greek lamb for a large mouthful.

Putting his spoon on the table and looking at Darius, Phar speaks with conviction, "Great King, I prefer the lamb."

"You prefer the Greek dish over the Persian dish?" exclaims Darius.

"Yes, Great King, that is what I prefer."

Phar senses the king's son, next to him, turning around in his seat.

Looking at Xerxes, Darius says, "It's been a long time since that was the answer, and a very long time since it was spoken without equivocation."

Xerxes replies, "Perhaps the young Egyptian emissary is hard of hearing."

Without showing any emotion, Darius makes a motion with his hand. Servants pick up his chair and turn it around and then follow suit with Phar's chair.

Once again facing the banquet guests and the copious food, Darius says, "Phar, you just told your Great King you prefer a Greek dish over a Persian dish. Your answer is most uncommon and obliges your Great King to make a clarification that is equally uncommon. The lamb you preferred is actually a traditional Persian dish. The pork is a Greek dish and the simple recipe—blood, pork, vinegar, and salt—comes from the city of Sparta where it is known as black broth. The Spartans have a well-deserved reputation for eating very bad food."

Phar works hard to disguise his glee. He also wonders about the apparent differences between Darius and Xerxes. Darius is a ferocious warrior who can be vicious when he is displeased. But his wisdom also is broadly recognized. Xerxes, however, seems to have no tolerance for anything, and his wisdom is suspect. Phar wonders why Xerxes is the Great King's favored son.

Darius continues, "Earlier, you asked why the servants whisper to your Great King about the Greeks."

"Yes, Great King."

Darius stares at Phar but does not respond. As the silence lengthens, the Great King's expression gradually changes. Phar does not like what he sees. Then Phar notices that Darius' hands are gripping each other. The grip is hard—too hard. All of his knuckles are white but the backs of his hands are a dark angry red. Phar takes a deep breath but his voice is paralyzed.

Darius also takes a long, slow breath and whispers to Phar, "Your Great King hates them."

CHAPTER EIGHT

THE QUICK MARCH BEGINS

While the rally horns blare, Themistocles and Sicinnus push their way through thousands of men—every able-bodied male in the city—as hoplites and their body slaves congregate in Athens' agora before marching northeast to Marathon. A number of women have gathered a short distance away. Their presence is strictly forbidden, but the law is not being enforced and no one tries to stop them from sobbing. It's shortly before sunrise, and with torches blazing everywhere there is plenty of light for Themistocles to find the man he seeks—Miltiades.

Making his way toward him, Themistocles calls out, "Where's Callimachus?"

"Our warleader's long gone." Miltiades steps forward. "He's leading a flying column of the fastest hoplites; they're probably arriving at Marathon about now. Last night, when I went to his home after we got the report from your Sicinnus, he should have been asleep but instead was wide awake, sitting inside the door with his wife. As if they were expecting me. After I told him what was happening, he said he'd be at Marathon by sunrise with six hundred men, and they would take the short route."

"So," Themistocles says, "the short route. A normal man would skirt Pentelicon to the south. But not him—he takes his vanguard straight over a mountain on a treacherous trail in the middle of the night so he can save a little time."

"It's good he took the short route. We won't have to split forces and send a contingent to cover it."

Themistocles sees three hoplites approaching. Aeschylus is on the left.

Next to him is his younger brother, Cynegirus, who everyone calls Kye. He is a handsome youth, ten years younger than Aeschylus. Themistocles also knows Kye but does not recognize the third man, whose appearance intrigues him. With little facial hair, he looks barely old enough to be an ephebe, yet he's here as a hoplite. And the young man's physique is impressive even by the high standards of Greek males approaching the full bloom of manhood. Themistocles surmises he is not only devoted to the rigors of the gymnasium, but also descends from exceptionally hardy stock.

"Greetings, Aeschylus," shouts Themistocles. "I hope you realize, my friend, that your eloquence won't do you much good at Marathon. Persians are too crude to appreciate your work. And your poor writing stick will break into pieces if you try to stab an enemy with it."

The soldier poet smiles. "Next time you want to engage in a spear-throwing contest, you know where to find me. And no need to worry about my 'writing stick.' I'm keeping it in good shape for a new play I'm working on. Did I tell you I'm using you as the model for the protagonist?"

"So I'm to be a hero! Excellent choice and another example of why I tell everyone you're the smartest man in the city."

"Actually, the play will be a study of man's misery. At the beginning, the protagonist is quite an unpleasant sort and later he just gets worse. I think the most exciting action should be offstage, so the audience only hears noises and imagines the worst. I'm debating which animal will make the most awful sounds when it's on the receiving end of the beastly deed my hero will perform. Perhaps a nice, fat hog with high-pitched squeals and guttural grunts will hold the audience's attention."

"Humph. Doesn't sound too heroic to me, Aeschylus. I hope your brother covers his ears when you talk like this." Turning next to the poet's sibling, Themistocles smiles. "Greetings, Kye. I keep hearing good things about you, so apparently your brother hasn't corrupted you yet. And your companion here, I don't think we've met."

"He's new to the ranks but will soon be acknowledged as one of Athens' best, I'm sure of it. Themistocles, this is my partner, Arrichion."

"Arrichion!" Shifting his focus to the young hoplite, Themistocles continues, "You bear a famous name, and I'm sure you're asked about it often. Any relation?"

"He was my great-grandfather."

As he always does when meeting a young person, Themistocles instinctively focuses on the youth's eyes and the sensitive muscles around his mouth. He knows a genuine smile comes and goes slowly and is intense only briefly. A fake smile is just the opposite, arriving and departing quickly but maintaining its intensity longer. The proud smile that Arrichion can't keep from spreading over his face, vying with what looks like an instinctive modesty at mention of his famous ancestor, is clearly deeply sincere.

"Well, now, I am humbled," says Themistocles. "Athens is big, but I like to know who's who, and I should have learned of you. When were you named a hoplite?"

"Last week."

"So this will be your first time on the battlefield with opponents who actually mean to kill you?"

"Yes. And I'm ready." The youth sounds ingenuous to the middle-aged warrior. "I'm eager for glory. The last two years have prepared me well."

"You know, of course, that valor comes before glory." Themistocles gives the young man a steady look before continuing. "I have a few questions I like to ask ambitious men new to battle, if I may."

He pauses, and Arrichion looks at him attentively. "Of course."

"When our phalanx clashes with the Persians, and you have your first chance to show your bravery to everyone, what will be your first duty?"

"To hold my ground." Arrichion responds without hesitation.

Themistocles nods and says, "You say 'to hold your ground.' Instead, why not charge ahead, by yourself, and prove your valor by fighting the enemy, man to man?"

Sure of the answer he has been taught through two years of training, Arrichion says confidently, "Because that is no longer how to show valor. We have learned a better way. Today we have the phalanx. We fight together, not as individuals by ourselves, but as many who combine to become one. We demonstrate our valor by ensuring the phalanx is not broken. After the clash with our enemy, we strive to push forward, but we must never step back. We must hold our ground."

Themistocles nods again and says, "Yes, and who do you hold your ground for?"

"For my comrades. Especially for the man on my left, who I protect with my shield, just as the man on my right protects me."

"And the oath you swore as an ephebe?"

"I will protect my comrade on the battlefield, and I will not leave him."

"And for all the hoplites to protect their comrades, the phalanx must stay intact," observes Themistocles. "How many rows are in a phalanx?"

"The normal depth is eight rows. But that can vary depending on the length of the enemy's lines and how thin we must spread ourselves to match their lines."

"How do we protect the phalanx? How do hoplites ensure the phalanx holds together?"

"Keep the rows of the phalanx straight so that all of the hoplites can protect one another."

"Raise your voice and repeat the first half of that statement," says Themistocles.

"Pardon?" asks Arrichion.

"The first half of your statement—say it again, with vigor."

Arrichion shouts, "Keep the rows of the phalanx straight." The young soldier looks at Themistocles curiously and asks, "Did I say something wrong?"

"Not at all. Everything you said was absolutely correct, just as you were taught as an ephebe. But now the teaching is finished and the true learning begins. You will discover soon enough that keeping the battle lines straight is very difficult when the killing is real. If the lines are not straight, the shields won't do what they must. I asked you to repeat your words to help you remember. And I have a couple more questions."

"I'm ready."

"You are ready," repeats Themistocles, approvingly. "As a new hoplite you won't be in the first three ranks—the killing rows—when we clash with the Persians. So what will be your second duty after holding your ground?"

"Push. Put my shield between the shoulder blades of the man in front of me and lean into it with all my weight—push with all of my force."

"And what if the man in front of you falls?"

"Step forward and replace him."

"Yes, exactly," says Themistocles. "But if the man in front of you does not fall but instead shits all over the ground, then what?"

Pausing momentarily, Arrichion says, "Watch where I step."

Laughing, Themistocles continues, "However . . ."

"If I may interrupt," says Arrichion. "I want to correct what I just said. Watching my step won't be easy; it may be impossible. What I should have said is, I will keep my feet in a wide stance to maintain my balance so I won't slip and fall, whatever happens in front of me."

"Well, Arrichion, you answered my question before I asked it," says Themistocles. "You're right; you won't be able to watch your step. With sweat running in your eyes and your head covered by an eight-pound bronze helmet while everything around you is a blur, you will see next to nothing."

"And I am ready," Arrichion says without a pause.

"Yes, indeed, hoplite," says Themistocles, his own voice ringing out. "You are ready! And now I have a request about something else—your famous ancestor."

The sound of the rally horns changes, and the signal to depart reverberates throughout the city as the first rays of dawn appear. Thousands of men in Athens' agora are about to start a quick march—two paces per second for the twenty-six miles to Marathon.

"Enough talk for now," says Themistocles. "We need to save our breath for the next few hours. Arrichion, my request will come later for you to tell us more about your ancestor, who lives forever in glory."

～◡

Ares, the God of War, watches nine thousand hoplites march far below him. Their line looks like a long slithering snake. The fighters have been moving at double time for three hours and they stretch more than a mile along the main route from Athens to Marathon. They are circumventing Mount Pentelicon to the south; everyone is breathing hard and sweating heavily as the sun climbs higher in the morning sky. There is little conversation.

As they march, the hoplites wear or carry roughly half of their military panoply of bronze armor and weapons, while their slaves, traveling with them, carry the other half. Each man—both hoplite and slave—is thus responsible for about thirty-five pounds of the panoply's seventy-pound total.

As they press on, Themistocles and Sicinnus march alongside the same men they were talking with when they left Athens—Miltiades, Aeschylus, Kye, and Arrichion. Aristides has joined them.

"The sun is halfway up the sky." Aristides grunts after a sharp look upward. "We should be at Marathon by noon. You see, if you . . ."

"You talk too much," huffs Themistocles. "March."

Offended, Aristides answers in his maddening, schoolmasterish way, "Words of wisdom are always worth espousing. And for those with even minimal intelligence, listening to . . ."

At that instant, a bloodcurdling scream blasts from the direction of Mount Pentelicon, and several hundred of the marchers stop in their tracks. Themistocles looks toward the top of a large olive tree just beyond the rise above them, where the sound seems to have come from. The shriek was piercingly pained, as if something powerful was being killed. But it might have been a war cry.

The hoplites react as one—an instant of fear chased off by disbelief. How could they be under attack? Where are the Greek scouts? Then, disbelieving or not, they scramble, grabbing armor from their slaves and attempting to create a makeshift phalanx on rocky and irregular terrain that makes forming good lines for defense nearly impossible. As best they can, they prepare for an assault on their left flank. The same questions crowd the mind of each man: How did the Persians get so far from the beachhead at Marathon, how did the Greek scouts miss them, what happened to the warleader's vanguard?

"Stand fast!" shouts Miltiades, stepping out front, hands held high so the frantic men can see him. "Level spears. No advance. Hold your ground."

The ranks quickly take shape, now three rows deep. With an unconscious swagger, Miltiades tromps to the far right of the front line, the position of greatest danger and greatest glory. His jaw juts so far forward that he looks almost deformed. Unconsciously, his men contort their faces to mimic his. And they listen.

A few moments pass, and the men's alertness opens to curiosity. Another few breaths, and then Themistocles, next to Miltiades, snarls, "My man Sicinnus is right behind me. Let him go up and look. He's surefooted and the fastest runner here."

"Not as fast as a Persian arrow."

"He has his shield."

Miltiades pauses and then, thinking of no better option, says, "Send him up."

Themistocles immediately starts pulling off the armor Sicinnus is wearing as an honorary hoplite. As soon as the servant is stripped down to his shield and knife, Themistocles commands him, "Go."

Sicinnus dashes straight for the olive tree just over the rise. Themistocles starts to strip off his own armor. Then, without a word to the hoplites' commander, he races after his slave with the same lack of protection—nothing but a shield and a double-edged knife.

When Themistocles reaches the crest, he sees Sicinnus standing alone under the olive tree about twenty strides away. As he runs toward the tree he sees Sicinnus studying something in his hand.

Arriving, Themistocles says, "There's nothing here! What's going on?"

"I don't know, but look at this. I picked it up before you came over the hill crest." Sicinnus opens his hand; on his palm is a large, glittering feather. Themistocles carefully takes it for closer examination. He lifts it up and down; it is surprisingly heavy.

Themistocles looks up at Sicinnus and speaks softly, "Solid gold."

Sicinnus nods.

Still softly, Themistocles says, "We need to look for more feathers."

"I already have; there are no others."

"Where exactly did you find this?"

"Over there." Sicinnus points to a spot near the tree trunk.

Themistocles steps over to examine the area. There is a deep, irregular depression in the ground—a small, deformed crater—as if something hit there, hard. Themistocles does not like what he sees. He turns to Sicinnus and says, in a low voice, "Do not speak of this. No feather, no hole in the ground. Say nothing. I don't know what happened here, but this is our secret. We'll talk later. Come with me."

Slave and master run back toward the waiting hoplites. When the two men reach the top of the rise so the others can see them, Themistocles yells with a signaling wave, "All clear! There's no one here."

Miltiades, after shouting to the troops once more to hold the line, motions to Aristides, and the two of them run toward Themistocles and Sicinnus as Themistocles rushes down the rise, hoping to thwart anyone's ascent.

When they meet, Themistocles blurts out, "Some sort of animal probably killed something up there. That must have been the noise that sounded like screaming. But there's nothing there now, so whatever it was must have carried its victim away."

"Nothing?" says Aristides. "That's hard to believe."

"Hard to believe or not, that's what I saw—nothing. Nothing alive, anyway. We're wasting our time here."

"I don't know," mutters Aristides. "This doesn't make sense."

Themistocles takes a firm step toward Aristides. "Listen," he says, "if you want to snivel over nothing, go ahead. Forget about the Persians."

Themistocles motions to Sicinnus and they jog down to the bottom of the rise and then turn toward Marathon. Leaving his armor behind in the hands of other slaves, Themistocles intends to quickly work his way to the front of the long column. After matching strides, they begin talking together quietly in short bursts; Sicinnus, as the better runner, is less easily winded than his master.

Sicinnus, who witnessed the charade of anger Themistocles put on for Aristides, asks, "Why the secret?"

"One good question deserves another," says Themistocles. "What do you think about the feather?"

"I don't know. It's strange."

"Do you think it might be an omen?"

Sicinnus jogs a few paces silently, then a realization strikes him. "The goddess Athena sometimes appears as an owl of gold."

"So the patron of Athens drops a feather, and . . . we hear an awful scream on our way to fight to the death . . . for her city." Themistocles jogs a few more paces, panting. "What do you make of that?"

"Can't say I like it."

"That's why the feather is our secret."

"You want to keep the omen a secret from the men . . . even the leaders?"

"The leaders above all."

After a silence, Sicinnus says, "Why keep an omen, whatever it means, secret . . . especially from the leaders . . . who should know best how to interpret it . . . if it *is* an omen?"

"We're a long way from the Oracle of Delphi . . . You say our leaders . . . know best how to interpret an omen. So which of our leaders . . . will be most responsible for interpreting it?"

"The warleader, Callimachus."

"And what he thinks it means . . . will be influenced by the war council . . . the ten generals."

"You're one of them."

"But just one. The question . . . for him and the war council . . . will be simple."

He goes silent and jogs ahead.

"And that is?" asks Sicinnus.

"What does this . . . *possible* omen . . . mean? The destruction . . . of the Greeks . . . or the Persians?"

The two men continue to jog in silence for a time, then Themistocles says, "Well?"

"I don't know."

"That's right, you don't and . . . neither will Callimachus . . . or the generals. They're all devout . . . take omens very seriously . . . often too seriously . . . especially Callimachus . . . I'm only one of the generals . . . I don't want to debate the issue."

"So you admit it *is* an omen?"

"I don't know . . . if it's an omen . . . and if it is . . . don't know what it means."

Themistocles stops talking long enough to gather his breath, and then says with grim conviction, "And I don't care. All that matters is what we must do and we must do it at Marathon." A few strides later, he adds, "Enough talking for now. I need to preserve my wind."

The two men settle into a steady rhythm and, keeping silent, move ahead along the column, advancing faster than everyone else except for occasional long-distance runners and scouts racing by in both directions, carrying messages between Callimachus at Marathon and Miltiades among the nine thousand hoplites. Eventually they work their way to the front of the column.

~~

Ares, the God of War, is still watching the hoplites. This is the Greeks' second race to Marathon. The warleader and his vanguard ran their race hours earlier. Ares knows more races will come.

He smiles, thinking of their scramble a moment ago to defend themselves against nothing. He listens to their talk about the 'omen' that he knows was no omen at all. As he contemplates what awaits them, his smile broadens. The recent moments of confusion had no consequences. What they are going to face at Marathon will have consequences lasting forever.

CHAPTER NINE

CRASH LANDING

Crouched atop Troy's collapsed southern wall, Athena takes a last look around the ruins. She is barely an arm's length above the ground, as the wall is almost entirely buried. She can see the Aegean Sea in the west and wastelands everywhere else. The ancient magnificence is history, like an aged hero's beautiful youth—glorious, then gone. Like Odysseus. The goddess launches into the sea-scented air. She won't be back for a long time.

She suffers from her passion for Themistocles. But she knows their future must wait a little longer. For now, she needs to focus on protecting Themistocles and her city. She must guard and guide him so he can do the same for his people and their progeny—the children of Athens whose survival depends on his success. And then the future beyond—what will that future be? Even she cannot know.

Before the great struggle begins in earnest, Athena will give herself a small pleasure—just a little diversion to be near Themistocles for a moment. It will take only an instant to get close enough to watch him strut past with the other hoplites on their quick-march from Athens. She smiles. Unlike her slow flight to Troy's ruins, meant to deceive Zeus and Poseidon, this flight will be done in an instant, quick as thought.

As she flashes by high overhead, she catches sight of the long, slender serpent shedding skin and sloughing scales as it slithers northeast. Seen from the clouds, the winding shape seems to undulate forbiddingly like a water snake maneuvering toward its prey.

The bright metal of weapons and armor is easy to see even from this height. But there is more than that; she can see the sheen of the sweat-soaked men marching at a near run in the late summer heat.

Athena looks toward the northeast, where the snake is headed, and she sees its prey. But that is no hapless quarry in the distance; it is a monster, and it is enormous.

The encounter to come begins to take shape. Two beasts will clash—the slim Greek serpent and the great Persian lion. Different features and different cultures, but each with the same intention—to kill the other.

The goddess imagines the impending clash but quickly shifts her attention when she sees her favorite mortal. Athena's timing is impeccable. Themistocles is approaching a large olive tree that will give her a perfect view as he marches past.

The goddess takes aim. Her arms flare and transform into wings with flashing plumes as she changes into a golden owl, and she plummets toward the earth, her talons forward and open. With a powerful swoop, she reaches out toward a limb of the tree, but then the unthinkable happens.

The limb vanishes. The entire tree disappears. Athena has to stop in midair—a challenge even for a goddess. She spreads her wings wide and somersaults to break her momentum, but the maneuver is not quite enough; she lets out a piercing shriek and lands face-first in the dirt. She looks up from the ground and sees the tree reappear. It seems to be smiling down at her, mockingly. Athena's owl-beak clenches hard. She knows who performed this little piece of divine trickery. Uncle Poseidon must be bursting with laughter.

And so the petty tit for tat between Poseidon and Athena continues. Athena bitterly recalls his mistreatment of her dear Odysseus during his ten-year struggle to return home after the Trojan War. The God of Waters harassed him with titanic waves and immense whirlwinds, and Athena had to use everything in her power to keep Odysseus from drowning. Now, thinking about Poseidon, she flies off again and soars up to find the winds that can cool her rage.

CHAPTER TEN

THE QUICK MARCH ENDS

At the head of the column of hoplites from Athens, Themistocles and Sicinnus are approaching the final hill on their route. Neither high nor steep, it will not challenge them to run up to its crest for a view of the plain of Marathon. They are looking for signs of the flying column that left Athens during the night and should already be here.

Themistocles, slowing down a bit so he will not arrive winded, sees several hoplites standing on top of the rise. It is still too far to identify any individuals except one. A large man, tall and solid, starts walking down toward him. Themistocles knows the warleader's gait, strong yet nimble.

When they get within shouting distance, Themistocles hears the question he expected: "What took you so long?"

"We took our time so you could have the glory of slaughtering our guests by yourself."

"Thanks for thinking of me," says Callimachus with a grin. "But what kind of glory are you after? No shield, no armor, no spear—just a knife. That's a strange way to fight."

"When the time comes, I plan to be naked to make it a fair fight, wave my knife at their crotch and make them scamper off, bleating like sheep."

"Beat you to it," Callimachus says with a grunt. "Sounds like what I did a little while ago when some Persian scouts came up here. Didn't stay long. Raced back to tell their mothers nasty stories about those uncivilized Greeks!"

Themistocles drops his bluster. "So the Persians have already been up here?"

"Just scouts," says Callimachus. "By now they should have report-ed back exactly what we wanted them to see: the Greeks already here, and on the high ground. When our vanguard arrived first thing this morning, we spread ourselves over the conspicuous spots so we'd look like thousands. The Persians don't know the lay of the land, except for that vile ass Hippias, and by the time he tells them what to do and the scouts report back a second time, all our hoplites will be in place. Our scouts tell me the rest of our army isn't far behind you."

"Then all is well, so far?"

"Could be worse. We got here in time so at least we aren't racing back to Athens to defend ourselves—yet."

Themistocles pauses at the word "yet" but his contemplation is cut short when Callimachus says, "Come with me."

The two men walk quickly up the slope, with Sicinnus following. As they near the crest, Themistocles anticipates the view he has seen here so often. The plain of Marathon is a magical place sweeping toward the sea. Fertile fields of fennel with small yellow flowers and delicious aromas gradually descend toward the main attractions—the long, white beach and the emerald-blue bay, protected by a thin, twisting peninsula that stretches outward at the bay's far eastern end. Looking down from the hills toward the lowlands, the beauty of this place usually brings tranquility and meditation.

But this time, when Themistocles reaches the hilltop and stares at the sprawl before him, he is overwhelmed by shock, not serenity. The blue bay is covered by a thick gray crust—hundreds upon hundreds of warships and cargo barges. And the beautiful white beaches swarm with Persians by the thousands, everywhere. Still farther away, beyond the Great Marsh, horses are being unloaded from barges lined up as far as his eyes can see. Miltiades, who once lived among the Persians, has told horrific tales about the devastation these animals and their riders can inflict on an enemy's flanks.

Only one area is clear of the Persians and their warhorses. The Great Marsh is a short distance inland from the seashore and extends along much of the narrow beach. Unspoiled by the invading men and animals, the marsh and its greenery look alluring from the vantage point of the hills, but up close the marsh is deadly. Its mud traps the unwary like soft tar. The only movement it allows is downward, as intruders sink and disappear beneath the sludge.

Momentarily speechless, Themistocles finally asks, "How many?"

"Eighty thousand, more or less," Callimachus says. "That includes the ships' rowers, who probably won't fight. So, of fighters, only about forty, forty-five."

So we're outnumbered *only* four to one!"

"Well, our friends in the good city of Plataea are sending us a thousand hoplites, all they have, and they should get here today. And if the fight holds off until the Spartans arrive, I don't think we'll be outnumbered by any *more* than four to one."

"That's a comfort."

Both men stay silent for a moment as they survey the staggering scene. Finally, Themistocles asks, "How many horses?"

"About a thousand."

"Outnumbered four to one, *and* they have a thousand horses," Themistocles says with a deep sigh. "So now what?"

"We wait."

"For what?"

"A mistake."

"And if they don't make one?"

The warleader is silent, but Themistocles knows what his silence means—a return to Athens. He is unnerved that Callimachus is even considering it.

"Time is on our side," Callimachus finally says. "And we're lucky to be near pastureland with plenty of grazing animals."

"What do you mean?"

The warleader points toward the river and springs that water the plain below them.

"Notice anything about them?"

Themistocles looks at them intently.

Callimachus glances at him with satisfaction. "Don't know about you, but I like putrefied pigs best. But sheep work almost as well. If we can get our hands on some of those fancy Persian horses, they'll work fine too, once they're gutted."

A smile begins to appear on Themistocles' face.

The warleader continues, "We let them ripen in the sun. Then we throw them into some of those streams. We can't ruin all the fresh water, but we can foul enough to make some of our guests sick, maybe a lot of them. Men with the runs make poor fighters. After the rest of our men arrive and we position ourselves to truly cover the high ground and the two routes to Athens, our next job will be to round up and kill all the animals we can."

"It's late summer so the water flow is low," says Themistocles, taking up the warleader's idea. "That should make it easier."

"Right. The river would be the easiest to poison, but it still flows high, perhaps too high. The lesser flow of the springs makes them more vulnerable." Callimachus narrows his eyes to stare at Themistocles, and asks, "How often do you crap?"

"How often do I take a shit?"

"No need to be uncouth," Callimachus says with a smile.

Laughing, Themistocles responds, "Ah, yes, I forgot—we must be prim and proper for our warleader, the prestigious Polemarch." He puts his hand on his chin and rolls his eyes in mock contemplation. "I'd say once a day, give or take."

"And how much does it weigh?"

"My crap?"

"That's what we're talking about. And I don't mean the stuff that comes out of your mouth."

Themistocles rolls his eyes again and grins. "That's a harder question. Can't remember the last time I hefted it. Maybe a half-pound."

Callimachus turns to gaze again at Marathon's beach. "Down there we have eighty thousand Persians. That's forty thousand pounds of crap every day. Plus a thousand horses. A healthy horse craps fifty pounds a day, and if the animal has diarrhea it will crap eighty pounds a day until it recovers or dies. For our purposes, one sick horse is worth more than a hundred sick Persians."

"I didn't know you were so good with numbers," says Themistocles. "And I didn't realize you spend your waking hours studying such things. But we aren't going to win this fight because their bowels won't hold."

"Misery is the point. Misery breeds mistakes. We need the Persians to make a decisive mistake. And so we want to make them as miserable as possible."

Themistocles falls silent, heartened to hear Callimachus acting like the renowned warleader he is, contemplating tactics for winning instead of reasons to retreat.

"I have a different question," Callimachus says, staring at him again. "The runners tell me while you were marching here, you came to a large olive tree where your men were shocked by a terrible scream. After you investigated, you told Miltiades there was nothing there. What do you think I should make of that?"

Themistocles shows no reaction to the question. But the warleader sees Sicinnus flinch, a few paces away.

CHAPTER ELEVEN

DOUBLE TROUBLE

Hippias stands on the beach, brushing the sand from his hands and knees. The sun is well above the horizon now and there are puddles of blood at his feet. He seems composed.

Datis rushes up to him. "What's happening?"

"We need to get off the beach and onto solid ground." Hippias sounds cool-headed and matter-of-fact. "And we need to get to Athens."

"What are you talking about? My men said you were vomiting blood and asking for your mother."

"I had a coughing and sneezing fit. I'm better now."

The commander looks at him skeptically.

"There's blood all over your face and the sand. And what are these holes in the ground? What were you digging for?"

"I said I was having a fit and it hurt so I pawed at the ground. It's happened to me since my childhood, it's nothing. When you're as old as I am, you'll be happy to still be able to dig in the sand on your hands and knees."

"Why were you crying for your mother?"

"I was having a fit, I told you, and I invoked my mother. It's over."

Datis looks at the two soldiers who saw what happened. With shaking heads, they signal that Hippias was not just invoking his mother; there was some other meaning, something unknown.

"We have to get off the beach to solid ground," Hippias says again.

"That is exactly what we are working to do," says Datis, exasperated. "Why are you squawking about it now?"

"You're Persian and won't understand," says Hippias. "But let me try. For you, the beach is nothing more than an area to cross between sea and land. On the sea, the Persian fleet cannot be successfully challenged by anyone, anywhere. And on solid ground, your soldiers and archers and warhorses can devastate the enemy. But the beach is the in-between place—the place of uncertainty."

Datis spits and scoffs, "You're talking nonsense. But you're right about our Persian fleet on the sea; we're invincible. And while solid ground is always best, our archers and warhorses are effective on any shore, as long as it's flat, and Marathon is, as you can see." Datis gestures sarcastically toward the level plain before them. "We made sure of that before we accepted your advice to disembark here. So whether it's a beach or solid ground, the result will be the same. We are unbeatable."

"You don't understand. We Greeks draw strength from the joining place of ocean and earth. But the shore is a place of uncertainty and it's dangerous, especially for foreigners."

Datis spits again, "The beach is the in-between place; it gives you strength. What are you talking about? I thought you Greeks were rational!"

Before Datis can say more, a sweating Persian scout runs up, kneels, and gasps, "Forgive me, Commander! Do not strike me! I have news."

The scout waits with his head bowed.

"Well?"

The scout pauses fearfully before speaking. "The Greeks are here."

"What?" Datis raises his hand as if to strike the man. "What are you talking about? Where?"

"In the hills, all over them, everywhere up there."

"How many?" Datis asks, lowering his arm.

"Hundreds in plain sight. There may be thousands more in the hills behind them."

Turning around toward his ships, Datis shouts, "Form up, form up!

Position the archers. Prepare for attack."

When Datis starts to run toward the ships, Hippias shouts, "Datis, hold up!"

Datis wheels around. "What? A moment ago you were babbling about your mother, and now the Greeks are here. We still have thousands of men to unload, and the horses aren't ready. We're vulnerable."

"Something doesn't make sense. If the Greeks were here in force, they would already be on us. Look over there, near where the horses are being unloaded." Datis looks where the Greek is pointing. "Off toward the north, there's a path to a hilltop that should give a clear view of the Greeks' position on the other side of the hills. Fast runners can get up the hill in half an hour. Send those with the best eyes."

"I'll send scouts on horses."

"Use runners. The path up that hill is too rugged for horses."

"It will be done," says Datis. "Anything else?"

"Yes. We should hear if the scout has more to report."

Datis yells at the scout, "What else?"

The scout hesitates again, then says, "I got close enough to make out a man who looks like their leader. A big man, tall and broad."

Hippias listens closely.

"He pointed at me and then at his groin, back and forth several times. Then he turned sideways and bent over and pointed at his—with respect, sir—at his butt. Then he stood up and pointed back at me and motioned me to come to him. He whistled, the way you call a dog."

"That's the Greeks for you," says Datis, "Your Greeks, Hippias."

"More to the point," Hippias responds, "that's Callimachus."

"The warleader you told me about?"

Hippias nods. "We have to get off this beach. We need to move fast."

Datis turns back toward the ships and shouts again, "Form up, form up!"

As the Persian commander sets off at a run, Hippias calls out to him,

"You should send a thousand soldiers straight at Callimachus right now. We have no time to wait. Attack Callimachus now!"

Datis does not look back.

CHAPTER TWELVE

BANQUET LESSONS

Phar cannot take his eyes off the Great King's knuckles. The young Egyptian heard Darius whisper his hatred of the Greeks but does not understand why that hatred is so intense. He realizes, however, that it is best to stay silent and listen when the Great King's fists are gripping each other so hard his knuckles are white.

Darius speaks aloud, to himself, "Remember the Greeks."

Phar looks up and sees that the king's eyes are closed.

Darius continues. "Hate must be remembered because hate requires retribution. Some say otherwise, but they are not the Great King."

The king's eyes snap open as if he has broken a trance. He relaxes his hands and his face and takes a long, slow breath. He seems to be deep in thought.

"The answer starts twenty years ago. The Athenians ousted their tyrant, Hippias—a good man, at least for your Great King's purposes, and they created a new, strange way to make decisions and rule their city. Phar, have you ever heard of democracy?"

"No, Great King, I do not know the word."

"Don't try to figure it out; it is of little consequence. Do you know what it means to vote?"

"Do you mean, Great King, counting the opinions of the advisors to a ruler?"

"Yes and no. Counting opinions is correct, but the opinions are not to advise their ruler. Athens no longer has a ruler. After they exiled Hippias, the Athenians began to make decisions by counting opinions. Whatever opinion has the most votes becomes the decision."

"Votes make decisions, Great King? I don't understand . . ."

"Don't try," Darius interrupts. "Stupidity and insanity are impossible to understand unless you are senseless and crazy yourself. Besides, there is only one democracy in the world and it will soon disappear. In a short time it will succumb to the invasion of Datis, and the thing called 'democracy' will be gone for good."

"Based on what you say, Great King, gone for good sounds good," says Phar.

"Now your Great King will explain why the Greeks must be remembered." Darius looks at the young Egyptian with an almost avuncular smile. "When Hippias was exiled from Athens, he wisely came to Persia and offered his services to your Great King, and your Great King accepted him. Then the Greeks continued to do what they so often do—fight among themselves."

Darius pauses briefly. "Listen carefully, Phar. In a moment, you can answer the question: Why do his servants tell the Great King to remember the Greeks?"

"Great King, I am listening carefully."

"After the Athenians got rid of Hippias, they struggled with their new democracy and, not surprisingly, had difficulty making coherent decisions. The Spartans, long their rivals, decided it was a good time for a full-fledged attack. Wisely, Athens sent envoys to your Great King seeking assistance. In response, your Great King asked the Athenian envoys to offer earth and water as signs of submission, which they did. Your Great King's envoys then advised the Spartans that the Great King's pleasure was for the Spartans to stand down, and they wisely assented."

Darius leans back in his chair and smiles. "The Spartans are militant thugs, but they are not stupid. They know when to fight and when to refrain. Phar, do you understand?"

"Yes, Great King, I understand. I know people like that—vicious but cautious. They can be dangerous."

"Yes, very dangerous," replies Darius. "Especially if they are treated with no respect. When the Spartans complied with your Great King's request, they said they wanted Hippias to return and rule Athens once again, and your Great King approved. But the Athenians refused. A while later there was a revolt in the far western reaches of the Persian Empire near the Great Sea, in the land of Lydia. This is an area of Greek colonies our armies subjugated three generations ago. The colonies in revolt were supported by their Greek brethren across the Aegean Sea—mainly by Athens.

"Later, your Great King's massive army approached the colonies intending to crush the revolt. The Athenians abandoned their effort, but before they departed they sacked Sardis, the capital of Lydia, and burned it to the ground—a treachery and an insult that reverberated throughout the empire. Finally, just a year ago, your ever-patient Great King gave cities throughout the land of the Greeks one final chance to submit by offering your Great King's heralds earth and water. Many cities complied and some others equivocated; only two cities clearly rejected the heralds' requests. In Athens and Sparta the Great King's heralds were told to find their own earth and water and thrown down a well to their deaths. These heralds were under your Great King's personal protection and deemed sacred under laws recognized everywhere."

Darius pauses and looks off in the distance, while stroking his beard. Finally, he says, "Your Great King's summary of the last two decades is finished."

Phar is so shocked that he briefly forgets he is supposed to answer Darius' earlier question. "You are the Great King. You are Darius the Great. The Athenians rejected your instructions to take back Hippias. And they killed the sacred heralds under your personal protection. This is all hard to believe."

"And your answer to your Great King's question?" asks Darius.

"Why your servants remind you to remember the Greeks?" says Phar. "Great King, I am not certain, but my guess is the burning of Sardis."

Darius nods his head in silence. He then turns to Xerxes and asks, "Did you hear his answer?"

Xerxes has been watching the banquet guests, seemingly indifferent to the conversation between Darius and Phar. Now he leans his head back so he is looking down his nose at the young Egyptian. "I heard," he says.

Darius turns back to Phar and asks, "Why is your answer the burning of Sardis?"

Phar replies, "Great King, I cannot say why I suspect the burning of Sardis is the reason you want to remember them. There may be an explanation for what I think, but my answer is based on instinct."

"Your instinct is good," says Darius.

Darius turns his head toward the feast, but after a moment Phar realizes Darius is looking beyond the banquet guests toward three men who are walking toward them. The men are wearing identical garments—pure white robes with their heads wrapped in red cloth. Each also wears a white veil over his nose and mouth. When the men arrive, they stand before a table that has been left unoccupied for them.

Darius stands up; immediately all the seated guests do likewise. Everyone falls silent. Looking straight at the new arrivals, the Great King solemnly intones, "Ahura Mazda."

In unison, the banquet guests chant, "Ahura Mazda." The white-robed men look to the Great King, who sits down. The three men then take their seats, as do the rest of the guests.

Anticipating Phar's question, Darius says, "Magi, Persian priests of the religion of the prophet Zoroaster."

"Great King, is Ahura Mazda the religion's chief god, the supreme deity?"

Darius narrows his eyes and his expression turns to a scowl, "Phar, you just made a mistake—your first one so far. You are human—and young—

and your Great King will tolerate this one mistake, but do not repeat it. Ahura Mazda is not a god. He is *the* God. Ahura Mazda is the *only* God."

Phar is surprised. In Egypt, his countrymen worship countless gods. Almost a thousand years earlier, a sickly, deformed pharaoh who recognized only one god had tried to impose his will on his subjects, but he has been largely forgotten except for a few writings on the walls of ancient tombs. If the Great King is correct, the idea of one and only one god prompts an unanswerable question: What happened to all the other gods?

Phar opens his mouth but he is not sure what to say. Darius cuts him off by raising his hand for silence.

Looking off to his left, Darius says, "This conversation will continue in a moment, but there is another matter I must attend to now. Observe your Great King as he renders justice."

Darius moves his hand and immediately a herald presents himself. Darius nods and the herald speaks, "Great King, today's message from Datis has arrived."

"The courier's time?" asks Darius.

"He was late, Great King," the herald replies, as he swallows hard. "He was due at noon, when the sun is straight overhead and there are no shadows to east or west. The shadows had just begun to lengthen, so he was late—but only slightly."

Phar watches and listens intently, although he does not understand the meaning of the Great King's question or the herald's answer. Phar senses a hesitation—perhaps a quaver—in the herald's voice. This is surprising because the herald's initial bearing was solid and certain, reminding Phar of his own father. And the herald also appears close to Phar's father's age, in his mid-forties.

"Return the message to the courier and bring him here," says Darius. "He will deliver the message in person."

There is a fleeting twitch on the herald's face, but he says nothing and promptly departs.

Knowing the young Egyptian is bewildered, Darius explains, "Every day, your Great King receives a message from Datis, the military commander who has sailed west across the Aegean Sea two thousand miles from here. The Greeks call the Aegean the wine-dark sea, but soon everyone will call it the Sea of Darius the Great. As I speak, Datis is being guided by a mean-spirited old man, none other than Hippias the Greek."

Darius continues, "Your Great King gave Hippias protection twenty years ago and now he is returning the favor. He will be richly rewarded because your Great King has designated him to be satrap of all the Greek lands. A perfect man for such rule. Consumed by the desire for vengeance, he has not aged well. Hippias will be a bane to the Greeks, but he is too old to survive for long. His successor will be such a relief to the Greeks that they will praise the wisdom of their Great King. That is when their tribute to the empire's treasury will double."

"Fascinating, Great King," says Phar. "But what were you saying about the courier being late, and why is the courier required to give you his message in person?"

"The message from Datis is due here every day by noon, when the sun hangs straight overhead. Everyone has obligations in life. Your Great King's obligation is to serve the One True God, Ahura Mazda, and expand the empire. If another man's obligation is to deliver a message to the Great King on time, and if that man does not fulfill his obligation, there is a failing. Such a failing must be judged and the Great King's justice must be rendered. Does that make sense to you?"

Confident he knows the correct answer, the emissary emphatically says, "Indeed it does."

"Good," says Darius. "Your Great King trusts the next few moments will not be too troubling or disturb your appetite, because the banquet is just beginning."

"I have a strong constitution, Great King," says the young Egyptian, with feigned bravado.

Although the emissary tries to put on a good front, his mind races with the image of a well-known example of Darius' justice. Some years earlier a man named Fravartish strongly displeased the Great King and had his nose, ears, and tongue cut off and one eye dug out. The other eye was left intentionally, to deepen his misery. Then Fravartish was chained outside the palace entrance for all to see. When he had recovered sufficiently to fully appreciate more pain, he was flayed alive, screaming and flopping like a flounder. Finally, his flayed corpse was impaled outside the palace next to another impalement—his own skin stuffed with straw. People who came to gawk at the grisly scene were asked to pick their favorite Fravartish.

"Great King, I have one more question," says Phar. "I saw the herald flinch when you told him to bring the courier to you. He seemed apprehensive, especially when he told you that the courier was only slightly late. Why did he act like that?"

"Because he is a father," Darius says, his voice devoid of emotion. "Parents can be like that. The courier is his son and only child."

CHAPTER THIRTEEN

THE INTERROGATION

Callimachus stares at Themistocles, waiting for him to explain the scream near the olive tree. As a master of intimidation, the warleader is adept at implying that he already knows the answers to his questions. But Themistocles is a master of human nature and knows how to read a bluff.

The two men are standing on the hill above the plain of Marathon, and Sicinnus is nearby. Every so often, a breeze from the sea brings with it the murmur of the Persian forces disembarking onto the narrow beach. The men pretend to ignore those sounds. Hoplites stand at intervals along the hills around them. The sun blazes near its zenith.

"I'm surprised Miltiades spent precious time trying to figure that out," says Themistocles. "And even more surprised he thought it important enough to send a runner to you about what was plain enough, at least to me. Some animal killed another and carried off its prey. There was nothing there. Certainly no Persians."

"That's what the runner told me you said." Callimachus keeps staring. "Actually, it seems Aristides was more concerned than Miltiades. The runner said Aristides wanted me to know the scream was terrible, quite unworldly. And that our men were unnerved."

"Well, I wasn't," says Themistocles. "Like you and Miltiades, I go back a long way with Aristides. He's an honest man. They don't call him 'The Just' for nothing. And he's brave, without a doubt. But sometimes he acts like an old grandmother wringing her hands, and this is one of those times."

"Perhaps," says the warleader. "Still, it's a strange story. I'm told there was no blood on the ground, no trail showing an animal was dragged off.

The runner said Aristides wanted me to know the details." He pauses for confirmation. Themistocles nods, coolly. He had not said any of that, but he would allow for the implication; Aristides always liked to pile things on.

Callimachus goes on, still watching him. "The runner also said your slave was the first on the scene. Sicinnus is his name, I think?"

"True."

"In the past you have spoken highly of him, didn't call him a slave, instead called him 'your man.' I would like to talk to him."

"Of course." Themistocles motions for Sicinnus to step forward.

This is a development that Themistocles did not anticipate. Briefly turning toward Sicinnus as he approaches, Themistocles' widened eyes and raised eyebrows send a clear message: watch yourself. Although Themistocles is confident of Sicinnus' quick wit, the slave is confronting a citizen of Athens, and any slave who speaks an untruth to a citizen looks death straight in the face.

"Sicinnus, I know of you," says Callimachus. "Your master has spoken about you. So has the city's best runner, Phidippides. I remember him calling you the best runner he knows. With proper training, he says you might be even better than himself."

"I am honored to hear those words," says Sicinnus. "And also honored to know Phidippides well. He has my highest respect. But he can be too humble. I have no illusions of matching his feats."

"Well said. Themistocles told me you are well-educated. You tutor his children. How did you come by your training?"

"As a youth, until age sixteen, I was educated in Persia. My father was a successful merchant, so all his children had the best educations, even my sisters."

"You are Persian?"

"By birth, yes."

Callimachus nods thoughtfully. "And you've lived in Athens how long?"

"Eight years."

"And you remain fluent in the language of Persia?"

"Yes."

"You've lost nothing since you left so long ago?"

"I have lost nothing. I can speak and comprehend as if I never left."

"Interesting."

Listening to the conversation, Themistocles is becoming uncomfortable. What is Callimachus up to? Is he trying to distract and confuse? Is he setting some sort of trap?

"So, eight years in Athens," the warleader continues. "And you were with Themistocles that whole time?"

"Yes. Themistocles saved my life and brought me to Athens."

"Saved your life?"

"Yes. Also, the life of my wife."

"And your wife's life."

"We weren't married at the time. We married three years ago."

"So you must feel a strong loyalty to Themistocles?"

"A loyalty and a bond of obligation."

"A bond of obligation," repeats Callimachus as he looks at Themistocles.

Themistocles thinks the look is an invitation to say something—bait he decides to ignore. He is ill at ease about where this conversation is going.

Looking back at Sicinnus, Callimachus says, "Your story is most interesting, and one day I'll hear more of it, but now I have another question. You say you came from a rich Persian family. Did your family— your father—know any of the royalty of Persia, any of the rulers and clans involved with King Darius?"

"No, the only times I remember him talking about the rulers were when he grumbled about their constant intrigues. He told me many times, 'If you want to be happy and earn a fair profit, avoid schemers, no matter who they are.'"

"Excellent," Callimachus says softly to himself.

Themistocles finally understands what this conversation is about, or at least what it is not about. Callimachus is not focused on some action at the olive tree. The warleader is not concerned about what happened in the past, even a couple of hours ago. He is doing what he always does—looking to the future, thinking about the battle to come, calculating, plotting.

The warleader continues, "Our entire army will begin arriving shortly and we will become very busy very fast. But before they get here I'm interested in one more issue—the gods. Sicinnus, you grew up in Persia and have lived longer there than in Athens. Whose gods do you worship?"

"I accept the gods of the Greeks," says Sicinnus.

"Good. I thought perhaps your loyalty to Themistocles might have made you somewhat skeptical, perhaps even a bit corrupted in your way of thinking." With a dry smile, Callimachus glances at Themistocles.

"I am not at all skeptical," says Sicinnus. "I pray to the gods of the Greeks." Sicinnus wants to say more in defense of Themistocles' faith but decides to hold his tongue.

"Does that mean you have rejected the gods of Persia?" asks Callimachus.

"In Persia the prophet Zoroaster says there is only one god—Ahura Mazda. I do not believe that."

"I've heard about the Persians' belief in only one god. Hard to understand. I can't imagine any religion like that lasting very long."

"Actually," Sicinnus says, "Zoroastrianism is very old. And there is another old religion that promotes only one god—the religion of the Hebrews."

"Never heard of them. And what do they call their god?"

"Yahweh, but they won't say the name out loud because it is too sacred to them."

"Ahura Mazda is the only god, and Yahweh is the only god, and you can't speak his name. And no goddesses at all! Too strange for me."

Callimachus turns to Themistocles with a knowing smile. "Your man, Sicinnus, is well-educated indeed. He knows about obscure people and strange religions I've never heard of. We may continue this conversation later, but for now, look behind you. Our men are arriving and in the lead is none other than your good friend, the 'grandmother.'"

Themistocles is glad to see his pedantic friend, Aristides, approaching. Callimachus' final questions about different religions and curious gods were giving him a headache.

Callimachus heads down the hill to greet the arrivals.

"What was that all about?" asks Sicinnus.

Themistocles laughs and says, "Callimachus is an odd man. That's part of what it takes to be warleader. The key was when he said 'excellent.'"

"You mean when I told him my family was not involved with the rulers of Persia and the men surrounding the Great King?"

"Yes. Were you telling the truth?"

"Of course," sputters Sicinnus.

"I thought so—just checking."

"So when he said 'excellent,' what did that tell you?"

"It told me what he was focused on—you. He cared about your answer and the fact that your family had no connection with Persian royalty. He also seemed very interested in your fluency in the Persian language."

"Callimachus was focused on me? I don't understand."

"He's going to talk to you again, but it'll be about something entirely different. He has a battle plan or is developing one, and it appears you may play a role in it."

"How do you know all this?"

"Because I know who and what Callimachus is," says Themistocles. "He wants what we all want—glory—but his lust to be remembered is beyond all the rest of us."

"So what is his plan for me?"

"I don't know. And I doubt if he himself fully knows yet. But whatever plan he devises, it may give you glory. And that, of course, means his plan for you will be dangerous, likely very dangerous. The greater the danger, the greater the glory. I'm envious."

CHAPTER FOURTEEN

MANEUVERS

The advantage of high ground can be crucial. Both sides know this. Down on Marathon's beach, Hippias wants the Persians to move immediately into the hills and challenge the Greeks.

But Datis has a different priority. He runs back toward his ships after talking to Hippias, shouting, "Form up, form up!"

Hurrying to keep up with him, an officer asks, "Commander, do you want to send a contingent into the hills to test the Greeks?"

"Not yet. Maybe Hippias is right and not all the Greek forces have arrived. But the risk is too great if he's wrong; our Persian fighters are still disembarking and vulnerable. Unload the horses and archers as fast as you can. We need to get the cavalry in place to hit their flanks if the Greeks come down from the hills. And get the conscripts behind the archers. Use your whips if you need to. Also send a scout on horseback up that hill." Datis gestures toward the hill Hippias pointed out. "Forget what the Greek said about the path being too rough. On foot is too slow."

Datis shouts again toward the ships, "Form up, form up! Archers in front, prepare for attack."

～੭

In the hills, the Greeks are maneuvering. The long column of Athenian hoplites is arriving. Callimachus gives orders to make themselves fully visible to the Persians below, and the soldiers begin to concentrate their forces along the heights, near the two paths from Athens. Callimachus, with Miltiades and Aristides, returns to Themistocles and Sicinnus on the hill crest. Miltiades and Aristides survey the Persian horde.

"Like an invasion of ants," says Callimachus.

"Daunting." Aristides looks grim.

Callimachus gestures toward the activity on the beach. "Their maneuvers are becoming clear. Their archers are forming up and they're rushing to unload the horses."

"Preparing for our possible attack," says Themistocles. "Arrows to greet us from the front and more arrows from their horsemen on our flanks."

"But no sign they're coming up here," Aristides adds.

"They don't know our strength," says the warleader. "If we don't go down there, they'll have to decide whether to come up here to challenge us on the high ground."

"So they don't know how many of us there are?" Themistocles asks.

"Not yet. They're trying to figure that out as we speak. My guess is they have scouts running up that hill over there to get a good look. Hippias knows the terrain; that's what he should have told them to do." The warleader lets out a nasty laugh. "When our vanguard first arrived here, I sent a little welcome party to that hill."

Miltiades points down at the beach. "See the weakness I told you about?"

"The whips?" asks Callimachus.

"Used on the men forced to fight," says Miltiades. "Foreign conscripts. They don't fight well."

"Maybe not, but it looks like they can't run away either," says Callimachus. "If they try to, the Persians will kill them."

"Look at how fast the Persians unload those horses," says Aristides.

"So?" says Themistocles.

"They know what they're doing. And it's not just the horses. It's all their men, too. Watch the Persian organization and speed. Efficiency."

"Efficiency," Themistocles snorts.

"I don't care about efficiency, I care about discipline," Callimachus says. "The Persians show plenty of that unloading their ships."

"It built their empire," says Miltiades.

"Formidable," says Aristides.

"But not invincible," Themistocles adds.

"Maybe, maybe not," says the warleader. "But given what I see, we need to pray to the gods." Then he spots two hoplites running up toward them. "At least we're about to get an answer to one important question."

The hoplites arrive drenched in sweat and splattered with blood.

"Greetings, comrades!" exclaims Callimachus. "You return from the hill sooner than expected. The other two men in your party, did they also return alive and well?"

"All four of us," says one hoplite, nodding. "And we bring you success. You were right, warleader. The Persians sent a scout up that hill to get a view of our troops. Apparently, he got it, but the poor fellow will never report what he saw."

"Just one Persian scout?" asks Callimachus.

"And just one horse," says the hoplite. "We came across it tied to a tree, so we knew the scout must have climbed the rest of the way on foot."

"And?"

"A short while later, we saw the Persian racing down to retrieve his mount. When I jumped out in front of him I thought his eyes would leap from his skull. He turned away and ran straight into my comrade's waiting arms."

The other hoplite grins. "One of my best sticks ever—skewered him with a spear through both legs. He still tried to run—lots of quick little steps. But he didn't get far. Quite a sight to see that spear seesaw sideways."

All the men bellow with laughter except Sicinnus, who manages an unconvincing smile.

"Then what?" asks Callimachus.

"We put him out of his misery and made sure he delivered your message."

"The warleader's message?" asks Themistocles.

"The warleader's words, copied exactly," replies the hoplite. "We tied the scout's body on his horse and sent it back down the trail. Your message is stuffed in his mouth. The Persians will be impressed."

The men guffaw again, except for Sicinnus.

~

Back on Marathon's beach, the Persians continue to organize their formations in front of the ships. Hundreds of archers are backed by a few thousand conscripts who, in turn, are backed by well over a thousand elite soldiers. Unloading the horses is more difficult, but two hundred are already mounted and ready—enough to torment any Greeks who might attack.

Hippias asks Datis, "Commander, how much longer before you send troops into the hills?"

"Not long. We need another fifty horses in place."

"It's taking too long," Hippias objects. "If the Greeks haven't attacked us yet it means they're not here in full force. But they're coming, that's for sure. You're going to miss your chance to get off this beach without a full-fledged fight. We need to attack now."

"We'll be ready soon and *then* we'll attack."

"You'll miss your chance!"

Datis snarls, "Look, you know the terrain here and how those Greek bastards think, but I know how to prepare my men for battle. I've told you what we need—we must disembark safely. Soon we'll no longer be vulnerable. After that I don't care about getting off the beach without a fight—it's a fight we will win, whenever and wherever it comes."

A soldier next to Datis points north and shouts, "A runaway!"

A wild-eyed horse is galloping straight toward them. Hippias calls out, "What is it carrying?"

The grim answer quickly becomes clear as a Persian horseman catches up and reins in the animal. By the time Datis and Hippias reach them, the dead scout has been untied from the horse and laid on the ground.

"What's that sticking out of his mouth?" asks Datis.

A soldier yanks out the knife under the dead man's chin. When the jaw falls open the soldier pulls out a bloody piece of leather. Grabbing a goatskin full of water, the soldier rinses the leather and says, "There's some sort of writing on it."

The soldier hands the leather to Datis, who studies it momentarily and hands it to Hippias, saying, "It's Greek. What does it say?"

Hippias stares at the leather longer than necessary to read it.

"What does it say?" repeats Datis.

"It's an insult," says Hippias. "And a challenge."

Exasperated, Datis yells, "I don't want your explanation; I want to know what it says."

Hippias reads slowly:

PERSIAN SLAVES ALL OF YOU. IN BED WITH YOUR MASTER THE GREAT WHORE DARIUS. YOU WILL SOON DIE FOR THAT WHORE. HE DOES NOT KNOW YOUR NAME. HE DOES NOT CARE. POLEMARCH.

Except for Datis, the listening soldiers are stunned into silence at the words "Great Whore Darius."

For a moment Datis is silent too, and then he says scornfully, "What does 'Polemarch' mean?"

"That's his title," says Hippias. "Warleader. It's from Callimachus."

"Where will he be when we fight?"

"On the battlefield he will be on their far right. In their first row, the last man on their right, where his shield can only protect his left side, with no protection on his right. The place of most danger and greatest honor."

"Then that is where he will die."

Datis looks up at the distant enemies in the hills. He can barely make them out, so he does not know he is looking straight at Callimachus. Or that Callimachus, also without knowing it, is staring back at him. The two commanders are thinking similar thoughts: Today's race is a draw. One or two hours either way would have made all the difference. If the Greeks had arrived earlier they could have slaughtered the unprepared Persians and set fire to their ships. But if the Persians had arrived earlier, by now they would be advancing toward Athens.

Datis and Callimachus also think about what is going to happen. The Greeks have the advantage of high ground. But that advantage will diminish as the Persians continue their preparations and organize the rest of their fighting forces. The Persians' overwhelming numbers, their warhorses, and their archers will make it impossible—suicidal—for the Greeks to attack. The Greeks will have only one option. Defense.

Datis and Callimachus silently ask themselves the same question. Will the high ground be enough to save the Greeks? Their answers are the same. Datis smiles. Callimachus does not.

CHAPTER FIFTEEN

THE GREAT KING'S JUSTICE

The Persian banquet continues, and Darius' attention turns to the sweets. He carefully inspects a dark red cherry. Persians believe that fully ripened fruit, harvested at its peak, has a purity that cannot be bettered through culinary art. Darius tosses the cherry into his mouth. He promptly spits out the pit, catching it on the flat side of a knife blade he holds at arm's length in front of him. Phar's eyes widen at such adroitness. Xerxes, however, looks unimpressed.

A short distance away, two men stand together off to the side of the banquet—the Great King's herald and the herald's son, the overdue courier. Darius motions with his hand and the herald promptly walks forward.

"Instruct the courier to bring your Great King his message," says Darius. "Instruct him to approach alone."

"Yes, Great King," replies the herald.

When the courier arrives, he genuflects until Darius commands, "Arise and give your Great King the message."

After reading the message, Darius abruptly stands. All the banquet guests also stand and fall silent.

"My eminent slaves," Darius begins, "Datis and the Great King's fleet landed on the island of Euboea just off the Greek mainland. They laid siege to the city of Eretria, and the siege will last no more than seven days. Then all Eretrians who survive will be enslaved and the city will be destroyed utterly. Thus says Datis to his Great King."

Xerxes shouts out, "Great King Darius!"

Darius raises both hands for silence and continues, "There is more.

When Commander Datis departs the island of Euboea, the Great King's fleet will be guided by the former Tyrant of Athens, Hippias, to the shore of a place you do not know—it has a name fit only for savages and lies on the east coast of the Greek mainland. From that place, Datis and the Persian Empire will advance to Athens, which will be utterly destroyed and any survivors enslaved. Then, over time, my empire will continue to advance and conquer all the peoples from Athens to the immense ocean rumored to wash the farthest edge of the world, where the sun each day descends into its waters. All lands, everywhere, will belong to the Empire of Persia. Thus says your Great King."

Darius gives a slight nod toward Xerxes, who shouts, "Great King Darius! King of all Persia. King of kings. Euboea. Athens. The Empire of Persia. Great King Darius!"

All the banquet guests and Xerxes repeat the sequence. "Great King Darius. King of all Persia. King of kings. Euboea. Athens. The Empire of Persia. Great King Darius."

Once again Darius raises his hands for silence. He surveys the entire banquet scene and looks many of his guests in the eye. Then, looking high above them, he chants, "Ahura Mazda."

Hearing the name of Persia's one and only God, all the guests and Xerxes bow their heads. The young Egyptian emissary, taken by surprise but quick to understand protocol, does likewise while keeping an eye open to make sure he follows the next move. It comes quickly; everyone raises their heads and looks up at their Great King.

Darius chants, "Ahura Mazda, the Wise Lord, the Uncreated Creator. Ahura Mazda, who demands Truth and Good Works and, in return, gives us Order out of Chaos. Ahura Mazda, who uses Fire to banish Darkness. Ahura Mazda brought me help, and by the favor of Ahura Mazda, I rule as your Great King, King of kings, King of the Empire of Persia, King of all countries."

Darius sits down and the guests follow suit. The banquet festivities resume.

Staring at the courier, Darius asks tersely, "Why were you late?"

"Great King, my horse went lame," replies the courier.

"So the horse is to blame." Darius pauses, looking hard at the courier. "Do you want me to punish the horse? Perhaps draw and quarter the animal? That has been done before. The sound is impressive. Louder than any man's scream—far louder."

"No, Great King, the horse deserves no punishment. I was the rider. I am responsible."

Again the Great King silently stares at the courier, and then commands, "Explain."

"Great King," the courier replies, clearly trying hard to control the tremor in his voice. "After I changed horses at the final station before heading here to Susa, I traveled some distance and my horse went lame. I was much closer to the station than to Susa so I ran back to the station and started again with a fresh horse, but my attempt was not fast enough to arrive here on time."

"Did you put the lame horse out of its misery?" asks Darius.

"No, Great King. The horse could not carry my weight but it could keep up with my run, so I brought it back to the station."

"So the horse is still alive?"

"Yes, Great King. The men there must decide if the horse can be saved."

Again the Great King stares silently at the courier. Then he slowly nods.

"You are dismissed. You may return to your . . . to the Great King's herald."

Darius leans back on his chair and, looking to his right, asks Xerxes, "The courier's fate—how would you rule?"

"Death, without question." The face of the Great King's son is as cold as a mask. "He must be an example to everyone. Failure to fulfill a duty to the Great King is not acceptable."

Darius slowly turns his head and looks at the young Egyptian emissary. Phar feels a twinge of panic; he assumes he knows the question to come. Phar casts his eyes down in an awkward effort to disappear. But Phar's assumption is wrong.

Speaking softly, Darius says, "Wisdom sometimes reveals itself through silence."

Darius turns back to the banquet guests and again stands up. All the guests rise. Darius speaks with the full resonance of his authority and once again intones, "Ahura Mazda."

All heads bow again and Darius continues, "The Uncreated Creator demands we do Good Works. Mercy is a Good Work. As mercy is granted by Ahura Mazda, mercy may be granted by the favor of your Great King."

Darius stops speaking and looks out at all the banquet guests. Phar glances past Darius and sees Xerxes almost imperceptibly shake his head once. Darius slowly sits down. He moves his hand and the herald quickly walks up and stands in front of him.

Leaning toward the herald, Darius says, "This evening you and your wife shall be with your son. Then you will say farewell."

The herald cringes, but Darius continues, "Your son wants to be a soldier in our army—is that true?"

"Yes, Great King, that is his strong desire."

"Tomorrow morning your son will be placed in our army and will immediately depart for Scythia far to the north. He will be away for a full year. After that, his future will depend on his actions as a soldier. If he proves to be his father's son, your Great King will be satisfied. Now inform your son of the Great King's decision, dismiss him, and wait here."

The herald's face is flushed with emotion, and his gratitude is almost palpable. He turns and walks away with a firm stride.

Turning to Phar, Darius says quietly, "A loyal man."

Phar thinks, completing the king's meaning: *Now even more so.*

"I see you have questions."

"Many, Great King."

"I expected so. This is a good time to practice priorities. Ask one question and assume that is the only question to be answered. What is the question that has your highest priority?"

Phar has no intention of asking about the courier and the mercy Darius just granted. Xerxes is within earshot and, after Darius' explicit repudiation of his son's advice, Phar wants to avoid any entanglements with him.

Phar asks, "Why did Datis say with such confidence the siege of Eretria would last no longer than seven days?"

Darius nods and smiles in a way Phar has not seen before—the expression is uncomplicated, almost gentle, and knowing. Phar is reminded of how his own father sometimes looks at him.

Darius replies, "Well, well, your question is not what most men would ask. Why do you ask this question?"

"Great King, I know something about sieges against walled cities; they can last months and often fail. How can Datis know the siege will be so brief, how can he be so certain about the number of days it will last, and how can you be so confident in his prediction that you say so publicly?"

"You say you know something of sieges," replies Darius. "How are sieges usually won; what brings victory?"

"Break the walls, or go over them, or tunnel under them if you can, Great King," says Phar. "But that often is impossible, so victory may come from cutting off the city's food and water. But starving the inhabitants can take a long time—many months perhaps."

"You are correct for most sieges by most armies. But we are talking about the Great King's army, and the Great King's first tactic, always, is treachery. The betrayal of Eretria is set. It is certain that Datis has conferred with some Eretrians—no doubt nobles, as they tend to be the most traitorous lot—and offered them and their families lavish rewards, which they will receive for their faithful service to the Great King. If our army does not slaughter them, of course, in the general mayhem that goes with destroying a city."

"I understand, Great King, I think," says the emissary. "It seems you are telling me military secrets."

Darius does not respond. Instead, he stands up and walks away toward the waiting herald. Surprised, Phar is not sure what to do, so he looks out at the banquet guests. He glances over to see what Xerxes is doing. Phar is relieved that Xerxes is staring straight ahead and not glaring at him.

Darius returns and sits down. Looking at Phar, he says, "Lessons and secrets make good conversation. And when evening comes, fine wine adds to the pleasure. Before you return to Egypt, you will be summoned."

"Great King, I look forward to your summons," Phar replies.

"For now, you may depart with your escort."

Phar realizes someone has come up behind him. He looks over his shoulder and sees the herald.

Phar stands up, bows toward Darius and says, "By your command, Great King." Then he and the herald walk off, and when they are a good distance from the banquet, the herald stops and turns to Phar. "By the Great King's first command, I will be your main bodyguard while you are here, and there will be others you will not know about."

"The first command; is there another?"

The herald seems to hesitate before deciding to speak.

"The Great King's second command," the herald says, looking steadily at the Egyptian, "is that you are never to be alone with his son, Xerxes. Ever."

CHAPTER SIXTEEN

THE LONG RUN

The runner rinses his mouth and spits. Another sip, this time to swallow. Returning the water bag to his pack, he starts off again. Twenty hours into it and at this stage of the run he will stiffen up if he stops for more than a moment. He feels good, but he always feels good after vomiting. The nausea is temporarily gone.

When he felt the sickening sensation gradually coming on, he knew not to fight it. A disciplined professional, he understands how to use his mind—not to dominate the feeling, but to make sure it does not dominate him. He knows when to stop and let himself retch.

Years of training have taught him how to sustain himself through such long runs—how much water to carry, along with the proper mix of salt, bread, fruit, and dried fish to bring in the light bag laced securely across his back.

Drinking water is trickiest. Too little and the leg muscles spasm, or dry heaves bring up nothing but bile. He also knows from painful experience that the strain of dry vomiting cramps a runner's testicles like a tightening vise.

But too much water is the more serious problem. Distance runners always want too much. Water is a Siren whose song can kill. During his runs, Phidippides never drinks directly from a flowing stream where water nymphs might tempt him to death by caressing his parched throat and whispering, "more, just a little more." Better to put the precious liquid in his bag and let it warm a bit to lessen the temptation.

It is well past midnight. In another seven hours he should make it to

Sparta. He left the agora near Athens' acropolis at five yesterday morning. Part of his ritual, almost a superstition, is to always begin a long run at the agora, the open market and meeting place that draws thousands of Athenians daily. It is there that they take gossip to its highest form, debating and voting on everything conceivable according to the rules of their fledgling system of government—rule by the demos. Democracy.

It was still dark when Phidippides left the agora, and the running was easy and safe along well-used pathways. When the sun, Helios, came up, he focused on the horizon and used only his peripheral vision to watch his steps. The long-distance view helped delay the nausea.

When the sun rose higher, he covered the back of his neck to prevent sunburn. Blistering his feet would have been worse, but one of Phidippides' strengths is that his soles are so callused they act like thick leather pads. And despite the calluses, his long toes are flexible and sensitive enough to give him excellent balance. He can feel the terrain under his sandals as they pound the earth in a relentless, steady rhythm.

His mind goes back to a disturbing conversation he had a couple of days ago with Callimachus and Miltiades. Callimachus commanded him to, "Beseech the Spartans, if you must. You must convince them. They *must* help us."

Callimachus also told Phidippides to explain to the Spartans that the Persians' imminent attack would be unlike anything the Greeks had ever experienced. Nothing like the frequent fights among Greek city-states over disputed borders or where they could plant olive trees and grape vines or graze their livestock. He was to stress that as the most influential of all the Greek city-states, Sparta and Athens must set aside their differences and fight together to repel the enemy. Otherwise, if Athens fell, Sparta would fall next.

Callimachus' message makes Phidippides shudder. He cannot forget the word "beseech." The warleader did not say "beg," but that is what it sounded like. Does Callimachus fear the Persians so much that he would beg Sparta for help? Is there anything that justifies an Athenian groveling before a Spartan like a craven dog?

Phidippides steps on a small rock he did not notice and snaps his full attention back to the ground just ahead of him. He studies the terrain and tries to keep his thoughts from wandering again, but he cannot stop thinking about the message he was ordered to deliver. Callimachus had spoken first, but when it came time for the second-in-command to speak, Miltiades' tone was grave.

"Phidippides, what you say to the Spartans may be the most important message you ever convey in your life. Speak to them in ways they can best understand. You know how the Spartans long ago subjugated the nearby land of Messenia and made all the people helots; the Spartans call them serfs, but helots are really slaves. Tell the Spartans that the Persians are coming to turn all Greeks into helots. All of us. They will destroy our temples to the gods—be sure to mention that because Spartans are so devout. And make it clear that Persian domination will be permanent, or at least will last far longer than the Spartans have dominated Messenia and the helots. That is what empires do. That is how the bastard Darius—the Persians' so-called Great King—that is how he thinks. Finally, remind them of what Callimachus just said: If Athens falls, Sparta will be next."

Miltiades had paused for a moment then, as though unsure whether to say the rest of what he was thinking. Finally, he concluded, "Tell them the Persians come not in thousands, but in tens of thousands."

Phidippides is uneasy about whether he will be able to convey the message properly. He will need to think this through again as he gets closer to Sparta. For now, he refocuses on the rugged terrain around him to try to clear his mind.

He has run two-thirds of the one hundred and fifty miles between Athens and Sparta. The faint moon creates hazy shadows around him. He has eyes like a cat; few can match his night vision. Still, the pale light's changing shades can be deceptive. Rocks of all sizes are everywhere. Holes are nearly invisible, even to him. There must be no false steps.

The runner rests his mind but stays focused on the ground ahead. A few hours ago he passed near the city of Corinth, leaving behind northern Greece and Attica, the area around Athens. Now he is well into Greece's southern half, the Peloponnesus. He feels the path under his feet rising gradually and steadily and knows exactly what is happening; he is ascending Mount Parthenium, whose peak stands almost a mile above the Aegean.

The moonlight is a pleasant distraction. Phidippides enjoys its shimmering effect on the flora along the trail. The soft, scattered light, faint and flickering, reminds him of being under water in the Aegean Sea, far below the surface in forests of swaying kelp, feeling the power of the tides deep down. He can hold his breath for a slow count to two hundred. The back and forth movements and unhurried circular swirls of the kelp are so strong, yet so gentle. And quiet. He feels the quiet again now, in the depths of his repetitious motion. No noise at all. Just the silent rhythm of running.

Something is wrong. He listens and turns his head slightly back and forth to better gauge the source of a new sound from far behind him—where is it, how far away, and what?

The sound gradually grows louder. It is following him. Animal or man? A quick glance back reveals nothing. What can possibly be out here now, well after midnight? It must be an animal. Maybe he is its prey.

He starts to scrutinize the ground along both sides of the path, looking for a heavy stick. He surely does not want to fight after running so far, but he may have no choice. He carries a short knife, but a big stick might be better. Another quick glance over his shoulder and still nothing, but the noise is gaining on him.

Phidippides detects something familiar in the sound. The steady clomping of a horse with a loping gait, but lighter, as if the horse had only two hooves—but how could that be? And how can there be a horse here in the mountain forest? If it is a horse, there must be a rider, and that means danger.

He wants to maintain his pace, but he also needs to find something to use as a club. He will have to stop and turn if the sound gets close; he cannot let whatever is after him take him from behind.

It's too late—the sound is here now, right beside him, just inches away and pacing him step for step. Phidippides is shocked. For an instant his mind goes blank. Then he realizes it is not a horse, but a man. And the clomping sound is indeed coming from two feet, not four. Phidippides stays focused on his own feet and then slowly—ever so slowly—looks to the ground next to him. There they are, two of them, but hooves, not feet. Somehow a horse after all?

Phidippides flashes to the only possible explanation—he has lost his mind. He looks again at the hooves and, yes, they are the size of a horse's hooves, but they are split—cloven. The hooves of a goat—a giant, two-legged goat.

There is another noise and it is loud. "Phhhhhh." Its resonance is powerful. Not the sound of something exhausted. More like the exhalation of a muscular athlete lifting heavy weights.

"Phhhhhh" comes again. And a third time. Then the sound becomes a name—"Phhhidippides."

At that, the runner cautiously turns and looks straight into the eyes of a god.

It is the God of Mountain Wilds. Without saying a word, the runner quickly turns back to watch his own feet and concentrate on his knees to make sure they do not buckle.

"Phidippides, you are a long way from home," says Pan. "Do you know where you are?"

The runner does not answer.

"You are in the forests of Arcadia," says the god. "*My* forests. You are climbing Mount Parthenium, *my* mountain. And after you top it, the rest of the way will be downhill, to Tegea, then Sparta."

The runner still says nothing.

"You ignore me, just like all the other Athenians. Why? I am a friend of your city; I have helped the Athenians in times past. And I will again."

The runner knows he must speak but is not sure what to say. Whatever words he chooses must be truthful.

"God Pan," the runner speaks in his mind. His lungs are too exhausted to speak aloud, but he senses the god can hear his thoughts. "I do not know how to answer. I do not mean to ignore you. I respect you just as I worship the other gods."

"Ah, there you said it. Just what I suspected. Those other gods you worship—Zeus, Hera, and the rest of the Olympians. But I am not one of them, and I am seldom invited to mighty Mount Olympus, so you worship them and you just *respect* me—if you remember me at all."

"No, no, Pan," the runner protests in his mind. "I worship you, too. If I have failed you in my devotion, I am sorry. I will make amends."

"I am pleased to hear you say that, but I still wonder about the rest of the people of Athens."

"Please, Pan, tell me what I should do, what my city should do. Whatever you ask, I will convey it to the Athenians and I know they will join me in satisfying your wish, whatever it is."

"I am pleased to hear that, too. Not long ago I was wondering about the last time the Athenians built a temple dedicated to me—to me alone—for the past favors I have granted you and the help I will give you again, soon. But you and your city must decide how to express your worship."

"God Pan, you have my promise, my covenant. When I return to Athens I will convey the question to all Athenian citizens, to the full Assembly. They will decide the best way to express our devotion to such a praiseworthy god, and you will be satisfied. You deserve to be indulged and you will be gratified by the city's decision, I am sure of it, though I am only a runner. I will suggest they build a temple dedicated to you alone—a splendid temple for a glorious god."

Pan nods approvingly and says, "Your covenant. Athens' covenant. Covenants are good."

"But almost all the citizens of Athens are away, so I cannot convey the message to the Assembly until they return."

"At Marathon."

"You know?"

"Lean toward me and slow your pace," the god says in a hushed tone. "I will help you speed up again after we finish our talk."

Pan moves so close their shoulders touch. He places a hand on the runner's hip. The touch is gentle and intended to ensure that they will continue running in exact unison, step for step. In the wavering moonlight, man and god are joined.

As the runner leans toward the god, a potent smell hits his nostrils. It is a complex odor, a powerful scent of the forest, as if he is both drinking and inhaling a pungent mixture of the essence of trees—moist, crushed pine needles and fresh, oozing sap—and dirt. But the dirt smell is not appealing, not at all. More like night soil with a unique stench. The combined, confused aromas are simultaneously perfumed and putrid.

Pan smiles because he knows exactly what the runner is experiencing. The god has seen this many times before when he has been intimate with mortals. His hand tightens on the runner's hip. With his face barely an inch from the runner's ear, Pan whispers, "The Goddess of Wisdom and of War visited me. Are you listening?"

"Yes, god Pan, I am listening."

"Then hear this. When Athena came to me she asked that I give you our message—a message from the God of Mountain Wilds and the Goddess of Wisdom and War. Are you listening?"

"Yes, Pan, I am listening."

The runner feels Pan's hand move across his lower back and grasp his waist as the god's lips touch his ear. "We will be there."

Phidippides realizes Pan is gone. He feels his legs lighten and his pace increase. He tops the crest of Mount Parthenium and begins the long descent. Less than seven hours to go. When he returns from Sparta, he will follow the instructions Callimachus gave him. He will stop at Athens and say the Spartans are coming to help against the Persians, no matter what the Spartans actually decide to do. His message to Athens will strengthen their courage and, hopefully, give pause to any potential traitors in the city. But when he finally arrives at Marathon and reveals Sparta's true response, what will it be?

CHAPTER SEVENTEEN

REASON TO WORRY

Themistocles walks a short distance away from all the other men on the hilltop overlooking Marathon. His mind is always racing and sometimes he needs to slow down, breathe deeply, and avoid talking to anyone. Especially when he is worried.

He remembers a time more than a year ago when Miltiades had just returned to Athens after his adventures in the east and his deceitful alliance with Persia's Great King Darius. He also remembers the moment when Miltiades told him that he heard talk in Darius' royal court of an aristocrat in Athens—Magacles—who continued to befriend the city's former tyrant, Hippias. This meant Magacles might be a potential Persian ally.

Themistocles and Miltiades had decided to confront Magacles. A pudgy man in his late fifties, Magacles' intensity could be intimidating. He had the unnerving habit of staring from the corners of his eyes.

Themistocles and Miltiades had agreed that Miltiades would do the talking and would immediately get to the point so Magacles would have no time to think about his answers. Miltiades was calm but quick. "When I was with the Persians, I heard your name more than once and they always spoke well of you. They usually also mentioned Hippias and the fact that the two of you remain friends. What do you say to that?"

Remaining composed, Magacles immediately said, "When Hippias ruled Athens I was, indeed, his friend. I never imagined he would become a traitor."

"I'm asking about a period of time after Hippias was banished from Athens," Miltiades continued. "The Persians said the two of you are *still* friends."

Themistocles remembers that Magacles seemed relaxed when he replied, "Since I wasn't with you when you were so taken by what the barbarians said, all I can tell you is that, at best, they were confused. While there is some truth to my initial feeling of regret that Hippias could not think straight, treachery is a very different matter. He is no longer my friend, and I want nothing to do with him."

"Have you been in contact with Hippias since he left Athens?" After asking his question, Miltiades immediately raised his hand and said, "No. Instead, my question is have you been in contact with Hippias during this past month?"

Themistocles clearly remembers this point in the conversation. The twitch in Magacles' expression, a facial flash so fast that few people would have detected it. And a brief bulging of veins in his throat along with a quick, hard swallow.

Then, once again apparently unruffled, Magacles replied with a firm, "No." He crossed his arms and continued in a lower voice, "Have we arrived at the point where you are going to make an accusation and, if so, will your contention, whatever it might be, also be based on the talk of barbarians?"

Miltiades crossed his arms too and silently studied Magacles.

After a long moment, Magacles said, "You have walked up to the line of making an allegation, but not crossed it. However, as you know, what we are talking about is a most serious denunciation. If you believe there is justification for it, I suggest you put the matter before the whole Assembly. And our reputations will be on the line."

Magacles looked hard at Miltiades and then gave the same look to Themistocles. Turning back to Miltiades, he went on, "Yes, our reputations, an aristocrat versus one man renowned for deception and another of low birth. And when the Assembly renders its decision, I propose that the losers be ostracized. Or perhaps better yet, if the

Assembly prefers, put to death."

Magacles abruptly started to walk away, then stopped and glared at them over his shoulder. "And if anyone else in Athens mentions what you have been talking about, it will be clear how they know. That will give me the right to bring my own charges to the Assembly."

Turning once again, Magacles was gone.

Themistocles remembers how he and Miltiades looked at each other and the exact words they spoke. Miltiades shook his head. "I don't know if I want to apologize, but perhaps I should at least tell him I am satisfied he's not a traitor."

"Only if you know you're lying to him."

"What?" exclaimed Miltiades. "You didn't believe him?"

"He's good, very good. But there were enough small signs to make me think he's a liar, through and through."

"His eyes?" said Miltiades. "The way he looks at you from the corners of his eyes?"

"Actually, not his eyes," replied Themistocles. "It's the muscles around the eyes; they can move and twitch even when the eyes hold steady."

"What else? Something he said?"

"Not what but *how* he said it."

"I don't understand," said Miltiades. "He gave quick answers, which means he didn't have to think about it. That indicates he was telling the truth."

"Answers can sometimes be too quick. His answers were prepared. He thought them through long ago, probably memorized them. He would have known that someone, sometime, might ask him the same questions you just put to him. He would have known that because he's guilty."

After pausing to reflect, Themistocles continued, "And when you asked him about making contact with Hippias, his reaction . . . it could have been that the insult was becoming too much and changed the way he acted, but I don't believe that. You were getting too close to his guilt."

"But you can't be certain, can you?"

"No, I can't."

"And we can't prove it."

Themistocles' memories evaporate as he hears footsteps approaching from behind. Miltiades walks up and says, "The most extroverted citizen of Athens also likes his time alone. You're a strange man, Themistocles."

"Very true and I'm proud of it. Being strange prevents me from being boring."

CHAPTER EIGHTEEN

TWO WOMEN MAKE READY

"Archi, why do they do it?" asks the young woman sitting next to Archippe. "Your Themistocles, my Sicinnus, all men are crazy. Free citizens love to fight, and men who are slaves want to fight. I understand what's happening now. Our survival is at stake, so fight they must. But it's not just now. It's always; it's never-ending. Something strange inside men drives them."

The two women sit in Archippe's courtyard in Athens, watching the younger woman's—Lela's—toddler play outside. Alyssa runs around and repeatedly plops down. With every harmless fall, Alyssa looks to Lela, who waves encouragingly so the toddler gets up again to repeat the adventure. Bounding beside Alyssa is Archippe's puppy, Argos. A Melitan lapdog, Argos is small, white, and fluffy with upright ears and a long furry tail curved over his back.

Alyssa and Argos stop their frolicking. Alyssa is investigating something near a small rock while the puppy watches. Both she and the puppy are delighted as a warm late-afternoon breeze wafts around them. But, for the two women, the waning of the day brings worry.

Lela and Sicinnus have one child, Alyssa; Archippe and Themistocles have four. The three boys are at the gymnasium, and their daughter is weaving cloth on a loom in the back of the house. Their first born, Archeptolis, is twelve. His nickname, Arch, takes after his mother, who goes by Archi among those close to her.

Archippe is thirty-six with thick, light brown hair. During the summer her hair lightens with tinges of streaked copper. She lets her hair flow down to cover her breasts. In public, she is the image of confidence and fortitude. At home, that image softens as her sensitivity reveals itself.

Although Lela is twelve years younger than Archippe, their personalities, inner strengths, and strong heads mirror each other. The two women are like sisters, even though Lela and Sicinnus are slaves to Archippe and Themistocles.

Before Archippe can answer Lela's complaint, Argos starts to yelp while Alyssa squeals for her mother's attention and points to a mystery near the rock. Lela knows the toddler's sound means delighted curiosity, so danger is unlikely. Still, things under rocks deserve a mother's swift attention. Light-footed Lela quickly reaches her daughter and looks where she is pointing.

Out of a small hole in the dirt, ants are streaming in a frantic column. Curious little Alyssa is stirring about in the hole with a short stick, wreaking havoc among the disoriented insects. Half a dozen ants dash up the little stick and onto the toddler's hand, and with a screech Alyssa tosses her tiny stick into the air and starts wailing in panic.

Argos jumps up and down and tries to howl but manages only a high-pitched yapping. With a laugh she can't restrain, Lela brushes the rude insects away, hoists Alyssa up, and begins the rocking motion and soothing words she knows will quickly end the little trauma.

By the time Lela returns to sit with Archippe, Alyssa has fallen silent, although she maintains her tight grip around Lela's neck. The women smile together at Alyssa's antics. Then, simultaneously, their smiles leave them.

"Arete and kleos," says Archippe.

There is another pause before Lela responds with a deep sigh, "Valor and glory. I know, I know. Sicinnus doesn't say it out loud, but it's always there. The same with Themistocles, I'm sure."

Archippe takes a deep breath and nods.

"So why?" continues Lela. "Why are they made that way? It's so self-centered. I can relate to arete—valor—up to a point. Though it's a concept I had never heard of until I came to live among the Greeks. And the word has so many meanings it makes my head spin: courage, virtue, the pursuit of excellence, achievement. And kleos—glory—which is all about being remembered after you die. What's the good of that?" She gives a little snort. "Everyone acknowledges that Greek women have valor, but it's only the men who go on and on about glory. Why can't they live for the here and now? I won't say that to Sicinnus, but that's what I think. What does glory have to do with husbands and wives and their children? Why can't men stay focused on living life?"

"You already answered your own question. It's how they're made. They care so much about what other men think." Archippe continues, pensively. "The other part isn't the here and now; it's the hereafter. Everyone fears death, of course, although men want to conquer death, to be immortal, like the gods. But even a man with half a brain knows that can't be. So the closest they can get is to be remembered. It's three steps, with one leading to another—to be respected, then recognized, then remembered. Forever."

"Insanity," says Lela. "Children are the real legacy. Isn't having children enough for them?"

"I guess not."

The two women pause, watching Alyssa, who has crawled down from Lela's lap and, having forgotten the rock and ants, sits playing with a small clay doll.

"It's insane!" blurts Lela.

"Who am I to disagree? Themistocles says men fight for the same reason roosters do—because neither will give way to the other."

"So our husbands are just crazy cocks."

The two women laugh out loud and nod their heads in the mutual appreciation that they sometimes understand their husbands better than the men understand themselves.

"But I think you're being harsh, at least a little, Lela," says Archippe. "Men may be crazy, but that doesn't mean they're bad, at least not all of them. My Themistocles and your Sicinnus are good fathers—and husbands. Crazy but good."

"Yes, yes. I know." Lela sighs. "But I'm so scared, Archi. I've been through a lot in my twenty years, but nothing like this."

"None of us have." Archippe pauses. "You know my children well. If we survive, I'm sure Themistocles and I will have more."

"*If* we survive," repeats Lela. "Everything I hear says we won't." Lela pauses but then continues, "Except for Sicinnus. He says we will; he's certain."

"I'm glad to hear that," says Archippe. "Themistocles pretends to be confident, but he knows I know he's pretending. Over the last few days he finally opened up and told me about his big concern, his greatest fear."

Before Archippe can continue, Alyssa climbs back onto Lela's lap and starts fussing, arches herself backward, and begins whimpering.

"Hungry?" asks Archippe.

"No, sleepy. She didn't have her nap today."

Following Lela inside the house, Archippe sits on a stool by the cool hearth while Lela carries her daughter into the bedroom. Archippe mulls over what she is about to say. She knows Lela will be shocked, but the best way to explain is to go straight at it. This is no time to be subtle.

She shuts her eyes and breathes deeply. In a strange way she is pleased that over the last few days her anger has grown stronger than her fear. She is better at dealing with anger.

"That, at least, was easy." Lela returns and sits down. "When Alyssa misses her nap, she can be hard to console and get to sleep. But not today, fortunately." She looks over at her friend, surprised that Archippe is keeping silent on her stool in the shadows. Argos is yipping outside. "Archi, you were about to say something."

Archippe gravely raises her eyes to Lela. "I want to tell you what I recently learned from my husband. But understand that our conversation now, yours and mine, will be between us only." Archippe stares directly into her best friend's eyes, and Lela acknowledges the statement with a slow, silent nod.

Archippe continues, "I have a very personal question, and I know it will sound strange. At first, the question was going to be have you ever thought about having sex with someone other than Sicinnus? But then I thought, no, that's not really the question. So instead my question is this: Do you know how to flirt? More than flirt. Do you know how to play the seductress, how to make a man think you want him, and that you want him to have his way with you?"

"Well, that's quite a question," Lela says slowly.

"I know. I'll say again that only I will know your answer. And this isn't a joke."

"No, Archi, I understand it isn't a joke," says Lela. "I'm not sure what to say. Sicinnus and I haven't made love in almost two years, since before Alyssa was born. Two years! When you asked your question, the thought flashed through my mind that you knew about us, maybe Sicinnus told Themistocles who told you. But that's not likely, is it?"

"No, I didn't know. Themistocles said nothing. I expect that's because he doesn't know either."

"I'm sure you're right. It's not something Sicinnus would talk about, even to Themistocles."

"At some point you and I should talk about it. Perhaps I can help," says Archippe. "But right now, we need to deal with my question. Right now, we need to focus on our children, yours and mine, and whether they will live or die."

"My desire to have sex with another man, or my ability to act like a temptress—how does that have anything to do with the lives of our children?"

"Let me explain. Move closer, Lela, because what I am about to say isn't . . ."

Lela shivers and jumps up.

"Did you hear that, or feel it? Someone is here."

"I didn't hear anything," says Archippe.

Lela bolts toward Alyssa's room. She returns after a moment. "Nothing. But I felt a gust of wind. It moved against the direction of the breeze outside. As if someone came into the house. I'm sure of it. I still sense it. But there's nothing. You didn't detect anything? Are you sure?"

"Nothing," says Archippe.

Two invisible apparitions stand in the back of the room. They are motionless but attentive. Both are focused on Lela.

Lela looks around one more time and sits down, saying, "Amazing. I was so certain. I've never felt anything like that. Maybe the stress."

"The stress and the fear," says Archippe. Straightening her back, she continues, "Actually, we are all worried sick and I mean to do something about it, with your help, I hope. Are you ready to hear me out?"

Lela's eyes sparkle and a surprising grin brightens her face. "So I'm to be part of a big solution?" Tossing her head to the side to flip back the long bangs on her forehead, she adds, "Sounds like you have some sort of intrigue in mind. I like intrigue."

Archippe smiles. "Such a coy look. And so natural. And you say you don't know how to flirt! Are you trying to tell me something? Something about your hidden ways?"

"Hidden except from Sicinnus," says Lela. "You asked if I'm ready to hear what Themistocles told you. I'm ready."

"Very well. Themistocles is almost certain there are traitors among us, and if so they will try to betray the city to the invaders."

Lela's coy expression vanishes.

"I was aware of this. Sicinnus told me. He swore me to silence."

Archippe nods, "I'm not surprised; I thought Themistocles would have told Sicinnus, although there isn't much talk about possible traitors, at least publicly. But Themistocles told me everything he suspects. He said the most serious worry by far is what happened when he and

Miltiades met with . . ."

Archippe pauses and carefully studies Lela's face. Then she asks, "Do you know the man called Magacles?"

Curious, Lela tilts her head to the side and says, "Strange that you ask. I don't know him, but once or twice in the past Sicinnus mentioned him, and what he said wasn't good. Then, just before he left for Marathon, he mentioned Magacles again and said, if by some chance I encountered him, I should quickly excuse myself and leave. Sicinnus said he's a very bad man."

"Is that all he said?"

"Yes. But the way he said it, and when he said it—just as he was leaving—well, his words were unsettling."

"Themistocles said that if there are any traitors in Athens, he believes one of their leaders will be Magacles."

"But how can he be so sure?"

"He isn't sure, but he strongly suspects. And if my husband has a serious suspicion, he's probably correct. I know his abilities."

"But why didn't Themistocles warn other people about Magacles? And why don't you tell someone now who is in authority here in Athens?"

"Without proof, such a public allegation will accomplish nothing and could have disastrous results for the accuser. Themistocles did speak to two old friends of his father who are here in Athens and asked them to keep an eye on Magacles. Though he stopped short of accusing Magacles of being a traitor. He didn't tell me who the old men are. They're men he trusts, but from the way he shook his head when he mentioned them, I could tell he wasn't confident they're up to the task."

Repeating her earlier question, Lela asks, "But why not tell someone in authority here in Athens?"

Archippe answers with her own question, "If there is one traitor, there almost certainly are others; what if I guess someone in authority is trustworthy and he's in league with Magacles? No, that's not how to proceed. My plan relies on women, not men. Women led by you and me."

"Did your husband say anything about other traitors?"

"No," Archippe concedes. "All he said was there may be men among us who are ready to betray us to the Persians, and, if so, Magacles is probably one of the leaders. Common sense dictates the rest—we must take matters into our own hands."

Lela nods. "So what is your plan?"

"Stop them."

"How?"

"By distracting them."

"Distracting them?"

"With our bodies."

"Sex?" exclaims Lela.

"Use our wiles to inflame their fantasies."

"Fantasy or reality?"

"Fantasy," Archippe says. "The idea is to play on their imagination and desires. Like holding succulent food just out of reach of a starving man. Once he understands what we want in exchange for what he craves, he'll give it to us willingly. And what we want will be easy for him to give—just a little information."

"Why do you need me?" asks Lela. "You are one of the most beautiful women in the entire city."

Archippe leans her head back and smiles. "Let me remind you of something you already know about men. Some of them are attracted to women with mature beauty. I am thirty-six years old and I don't deny your compliment. I know men ogle me when they get the chance. They stare at my large breasts, which I cannot disguise no matter how thick my garments. But there are other men who prefer a different look, a younger woman with small, tight breasts. So I think you understand why I want you to help me. And help all of us, including Alyssa."

"I understand you." Lela pauses. "But let me speak frankly."

"I think you always do, especially with me."

"You and I are best friends. When you and I and Themistocles and Sicinnus talk among us, you treat Sicinnus and me as equals. But the reality is that Sicinnus and I are slaves. Isn't that a reason you want me to help you?"

Archippe silently nods in agreement.

Lela continues, "If a man of Athens wants to seduce a woman of Athens, and that woman happens to be the wife of one of the most powerful Athenian citizens, the seducer might hesitate. Less so if the woman is a slave."

"Again, yes." Archippe pauses and looks straight into Lela's deep black eyes. "Does that make a difference?"

"No, I just wanted to say it. But I am very unsure about this. Can it work?"

Lowering her voice further, even though she thinks they are alone except for the child sleeping in the next room, Archippe says, "Listen carefully . . ."

Before Archippe can continue, Lela jumps up as she did earlier and looks around. And, just as before, she quickly walks to the room where Alyssa is sleeping. Lela returns, shaking her head. "I've lost my mind. You didn't hear or feel anything—that small gust of wind?"

"Nothing."

Lela sits down in silence, breathing hard.

The two invisible figures in the back of the room float forward and stand behind the women. The apparitions listen intently; they want to hear Archippe's plan. Their eyes are concentrated on Lela.

On the floor behind Lela, a small shadow slowly twists and turns. The women do not see the snake slithering back and forth over the feet of the watchers.

Countless mortal years have come and gone since Demeter, the Goddess of Fertility, and her young daughter, Persephone, visited the snakes down in the cave of Eleusis. Persephone has come of age, and her youthful radiance and allure catch the eye of many a god.

The time has come to fulfill the wish Persephone made eons ago when she left the cave. She wanted to see the snakes again, and they are coming. Soon they will rise to the earth's surface because Demeter decided long ago to summon her snakes from the cave of Eleusis when mortals confronted their greatest need.

~⁓

Lela is unaware that the apparitions behind her are Sicinnus' patrons and the protectors of his wife and child. Only gods and goddesses know why they decide to help some mortals and hurt others.

CHAPTER NINETEEN

FIGHT UNTO DEATH

As the first day at Marathon draws to a close, it is clear the Persians are not yet ready to challenge the Greeks on their high ground. The Greeks stand guard and prepare to settle in for the night.

The Greek fires are low; there is no need for heat on this sultry evening. The reason for the fire is simply to be mesmerized by the flames, the sparks zigzagging up, the occasional small spit of hot, dancing light, and the popping, snapping, and soft sounds of spent wood settling and yielding to the inevitable. A tended fire invites meditation and a commonality of feelings—thoughts of promise and hope. Sometimes the promise is kept in the here and now, as with lovers holding each other. But often the promise points to the future. The Greek warriors ponder their promises as the flames defeat the surrounding darkness.

Two men sitting near one of the smaller fires silently alternate between gazing at the fire and looking into each other's eyes. Kye finally speaks to his young partner. "Arrichion, during your two years of military training as an ephebe, you were told over and over that we fight in the phalanx for one another first and foremost, not for ourselves. Do you believe it?"

Arrichion gives Kye a quizzical look. "Of course, I believe it. Don't you?"

"Yes, you and I imagine ourselves fighting for a friend, for each other. But what about all the hoplites who aren't our friends?"

"We fight for them too. It's our duty; you know that."

"Yes, of course. I guess what I'm trying to do is think through . . . I'm trying to understand friendship. What about this: Can you imagine yourself befriending a Persian?"

Pausing for a moment, Arrichion responds, "You sound like your older brother with questions leading to more questions. My first thought was about the Persians down on the beach, our enemies. But then I thought about Persians who live in Athens. Some of them have been in the city for a long time, perhaps most of their lives."

"And?" asks Kye.

"Can I imagine having a Persian friend? Yes, it's possible."

"So a Persian living in Athens might be a friend, but what about a Persian enemy, as you just mentioned?"

"You will be hard pressed to find any Greek who can imagine befriending a barbarian enemy."

"But I'm not asking any other Greek," says Kye. "I'm asking you." Arrichion does not respond and Kye finally breaks the silence. "It's a difficult question for both of us, and the answer will have to wait. My brother is coming."

Aeschylus and Themistocles walk out of the darkness and sit down near the two youths. Turning to young Arrichion, Themistocles says, "Before we started out this morning, I told you I wanted to hear your story about your great-grandfather and namesake. Might this be a good time to tell your tale?"

"I can't imagine a better one," says Arrichion. "Your request does me honor." With a glance at his friend, who nods encouragingly, he begins, "Well, as you know, the story about my great-grandfather involves pankration.

"As you also know, pankration is the deadliest sport of the Olympian Games. It is a war sport, combining the combat sports of wrestling and boxing, but with this difference—it has only two barred maneuvers: no biting or using teeth to tear off flesh, and no gouging out an opponent's eye. All other tactics are allowed, including kicking, strangling, striking a man's groin or any other part of his body, and breaking any and all bones.

"My namesake, my great-grandfather, Arrichion, was, is, and always will be the champion of all pankration champions of all the Olympian Games. He first became champion over eighty years ago, in the 52nd Games, then again four years later, and once again four years after that."

"And he lived in the town of Phigalia?" asks Themistocles.

"Yes. Two days walk north of Sparta and two days south of Olympia."

"Married with how many children?"

"Arrichion and his wife, Arcadia, wanted a full family, ten children at least. But at the time of his third championship, there was only one child, a son—my grandfather."

Sensing there are no further questions, Arrichion continues. "As you know, adroitness—lightness of foot and the ability to leap, dart, and dodge—are techniques that pankrationists make into a fine art, a dance. Among all pankration champions, Arrichion was unsurpassed at dancing on a hoplon shield. Because a hoplon is shaped like a shallow bowl, when it is on the ground with the concave side up, it moves at the slightest touch. The hoplon dance requires a pankrationist to jump onto the shield's opposite edges so the shield will not move. And then to execute a full circle jump dance around those edges while the shield stays perfectly still. Arrichion did it blindfolded.

"He never lost a single pankration match at the Olympian Games. He won most matches within just a few moments. Only once did he take longer—in his final match for the championship at the 54th Games. That was when Arrichion fought a huge challenger with no name. His opponent was more than a head taller and over a hundred pounds heavier than my great-grandfather.

"Arrichion focused on two tactics—attrition and fingers. He was trained to fight all day and no one had better stamina. And the easiest bones to break are fingers. That's how Arrichion planned to weaken his opponent.

"After a full hour in the pankration pit, Arrichion's tactics had accomplished nothing. No broken fingers and his hulking opponent showed no fatigue. Under the hot sun they fought on, hour after hour. Finally, during the sixth hour, Arrichion slipped but didn't fall. However, that small mistake was all the hulk needed, and he was on Arrichion's back. Arrichion struggled to hold up the huge challenger and avoid falling, but the massive weight was not the main problem. After jumping on Arrichion's back, the challenger had wrapped his legs around his waist and locked his feet onto Arrichion's thighs. The squeezing of the scissor grip was extreme, and the challenger had also bent his right arm around Arrichion's neck in a strangling chokehold. It was a death grip. With both air and blood flow completely blocked, the end was only a few heartbeats away.

"Arrichion's eyes blurred and started rolling up. His hearing was failing but he was not yet deaf, so from somewhere seemingly far away he heard the challenger's trainer howl, 'Nike! Nike! Victory! Victory! You have him. The glory is ours. Finish him off! Nike! Victory! Glory!' Everyone heard the braggart. Arrichion's mistake could have determined the end of the match, but it was the trainer's taunting chant that actually goaded Arrichion to a last burst of strength.

"His next maneuver was the hardest. With his challenger still wrapped around him, choking him, Arrichion bent forward, which put even greater pressure on his throat. It is almost impossible to imagine, but somehow he reached below his groin, grasped his opponent's ankle, and pulled his foot forward. Then Arrichion twisted the ankle—hard. The pain forced his challenger to slightly loosen his scissors lock, and that was all Arrichion needed. He crouched farther down for leverage and wrenched the ankle with such force that it burst from its socket. Now totally deaf, Arrichion could not hear the challenger's shriek.

"From a full squat, Arrichion jumped up and backward. In midair he shifted his hand away from the broken ankle and in one quick motion grabbed the challenger's big toe, bent the toe sideways, broke it, ripped it off the foot, and pulled both the toe and the attached skin down the full length of the foot. The brute threw his head back and screamed, pointing a finger high overhead to signal submission. As the two of them crashed to the ground, the challenger landed on his spine without releasing his chokehold, and Arrichion's head snapped backward.

"The referees rushed up to make sure the contestants released their grips, because the match was finished. The challenger had let go and was covering his face and moaning. Arrichion lay motionless, with the bloody toe and long strip of skin still in his hand. The referees thought he was unconscious and began slapping his cheeks to rouse him. Only then did they realize his neck was broken. Arrichion was dead. The victor's reward—a wreath of wild olives—was placed gently on his head.

"When they returned from Olympia two days later, the men of Phigalia brought their champion home with them. The pankration champion of the Olympian Games three times in a row. Glory! He will be remembered forever. What more can a man ask for?"

CHAPTER TWENTY

INFILTRATING THE GREEK CAMP

Shortly after dawn, the Persian commander paces the beach near his tent, weighing his options. Persian ships line the long shoreline like an enormous pod of beached whales, their masts like crests and their oars cocked skyward. Tents lie scattered along the long, narrow beachhead, with wisps of campfire smoke winding into the early morning sky. It is his army's second day at Marathon.

"We're a little too far away from Athens for my friends to invite us in. So now what?"

Datis looks up to see the sarcastic Hippias walking toward him.

"We pause and take stock," Datis says, "after thanking Ahura Mazda because we disembarked safely."

"Pause for how long?"

"Before you interrupted me, I was considering that question." He gives the Greek an appraising look. "Attacking the high ground is not out of the question, but our warhorses will be almost useless, our archers scattered, and their hidden targets dispersed and difficult to hit. But you just gave me an idea."

"Pleased to be of service."

"Perhaps you should talk to one of the Greeks up there." Datis gestures toward the hills.

"You're serious?"

Datis stays silent.

Hippias grumbles. "When I play cat and mouse I prefer to be the cat. Your point?"

"You say your friends will let us into Athens. You say Athens is stuffed with your friends. Maybe there's an overflow of your friends up in those hills."

Hippias exhales loudly. "You want me to sneak into the Athenian camp to find out?"

Datis continues, pretending to ignore Hippias' question. "What would the Great King do? When thinking things through, that's always a good question to ask."

Hippias says nothing. A seabird sails past them, silent on the cool sea wind.

Datis answers his own question. "I think the Great King would say there are few friends of Hippias, the Tyrant of Athens, among the Greeks watching us up there. But maybe there is one. And one is all we need."

After Hippias considers this he grunts his grudging respect for the commander's idea. "Do you have spies who can get in and out of the Greek camp?"

"Of course. Do you have the name of a so-called friend they should seek?"

"Tell them to find Euryptolemus, son of Magacles. He goes by the name Eury."

Datis repeats, "Euryptolemus, who goes by Eury, the son of Magacles."

Hippias snorts, spits out a glob of blood-tinged phlegm, and laughs loudly. "He is of the Alcmaeonid family."

"Why do you laugh?"

Hippias leans back and looks up to the sky. He raises both arms high over his head and shakes his fists violently. Then he lets out a shrill howl that makes Datis remember yesterday on the beach when Hippias was babbling about his mother. *The soldiers were correct. The old man's mind comes and goes. Soon enough, his head will be totally useless.*

Hippias drops his arms and steps forward again as if nothing had happened, and says, "The irony of fate. Before I was forced into exile,

Athens was ruled by different aristocratic families. Plenty of intrigue, some outright murders, but it worked well enough. I am of the Pisistratus family. My family ruled Athens off and on for over a hundred years. But we always confronted other families that desired power, especially the Alcmaeonids. The Athenian who conspired with Sparta to overthrow me was Cleisthenes, an Alcmaeonid. After his victory he changed everything. And an unwieldy new system of rule was enacted to allow all citizens to assemble and vote to decide just about everything. One result of Cleisthenes' games was that *all* aristocratic families lost power. So now we come full circle; today the Alcmaeonid family of Cleisthenes includes some of my best friends."

Hippias pauses and looks away, as if contemplating something. He smiles, but the smile turns sinister when he says, "Now your spies will seek Eury, son of Magacles, one of my closest friends when I lived among the Athenians. He is in Athens, waiting for me and your army. He's also the nephew of Cleisthenes. Magacles' father was Cleisthenes' brother. Does that surprise you?"

"The irony of fate indeed," replies Datis. "Because you are talking about intrigue and an occasional murder, I'm not surprised at all. Coming full circle is to be expected. That is what men do."

CHAPTER TWENTY-ONE

SPARTA

Phidippides sits in a small, open air arena carved into a rocky hill at the edge of the city of Sparta, watching the wrestling matches. He has delivered his message to the Spartan leaders. All he can do now is await their answer and recover from his long run.

He is fascinated by the wrestlers. He has long heard about such matches but never before seen them. Five simultaneous contests. Ten naked bodies turning, twisting, writhing in constant motion. From head to foot, they are covered with thin coats of oil so their tanned skin glistens in the bright sunlight. Their vitality is striking—vigorous grabs and speedy escapes. How adroitly they trip each other and recover with fast flips that leave them upright, balancing on one foot. It's like watching an exotic, vicious dance, for vicious it is. A match ends only when a wrestler loses consciousness or cannot bear the pain and raises a finger to submit. The victor is allowed a brief display of pride and raises both arms high. The loser is not helped off the field unless she is unconscious—if so, she is dragged, not carried. Then two new girls step in and another match starts. The struggles go on for hours.

To accommodate a small audience, stone benches have been cut from the hill next to the wrestling pit. Phidippides is surprised that the benches are mostly empty. If this were Athens, they would be overflowing with men pushing each other for a view of the participants.

Turning to the Spartan sitting next to him, who he knows is an ephor—an official of the council that helps govern the city—Phidippides says, "Impressive. There is nothing like this in Athens. Out in public, where anyone—everyone—can watch. Your girls don't seem embarrassed or self-conscious at all. It's hard to believe."

～

Phidippides is also thinking about yesterday, when he conveyed his message to the council of ephors and made his plea. Exhausted by his run from Athens, he genuflected in front of the five overseers. His first impression was of the ephors' extremely long hair. All Spartan men wear their hair long, but the ephors' hair is far longer and worn in the old tradition, with four braids hanging down the front of the chest, a separate mass of hair gathered behind the head, and the rest hanging halfway down the back.

The ephors sat on a long rock bench in identical crimson robes. Phidippides could tell the garments were thin, and he had heard that the ephors wear the same light wraps in winter and summer to demonstrate Spartan toughness.

Staying on one knee the whole time, Phidippides appealed to Sparta to come to the aid of Athens. He stressed that if the Persians defeated the Greeks, they would destroy the religious temples and treat the Greeks worse than the Spartans treat their helots. And he put his greatest emphasis on the argument that if Athens were defeated, Sparta would be next.

None of the ephors looked directly at him. Two had their eyes closed and the other three seemed to be abstractly staring off into the distance. Phidippides suspected all of them were listening intently, but he could not be sure.

When Phidippides finished making his case for help, the ephor in the center of the five slowly turned his head and looked at the Athenian. Showing absolutely no expression or emotion, he said in a rigid tone, "Athens shall have our answer the day after tomorrow, at dawn."

That ended his meeting with the ephors, and Phidippides remembers thinking: *These people are strange. Very strange.*

～

The ephor sitting next to him now looks at him to respond to his comments about the wrestling girls. He neither smiles nor frowns. "You find our Spartan ways curious, just as we find your Athenian ways—how you abuse your girls and women."

Phidippides is uncertain how to react to the sarcasm, but then realizes the Spartan is not being sarcastic. "Abuse?"

"When a Spartan girl shows signs of following a path of misbehavior, we tell her if she continues she will be sent to Athens. We need say little else to make the girl do a quick about-face."

"Interesting," says Phidippides carefully. "But we Athenians care for our girls and women just as I am sure you Spartans do." Phidippides is thinking hard because he does not want to give any offense.

"You speak of love, I assume."

"Yes, exactly. It is just that we Athenians seem to emphasize . . . I'm not sure of the best word. Protection, perhaps. The safety of our girls and women. Men are stronger than women and can do them harm. A man and his lust. I'm sure you understand."

"I am sure I understand. Our girls and women do not fear Athens because its citizens lack love. And our girls and women are not afraid of a man's lust, at least in Sparta. I trust you know Spartans are a disciplined people, both men and women. We understand that harsh punishment, inevitable and swift, usually thwarts temptation, even the lure of lust. Beyond Spartan lands, our men may do as they will. But here in Sparta, failure of self-control leads to a choice—banishment from our city, or death. Given that choice, most men choose death."

"And how is death administered?"

"Usually through starvation."

Phidippides almost smiles at that answer but stops himself in time. He has already had a taste of Spartan fare and is not sure starvation could be much worse.

"So when choosing between starving to death and exile, most Spartans would rather starve."

"Not the likely choice of most men in your city, I expect."

"In Athens we honor the individual. Life. Happiness."

"In Sparta, we honor Sparta. To praise life is beside the point. And happiness—what is that? The real question for us is not complicated. What deserves the higher honor—you as a self-centered individual or the entirety of your magnificent city?"

Phidippides realizes he is being pushed into a corner and tries deflection. "I know Sparta's reputation, but what is it about Athens that Spartan girls fear?"

"The separation," says the Spartan.

After waiting for an explanation that is not offered, Phidippides says, "I don't understand."

"You want Athenian girls to stay home with their mothers to keep house, cook meals, weave cloth. You want to protect mothers and daughters from men's prying eyes and pawing hands."

"Yes, fair enough."

"And while your girls stay home and stay safe, your boys run around outside in the sun doing what boys do, which sometimes is not safe."

"Yes, also fair enough."

"And for formal exercise, daily drills and the gymnasium, your girls receive little or none."

"True," says the Athenian. "The boys must grow to be fit."

"We are talking about the girls," retorts the Spartan. "And education—learning to read, write and think—much less for the girls, I expect."

"Yes, of course, that's logical because girls need less education."

133

"Logical in Athens, apparently. In Sparta we educate our girls as well as the boys. Two more questions, not about your girls, but your women. In Athens, do the women drink wine like the men?"

"Oh, no, that is not acceptable in Athens. Do the men of Sparta let their women drink wine?"

"I'm sure you appreciate the relationship between Zeus and Hera. The God of the Sky and Thunder makes every attempt to avoid confrontations with the Goddess of the Marriage Bed, which keeps him busy indeed, but his efforts are more than worthwhile when he's successful. The men of Sparta recognize the wisdom of having a satisfied wife. The women of Sparta drink wine as they please."

They pause for a moment, lured by the spectacle in the arena beneath them. Phidippides must admit these girls not only are in the finest possible physical shape; they also look like they are in the highest of spirits, as fiercely as they fight one another. They look remarkably—happy.

"One final question," says the Spartan, turning back to the Athenian. "I understand that Athens has many brothels, especially in the port of Phalerum a short distance from your city. I think you call them houses of pleasure where prostitutes called 'pornai' live. True?"

"Yes, of course. But that's true for all the Greeks. It's better in Athens because a century ago our lawgiver, Solon, laid down rules of equality. The costs of the women's favors were regulated by Solon and remain so. No more than a man's daily wage. So in Athens wealth does not have special privileges for these women's favors. Athens is egalitarian. We are the city of equity."

"I see," the Spartan replies dryly. "The next time we have a wayward-thinking Spartan girl on our hands, perhaps you can come and explain all this to her. Your clarifications could be most useful."

The Spartan pauses, leans toward the Athenian, and says, "But if you do come to help us with a wayward girl, you will want to correct one thing you just said. The houses of pleasure where pornai dispense their favors, as you call them, those houses do not exist in Sparta."

Phidippides desperately wants to change the subject. He feels he is treading on eggs. He hopes that yesterday's appeal to the ephors will be successful, but he is not optimistic. Just before he left Athens a few days ago, Athenian spies told him about the current state of affairs in Sparta, where there was unrest that could thwart the Athenians' call for help. A serious problem was complicating Sparta's military operations, and a second problem was inhibiting Sparta's ability to make political decisions.

The military problem is a revolt by the helots in Messenia, west of Sparta. Roughly once a generation, the helots rebel against their Spartan masters. Then the Spartans must repeat their suppression and subjugation. The outcome is always the same, but it is a distraction.

The other problem has to do with internal politics. One of Sparta's two kings, Cleomenes, is insane and has been put in chains. His succession is still undecided.

Sparta is an oligarchy with seven rulers; in addition to the five ephors, there are two kings. The ephors make initial decisions about Sparta's actions, and the kings implement the ephors' edicts. The arrangement among the ephors and kings invites intrigue, especially when a king must be replaced and it is unclear who will replace him.

As Phidippides mulls over his concerns about Sparta's distractions, he sees a tall Spartan walking toward him. Even by Sparta's high standards, the approaching man has a superb physique, with an exceptionally large chest and rippling muscles that his tunic does little to hide. He has the sturdy stride of self-confidence, and Phidippides estimates he is about fifty years old. The man wears his long dark hair and short beard in the simple style of most Spartans. As he approaches, Phidippides notices the man's constant slight smile. It is not directed at him, or at anyone for that matter, but seems to be integral to the man's face. Phidippides suspects the smile is neither genuine nor false; it is simply there.

The ephor bows to the new arrival and discreetly leaves, without a word to Phidippides. This surprises the Athenian, though he is quickly learning to expect strangeness in the Spartans' ways.

"Welcome to Sparta, Phidippides," the smiling man says. "Come. Let's walk over to the side here. The spectacle is one of our finer pleasures," gesturing toward the fighting girls, "but it gets a little noisy for me when I want to talk."

The two men walk a short distance away from the arena. The sounds from the wrestling become muted and the number of watchers, already few, diminishes even more.

"I see you had the opportunity to hear the wise words of an ephor. You are fortunate. I also hear you slept from late yesterday afternoon until midmorning today. Understandable after running here from Athens in less than two days. Impressive. You look fresh and recovered—also impressive after only one sleep. I am Leonidas."

Phidippides knows of Leonidas, a younger half-brother of the mad king, Cleomenes. Because Cleomenes has no heir, one of his brothers or half-brothers will replace him. Rumor has it that Leonidas is most likely to inherit the role.

"I gladly accept the hospitality of Sparta," says the Athenian. "You're right, I had a good sleep and my recuperation is a gift from the gods. I'll be ready for my return run tomorrow."

"After the ephors give you Sparta's answer," says Leonidas.

"Yes. Immediately after their answer at dawn, I must leave."

"I, of course, cannot say what their answer will be. Only the ephors speak to that. But I can say you're fortunate your plea for help didn't come much earlier."

"Oh?"

"When the ephors make decisions on behalf of Sparta, they consider many opinions, and that includes the kings' views. I'm sure you know King Cleomenes has been no friend of Athens, so any advice he might have offered would not likely have been favorable. But my brother is no longer able to offer advice anyone will heed, so Athens is fortunate. Of course, that doesn't determine what the ephors will decide."

Phidippides pauses before voicing his next thought, considering whether he is being indiscreet to do so. He decides to chance it. "I know of Cleomenes' long hatred of Athens, but, speaking frankly, I don't understand it."

Leonidas' smile becomes so thin it looks like a crease across his face, "You know the history of our cities' opinions of each other began long before my brother was born and will continue long after his death."

"Of course. But I'm interested in the reason for King Cleomenes' view—if you're willing to tell me, that is. It baffles me."

"The reason began with disrespect," replies Leonidas. "Twenty years ago, some aristocrats from Athens came to the Spartan ephors and asked for help to overthrow the tyrant, Hippias. The ephors agreed and King Cleomenes, who was then young and sane, led our hoplites to Athens, where we surrounded Hippias on your acropolis, captured his children, and told him if he wanted to see his family again he must accept exile. He accepted exile and was gone."

"And I am told the Athenians were most grateful to your king and the Spartans."

"That is what they said to Cleomenes and apparently still say today. But actions are what count, not words. The leader of the Athenian aristocrats, Cleisthenes, paid no attention to Cleomenes' advice on how to rule Athens. It is a high insult for the saved to totally ignore their savior. And Cleisthenes did something worse—far worse. Do you know what that was?"

"I'll venture a guess you're talking about the way the citizens of Athens rule themselves—our self-rule, rule by the demos."

"So you know," says Leonidas, nodding. "Yes, the so-called 'democracy' that Cleisthenes created, an unheard of innovation. Athens overturned proper rule."

"But the ephors of Sparta are elected by the citizens."

"That is not the same thing. They are elected and make decisions affecting Sparta, decisions that are enacted by the kings. And the most important of all decisions invariably relate to war. On the battlefield, Spartan kings are supreme. Your citizens are farmers and our citizens are warriors, and both must have absolute rulers. Your democracy has no place for kings. Cleomenes was then and still is a king of Sparta."

"He is also mad," Phidippides adds.

"That's of no consequence," Leonidas replies, stiffly. "If the idea of your democracy spreads beyond Athens, it will become more than an insult; it will become a threat. Therefore, Cleomenes detests your democracy. Does that answer your question?"

"Your answer is clear enough. It makes me want to ask another question."

"Before you ask it, answer mine, if you will. We Spartans thought that when your Cleisthenes died several years ago, the nonsense of your democracy would also die. But it hasn't. How long do you think your system of rule is going to last?"

Phidippides looks down gravely when he hears this. It is indeed a question that has been discussed not infrequently in Athens.

"Democracy has many enemies outside Athens," he says, looking up again at the Spartan.

"And also some enemies within it," Leonidas interjects, "or so I am told."

Phidippides nods.

"If you ask how long democracy will last in Athens, my answer is, I don't know. But you also referred to the death of democracy. I suspect the idea of democracy will never die. Once citizens know self-rule, they will not easily abandon it. It may go dormant, but I do not think it will die."

"Ah, you Athenians and the way you manipulate words. Your answer is satisfactory, with an added point—when something goes dormant, sometimes it never wakes up. And now I think you have another question for me."

"Yes, I do," says Phidippides. "How do you view Athens? What is your own opinion of its democracy?"

Leonidas slowly turns his head away and looks off in the distance. The Athenian realizes the Spartan has shifted his thoughts away from the conversation.

Leonidas speaks softly, "Before the ephors voted a few weeks ago, I told them my brother should be put in chains. I did this for Sparta. He is my brother, but Sparta is superior. To us all." After a brief pause, Leonidas continues, "If I die today, what will be remembered is that I said my brother should be put in chains. I will have no glory. But I will not die today, so perhaps the gods will find a way to grant me glory."

Pausing once again, Leonidas looks at Phidippides and says, "I give little thought to small matters, such as the democracy of Athens, because I do not share your belief that it will last, either in practice or as an idea. Your system of rule makes no sense; I dismiss it. But I don't hate it the way my brother does. I reserve my hatred for matters of consequence. Does that answer your question?"

Phidippides nods and answers with a simple, "Yes."

"Good," says Leonidas. "With that I must leave you." He gestures toward the arena. "Enjoy our sports."

Leonidas, with his uncanny smile, turns and walks away. Phidippides wonders if he offended him and goes back to watching the young Spartans wrestling in the pit.

A moment later, Phidippides hears a sound of chanting and turns with many in the arena's audience to see a procession passing close by. A youth no more than twenty years old strides proudly in the lead, wearing a garland of brightly colored flowers in his hair, followed by five more youths with clusters of grapes draped around their necks and shoulders. Behind the youths comes a larger group of unadorned and sober-looking older men.

One of the men is leading a large ram, also bedecked with fruit and flowers. Members of the procession are chanting a soft, low song that sounds both happy and strangely sorrowful.

As Phidippides watches the group pass, the ephor who accompanied him earlier, and had remained at the arena, comes up to him.

"You are here in Sparta at a special time," the ephor says. "We are in the midst of Carnea, our Festival of Atonement. I expect you know of it?"

"Does it have something to do with those men passing by?"

"Indeed," says the ephor. "They will soon engage in a most important ritual—the race of sacrifice. The youth wearing the garland will run off, and after he can no longer be seen in the distance, the grape-cluster runners will race after him. If they eventually catch him, that will be a good omen for the city. In the old days, long ago, it also would have meant the garland runner's death, a high honor and sacrifice he would have volunteered for. But in this era, if the garlanded runner is caught, the ram takes his place as a sacrifice to the gods."

Phidippides knows that Sparta takes religion, and the proper worship of the gods, very seriously—more seriously than Athens or any other city throughout the land of the Greek-speaking peoples.

"During Carnea," continues the ephor, "Sparta does not engage in military campaigns beyond our borders. It is prohibited as a violation of proper worship."

"No matter what the reason?"

The Spartan stares hard at him and says, "Unlike so many other Greeks, Spartans are not in the habit of setting aside religious obligations when they are inconvenient."

"Yes, of course. But when does the festival end?"

"With the next full moon."

"The next full moon?"

"Six more days."

After taking this in, Phidippides says, "I find Leonidas very impressive."

The ephor looks straight at the Athenian but says nothing.

Phidippides continues, "Perhaps when I meet him again he will be a king."

The ephor remains silent. The runner offers a slight smile and turns back to watching the wrestling matches. He must tread carefully here. The ephor may not be a supporter of Leonidas' kingship. He turns back to the ephor and says, "You will excuse me. I need one more long sleep to be ready for tomorrow's run. We will meet again at dawn."

The ephor continues to watch the girls throw one another around and does not look over at Phidippides. The Greek wants to say something positive, something pleasant. But he thinks better of it. Parting without showing any such emotion seems more appropriate here in Sparta.

As Phidippides walks through Sparta heading for his final meal of the day, he looks around at the small, sparse buildings he is passing. They are solid and simple, nothing more. The common structures of Sparta are made from the same materials as those in other Greek city-states— sun-dried mud bricks and red clay roof tiles. And like other Greeks, Spartans usually paint their buildings white to reflect the hot sun. But while almost all Greeks avoid ostentatious construction, Spartans take austerity to an extreme; their residences are smaller, have only one story instead of the two stories that are common elsewhere, and lack adornment of any kind.

Phidippides is most intrigued by what is missing when he surveys the city's panorama. Almost all Greek cities are surrounded by high defensive walls. No structures are more important; the survival of the entire city and all of its inhabitants can depend on those walls when the city is under attack. Walls are the fundamental defense against invasion. But Sparta has no walls around it, because it does not need them. Sparta's defense is its reputation.

As the Athenian nears the building where men eat their meals together, he is not optimistic about the food. His first meal in Sparta yesterday was black broth, the city's staple—pork boiled in blood with vinegar and salt. He had never eaten it before, but he had certainly heard of it. In Athens and elsewhere, black broth is touted as proof of the Spartans' backwardness. To Phidippides' surprise, his first taste of the concoction had been tolerable enough. But as famished as he was after such a long run, even mud would have tasted like ambrosia. Earlier today when he ate it again, he realized black broth is awful.

On entering the hall, the potent smell of black broth hits his nostrils and makes him cough. Again he will be confronted with what he hoped to avoid—nothing more, nothing less.

As he force-feeds himself, Phidippides ruminates on the ephor's words about the Festival of Carnea. The Spartans cannot come to Athens' aid for six more days. And then a quick march from Sparta to Marathon will probably take an additional five days. He tenses as he considers the bigger problem—will the Spartans even come at all? What will the ephors say at dawn tomorrow?

CHAPTER TWENTY-TWO

A SUSPICIOUS MAN

Athena soars in broad circles above her namesake city. Her thoughts swing between worried plotting and calmer appreciation of Athens' expanse, now that it is the Greeks' largest city-state, home to more than one hundred thousand people.

She cannot shake off the memory of Troy's final destruction with the death of so many children. Athens could fall as Troy did, and that must not happen.

To soothe herself, she tries to focus on the city below her. Her first impressions are two distinct colors—red, from the red tile roofs, and white, from the paint on almost all of the houses and structures.

Next, the city's most prominent natural feature claims her attention. Athens' acropolis rises from the city center, its primordial essence unmistakably clear. The great rock has been there in that exact spot since long before the gods created humankind. A giant, flat-topped mass of thick hard limestone, it towers over the city. Its steep sides are full of cracks, crevices, and caves, and deep inside it are soft mixtures of sandstone and other conglomerates. At the top it measures almost nine hundred by five hundred feet—more than seven jagged-edged but roughly level acres.

The giant rock's veined and fragmented stones continually change colors as the sun and clouds move overhead. Light blue prevails, with hints of soft gray. Pink also dances here and there. Sometimes a deep red, reminiscent of fresh blood, appears, then vanishes. Over the course of a day, the rock's colors and shadows gracefully merge and separate as they flow around its surface. The rock looks like a living thing and Athena delights in its display.

She nods approvingly at the monuments atop the acropolis. They are dedicated to many gods and goddesses, but one monument in particular draws her smile. She looks down at the grand temple recently dedicated to her—the Archaios Neos. Situated in the center of the acropolis, it is over one hundred and twenty feet long and surrounded by tall, graceful columns.

The magnificent temple is made even more splendid by her statue on its marble pediment. Unlike figures of her from the past, this Athena is no matronly, staid figurehead. She is a new goddess—a goddess of transition, shown in motion, leaning forward in a long, unhesitating stride. Her right hand points a sword toward the enemy. She raises her left arm to show the certainty of her power and inevitable victory. Her presence is dynamic and alive—a statue created by men who threw off tyranny to rule themselves. They have changed. So, too, their image of their patron goddess.

Still flying above her city, Athena briefly shifts her attention from the acropolis to the nearby agora, the marketplace thronged with her people. Yes, *her* people, who worship her above all other gods and goddesses, and who are threatened as never before—every one of them in the gravest jeopardy imaginable. Athena takes one more look at the bustling agora, and flies away toward Marathon.

~~

Far below, two women are walking together through the agora. As usual, the marketplace is filled with gossip and bartering. Parts of the agora have long stoas—covered walkways with tall wooden columns holding up roofs that provide welcome shade. But these touches of elegance are easily overshadowed by the prevailing bedlam. The agora is usually busy, but today it is especially crowded. People have been streaming into the city from the nearby countryside of Attica and elsewhere, hoping for safety behind Athens' walls.

Men usually far outnumber women in the agora, but today it is just the opposite. Of the men who are here, most are either sitting or shuffling around slowly because they are old or feeble from illness and disabling war wounds. The men who can fight are with the army at Marathon.

The two women speak softly as they walk together.

"Tell me, Archi," says Lela, her curiosity overcoming her caution, "how did—*he*—avoid going to Marathon? He can't be that old; he has to be less than sixty."

"He says he's sick," replies Archippe. "He pretends he's got a limp; if you catch him off guard, you'll notice he sometimes forgets which leg is supposed to be lame."

She guides Lela to a secluded alley off the agora and pretends to discuss a bit of her shopping with her young slave. "Now I need to tell you something important. Please listen closely to my instructions. They're simple but you must follow them exactly. Everything we're about to do depends on it. Understand?"

"I understand. And I'm listening."

"Good. When we find Mag—oh yes, isn't it a pretty krater? I hope my husband will like it when he gets back." She stops talking and pretends to admire the elegant piece of pottery she is holding up to the light as an old man with a pate as bald as an amphora hobbles by, and then she continues in low tones, with a pasted-on smile for the benefit of passersby.

"When we find *him*, I'll introduce you and say you wanted to meet him. I expect he'll ask why. If he asks me, I'll say you didn't explain and then turn to you. Or he might ask you directly. Either way, you'll answer. And your answer will be that your husband, Sicinnus, spoke highly of him and said if you ever had the opportunity to meet him, you should do so. After that, don't answer any more questions. If he asks more, just be as evasive as you can, and avoid details. No further talk is best, but if you must say something, make it vague. Do you understand?"

"Not really. There might be problems. I doubt Sicinnus even knows him. He may have just heard about him from Themistocles. And I doubt he is aware of Sicinnus."

"I'll deal with whatever he might say. When conversing with a man gets tricky, I just put on my ignorance cap and talk away in circles. Shuts them up every time. Talking in circles makes half the men listening shut up because they think they're so smart it's beneath them to listen to a woman who can't string her thoughts together. The other half are afraid the woman is saying something they don't understand. Those men think the woman might be smarter than they are—a very frightening thought. So, to avoid being found out, those men shut up too."

"But the way you want me to talk to him—or not talk—may come across as strange to him. Supposedly my husband tells me I need to meet such a wonderful man. Then I'm unresponsive when he wants to know more. Don't you think that will make him suspicious?"

"That's exactly the point. Suspicion leads to curiosity. That's what we really want."

"Curious about why I really want to meet him?"

"Exactly," says Archippe with a smile. "And when you sense that he's curious, you should wiggle your shoulders just a little."

Lela stifles a laugh. "I'm beginning to think you're as crafty as your husband."

"I accept the compliment of being crafty, but Themistocles is cunning. I'm good, but he's the best."

Turning her head to look directly at Lela, Archippe continues, "I'm thinking about what you said, so let me modify the instructions I gave you. You're smart and you know how to use your words. So be natural. But be careful. And remember my trick with the ignorance cap; it can work wonders."

They return to the congestion of the agora, staying quiet until Lela asks, "How do you know where to find him?"

"Themistocles told me he loves to gamble and does it constantly," says Archippe. "Hopefully, he's down at the far end, where the men still in Athens are at their games—most likely knucklebones, dice, five-lines, or petteia. If not, he'll be a short walk beyond there, at the arena they just built for the newest sport, if you can call it that—cockfighting."

"I remember that from long ago, as a child. Gave me nightmares."

"As a child, in Persia? Cockfighting started in Athens only a couple of years ago."

"Yes, I was with Sicinnus and both our fathers. Sicinnus' reaction was the same as mine. One of the reasons I liked him even then. And his attitude never changed as he grew to be a man. I don't really know if he dislikes cockfighting because it's so awful or because I detest it so much. Either way, he's a sensitive man."

"An uncommon trait for a man, very uncommon. I wish I could say the same for Themistocles. He took me to the cockfights once. I love him more than I can say, but sometimes I wonder why. There were no other women there, and the men looked at me like I had three heads. I lasted a very short time, with all the slashing and blood and flying feathers. Then I told Themistocles he could either take me home or I would go by myself. Wisely, he walked home with me. But then he went back to the cockfights alone."

The women edge themselves through the crowds and make their way to where the men are playing knucklebones. The game pieces are made from the knuckles of sheep and goats. The women know the game because children play it all the time by throwing the bones up in the air and trying to catch as many as possible on the back of one hand. But the men play it differently, by repeatedly throwing their four knucklebones on the ground. Each side of a bone has a different value. After every throw, they count up the values of the sides that are face down. Thirty-five throws complete a game, final numbers are tallied, and the highest total wins the bet.

Seeing that Magacles is not among those players, Archippe motions for Lela to move on. As they approach the dice games, a loud whoop goes up from the bystanders, all of them old men. The women look down at the three terracotta dice just thrown and see the reason for the all the noise. It is an Aphrodite throw—the highest toss, three sixes. But once again, the man they are after is not there.

When they approach the board games, several games of five-lines are underway. Two men compete in each game by first throwing dice that determine the number of pebbles each man can move from line to line. The women do not understand the rules, nor do they care to. Their man is not there either, so they move on again.

The popular petteia games are being played in a large area of their own. Petteia goes back at least seven centuries to the Trojan War. It is a game of pure strategy, and the women see two competitors just beginning to pit wits against each other. Their game board has eight rows with eight squares in each row to make a total of sixty-four. Each player starts with eight flat round stones in the squares along the row nearest him. Each player has his own color of stones, black or white, and the man with the black stones moves first. Opponents carefully alternate moves by shifting a stone one space forward or back or left or right. The goal is to take all of an opponent's stones by sandwiching them one by one. If a player positions two of his stones on opposite sides of an opponent's stone, he captures that stone.

Petteia can last for hours and fixates a man's mind. During the Trojan War, the two greatest Greek fighters, Achilles and Ajax, became so engrossed in a game of petteia that they forgot about the battle raging around them. Archippe and Lela, however, are not enticed by the games in front of them. Magacles is not here either.

Archippe mutters in frustration, "So we're off to the cockfights."

The women have covered barely the length of a spear throw when they begin to hear the noise. It steadily gets louder as they approach, and by the time the arena comes into view, they can hear individual shouts punctuating the constant din.

"They sound crazed," says Lela.

"Men," is Archippe's simple reply.

The women look around. The circular cockfight pit is surrounded by seven tiers of seats cut from earthen embankments created when the pit was dug. The seats are covered with large slabs of stone and can hold a few hundred spectators. Another hundred can watch while standing just beyond the highest ring of seats. It is late summer and the earthworks are brown and bone dry. All the seats around the fighting pit are filled with onlookers, but there are still places to stand and observe both the fighting and the almost exclusively male crowd. The two women survey the group, looking for the same thing—other women. There are a few.

"Pornai," says Archippe. "Prostitutes. Some are probably here from Phalerum. An uncommon outing for them, away from the stench of their home, if you can call where they live a home. And perhaps one or two of them will be lucky. If she shows her patron a good enough time, he might keep her in Athens for a while—perhaps long enough that if the Persians come, she'll have our walls to protect her. Unlikely that'll actually save her—or us—but there's no protection at all in Phalerum."

Lela is about to say something when Archippe stops her. "I see him," she says, looking toward someone across the cockfight pit. The pit is atypically quiet because of a pause between matches. The women walk until they are only a short distance from Magacles. He sees them and Archippe waves. He waves back and quickly comes over, walking with a limp that Lela suspects, and Archippe knows, is feigned.

"Well, well, Archippe, greetings," the man says, with a smile that fails to hide his smirk. "What brings you to a place where men make themselves such obnoxious fools?"

"And greetings to you, Magacles. I thought you might be here since you and my husband so love this awful sport. We were close by in the agora, and I wanted to introduce someone who would like to meet you. This is my servant, Lela."

Magacles turns to Lela and takes his time letting his eyes wander over her entire body. "Greetings to you, Lela," he says at last, in a slow, smooth voice. "Indeed, we have not met. I would remember that without question."

"My husband has spoken of you," Lela says, with a shy smile. "He calls you one of our city's most remarkable citizens. He described you to me just the other day in quite glowing terms—a true statesman, he said, a leader. I asked my mistress, if there were ever an opportunity, I would like to meet such a man. This is a real pleasure. And an honor."

Archippe is impressed, not just by Lela's words, but also by the way she says them. Archippe instinctively understands what Magacles does not. Lela is playing her role well—the awestruck young woman so impressed by the prowess of an older man and his grand reputation.

"What is your husband's name, my dear?" Magacles asks.

"Sicinnus. You probably don't remember him, a man such as you."

"Sicinnus? Sicinnus?" repeats Magacles in a quizzical voice.

"He's not very significant. But he made it clear to me you are the type of man who is not easily forgotten."

Archippe suppresses a smile. At first she was worried that Lela was about to overdo it, but no; she has tossed just enough bait to catch the fish's attention. The casual putdown of her husband was a nice touch, as long as Sicinnus never hears about it.

"Sicinnus, I think I remember the name," says Magacles. "A strange name."

"It's Persian. He is Themistocles' servant."

"Persian?" says Magacles in a raised voice. "Most interesting. And you?"

"I was born in Persia, yes. But I have lived almost half my life here in Athens. So, while my blood ancestors are Persian, I think of myself as Greek."

"I see." Magacles pauses, looking at the young woman appreciatively. "As I am sure you know, there are other Persians living here in Athens. I know some of them quite well. But certainly none of them have your— charms, shall we say. This must be a difficult time for you, or at least a complicated one. With the invasion underway and all our best citizens up at Marathon preparing for battle, engaged perhaps even as we speak."

He sighs as falsely as he smiles. "I am well represented at Marathon by my faithful son, Euryptolemus, my Eury. But you can't understand how much I would like to be with them myself. However, with my limp, it's not possible. Seventy pounds of bronze armor means I would be more burden than help. Even so, I have plenty of internal fortitude. I can be of genuine service here in Athens. To say nothing of the wisdom of experience. You may count on that."

Before Lela can respond, the crowd begins to shout and applaud.

"Ah, my big cock is here in all its splendor," declares Magacles. "This is something you will want to get a good look at. You'll be impressed; I promise you that."

Archippe's face freezes, but Lela smiles with apparent glee that Magacles seems to think is genuine.

"I call it 'Big Red,'" he continues, with a broad grin. "It's had more fights than any other rooster since cockfighting began in Athens. That's because it always defeats its opponent and does so very quickly—long before the second phase of a match, when the curved killer-knives are attached to the cocks' legs to create extra deadly talons."

Magacles turns to look down at the pit as Big Red is brought into the arena, carried in the arms of the bird's handler.

Lela and Archippe also look at the pit, and Lela says in an audible whisper, "It's huge." Although Lela wants Magacles to hear the words, her sentiment is genuine this time. She is staring at the biggest chicken she has ever seen.

"Speaking of Persia," continues Magacles, "let me tell you a special secret—just among us." Archippe refrains from shaking her head at his silly effort to impress and entice with such nonsense, but Lela opens her eyes wider as if to say, "How exciting, tell me the secret, please."

"Big Red's bloodline is Persian. I imported his father along with a brood of Persian hens. I paid dearly, but I have made far more money with all my bets on Big Red. And today I am making the largest wager of my life. Today I will become more than just rich; I will become a man of real wealth, which will make me a man of renown—even more than I am now. There is more than one way to attain glory."

The women realize Magacles is sweating and breathing hard, and then the crowd roars again. Big Red's opponent is being brought into the pit. The women stare at the strange sight and realize why Magacles made his bet of a lifetime. The new bird is pathetic, scrawny, and smaller than even a normal rooster. And the little bird's feathers look mangy, with patches of ashen, wrinkled skin exposed without any feathers. The bird looks sick, perhaps very sick. Archippe wonders how such a wretched creature is even allowed to fight, much less go up against Big Red. But Lela sees something Archippe does not, and that Magacles does not notice either. The new bird's handler is holding it very tightly. Lela understands that weak and pitiful birds do not need to be grasped so firmly.

The two handlers push the cocks' faces together so their beaks touch, and then quickly pull the birds away. The handlers repeat the action several times and then put the roosters on the ground. With their tail feathers gripped by their handlers, the birds start squawking shrilly and try to lurch at each other with their legs up and talons extended. Wild-eyed onlookers around the pit are shouting at the top of their lungs. The handlers pick up the roosters, walk to opposite sides of the pit, put the birds on the ground again, and let go.

In a blistering instant the birds are at each other, with feathers flying everywhere and piercing screeches that sound more like unearthly creatures than chickens. A moment later the birds back away but then charge each other again. Then again they back away and re-engage. They repeat the pattern over and over as their wings flap and feathers swirl, their squawks drowned out by the shouts of the frenzied crowd.

Then a change. The little bird backs away but does not attack again. When Big Red races forward, the little bird darts to the side. Big Red pivots and lunges forward; the little bird scurries to the side again. A new routine—Big Red attacks; its opponent evades the attack.

"You don't see that often!" exclaims Magacles. "That little chicken is afraid and wants no more of it. When Big Red catches him it will be over."

Lela nods in apparent agreement, but she is not so certain. She thinks there might be another way to interpret what they are seeing.

The attack-and-dart-away routine repeats until a referee enters the pit with his arms held high. Both handlers grab their roosters and more handlers join them. The roosters are held firmly on the ground while their legs are rubbed with garlic and then quickly wrapped with thread.

"This will be a first for Big Red," mutters Magacles. "I never thought that other bird would make it to the second phase of the match. But it will be good practice for my rooster. And it will be quick, that's for sure."

The two handlers are back on opposite sides of the pit, gripping their birds as they place them on the ground. Lela and Archippe see flashes of the curved, razor-thin killer-knives tied to the birds' legs. The long knives point straight back from the chickens' legs. The women realize Magacles is correct; this will not take long.

The handlers let them go again, and the clash is furious; no darting away this time. The birds seem to have merged and are spinning around and over each other. They are like a blurred ball, and it is impossible to make out what they are doing to each other as they whirl in a cloud of dust and floating feathers. The crowd is out of control with every man acting half-deranged, jumping up and down and screaming as loud as he can. The women too, except for Archippe and Lela, who are repulsed but cannot avert their eyes.

Then it happens. Something spurts and spins straight up through the churning dust and feathers. The onlookers' shouts are replaced by a unified gasp while the entire audience watches the rotating object rise and then fall with a splat. Everyone shifts their attention back to the birds. They have once again backed away from each other. Or, at least, the little bird has backed away. Big Red frantically flaps his wings and stamps his feet up and down, seeming to run in place. Then he takes off racing in a circle around the arena. The bystanders are mesmerized by the sight of the rooster with its head cut off, spraying bright red blood like a moving geyser. He completes a full circle around the arena, makes it halfway around a second time, and falls. Lying on his side, his legs keep trying to run and dirt flies everywhere. The bystanders roar their delight, all except for Magacles and his two companions.

Magacles slowly turns his head and glares blindly at Lela as his cock's handler enters the ring to remove the bloody carcass. The rooster is finally inert, a pile of tangled feathers. Its head is already being eaten by one of the local dogs that regularly haunt the arena for just such a chance; Magacles does not notice the dog's good luck.

The expression on Magacles' face is very dark. Lela stares at him anxiously; he seems to not even see her. Archippe is stunned into silence, but Lela wants to say something. She wants to go back to their conversation before the fight. As her mind races she decides to use both her instincts and Archippe's earlier advice.

"This is so terrible! I'm so sorry! I can't believe this." Lela slaps her hands over her face as if in shock and begins to moan. Then she pretends to sob uncontrollably. She peers through her fingers to gauge the reaction to her words. Magacles is still staring at her, but his expression does not seem as ominous.

What Lela fails to see is that her actions wake Archippe from her brief trance. The older woman is worried because she is sure Lela is overplaying her hand. Then Archippe looks at Magacles and realizes she is wrong. His expression is changing from anger to befuddlement. Perhaps she has been giving Magacles too much credit.

Magacles seems to snap awake and see the beautiful young woman standing before him, shaking with shock and grief. Reflexively, he touches her arm.

"Now, now Lela," he says in a smooth voice, speaking as though she were the one who needed comforting. "Don't cry, little one. It's all right. I have won and lost bets many times before. All things pass, my sweet, even the greatness of Big Red. He was a fine old bird, but there's no arguing with the Fates. Now, now, no more tears. Let us talk of more, well, pleasant things."

The words are music to Lela's ears; they are exactly what she was hoping to hear. She clenches her jaw to stop herself from laughing—and flinching from his touch. Archippe, whom Magacles seems almost to have forgotten, also has to concentrate to keep her true feelings hidden.

Archippe sees clearly that Lela is playing Magacles like the lyre she delights her mistress with on many evenings. The man still looks somewhat spellbound, but he is putting the cockfight out of his mind, at least for now. He seems not quite sure he is reading the signals correctly. Lela's tone and body language could hardly be better. Soft, vulnerable, not quite sultry, but close. However, Archippe is afraid Lela will go too far. *Whatever you do,* she thinks, *don't wiggle your shoulders.*

Magacles draws Lela's hands from her face. "But you were saying, before this unfortunate event, what a complicated time this is for you." He looks deeply into her eyes. "Of course, it must be, with your Persian background. The Persian army is now at Marathon and, who knows, maybe here in Athens soon! People are scared, with good reason. These are times for suspicions and scapegoats." He gently places his pudgy hands on her shoulders. "You should understand, I am not a prejudiced man, not at all. But that's not true for most of our citizens. Are you concerned about what people might think of you because of everything that is happening?"

Lela's mind lights up. She realizes he has just posed the perfect question for her purposes, but now is not the time to answer. She remembers Archippe's earlier admonition—do not engage in conversation; say your piece and then shut down further talk. Avoid being specific; stay vague. Put on your ignorance cap.

"That has not really been a problem," replies Lela. "Perhaps because I do not go out much. And perhaps because I spend much of my time with my friend Archippe who is like you—not prejudiced."

Lela looks over at Archippe. The timing of the look makes it appear to be completely natural, but Archippe understands Lela is asking for help.

"Magacles, we must be going," says Archippe. "We have taken up too much of your time, and I must get back to my children. Please excuse us."

Magacles gives Archippe a blank look, as though he had completely forgotten she was there. "Of course," he says, with a slight bow. Then turning back to Lela, he says, in his gentlest voice, "Perhaps we will meet again."

"I would like that," says Lela. "Perhaps sometime soon. And," she adds, giving him a deeply sympathetic look, "I am truly sorry about your cock."

The two women turn and casually walk back toward the center of the agora with its congested hustle and bustle.

When they are a good distance away from Magacles, Lela huffs, "He is a pig! A lustful old fart! What an awful human being!"

Archippe can't help chortling at Lela's indignant putdown as they walk together toward the farther edge of the agora.

"Did you see his eyes before he spoke his first words to me? Talk about being undressed then and there!"

"Now, now," says Archippe in a motherly tone. "Don't get carried away. Since when does drooling desire distinguish one man from another?"

"That's not my point and you know it. He is disgusting. He is demeaning. He wanted to make it obvious, the way he looked at me and spoke those stupid words, 'my big cock' indeed, playing as if I should read between the lines of his vulgar, foolish babbling, he's—he's—"

"You don't need to hunt for words; I know what he is. And he certainly made you feisty."

"You knew he would do that to me, didn't you?" Lela's eyes flash at her mistress.

"Well, I have to admit the thought crossed my mind. But you seemed to enjoy the cockfight."

"Ugh!" Lela grimaces in disgust. "You know better."

"Still, you laid it on thick."

"You gave me an assignment; I tried to do what I thought you wanted. Did I go too far?"

Archippe laughs out loud, "One thing it is impossible to do—flatter a man like that too much. For a moment, I wondered if you were going to wiggle your shoulders."

"I was concentrating so hard I forgot. Should I have?"

"Absolutely not. Your instincts are good; you're a natural. I'm starting to wonder if you have more experience than I realized."

"I have lots of experience."

"Oh?"

"With Sicinnus. I told you earlier, he and I have passionate desires. We live for each other, and now our daughter."

"I won't tell Sicinnus what you said about his significance."

"When those words came out of my mouth, I couldn't believe I actually said them. I shocked myself. That's the one thing I feel truly bad about."

"Don't fret. He'll never know. And it was an especially good touch." She pauses, then asks, "Do you know who Aeschylus is?"

"The man who writes dramas? Sicinnus once took me to one of his plays. I was astonished; I had no idea a few people speaking on a bare platform could affect me so deeply."

"Aeschylus is a close friend of Themistocles. The playwright sometimes talks about the men who act in his dramas. He says the best actors are absorbed by their work. During the performance they become the person they portray, and then afterward they return untouched to their ordinary selves. It seems as though that just happened to you; for a time you were no longer Lela, wife of Sicinnus. You were simply the Seductress. What came out of your mouth meant nothing to or about Lela. The only purpose of your words was to entice a suspicious man. You did it. The next time I see Aeschylus, I'll tell him if they ever decide to let women participate as actors, I have a recommendation."

"You make me feel better, you're good at that," Lela says, with a smile. "But I made a mistake. I shouldn't have called you my friend."

"Yes, better to lie about that. But at least you didn't refer to me as Archi. Calling someone a friend means little. But using a nickname only real friends use makes the relationship undeniable. You did well."

After taking this in, Lela says, "You're a wise woman, Archi."

"You and I both are. Even more important than being wise, we're going to act—and not in a play. Our men at Marathon will show valor. I am sure of that, and I am sure of something else. Valor applies to women as much as men, and it applies especially to you."

Lela stops in her tracks, which brings Archippe to a halt. "Valor? Me?"

"Yes," says her mistress. "The next time you encounter him, you'll be by yourself. I won't be with you."

After pausing to consider the implications, Lela responds with the naive courage of youth. "I can handle myself."

CHAPTER TWENTY-THREE

THE GREAT KING'S STORY

For thousands of years the Persians have been nomads, and Darius remains a nomad at heart. A restless man of immense power is well advised to control himself, lest impatience and agitation lead to serious mistakes. The Great King soothes and restrains his impulses by constantly moving his residence. Tonight, he and his personal guards—the Ten Thousand Immortals—are camped one day's ride from the city of Susa. The personal guards are called Immortals because whenever one of them is killed or otherwise unfit to serve, he is immediately replaced, so their number stays fixed at exactly ten thousand men.

Inside his huge tent, Darius is slowly walking in broad circles on beautifully woven carpets spread over the ground in overlapping layers. Although it is late at night, the tent is well lit with flickering oil lamps; shadows dance over the silk walls, which stir lazily in the night breeze as if the tent rested at the bottom of a twilit sea.

It is a few days after the banquet in Susa. Phar, the young Egyptian emissary, was invited to accompany the king's entourage to the camp, and Darius has just summoned him. While he waits, Darius pours water from a solid gold jug into a golden chalice. He replaces the lid and puts the jug back on a polished cedar table. Next to the gold jug is a blue ceramic one filled with wine, and two matching cups. Holding his chalice in one hand, the king fingers five small metal disks in the other.

An Immortal enters the tent. "Great King, with your permission, the emissary from Egypt is outside."

Darius nods and the Immortal withdraws. A moment later, the

Egyptian is bowing low to the Great King.

"Arise, Phar."

As Phar straightens up he sees an enormous black dog near a chair at the side of the tent. The animal was sitting but stands up now and wrinkles its nose and upper lip as if to snarl. The dog remains silent but fixes its gaze on Phar. It is a Persian mastiff, and Phar guesses its weight is more than two hundred pounds. He also suspects the dog is a man-killer, the Great King's intimate body guard.

Darius makes a slight motion with his hand and the dog sits back down, its eyes on its master. The king points to the polished cedar table in the middle of the tent. "Help yourself to wine and follow your Great King."

At the table, Phar instinctively selects the blue jug.

Darius resumes walking around the expansive tent while Phar follows a few steps behind, listening to the king play with the small metal objects in his hand. Every time Darius drinks from his chalice, Phar sips, or pretends to, from his cup.

After a short while, the Immortal re-enters the tent.

"Great King, your son, Xerxes, requests permission to enter."

Without looking at the Immortal, Darius says, "Tell him to wait."

Darius slowly walks another full circle around the tent, followed by Phar, and then stops and turns to face the Egyptian.

"The dog's name is Brute. His loyalty and empathy are unsurpassed. They go together, you know. When your Great King wants him to be gentle, there is nothing gentler. When your Great King wants him to be something else, his capabilities are most impressive. I think it is fair to say that you will never have the pleasure of meeting a better 'brute.'" Darius smiles and looks at Phar, who smiles back somewhat awkwardly.

The king raises an eyebrow as if inviting Phar to say something, but Phar does not know what to say, and remains silent. Darius continues, "Fill your cup again. Then have a seat in the chair next to Brute, but do not touch or speak to him. Only your Great King does that."

After refilling his cup, Phar reluctantly walks toward the giant mastiff. Phar avoids eye contact with the frightening creature, but from the corner of his eyes he realizes the dog is not paying any attention to him. Brute is fully focused on Darius.

As Phar begins to sit down, he sees Darius signal with his hand and Brute responds with three earsplitting, ferocious barks, causing Phar to spill some of his wine onto the carpet beside his chair.

The Immortal immediately steps into the tent and Darius walks over to him. Speaking softly so Phar cannot hear, Darius says something into the guard's ear. This takes so long that Phar begins to feel uneasy. He is listening hard to try to make out what Darius is saying to the Immortal. But the only words he hears are, "Summon the herald."

The Immortal departs and Xerxes comes in. The mastiff stands and wrinkles his nose and upper lip. Brute surely has encountered Xerxes hundreds of times, but the animal is acting toward him just as it did toward Phar.

"And to what do I owe the pleasure of a visit from my favored son?"

"Father, before I retired for the night I wanted to stop by and see how you are. But now I see you have a guest. I trust I am not interrupting."

"How thoughtful. Well, I will tell you how I am." Darius pauses and drinks the rest of the contents of his chalice. He turns his back on Xerxes, walks to the cedar table, refills his chalice from the gold jug, and walks back to Xerxes.

"I have changed my mind," he says. "When a man drinks in abundance, he is well advised to avoid talking about himself."

Darius stops and waits for Xerxes to say something. Brute continues to stare intensely at Xerxes and Darius. Phar's discomfort increases.

Xerxes says nothing, so Darius continues, "I am about to give some advice to the emissary from Egypt. I am going to tell him the story of how to be a Great King—how a Great King acquires and maintains power, how a Great King expands his empire. You know the story well. Do you wish to hear it again?"

"If it gives you pleasure, Father."

Darius turns away from Xerxes again and takes a few steps toward Phar and Brute. Phar sees that the king's face is flushed, though it is unclear whether from wine or anger. Brute growls softly.

Turning back to Xerxes, Darius says, "My pleasure is no different either way. Answer the question."

"Yes, Father, I would like to hear the story again," Xerxes promptly replies. "And I have a small request."

"Ask it."

"Brute appears to be extremely tense. Perhaps it would be best to allow him to relax."

Darius gives his son an amused look. "Perhaps Brute would like you to pat him on the head? Maybe rub the side of his nose near his teeth?"

Xerxes stares coldly at his father before answering. "Perhaps another time."

"Perhaps," Darius nods, "when it gives me pleasure."

Darius makes a small motion with his hand and Brute sits down. Darius drinks from his chalice. The king and his son walk to the table and the king motions for Phar to join them.

As Darius fills his chalice and Xerxes and Phar fill their cups, the king says to Phar, "You may join Xerxes on the other side of the tent. He prefers to sit as far away from Brute as he can."

The three men walk to the side of the tent opposite the mastiff. It crosses Phar's mind that he would rather sit next to Brute than Xerxes. After they sit down, Darius hands Phar the five small disks he has been rattling in his hand.

"What do you make of these?" asks Darius.

"They are very strange, Great King," replies Phar. "They look like gold, and they are impressed or somehow stamped with the face of a lion."

"Over fifty years ago, they belonged to Cyrus the Great."

"The first Great King?"

"Yes, the creator of our empire. What you hold in your hand are coins."

"Coins. I've heard of them. They give wealth, like cows and wheat."

"Your Great King's story begins in the early days of the empire when Cyrus got his hands on these very coins," Darius continues. "Cyrus was conquering lands in the west, close to the Aegean Sea. He was approaching another empire—the Empire of Lydia ruled by King Croesus. The coins in your hand were made by the craftsmen of Croesus. He was a very sly man. You said the coins look like gold, but they are actually made of electrum, which is only partly gold. Coins like these made Croesus the richest man in the world."

"Croesus gave these coins to Cyrus the Great?"

"Croesus did not give—Cyrus took. They fought a war and Croesus lost. Both men were military geniuses, but Croesus made one mistake, and one mistake is all it takes when one genius is up against another. Before they went to war, Croesus was unsure whether to attack or to defend. He sent his emissaries to the oracle at Delphi to hear the advice of the priestess. She said that if Croesus went on the attack he would destroy a great empire. Croesus attacked and just as the oracle predicted, he destroyed a great empire—his own."

Darius pauses and drinks. Phar hears Xerxes gulping. Darius fills his chalice again, and Xerxes fills his cup. Phar realizes Xerxes is extending the wine jug to him, so he feels obliged to do exactly what he does not want to do. He guzzles the rest of his wine, then holds out his cup to Xerxes, who fills it so full Phar must carefully bring it to his mouth and sip with his lips puckered to avoid spilling. It helps that this time, Brute is not barking.

Darius continues, "So Great King Cyrus captured King Croesus and took all his coins. Now for a question."

Phar flashes back to the banquet a few days ago, and he remembers all the questions Darius asked. He thinks he should keep his mind alert. He also thinks so much wine must soon affect the king's mind and wonders when he will start slurring his words.

"Tell me, Phar, what do you think Great King Cyrus did with Croesus?"

After mulling over his reply, Phar says, "Normally a captured enemy ruler is killed by the conqueror. Defeated rulers can be dangerous if they remain alive. And, Great King, you said Croesus was a military genius, so he could be especially dangerous. But for some reason I don't think Great King Cyrus had him killed."

Before responding, Darius looks at Xerxes for a reaction. Xerxes does not acknowledge his father's look, and instead stares fixedly into his wine cup.

Looking back at Phar, Darius says, "Everything you say is correct and your instincts are good. Most everyone in the Empire of Lydia assumed King Croesus was killed by Great King Cyrus, and many still think so today. But they are mistaken, because Croesus in fact lived a long life. He became the Chief Counselor to Great King Cyrus. And later aided Cyrus in his conquest of the world's most magnificent city."

"Babylon."

Darius and Phar look at Xerxes, who spoke that one word without lifting his eyes from his chalice. And now refuses to meet his father's gaze.

"Yes," says Darius, turning back to Phar. "For over a thousand years, the Babylonians worked to strengthen the walls that surround and protect their city. Two great walls, each one eighty feet thick and more than three hundred feet high. The double walls made Babylon invulnerable for centuries. Then a hundred years ago, along came Nebuchadnezzar. Do you know of him?"

In his mind, Phar curses the Great King's never-ending and arcane questions about people he has never heard of.

"No, Great King, I must admit I never heard the name."

"Well, you should learn about him. Nebuchadnezzar was a mighty king of Babylon. Almost as great as Hammurabi. You know of Hammurabi, of course."

Phar again silently curses while murmuring, "Why, no, Great King. I have not heard that name either."

"Egypt believes civilization began with her." Darius shrugs. "Egypt is too proud. Civilization did not begin with the pharaohs. It began with the idea of justice. Hammurabi was king of Babylon a thousand years ago. He wrote the first laws to govern everyone in the land, regardless of their status. His laws still exist. They look like a giant phallus."

Phar pauses and hopes the look on his face does not appear too foolish.

"Excuse me, Great King, you are saying the laws look like a . . . you mean like . . ."

Darius interrupts, "Fully erect! Have you seen it?"

"No, Great King, I have not seen it, I am trying to envision it, but what I see . . . perhaps the wine . . ."

"Hammurabi had his laws carved on a column of black stone," Darius continues. "The dense rock is basalt with a smooth, shiny luster. It is more than eight feet tall and almost two feet thick. Its weight is beyond most people's imagining, and nearly three hundred laws are carved on the stone's surface. The laws imposed different punishments for different crimes. If a man was guilty of slander, his head was marked with a cut for all to see for the rest of his life. If a man was guilty of theft by robbery, he was put to death. Your Great King's favorite is the best example of all the laws: If a man destroyed the eye of another man, the destroyer had his own eye destroyed."

"An eye for an eye," says Phar.

"Exactly."

"I have heard of that law."

Darius smiles.

"So, Great King, you say that Babylon—and civilization—began over a thousand years ago with the laws of Hammurabi."

"Yes," Darius says. "But we were talking about expanding the Persian Empire, so let us return to Babylon's Nebuchadnezzar. Like your people of the pyramids, he liked to build—temples and towers and arched gateways and hanging gardens and ziggurats. Wonders of the world. And Nebuchadnezzar built something else that, more than a generation later, became a problem for Great King Cyrus of Persia."

Darius pauses and stares at Phar, who silently curses yet again. He is sure the king will ask him to guess what Nebuchadnezzar built that later created a problem for Cyrus. However, Darius again drains and refills his chalice. Xerxes gulps his wine, refills his cup, and holds the wine jug out toward Phar. Thinking this cannot go on much longer, Phar swallows all his wine again and holds out his cup to be filled.

"A third wall," continues Darius. "Nebuchadnezzar built it around Babylon, so the double walls became triple walls. Then years later along came Cyrus the Great, intent on conquering the most magnificent and best defended city in the world. Babylon had been impregnable with two walls, and now it had three. So Cyrus the Great turned to his Chief Counselor, Croesus, and asked, 'How shall we do it?'"

Darius pauses and once again stares at Phar, who grimly expects to be asked to guess the answer. Instead, Darius says, "Enough for this evening."

Xerxes abruptly stands up, swallows all his wine, and bows deeply to Darius. Caught off guard by the unexpected halt to the story, Phar rises too quickly and, feeling lightheaded from the wine, rams into Xerxes so hard they both almost fall to the ground. They catch themselves and Phar bows toward the king.

"You did not finish your wine," Xerxes snarls, glowering at Phar.

Smiling and raising his cup to his mouth, Phar says, "You're starting to sound like Brute."

Xerxes gasps in disbelief at the comparison.

Darius commands, "You are dismissed."

As they leave the tent, Xerxes continues to glare at Phar while Phar smiles back.

Alone again, Darius resumes his slow perambulation around the tent, his face tense as though he is listening. After the steps of his two visitors fade away into silence, the king raises his hand slightly and a muscular soldier immediately emerges from an invisible partition at the back of the tent. He holds a sword in his hand and has a long knife strapped to his hip. The soldier serves as Darius' other ever-present protector.

"Inform the Immortal that your Great King is ready to see the herald."

The soldier quickly walks to the front of the tent and steps outside. A moment later the soldier walks back through the tent and disappears behind the partition. Darius continues walking in circles until the Immortal steps into the tent and says, "Great King, the herald requests permission to enter."

Darius nods, the Immortal departs, and the herald walks in, the father of the young man whose life the king spared at the banquet a few days earlier. The herald is also the man who Darius made responsible for monitoring and protecting Phar.

Darius asks in a completely sober voice, "You are confident your approach to your Great King's tent was discreet?"

"Yes, Great King," replies the herald. "Xerxes did not see me. He is gone from here."

"But perhaps his spy saw you."

The herald hesitates, then asks, "Great King, are you saying there is a spy in our midst who has a higher allegiance than to our Great King?"

"That is exactly what your Great King is saying. Here are your instructions. Tomorrow night your Great King will again summon Phar. That will cause the spy to inform my son. You are to identify the spy. Provide your Great King with the spy's identity immediately, before my son arrives, as he will. Then your Great King will instruct you on how the spy is to be dealt with."

As the herald leaves, Darius throws out the water in his chalice and fills it with wine from the blue jug.

CHAPTER TWENTY-FOUR

LEAVING SPARTA

Once again Phidippides is running with his constant companion—his mind. He is only an hour out of Sparta, but the harangue in his head is starting earlier than usual.

Why do I do it? Run all day long, then all through the night, then again the next day. Everyone asks me the same questions. But they're never satisfied with my answers.

Running more than one hundred and fifty miles from Athens to Sparta would cripple other runners for days, sometimes weeks, sometimes for the rest of their lives. Now he is running the same distance back, plus another twenty-six miles from Athens to Marathon. No one, including him, can fathom his recuperative power. A gift from the gods.

Phidippides and his mind circle each other, looking for a weakness. Occasionally his self-questioning is a no-holds-barred pankration match, but for now it is just a scuffle.

I don't run for the glory, to be remembered after I die. Glory comes from valor, and valor is holding your ground in the phalanx or winning at the Olympian Games. But at Olympia they run for speed. The same sprint they've been running for three hundred years. Just one stade! Now they have more races, but the longest is still only twenty-six stadia—three short miles. That's not what I do. I'm not even good at that. But I can keep running, on and on. Farther and longer than anyone.

As his legs churn, Phidippides' thoughts pause for a moment and then continue.

What my teachers said is true. The gift alone is not enough. Skill is earned with discipline and drills. To attain glory, skill and valor must unite.

He smiles.

And then there is cunning—such a potent skill. I wish I had more of it, like Themistocles. I wonder if Themistocles will attain glory.

Phidippides returns to wondering about himself.

I know what they think, some of them. They think I'm a coward. But the leaders don't want me in the phalanx; they want me to run and carry their messages. When I get to Marathon I'll make them let me fight. I'll demand it. I deserve it—the chance to show my valor. I'm not a coward. I can do both—run and fight. I can hold my ground with the best of them. Maybe die. For glory.

Finally, Phidippides' mind eases. He hopes the brightening day will clear his thoughts. It has been just over an hour since his dawn meeting with Sparta's ephors. He intentionally arrived early, but all five of them were already there. He wonders how many hours they were waiting. All night, perhaps. But what they had to say was brief and blunt.

His thoughts shift to something he knows Spartans do not view the way he does—how much Sparta has changed. Athenians talk about it. Some laugh, but most Athenians think there is nothing amusing about it. Spartan food was not always terrible. Sparta once had beautiful statues and monuments. They used to care about culture and the intellect. Not anymore. Why?

The answer came to him yesterday while eating that awful black broth again. The Spartans did it to themselves. Long ago, when they subjugated the helots of Messenia. That was when war, and victory in war, became not just an attraction or obsession, but their supreme love—what they valued above all things. When Sparta destroyed the culture of Messenia and enslaved the helots, the Spartans destroyed their own culture and enslaved themselves.

Phidippides' attention turns again to the morning sky. In the far distance, he begins to make out a multitude of objects clustered together.

Clumped rows of plants tended by the helots, perhaps. *Are those stocky shrubs red? Or is the red just an illusion from this distance? Their color doesn't make sense. They look like blurred blood. Some kind of vines, perhaps? Curious.*

Phidippides looks away and goes back to what he was mulling over earlier.

I run because it's like wine, but even better. I don't tell anyone that; it sounds like sacrilege, an insult to Dionysus. Everyone knows how he comes to them in their wine, but they don't believe running can be like that. They don't understand. The God of Wine and Ecstasy shows he loves us with the gift of wine and the gift of running long distances; he's one of us.

Phidippides is startled to realize the red objects in the distance are moving—in unison. This could be a serious problem; it is far too soon for him to be hallucinating. Many hours from now, in the dead of night, he will expect some confused fantasies. But not now.

He scrutinizes the objects more closely, and their synchronized movements. They are not rows of plants, but rows of men—Spartans marching in military formation. A phalanx.

For an instant, Phidippides is relieved that he is not hallucinating, but then he hears the peculiar music that is driving the march.

⁓

The music does it. Suddenly his mind leaps ahead, straight into the midst of the marchers.

Startled by this complete shift in perspective, he can sense that his body is still running, steadily closing its distance to these men. But 'he' is inside the phalanx now. He can feel the shoulders and arms of the men beside him. It is claustrophobic; he is squeezed among them. And he sees everywhere the brilliant crimson of the Spartans' cloaks, dyed to conceal the blood of battle.

The Spartan phalanx is moving in the uniquely Spartan way, very slowly, to maintain flawless formation and perfect unison. The Spartan hoplites' measured steps require not thought, but rhythm. Phidippides is fascinated by the strange flute-like sounds of the double aulos, two long hollow reeds connected with a single mouthpiece. He knows the instrument, but this is not Athens. Back home in his refined city, the aulos is played by half-naked young women for the entertainment of philosophizing men, who lounge on couches and drink wine during their sophisticated symposiums and pretend their intellects matter while they ogle the maidens and call for more wine.

The aulos Phidippides hears now sounds nothing like the Athenians' instrument; the Spartan aulos produces a shrill, high-pitched cry that carries a long distance. Then he remembers—there will be something more. He has heard stories of the Spartan phalanx and there is always a second sound. He listens, and soon it comes, another aulos, but with a much lower pitch. The two combine and compete, the high-pitched female and low-pitched male. The high pitch excites while the low pitch calms.

Phidippides thinks about the Spartans' strangeness. Athenians and other Greeks use horns and trumpets when they march on the battlefield. That makes sense. The Athenians step to the beat of the war trumpet salpinx, a long, thin brass tube with a bulb at the far end to control its piercing blasts. The salpinx is a rallying instrument. It requires such hard blowing that it makes a player's head hurt. Its sound is simple, clear, and loud. But that is not the Spartan way. The combined sounds of the Spartans' auloi are complex and conflicted.

Despite his thoughts, the aulos music begins to take hold of Phidippides, transforming him along with all the other hoplites in the phalanx. It is pulling all of them together, unifying them, morphing them into a single machine of war. The music's external, pulsating rhythm becomes internal—a shared throbbing deep in their gut. The men are changing from individuals into a fearsome whole.

Phidippides is over the edge now. His body paces itself to the sound, speeding up to triple-time with a cadence of three long strides for each of the Spartans' stomps. But in his mind, he is slow-stepping in the phalanx. At this pace his mind could go on forever, but his body will break.

Completely enraptured, Phidippides' mind readies itself for the imaginary clash. The Athenian hoplites and other Greeks rely on momentum when they attack their enemies. That is not the Spartan way. The Spartan way is to be immovable. Never step back. Stand, hold, and then one step forward, just one—now. The immovable Spartans stay calm. Emotions controlled. The clash comes, then the pause. There is always immobility just after the impact. It is a completely different fighting style. Pushing and crushing with no advance forward. The awful pressure, blood-spitting stabs in the first three ranks, choking gasps, fathomless ferocity.

In Phidippides' mind, an enemy soldier goes down, stuck in the groin by an underhanded spear thrust. Another thrust at the fallen enemy, straight down from a spear's butt end with its sharpened pike point. Then the fade to trampled blackness. Stomping feet. Up and down, over and over. An enemy smashed to pulp. Still no progress for the Spartan phalanx, no advance. But then it comes. The female aulos. A protracted shriek. This time the high pitch is meant to remind the Spartans of their mothers. It is a Spartan mother's strident scream, "Come home with your shield—or on it." That is the signal for the Spartan king to shout, "One step forward, just one—now!" The stalemate flexes; the Spartan monster pushes, and a small crack appears in the enemy's front ranks. Almost imperceptible, but inevitable. The enemy tries to adjust; the movement and fear are felt all the way to the rear. The enemy shudders. They have not been forced back yet, but they sense what is coming. A slight letup in the rear, ever so small but this time everyone perceives it. Panic has not started yet, but the end begins. The shriek of the female aulos has done her job. The low tones of the male aulos keep the Spartans steady.

Once more the Spartan king's command follows the mothers' cry with

"One step forward, just one—*now*." The immovable Spartans heave again. The irresistible enemy falters. Another enemy in the front line goes down. Then another. The crack widens, splits. The downed men are trampled as the oncoming Spartans fill the expanding void. Now the Spartans stab sideways at undefended flanks. The gap deepens. The doomed men in the rear cannot see it through the dust and flying dirt, and they cannot even hear it above the awful din. But they feel it. They know. They think about their wives, their children, and themselves. They turn and run.

Phidippides' mind starts to shift back to his own body. He is near the phalanx now, and reality begins to set in. He can already make out individual Spartan hoplites instead of just the blood-red blur, and he sees the flashing wall of round bronze shields. Now he hears a new sound. A male sound, but not the low-pitched aulos. It is a man's thunderous shout. Not just a yell, but a plea, a supplication. The Spartan king is screaming the wail of each man's mother on behalf of her son. A cry to the sky, to the gods. The word "Apollo" is clear. And now comes the sound of other voices, all of them—the entire phalanx. Singing, full-throated, the paean:

> Close—hand to hand,
> Shield—to shield,
> Helmet—to helmet,
> Crest—to crest.
> Valor! Glory!
> Home—to Sparta
> With my shield—
> Or on it!
> Apollo—give me
> Strength—and glory!
> Home—to Sparta
> With my shield—
> Or on it!

Phidippides speeds up even more, running quadruple time—four strides for every Spartan step. He is sprinting as fast as if he were in the Olympian Games. If he continues, this will kill him. But he wants another moment. He needs another moment. Ecstasy—just one more moment.

> Close—hand to hand,
> Then—and now,
> They were—there,
> I am—here!
> Valor! Glory!
> One step—forward,
> One step—now!
> Earn—the god's gift,
> Stand—or die!
> Glory! Glory! Glory!
> Home—to Sparta
> With my shield—
> Or on it!

Phidippides is right beside the phalanx now. He sees the hoplites clearly. There is no enemy here. The Spartan hoplites raise their hands over their heads as if they have spears, but they do not. Then an overhand thrust. The imagined spears jerk back away from imagined victims. The spears spin in the hoplites' hands so the butt ends face forward. Each spear's long, narrow blade becomes a pike's short, sharp point. The point aims at the ground, at the fallen enemies. A downward thrust; all the pikes stab into the ground at the same time. One final step and all the hoplites stop with a thundering stomp. Phidippides sees it, hears it, feels it. The human war machine comes to a halt, but the runner goes on.

When the phalanx is behind him he does not look back. He focuses on his legs and slows down to the proper pace. He is mystified by what just happened to him. A drill, some sort of practice, perhaps. Part of the religious Festival of Carnea? Spartans are not supposed to engage in battle during the festival, but that does not stop their never-ending war preparations. Or was the whole experience a dream?

The Athenian knows he may never understand, but he has a far higher priority—the ephors' answer. He must convey it to Marathon. And before that, he must tell Athens what he was instructed to tell them. Whatever just happened to him cannot happen again. He must regain and maintain his self-control. This will be a long run. The longest run in his life. And he is not ready to die.

CHAPTER TWENTY-FIVE

THE FALL OF BABYLON

Tonight Phar, again, receives a gracious summons from "your Great King." When he enters the capacious tent, he sees Darius hunched over the large cedar table. The king is facing away from Phar and does not look around when he enters. The black Persian mastiff starts to stand but Darius motions with his hand and the dog sits back down.

With his back still to Phar, Darius commands, "Arise."

Flustered because he had forgotten to bow, Phar quickly bends down and straightens up. He sees the king's gold chalice and two blue cups on the cedar table, just as they were last night, but instead of two jugs there are three—the king's gold jug plus two blue ones. And all three jugs are larger than those from last night. Phar grimaces.

Darius stands and turns around. In his hands is a large piece of parchment. "See," says Darius, "your Great King wants to ask you about this."

The incessant tricky questioning is starting even sooner tonight.

Darius turns and replaces the parchment on the table. Sweeping his hand over it, he says, "Look here."

Phar approaches and sees that the parchment is a map, though of what is at first unclear in the flickering light of the oil lamps.

"Look carefully," Darius says, pointing to each region of the map as he describes it. "These lines show the Tigris and Euphrates rivers, which come together as they flow southeast. On the left you see the land of Lydia next to the Aegean Sea, the far western edge of your Great King's empire. Then south from there, down across the narrow strip of Phoenicia beside the sea, is your home, land of the pyramids, and farther down is the mother of

Egypt, the eternal Nile."

Staring at Phar, Darius asks, "Why does your Great King spend so much time studying this map? What is most important about what you see?"

Before Phar can reply, an Immortal enters the tent and says, "Great King, your herald waits outside."

"Have him enter now," says Darius. "Phar, while your Great King confers with the herald, study the map and use your imagination."

The herald enters breathing hard as though he has been running. Turning his back to Phar, Darius walks over to the herald and they begin to confer in a whisper.

Phar tries to concentrate on the map while listening to what he can hear of the king's conversation. Before the herald departs, Phar is able to make out only one word: "torture."

Walking back to Phar, Darius asks, "Do you see what is important?"

"No, Great King, I am sorry. I am studying this map as hard as I can, but I do not."

"That is because you are not using enough imagination." Darius' voice is stern. "That is because you are limiting yourself to the map. That is not how a Great King thinks, and if you will one day be an advisor to your Great King, perhaps Chief Counselor as Croesus was to Cyrus the Great, you must think beyond the map."

In one swift movement the king's hand strikes the table beyond the left edge of the map, with his fingers extended as if to grab a portion of the world. The spot marks an area far beyond the western edge of his empire.

"*There* is where you should look."

Startled but still able to respond, Phar says, "But Great King, we know nothing about that land."

"Correct. Just as Cyrus the Great wanted Babylon, your Great King wants all of this land as well. Legend has it that it is washed by a great ocean somewhere in the distant west. But . . ."

Darius taps the table with the tips of his fingers.

". . . to go where your Great King wishes to go, there is a small problem."

He raises his hand above his head, clenches it into a fist and slams his fist down near the same spot on the table with such force that Phar staggers backward.

"The land of the Greeks!" Phar exclaims.

Darius nods. "A worthless land except for its location. My empire will expand west to the ends of the earth, and there are two ways to do that. Your Great King can pass north of the Greeks and ignore their land. But that would leave the Persian left flank constantly vulnerable, which is unacceptable even when the threat comes from such a lowly people. The other option is the only option, and it is well underway—to conquer the land of the Greeks and absorb it into the empire."

Phar looks up from the map and inquires, "And the Greeks themselves, what will happen to the people?"

Before Darius can respond, the Immortal enters the tent and announces, "Great King, Xerxes requests permission to enter."

Phar hears Darius mutter to himself almost reflexively, "As usual, too much haste." Then the king says out loud, "Send him in."

Xerxes enters the tent and stops just inside the entrance, glaring at Phar.

"The Egyptian emissary is again our guest," says Darius. "Welcome, my son."

Brute starts to stand but Darius motions to him to sit.

"Take your cup and a jug of wine," continues Darius. "Let us finish the story that began last night—the story of what it takes to be a Great King. My favored son will no doubt find it of particular usefulness."

The three men, each carrying a jug and drinking vessel, walk over to the same part of the tent as last night, away from the mastiff.

Darius begins, "So how did Persia's first Great King, Cyrus, conquer the unconquerable Babylon? The answer is by using religion and a river.

"Babylon was weakened and vulnerable because of religion—two religions, in fact. A generation earlier, Babylon had conquered a small country and its main city, Jerusalem, and taken its inhabitants captive to Babylon. By the time of Cyrus, many of these captive people, known as Hebrews, hoped to be freed from bondage because one of their leaders, Isaiah, had convinced them someone was coming to save them—a 'messiah,' an 'anointed one' who would be their savior and liberator. No one knew who the messiah would be.

"Hearing that, Cyrus knew exactly what to do. Persian spies infiltrated Babylon and met with Isaiah and told him Cyrus the Great was coming to save his people. More than that, they said he would help them return to their country and rebuild their most important place of worship, destroyed earlier by the Babylonians—a sacred temple where these people prayed to their 'One True God,' a primitive deity named Yahweh."

Darius laughs. "Isaiah eventually came to believe that Cyrus was, indeed, the messiah of the Hebrews. Apparently, Isaiah did not know that Cyrus worshiped the actual One True God of all Persia and the world—Ahura Mazda!"

Darius refreshes himself from his gold chalice and Xerxes and Phar do the same from their blue cups. The king is drinking the purest fresh water from one of Susa's deepest wells, while Xerxes and Phar are guzzling one of the Great King's finest vintages, a beverage impressive even to the usually abstemious Egyptian.

"Now for the other, far more important religion," continues Darius. "The oldest religion of Babylon, the worship of Marduk, the God of Water and Judgment. Several years before Cyrus arrived, Babylon's king, a fool named Nabonidus, left Babylon for a long time, and while away he became obsessed with the God of the Moon, Sin. While King Nabonidus was gone, he left his son, Belshazzar, to rule the city. But shortly before Cyrus arrived, Belshazzar went crazy and started seeing visions, such as a disembodied hand writing words on walls. So Nabonidus returned to Babylon, and the powerful priests of Marduk were appalled at the thought that Nabonidus would elevate the moon god, Sin, above Marduk. The priests considered regicide. Cyrus knew all of this too. And Cyrus knew exactly what to do.

"He sent spies to the high priest of Marduk to tell him the Great King, as a servant of Marduk, believed Marduk must retain his place as the primary god and patron of Babylon. The high priest sent back only a brief message in response. All it said was 'Hail, Marduk,' and Cyrus was certain of his man."

Darius waits before continuing, to let the implications of this sink in. Phar finds himself becoming more interested despite himself, and he sips more wine.

"Now, the Euphrates River flows through Babylon," Darius goes on. "Thus, it passes through the three walls surrounding the city. Those three walls all have river-gates made of vertical bars that open and shut to let boats through. Because the river-gates could move, Cyrus knew their bars could not be embedded in the river bottom; in fact, they went only a short distance below the surface of the deep Euphrates."

Darius' words begin to blur in Phar's mind; the story becomes like a dream while he quaffs more of the marvelous wine.

~○

Phar imagines Cyrus and Croesus standing along the bank of the Euphrates, studying the river carefully. It is the dead of night.

A long distance upriver, far beyond sight or sound of Babylon, Cyrus' engineers and laborers have been building barriers and dams around the Euphrates. The barriers were just destroyed a few hours ago to divert the river's mighty waters toward the dams and away from Babylon.

"The river diversion was successful?" Cyrus already knows the answer; this is the third time he has asked, but his nerves will not let him rest.

"Yes, Great King," says Croesus once again, "it was a complete success. But we must wait. It will take time for the flow of the river to be affected here, so far from the diversion."

It is the first night after the new moon. This is the moon god's monthly rebirth, when Sin is celebrated by Nabonidus and other apostates who have forgotten that Marduk is Babylon's supreme patron god. Tonight's crescent sliver of light is so thin that it casts less light than the surrounding stars; no dancing shadows or silhouettes mar the darkness.

Behind the two men stand thousands of Persian soldiers. Dozens more stand in front of them, close to the outer wall of the city. The soldiers near the wall carry large flat boards. The Euphrates still flows noiselessly past them and under the river-gate in the outer wall.

The night is warm and breathless. The waiting men alternate between listening to the distant clamor of the celebration of Sin inside the city walls and watching the Babylonian guard above the river-gate. If he were less distracted, Cyrus would smile at the thought that the priests of Marduk must be seething with rage at the dishonor the celebrants are showing to the city's patron god.

The Persians closest to the wall wonder about the guard high atop the three-hundred-foot barrier. Some of them can see the guard, but so far, the guard seems unable to see the Persians huddled in the deep darkness.

Great King Cyrus is also watching. Every time the guard walks across the top of the wall, Cyrus sees someone else near him, barely visible in the starlight. If the other figure is who Cyrus suspects, then Cyrus' request of the high priest of Marduk has been granted. But the Great King is uneasy. The wait is going on too long, and long waits can cause mistakes.

The Persians are at the northwestern river-gate where the Euphrates should drop first. Cyrus and Croesus look at each other again and then back at the river. Still no change.

A moment later, Croesus slaps Cyrus on the shoulder and points to the top of the wall. Cyrus looks up and spots the guard leaning over and looking straight down at the Persians. Then the second figure appears next to the guard. The two seem to blend into one. Cyrus is too far away to hear anything, but the Persians nearest the wall hear scraping and shuffling high above them, then a grunt and a gasp, and they look up in time to see something big falling toward them. They scatter before the body hits the ground, and then gather around the dead man. The corpse wears the uniform of a Babylonian soldier. A large knife has been shoved so far into his chest that only its hilt is visible, and even in the darkness the jewels on its handle glitter. The Persians whisper among themselves and wonder what happened, but Cyrus knows.

Someone says in a loud whisper, "Look at the water." And there it is—the river is sinking fast. Another loud whisper. "Look at the river-gate."

The bars of the gate no longer touch the water and the river is still dropping. Soon it will drain entirely, and Cyrus' vast army will walk under the gates of all three walls and into the heart of Babylon. It will be a muddy slog, but the men with the large boards will go first and lay down the wood as they advance, so the men behind them will not be mired in the muck.

The army pours into the city, surprised by what greets them—nothing. No opposition, no resistance. Cyrus tells his commanders to head straight for the festival at the other end of the city, subdue everyone using as little force as necessary, and prepare for Great King Cyrus' grand entrance into the city tomorrow. Then Cyrus is gone. Shortly after his departure, the noise at the distant festival becomes raucous. Then the sound gives way to stillness. The quiet fall of Babylon is complete.

⁓

Phar continues to slurp his wine. His thoughts begin to meander as if he were the Euphrates itself. His mind keeps floating and merging with Darius' retelling of the story.

~⌒

The morning after the fall of Babylon, Cyrus the Great formally enters the city and leads his imposing entourage onto the Processional Way. Cyrus stands in a war chariot and Phar is next to him. Croesus rides a horse beside the chariot. They all look straight ahead toward the Ishtar Gate dedicated to the Babylonian Goddess of Sex.

High walls stretch along both sides of the Processional Way. The walls are made of long bricks glazed deep blue and adorned with life-size golden lions. More than a hundred of these sculpted lions seem to steadily walk toward the rear of the procession. The lions are male, maned, and in their prime, each with a graceful tail that slopes down and away from the animal's body and turns up near the tip. Every lion's mouth is wide open and snarling, revealing the predator's fangs.

Cyrus' procession nears the Ishtar Gate, a soaring archway between two square towers that are eighty feet tall. Phar looks up. Along the tops of the towers and surrounding walls run rows of notched parapets designed to provide perfect cover for archers and spear throwers. The deadly ornamentation is high above and all around.

Under the great arch, the procession stops. Cyrus and Croesus climb the long stairs up the Gate, and Phar follows a step behind. As the new king of Babylon, Cyrus appears on top of the Gate. Facing toward the interior of the city, he looks out over the gathered people. He raises his arms in welcome, and the crowd's shouts fill the air.

Cyrus steps back out of his new subjects' view and takes in the spectacle. Phar sees an enormous tower south of the Ishtar Gate—a massive terraced ziggurat, measuring more than three hundred feet on each side. Rising like a flat-topped mountain, this stepped pyramid is the Tower of Babel.

Farther south, Phar sees the holiest place on earth, according to the Babylonians—the Temple of Marduk. Looking west, he focuses on a luscious green area about halfway to the Euphrates River. The Hanging Gardens, famous for luxury and lechery—a private place for Nebuchadnezzar of old and his many, many women.

Phar hears Cyrus say to Croesus, "Your Great King is ready. And our guest?"

"Everything is arranged," answers Croesus. "I will get him."

Croesus departs and returns a moment later with a large man wearing a black hooded robe. When they approach, the hooded man bows to Cyrus and says, "Welcome to Babylon, Great King and servant of the great god Marduk."

"Arise," responds Cyrus. "I trust you too are a servant of Marduk, as the great god's high priest."

"Yes, Great King."

Cyrus looks to Croesus, who holds out a large gleaming knife, freshly cleaned and polished. Although obviously deadly, the knife is also a ceremonial weapon with intricate and ornate carvings on its handle as well as sparkling, jeweled inlays.

Cyrus says to the priest, "Last night Marduk saw fit to give Babylon to his servant, Cyrus the Great, and one of your priests used this knife for a most pious purpose. I trust the priest is in good health?"

"Yes, Great King, he is in very good health—robust as an ox," the priest says. "He is the strongest of all the priests. That is why I selected him for the duty he performed."

"Do you think your worthy priest would like his knife returned?" asks Cyrus.

"No, Great King, he had no hesitation last night, and he has no concerns now. Indeed, he deserves and takes pride in his action on behalf of Marduk and Marduk's servant, Great King Cyrus. I suggest you keep the jeweled knife as a gift and reminder of your support from the priests of Marduk."

"Your Great King accepts the knife as a gift and reminder of your support," Cyrus says as the priest bows. "You may go. Tell all the priests to pray for the new king of Babylon, the servant of Marduk, the Great King."

After the priest departs Cyrus folds his arms across his chest and smiles at Croesus. Cyrus then turns to Phar and says, "So now you know. Now you understand how to become a Great King."

~~~

Phar is startled; he opens his mouth but cannot speak. It is one thing to imagine Cyrus conquering Babylon before his eyes as if in a dream, but quite another to hear Cyrus speak directly to him.

The young Egyptian shakes himself, then sees Great King Darius once again standing before him.

"Now you know how to become a Great King," Darius says again, not noticing, or pretending not to notice, the Egyptian's momentary confusion.

Darius pauses and drinks from his chalice. Phar glances at Xerxes out of the corner of his eye, but the king's son seems to have noticed nothing.

"Above all," Darius continues, turning full face to the Egyptian emissary, "a Great King must have a good advisor. And a good advisor will say what he thinks is true, not what he thinks the Great King wants to hear. Do you follow my words, Phar? Do you understand?"

Phar nods.

Darius continues, "And a Great King must know the best way to conquer an enemy—through treachery and betrayal. The supreme victory is a victory with no battles. When confronting enemies, a Great King's first goal is to find traitors among them, earn their loyalty, and then use them as weapons to cut out the enemy's heart. Do you understand, Phar?" Darius asks again, "Do you understand, emissary from our land of the pyramids?"

"Yes, Great King," Phar responds, his stupor finally behind him. "I understand you. The way to be a Great King, and victorious, is always to know the truth, even if it may not be to the king's liking, and to find traitors among his enemies and win their loyalty to his cause."

Darius turns to his son and says, with a cool look, "Spoken like a man who can advise a Great King because he thinks like a Great King."

CHAPTER TWENTY-SIX

A CURIOUS GAME

Hippias pokes at his fire. A ragged stream of smoke rises into the twilight as the Persian commander walks up.

"After all these years, you should know how to build a proper fire."

Hippias stares into the heat and does not answer. Smoke blows around them in the eddying winds.

"Every evening, as soon as the sun begins to go down, you do this without fail," Datis continues. "Here we are again, a warm evening, you build your fire and play with it. And still . . ."

Hippias ignores the Persian's remarks. "We need to figure out a way to get to Athens. Even without the delay of unloading our horses, the Athenians were here too soon. And we landed in the middle of night. I don't see how they did it. And what's wrong with my fires?"

"The smoke," says Datis. "So much you can hardly see the flames. If you know how to properly lay good, dry wood, it keeps it down. I'm surprised you've lived so long breathing all that smoke over the years. It's not good for your lungs, you know. Or your eyes. You should be blind by now."

"What about the spy you sent to the Greek camp?" asks Hippias, annoyed by where the conversation is going. "Any word on contacting Magacles' son?"

"When we have any word, you'll know." Datis pauses, then decides to continue irritating the old man. "Tell me, why *do* you like your fires so much?"

"The smoke," answers Hippias.

The Persian snorts in disbelief.

"The smell of wood burning comes from the gods," Hippias continues. "The finest aroma on earth, except for the fragrance of a woman. The smoke's scent relaxes me."

Datis responds with a cynical laugh, "I just figured out something about you—why you don't drink. Breathing smoke does for you what wine does for most other men—it loosens your head and makes you think about women. Ever been drunk in your whole life?"

"Once, a very long time ago. I threw up a hundred times before I passed out. I didn't like that. Then, when I woke up the next day I wondered if some animal had been sitting on my face and using my mouth to relieve itself. I didn't like that either."

"It's hard to trust a man who doesn't drink."

"Is that why you drink so much, to make men think you can be trusted?"

Out of the twilight beyond the fire, a Persian guard comes up. "Commander, one of our spies is here with a report."

Still looking at Hippias, Datis says, "Well, perhaps we'll learn something about the Greek camp and the son of your friend."

"No, Commander," says the guard. "The spy is not returning from the Greek camp. He ran down from the high hills overlooking the area they control."

"Bring him to me."

A moment later the spy stands in front of Datis. He is still slathered with sweat from his run and trying to catch his breath.

"Your location in the hills?" Datis asks, without preliminaries.

"Commander, my first position was close to the Greeks' main camp. But then I moved beyond the camp to observe their activities in a level area."

"Explain."

"An open plain akin to the area we control. Not as large, but the terrain is similar."

"And the activities of the Greeks?"

"I do not know the significance of my observations," says the spy, "but you said to report anything unusual."

"Correct. Continue."

"Four hundred Greeks assembled in the area. Some were throwing small spears, as if practicing or maybe for a contest because, after several men made throws, they seemed to compare the distances. Other men repeatedly threw something round and flat, about a forearm's length in diameter. They would crouch down, then spin around, straighten up, and throw."

"Games," says Hippias, still staring at his fire. "Throwing javelins, light-weight spears. The goal is to throw a javelin the farthest. Same goal for throwing the discus you describe."

"Interesting," Datis says, mulling this over. "The Greeks and their games. Were they also playing other games?"

"Yes. Some were grappling in the dirt, some were hitting each other with their fists. Hard to think of them as just games, but . . ."

"Yes, all games," Hippias interrupts, still gazing at his fire. "Wrestling, boxing—games of endurance and skill."

"A strange people, you Greeks," Datis says.

"On that point you're correct." Hippias turns from the fire to Datis. "We are strange to the Persians. Strange to barbarians who don't speak our language. Strange to all others in the entire world. We Greeks are unique, and one reason is what the spy describes. Greeks play games. Nowhere else in the world do people play games as we do, and with such fierce competition. Think about everywhere in your empire. Think about your province in the far south—Egypt. What do you think about when you think of Egypt? The pyramids. And what is a pyramid? A tomb. That's what the Egyptians live for—death. That's what their priests and god-king pharaohs say they should live for—death. Not the Greeks. The Greeks live for life. The Greeks play games."

"Like children," says Datis.

"Yes," replies Hippias. "Like children. With joy."

"Joy! You, the man who makes a high art of showing off his nasty temperament speaks of joy. Strange indeed."

"Allow an old man to drift back in time. I've been gone for many years, but I remember."

"Commander."

"Is there more?" Datis asks the spy.

"Yes. About the games, there were some others, but one in particular I want to tell you about. This one game, if that's what it was, involved about two hundred men, close to half of all the men there."

"And what were they doing?"

"Running."

"The oldest of all games," says Hippias, turning back to his fire. "The first Olympian Games started with running almost three centuries ago. How far were they running?"

"A little more than five, maybe six hundred feet," says the spy.

"A stadium's full length, the distance of the track for a one-stade sprint," says Hippias as he crushes a piece of charcoal with his stick.

"What I saw was no sprint," says the spy.

"Since the first sprint, many other foot races have been added to the Games."

"If you will allow him to finish his report," growls Datis.

"There were two strange things about the running game I watched," says the spy. "The first is that the runners were wearing armor."

"One of the less common games," says the old Greek as he fidgets with the fire. "The hoplitodromos. It was added to the Games just a few years before I left Athens. In all the other races the men run naked, but in this game they wear helmets and leg greaves and carry shields. I didn't pay much attention to it. I had more important matters on my mind."

"I'm certain you did," Datis says. *Such as staying alive while all of Athens plotted your overthrow.*

The spy interjects, "That may explain the armor. But there was something else strange. The men were in two long lines, one behind the other. Then both lines started running together. There didn't seem to be any intention for anyone to get ahead. No intention to win. At least nothing obvious I could make out."

"Curious," says Datis. "Hippias, is that how they run the game you mentioned?"

Hippias stops playing with the fire. "That's not exactly how I remember it. I assume it's some sort of variation. We like to change our games, modify the rules, invent new games. I've been away twenty years, and my recollection is hazy. Still . . ."

After turning to look at the spy, Hippias says, "A game without any intention to win makes little sense. Old or new, winning is the point of a game. We're missing something. How many men ran in each line?"

"About a hundred."

"So many!" Hippias purses his lips, ruminating. "Anything else get your attention?"

"One more observation, probably not significant."

"Proceed."

"The games I just described went on for about three hours. Then the assembled men departed in the direction of their camp, and another group of men, another four hundred or so, came into the clearing and engaged in the same games. That happened four times over a period of twelve hours."

"Hmm. Most Greek games are contests between individuals," says Hippias, half to himself. "But there are also contests between groups. So why aren't these groups competing with each other? Perhaps there were judges comparing their different runs. I wonder . . ."

"We're spending too much time making assumptions about games and their rules," says Datis, growing impatient. "What I care about is the coming battle."

"Or figuring out how to get your army to Athens regardless of any battle here," Hippias retorts as he turns back to his fire.

Datis tersely dismisses the spy as Hippias stares into the flames, muttering, "My assumptions make sense, but it's still a curious game."

Perhaps if Datis knew the Greeks better, or if Hippias had a younger and sharper mind, they would realize the curious game is no game at all.

CHAPTER TWENTY-SEVEN

THE GREEKS WAVER

From a height above the plain of Marathon, the two Greek friends stand together, watching hundreds of Persian archers show off by doing practice drills in full view.

In five long rows, the bowmen extend from the shore to well inland and onto the plain's solid ground. Open terrain extends nearly two miles in front of them. The sea is on their left. Right behind them stand twenty rows of soldiers—thousands of men shoulder to shoulder with their spears pointed skyward.

The archers launch their arrows together, all aimed at forty-five degrees for maximum distance—six hundred feet. They immediately nock more arrows to their bowstrings and continue shooting in unison over and over, a total of ten times, aiming a bit lower each time. They are tracking imaginary Greeks in a battle charge. As the men in the front two rows drop to one knee, they and the archers behind them angle the last few volleys to fly parallel to the ground. Straight at the onrushing enemies. Then the archers all but disappear as the Persian soldiers strut forward, level their spears, and prepare for a pretend collision. They brace for a clash with Greeks weakened by arrows. They also imagine their enemies being decimated by Persian cavalry attacks on the Greeks' flanks—maneuvers that real Persian horsemen practiced earlier in the day.

At the end of the drill, the archers run out to collect their arrows, run back, and prepare to start again. The two Greeks watching them from the hills shift their eyes toward the huge camp near the Persian ships. The scale of the encampment is alarming. Countless rounded tents made of animal skins litter the bright sand. Banners wave in the lazy sea wind and cookfires flicker. Brightly dressed soldiers move about or stand watching the archers practice. Occasionally one of them stares long and hard up at the hill where the Greeks are standing.

"Those archers are a nervy bunch," says Aristides.

"They know there's not much we can do about it," says his old friend. "Of course . . ."

"Of course what? What are your observations?"

"They're trying to intimidate us," Themistocles answers.

Aristides shakes his head and looks again at the enormous Persian camp.

"Our brethren from Plataea must be impressed," says Themistocles.

"A better word might be the one you just used—intimidated. When the Plataeans look down there, they see a camp ten times larger than their own entire city-state. I would not underestimate the unnerving effect of the Persian position."

"And what about us? As an Athenian, what word would you use?"

Aristides pauses before answering. "Our city is bigger in raw numbers, with perhaps half again as many people. But *they* are armed and organized to fight and kill. And Athens must subtract its women and children, and the old and decrepit, and foreigners, and most of the slaves. When you finish doing that, the answer to your question is, inevitably, 'daunting.'"

Frustrated because he agrees, Themistocles says, "The archers are back at their drills again." The two men watch in silence for a time.

"They're good," Aristides says.

"Very."

"I dare say," continues Aristides, "better than good. Their apical accomplishments are astonishing. Almost deserving of approbations if they weren't also such asses."

Without even glancing at his friend, Themistocles grunts, "You and your fancy words. 'Asses' was enough. I wonder if you'll ever learn to talk right."

Aristides inhales but before he can speak, he and Themistocles hear a familiar tramping sound behind them. They turn to see Miltiades rapidly approaching them, unmistakable with his ginger hair.

As he arrives, Miltiades growls, "I'm glad I found you together. We have a problem."

"The generals?" asks Themistocles. "I bet a few of them are pissing themselves. That always happens before a hard fight. So?"

"Worse than that," says Miltiades. "Sometimes men have cold feet and other times cold balls. And they've got the latter, bad."

"We dealt with all that back in the city," responds Themistocles. "We had a full Assembly vote."

"It's not the same when you're facing it. In Athens it was numbers and maybes; here it's ships and horses and men. Anyway, you know as well as I do when we're on the battlefield, the generals rule. They have the discretion to change any decision made in the city. And the generals' votes have changed or are about to."

Themistocles and Aristides trade glances.

Aristides asks, "Do you know the vote count?"

"A tie, five to five," says Miltiades. "In addition to the three of us, we have two other generals. They may hold with us but that's not certain. The other five are rock solid for returning to the city. They're spending all their time planning for a withdrawal, half at nightfall, the rest at midnight, with decoy sentinels left behind to look like we're still here. I expect a call for a council and vote before day's end."

Themistocles spits in disgust. "What did I say?" he exclaims to Aristides. "I guess the archery practice worked." Turning to Miltiades, he adds, "This is ridiculous. So, five to five. That leaves Callimachus. Does the warleader know what's going on?"

"I'm not sure what he knows," says Miltiades. "And I'm not sure about his mind. He may not be thinking straight."

"What's that mean?" snorts Themistocles.

"Remember I told you I went to see him late at night after we learned the Persians were landing at Marathon? But I didn't tell you the whole story. He was sitting there, wide awake."

"You told me that."

"And his wife was there."

"You also said that before. Was she laughing like she always does—the happiest grandmother in all Athens?"

"Not at all." Miltiades shakes his head. "When I told Callimachus the Persians were landing, he half-smiled in an odd way I've never seen before. Then the two of them looked at each other, and that was strange too. So I stepped out of the house to leave them alone. A little while later they came out holding hands."

"The old bull?" asks Themistocles, flabbergasted. "Right in front of you?"

"And they kissed. Put their hands behind each other's neck. Passionately, like newlyweds. Then he walked past me without stopping and said he'd be at Marathon by sunrise."

Themistocles stutters, "The warleader—kissing—in public."

"I'm going to find him now."

"I'll come with you," says Themistocles.

Aristides nods. "I'll come, too."

"No, not both of you. That's not how to deal with him. Three are too many. Too much of a heavy hand, especially with him."

"A good point," says Themistocles. "I'll go with you."

"No, it should be Aristides."

Themistocles opens his mouth to object, but Miltiades continues. "Themistocles, I'll be blunt. In the Assembly, you're the best, the master. And not just because you love to mingle and backslap, although you're the best at that, too. When you raise your voice in the Assembly, you know how to excite them, how to play to their emotions. You know how to tell them what they want to hear and then get them to support what you want to do. I admire your ability, but now we're talking about one-on-one with the warleader. And we're talking about your reputation, Themistocles. You're a complicated man."

Turning to Aristides, Miltiades says, "You've known Themistocles forever. Do you disagree with what I say?"

Themistocles makes a slashing motion with his hand and snarls, "There's no need to answer. The two of you go find the Polemarch, but before you leave I have some advice. And, given the exalted reputation I apparently have, you might be well-advised to heed it."

"I'm listening," says Miltiades.

"Tell Callimachus this. Tell him that the choice is between freedom and slavery. Tell him the freedom of Athens means the glory of Callimachus. If he makes the right decision, and the decision is his, he will be remembered for as long as there is an Athens. For as long as there are Greeks."

Themistocles pauses. Miltiades asks, "Is there more?"

"Yes. Tell him if we return to the city instead of fighting here at Marathon, if we take up defenses behind the walls of Athens along with the cowering old men and our women and children, we will be defeating ourselves. What will such a retreat do to the minds of our hoplites, to their sense of valor? The generals are deluding themselves if they believe anything other than this simple fact—retreating now will not delay defeat, it will guarantee it. Now is the time and place, the *only* time and place, to fight the Persians. Otherwise, all will be lost."

"And what about the real reason we can't withdraw behind Athens' walls?" asks Aristides.

"A good question—and a bad one," Themistocles replies. "Our real threat is traitors who might betray the city. But don't bother with that argument. The generals against us will make soothing counterarguments. They'll say that particular danger isn't real. And even if it is, they'll say the entrances to the city can be watched, opening the gates from inside can be prevented; they'll say it will never happen. They'll be wrong, but the main point for now is to keep Callimachus focused on valor and, ultimately, glory—the city's and his own."

Themistocles pauses again and Miltiades repeats his question. "Is there more?"

"Yes. When you're talking to him, compare Callimachus to . . . no, not Cleisthenes, not a statesman. Think warriors. But not Achilles. That's presumptuous. Ajax. Yes. After Achilles, he was the greatest Greek fighter in the Trojan War. A perfect match—Callimachus and Ajax. You and I live to prove our valor and deserve glory. That's normal. And normal men also live for other things, our families, our land. But Callimachus is not normal; nor was Ajax. For the two of them, the reason for life was, and is, glory. Period."

The three men stand in silence while Miltiades slowly nods his head. "You're very good, Themistocles."

"Very good, indeed," Aristides echoes.

"Democracy serves you well—you were born for it," says Miltiades. "Aristides and I will go find Callimachus. You should plan on a council of the generals before the day ends."

After they leave, Themistocles looks back at the Persians. A few moments later Sicinnus comes up the hill and walks over to him. Seeing the scowl on his master's face, Sicinnus asks, "What's wrong?"

"What's *right*?" exclaims Themistocles. "Aristides!"

"Ah." Sicinnus is familiar with this response, having heard it more times than he can remember. He is not anxious to probe further but feels obliged to. "Aristides is your best friend, or at least one of them."

"He is *not* my best friend; he's the friend I've known the longest."

Themistocles stops and stares at Sicinnus before adding, in a harsh whisper, "*You* are my best friend, and if you don't know that by now, you should."

⁓

Later that day, Miltiades' prediction materializes. The council of generals is well underway when Themistocles arrives. The other nine generals sit in a semicircle, and Callimachus is by himself, off to the side. Miltiades and Aristides are together and there is nowhere to sit beside them, which suits Themistocles fine; he doesn't want to be seen close to them just now. He is taking a seat at the end of the semicircle when a general rises and steps forward.

The general says, "Except for Themistocles, perhaps, the rest of you who wanted to speak have done so, and we are about to hear from our warleader. We know everyone's thoughts and it seems we are headed for a split vote that must be resolved by the Polemarch. I will be brief and simply summarize. My summary is based on the warleader's views. Although the warleader has not yet spoken at today's council, we all know his assessments of our situation and the enemy. I believe I can summarize his views with three words: hordes, horses, archers."

The general looks at Callimachus, who gazes back at him without motion or expression, neither acknowledging nor denying the general's words.

"I will stick to facts," continues the general. "Hordes. I believe it is fair to say that no one here has ever faced an enemy even close to this size. Not even Miltiades during his time among the Persians." The general pauses and looks at Miltiades, who does not react. The general goes on, "At least four-to-one against us, probably more, and that's not including the thousands of seamen manning their ships. If they add those to the fight, the odds against us will easily be eight- or even ten-to-one. I would vote to do battle if their advantage was two-to-one against us; a Greek is worth any two Persians. Even three-to-one, if we had advantages we don't have here."

The general pauses and then goes on. "In addition, there are the warhorses, a thousand of them at least. We know the reputation of the

Persian riders. Before they learn to walk they learn to ride. Their arrows are deadly accurate at full gallop. And, riding up and down our flanks, they won't come within a spear-throw as we drop like flies."

Leaning over to Aristides, Miltiades whispers, "He's exaggerating; the Persians learn to ride starting at age five. Unfortunately, everything else he says is correct."

"And speaking of dropping like flies, I trust we all watched the Persian archery drills," continues the general. "I don't need to elaborate. We all have the same goal. We must stop the Persians. What now must be answered is where to make our stand—here at Marathon or back at Athens where we will be supported by the walls of the city. I submit the facts, the same realities we know the warleader is focused on. The facts tell us, demand us, to return to Athens."

Themistocles is seething with his eyes closed because what he just heard sounds persuasive. Then he hears his name called. Opening his eyes, Callimachus asks him, "Do you wish to speak?"

Across the semicircle, Themistocles sees Miltiades silently shake his head "No."

Themistocles says, "No, I prefer to hear your thoughts, Polemarch."

Everyone is surprised by Themistocles' answer. Even Miltiades is surprised that his silent signal was accepted. Miltiades has forgotten what he himself said earlier in the day—that trying to read the indecipherable mind of Themistocles is usually pointless.

Callimachus rises slowly and steps forward.

"I fully agree with the facts just cited," begins Callimachus. "And I agree with the assessments."

Callimachus pauses and five generals smile.

"What I conclude from them," he says, "is another matter."

The warleader clasps his hands behind his back, and the five smiling generals stop smiling.

"This is a difficult decision," Callimachus continues. "When I am confronted with hard decisions, I like to ask what the best of our ancestors would do. The ancestors we will always remember. There are no better men to consider than those of the Trojan War, men such as Achilles, Odysseus, Ajax."

Themistocles puts his hand over his mouth, partly to cover his slight smile and partly to keep from nodding in agreement.

"Ajax would not return to Athens, of that I am certain. Ajax would say to you—if we run, we lose. And I say to you I will not run, and I do not intend to lose."

Callimachus pauses again and Themistocles abruptly stands up. His action is most unusual because the last person to speak before a council vote should be the warleader. Themistocles says nothing but looks at Callimachus for his approval. Instead, Callimachus raises his hand with the palm toward Themistocles, who sits back down as quickly as he stood.

"Here are my final words," says Callimachus. "Our situation is grim but returning to the city will not help. Miltiades knows more about the ways of the Persians than any of us, and he warned us. The fight before us will be different from any we have ever faced. Our old ways will not be enough. Returning to the city and using the walls for defense is an old way. It won't work. What we are about to encounter won't be what we know— phalanx against phalanx. Instead it will be our phalanx against their hordes and their cavalry and their archers. We must do something different from anything we have ever done. I have a plan and you will receive your orders at dawn tomorrow, assuming you are all still here after we vote."

Callimachus stops, looks at Themistocles and says, "If you wish to speak before we vote, your time has arrived."

Themistocles stands and speaks with deliberate calm. "I do not propose to add to the warleader's wise words or the words spoken by any of you. Rather, I speak to the dull subject of procedure—the vote. We have a choice. We can cast our votes to stay at Marathon or return to the city. Our votes will be known to all and remembered by all. But there is another choice. At this moment, nothing requires us to cast a vote. If one of you demands a vote, that is what we will do. And, of course, all will know and remember the demand, along with the votes we cast. The call for a vote and the votes cast will be remembered for generations to come."

Crossing his arms, Themistocles continues. "If we do not vote, the decision of the Assembly stands—confront the enemy on the open battlefield. I propose that our Polemarch adjourn this council now. Does anyone object?"

A long silence follows. Finally, Callimachus declares, "We are finished. You will receive my instructions at dawn."

CHAPTER TWENTY-EIGHT

RUNNER'S REPORT

Phidippides left from Athens' north gate just moments ago. His stay in the city was brief; he never sat down. He didn't dare. After running from Sparta all day yesterday, all last night, and most of today, he knows he must not stop and rest until he gets to Marathon. He told the Athenians that the Spartans were coming to help and would arrive at Marathon shortly—the exact message Callimachus instructed him to convey regardless of what the Spartans actually agreed to do.

Phidippides still hears the cheers ringing in his ears. Cheering for him as he left. Cheering for themselves because they think their chances of survival are better now.

He knows that around the next bend the path splits into two routes to Marathon, where the hoplites will be waiting for him. After the split the paths skirt Mount Pentelicon on opposite sides. The famous source of the most beautiful marble in all Greece, Mount Pentelicon is also the biggest obstacle between him and his destination. The shorter route passes over the north side of the mountain. That is how he initially planned to go, but its trail is narrow, rocky, and steep. Some of the ups and downs are severe—acceptable for a fresh runner but menacing to someone even slightly fatigued, and by now he is profoundly depleted. He decides instead to take the longer path on the right to skirt the mountain's southern slopes. In his condition, the longer route will actually be faster, and give him much better odds of not ending up writhing in the dirt with a twisted ankle or at the bottom of some chasm with a broken neck.

He watches the ground a short distance ahead and knows the next time he looks up he will see the path fork. His body hurts more than ever before.

Phidippides retreats into his mind. *Control yourself . . . concentrate . . . divert your thoughts . . . just twenty-five miles to go . . . this is nothing compared to what you've already done . . . more than three hundred miles . . . I must look awful . . . they gasped when I entered the city . . . but the cheers when I left . . . I'll tell the warleader and generals . . . what the Spartans really said . . . what the Spartans really promised . . . this pain is bad . . . never felt anything this bad . . . must be what the other runners felt . . . the ones who died . . . just twenty-five more miles . . . it's nothing . . . I'm sweating . . . good . . . I'm cold . . . not good . . . my nipples are bleeding so much . . . I'm alone . . . the only one here . . . I'm so alone . . .*

"Phidippides. Phidippides!"

He looks up and sees two women standing at the split in the path. They are by themselves. *Very unusual . . . women out here . . . no men around anywhere. Hallucination?*

As he pulls even with them one of the women cries out, "Tell Themistocles the children ask about him constantly. Tell him we love him."

He nods and runs past her, but the younger woman starts running beside him and cries, "For the sake of the gods, slow down, at least a little. You look bad. There's blood all over you. If you don't slow down . . ."

For reasons he does not understand, Phidippides tries to make light of what is happening. "I thought . . . your husband . . . was the runner in your family . . . I'm going to tell him . . . if the two of you are in a race . . . I'll bet . . . on you."

"Don't speak! I have a message for Sicinnus," says Lela. "Please, it's about our child."

She leans toward him and speaks into his ear. Then she slows, unable to match his pace any longer.

She stops and cries out, "Phidippides, slow down!"

Her voice drops as he speeds away, and she says to herself, "Please slow down. You have to slow down or you won't make it."

He does not look back. He does not slow down.

~

Three hours later, Themistocles is looking down at the Persians on the beach and inland plain. Sicinnus is beside him; they are both lost in thought. Themistocles is considering the fate of his family—Archi and their four children. Sicinnus firmly believes he and Lela and Alyssa will survive, but Athens could be destroyed. Then what? Themistocles breaks silence when Callimachus walks up.

"Back from the drills?"

"Yes," Callimachus says.

"And?"

"They're making progress, but it's difficult."

"Ready to add more men?"

"I just ordered that. The hardest part is for the men to control themselves once they see and hear the signal and make their move."

"When a man's heart is racing, it's hard to control his legs." Themistocles adds, "When the trumpets blow, his heart becomes a drum, driving him forward. That will be the real test of their discipline."

"Discipline comes with practice," says Callimachus. "Trumpets are an unfortunate necessity. The men in the front rows can see the signal, but the men behind depend on their ears."

Callimachus stops when he sees a messenger running up the hill toward them.

The messenger arrives, gasping. "Our men have confiscated most of the animals—cows, pigs, sheep, goats—from farms in the area. We have far more than a hundred waiting to be slaughtered over at the springs and the river."

"Did you invoke my name when you took the animals?" asks Callimachus.

"Yes, and we told the farmers Athens will pay for all the beasts and double the worth of the pigs. We told them our Polemarch took an oath on behalf of the city, and he has a special fondness for pigs."

"Good. And what about our own men's crap?"

"It's being gathered from the latrines and hauled to the springs. Awful stuff. Some of the men can't do the job, too much gagging."

"Tell them to breathe deeper and think about what the Persians will soon be drinking. We're getting there. It will take some time in the sun to cook the feast for our guests. Return to your post and tell the men to keep gathering as much livestock as they can. Tell them I'll join you all at dawn tomorrow to make the appropriate sacrifices and pray to Helios to keep things blistering hot for the next few days."

As the first messenger departs, Callimachus sees another hoplite almost sprinting up the hill toward them.

As he nears, the hoplite calls out, "Phidippides is here, down at the camp."

"Has he given us the answer from the Spartans?" asks Callimachus.

"He hasn't spoken. At least he hasn't said anything that makes sense. He's dying."

"What?" yells Sicinnus. "Is he up? Is he walking?"

"No, he's on the ground. He's convulsing and mumbling a goddess' name."

"We have to get him up!" shouts Sicinnus. "He has to move. I must go to him."

Sicinnus looks at Themistocles, who nods. Grabbing the hoplite by the arm, Sicinnus exclaims, "Take me to him, now!"

When Sicinnus and the hoplite reach the Greek camp, Sicinnus sees his friend on the ground, writhing and retching with dry heaves. Spasms make his knees jerk up toward his chest and then down as far as his legs can stretch. The whole time he keeps slamming his fists on the ground.

"Get him up! Help me get him up!"

Someone says, "He's about gone. There's no hope."

Sicinnus yells, "Help me get him up!"

They lift Phidippides from the ground and, with Sicinnus on one side and another man on the other, they wrap his arms around the back of their necks and begin walking slowly while his feet drag.

"Take a step," says Sicinnus. The half-dead runner's head hangs down as blood drips from his nostrils and mouth.

"Take a step," repeats Sicinnus.

"Kore," mutters Phidippides.

"That's what he's been saying since he got here," says the man opposite Sicinnus. "That and mumbling about running some race."

"Did I win?" Phidippides gasps.

"Win what?" asks Sicinnus.

The runner does not answer.

"Take a step," says Sicinnus.

Phidippides lifts a leg from the ground and moves it forward slightly before letting it drop.

"Yes," says Sicinnus. "That's how you win the race. Again."

Phidippides obeys, putting his foot a little farther forward this time.

"Good. That's how you win. Again. Again. Again."

Phidippides complies and Sicinnus calls out, "Water. Put a few drops on his lips, nothing inside."

When the drops of water are applied to Phidippides' cracked lips, he shudders and shakes his head.

"Good," says Sicinnus. "It hurts. It's supposed to, that's how you win. A little more water. A few drops inside his mouth this time, nothing more yet."

By the time Themistocles and Callimachus arrive, Phidippides is slowly walking on his own with Sicinnus by his side.

"Is he coherent?" asks Callimachus.

"It'll take a little longer; he's coming around," answers Sicinnus. "The spasms are behind him. He just needs to pull himself together and keep walking. Then a small amount in his stomach before some serious rest. Once he goes to sleep he will sleep for a full day, probably longer. I'll stay with him."

"So you think he's going to live?" asks Themistocles, shaking his head.

"He'll live. Unless something is ruptured inside him that we can't detect, but I don't think so. If he were broken internally, we'd already know."

"Protecting his life is most important, but I need to talk to him before he sleeps," says Callimachus, "if I can without serious danger to him."

"Talk?" asks Phidippides as he raises his head to look at Callimachus.

"Well, well," says Callimachus. "Yes, talk. Do you remember the Spartans, your run there and back to us?"

"I remember," Phidippides answers in a voice that is gradually growing stronger. "Thirsty. More water."

A pouch of water is quickly given to Callimachus who just as quickly holds it up to the runner's lips.

"Just one small swallow," says Sicinnus. "One at a time, slowly. No more."

"True elixir . . . of the gods," says Phidippides.

"Did you ask the Spartans if they are coming to Marathon, coming to our aid?" Callimachus presses him. "What did they say? Are they coming? When?"

"I asked . . . they answered." Phidippides pauses, and then says, "I want to fight . . . in the phalanx."

"What?" asks Callimachus.

"The phalanx," says Phidippides. "I have asked before . . . to be a hoplite in the phalanx . . . you know what I mean."

Callimachus leans forward slightly, squints at Phidippides, and roars,

"Son of a whore!"

Then the warleader lifts his head to the sky and blasts out a belly laugh so thunderous it startles dozens of men in the vicinity. Phidippides stands up straighter.

Callimachus turns to Themistocles. "The son of a whore is negotiating with me. A walking dead man wants to play hide and seek until he gets what he wants. He wants to be a hoplite instead of a messenger."

Turning back to Phidippides, Callimachus says, "And so you shall be. As Polemarch and on behalf of all Athens, I will be proud for you to join the ranks of the phalanx."

"You honor me. I will earn . . . your respect . . ." Phidippides sips more water and continues, his voice still halting but stronger, his stance surer. "I have news from Sparta . . . Sparta will march to Marathon . . . but not until six days from . . . when I left two days ago . . . they said . . . it will take them five days . . . to get here."

Themistocles snarls, "Which means a total of nine days from today. They expect us to maintain a standoff for another nine days? Why the delay? What's their excuse?"

"Religious festival . . . Carnea."

"What kind of an excuse is that?" sputters Themistocles.

"A very good one," Callimachus says dryly, going on to explain to Themistocles the religious reasons for the Spartan delay.

"Yes, yes, and I know you, too, are very devout, as a warleader should be. But we're talking about survival," Themistocles huffs, "and not just of Athens but of Sparta, too. They should know that. What do the Spartans think will be the Persians' next move if they destroy Athens?"

"I told that to the ephors," Phidippides replies.

"I'm sure you did," Themistocles says, his frustration unabated. "Telling the stupid bastards is one thing. Getting them to believe it is another. And Callimachus, I may be splitting hairs, but the Spartans are delaying their march to Marathon. We are talking about nothing but a

march. A march is not a battle or military engagement. Who says Carnea prohibits a march? You know what I think? I think the Spartans are
good at making something false seem true. Men do that by justifying a big
falsehood with a small truth. 'Oh, we want to help you. But Carnea
prevents us from coming right away. Just hold off the Persians for a length
of time beyond all reason. Then we'll come to your aid. We'll be there for
sure, eventually, maybe.'"

"Far be it from me to debate you about the way to be false and true at
the same time," says the warleader. "Especially you. But you're right about
splitting hairs. The Spartans made their interpretation of what Carnea does
and does not permit. We can lament the fact later tonight over a fire. For
now, I have a couple more questions. Phidippides, are you still with us?"

"I'm still here."

"You stopped in Athens before coming here?"

"Yes, only a short time." Phidippides' voice is still rough, but no longer
halting. "Then I took the longer route when the path split."

Looking over his shoulder at Sicinnus, he says, "At the split I met . . ."

Themistocles interrupts him. "What did you tell the Athenians?"

"I told them the Spartans were on my heels and will get to Marathon
soon."

"Nothing more?" asks Themistocles.

"Nothing more. Those were my instructions, correct?"

"Exactly so," says Callimachus.

"One more thing and then a little food and lots of rest," interjects
Callimachus. "So, nine days hence, if things go according to plan and
calculation, which they usually don't in my experience, the Spartans will be
at Marathon. Did they give you any details?"

"The ephors said the army will come in two contingents. The first will
be a flying column of two thousand hoplites. The others will follow soon
after."

"The ephors wouldn't lie," says Callimachus, with a short sigh. "If they didn't intend to come to our aid, the ephors would say so. And, for good measure, they'd spit in our faces." He is silent for a moment, and then looks at Sicinnus. "Take Phidippides to get some food and then, as you said, stay with him through the night."

As Phidippides and Sicinnus turn to leave, the exhausted runner looks over his shoulder and says, "Themistocles, I saw Archippe on the path. She wanted me to tell you the children keep asking about you, and they all love you."

Themistocles takes a deep breath but says nothing.

After Phidippides and Sicinnus are gone, Callimachus looks at Themistocles and says, "I agree with you. The Spartans are bastards. They're raised to be bastards. But this time, they are *our* bastards. They'll come. Though they may not get here in time."

"That's not the only problem."

"Well, just what I was thinking," says Callimachus. "Or maybe not. What is the other problem on your mind?"

"Persian spies."

"I was right," says Callimachus. "I thought I was the warleader around here."

"Hard not to learn a thing or two from spending so much time listening to you piss and moan."

"I'll take that as a compliment," says Callimachus.

"Take it as you will. So we're agreed, with Persian spies everywhere, and with the length of the Spartan delay, they'll probably learn of the Spartans' plans. The Persian commanders will know what we know before the Spartans get here."

Callimachus nods. "When the Persians learn the Spartans' plans, we want them to use that knowledge to make a mistake."

Smiling, Themistocles replies, "Polemarch, you surprise me. Yesterday, you told all the generals you had a plan, and today you started implementing it with running drills and a pile of dead pigs. But now you say you also need the Persians to make a mistake. Am I to understand you were not entirely forthcoming with the generals?"

"Don't choke while you gloat. I simply followed some sensible advice; it's usually best to tell the truth, but there is no need to tell everyone *everything* you know. I once heard that advice from the most cunning man in Athens. You."

Themistocles shrugs modestly, then asks, "Do you have a specific mistake in mind?"

"Not yet, but that mistake, whatever it is, must be critical. It must affect their key strengths. That means their lopsided numbers or the archers or the warhorses—or perhaps some combination of the three."

"When you finally identify the mistake the Persians should make, I suspect your plan will be dangerous. Probably very dangerous."

"There is no 'probably.' And it will be as dangerous for us as it is for them."

~

As Phidippides and Sicinnus walk together, Phidippides still feels very weak from his run. He leans toward his friend and says quietly, "When I saw Archippe outside Athens, your wife was with her. She asked me to give you a message about your child. Alyssa just spoke her first word."

Sicinnus abruptly stops and grabs Phidippides by both arms, then releases him and steps back, searching his friend's face.

"What did she say?"

"Kore. Lela said she repeated it several times."

Sicinnus stammers and repeats, "Kore?"

His shocked expression surprises Phidippides. "You probably expected 'Mama' or 'Papa.' But you look as if you were just hit over the head by a battle axe. Kore is the name of a goddess, to be sure, but a simple word for a child to say."

"Yes, a simple word," repeats Sicinnus, with a look of wide-eyed astonishment. "Easily said by a toddler."

"I'm the one who should be reeling in a stupor. You act as if you're the one who just ran here from Sparta."

"I can't believe it. I'm supposed to be so smart; how could I be so foolish? Why didn't I think of it? I should have figured this out long ago!"

"I don't follow."

"Kore is Persephone's other name. Her more ancient name."

"Every schoolchild knows that. But it doesn't explain why you look like you're about to flap your arms and take flight."

"What a mistake," says Sicinnus, ignoring his fellow runner. "Thank you. Phidippides, thank you. This is wonderful news. This is the best news since Lela survived Alyssa's birth almost two years ago. Thank you!"

"You're welcome, I suppose," says Phidippides. "Let's go. I'm hungry."

CHAPTER TWENTY-NINE

THE WOMEN'S SECOND MEETING

Early in the morning, Lela raps on the simple wooden door and lets herself in. She glances around the frugally but gracefully appointed room, with its carved chairs and hanging oil lamps, the decorative bouquet of mignonette in one corner, the small statue of an ephebe in another, and the white curtains covering the inner doors. But her friend and mistress is not there.

Themistocles and Archippe live with their four children in an eight-room, two-story home, built around a small, open courtyard. The house is made of sun-dried mud bricks painted white, and covered with a roof of overlapping red clay tiles. Lela glances up at the windows. Simple square holes set high and shuttered, they are more for ventilation than for viewing the outdoors. During the day in the summer, the windows are shuttered to repel heat. Later in the evening they are opened to release the warm indoor air to the cooler night.

As Lela scans the spare setting of the entryway, she smiles slightly, knowing there is a bit more to this house than its humble appearance suggests. Back in their bedroom, Themistocles and Archi keep several items that are not so modest. When they are being intimate, Themistocles likes to see Archi wearing the beautiful jewelry he gives her. And their bedroom walls display intriguing decorations, including tapestries and bronze plaques. On their bedroom chests are several beautifully painted vases as well as small, heavy statues made from polished rocks of different colors—green, gold, and gleaming black. Lela suspects they are worth a great deal.

Archi never talks to Lela about these luxuries. Lela suspects Archi is embarrassed about their extravagance. The enticing objects also never leave the bedroom, chiefly because Themistocles, even more than Archi, understands the minds of his fellow Athenians. Envy comes easily to them. Themistocles has a taste for the finer things in life, but he is considered a man of the people and he means to maintain that reputation.

Lela walks to the next room and sees Archippe, who has just finished talking to her three sons. The boys turn to leave for the gymnasium, which is their normal routine. Arch, the oldest boy at twelve, is in the lead. When he walks past, Lela nods, but he is frowning. The two younger boys keep their eyes cast down as they file past her, but at the last moment the youngest boy, Cleo, looks over at Lela and smirks.

"What's the matter with them?" Lela asks after the boys leave the house. "They act as if they just got a spanking. Especially Arch."

"A spanking with words. I heard last night he was seen touching a girl with a little too much affection, so I just explained what is appropriate and what is not." Archippe pauses and takes a deep breath. "A new phase of my life. A son thinking about girls. I don't have any gray hair yet, but I'm afraid it won't be long."

Smiling, Lela says, "You'll look good in gray. I can see the image clearly."

Archippe smiles back and says, "Thanks for the comforting words. But now we need to talk seriously before we go back to the agora. Is Alyssa settled in with the old woman?"

"She seems to quite like her. It's much easier lately. Used to be that if I didn't respond quickly when she called for me, Alyssa would panic. Now, she often doesn't pay much attention when I'm not there."

"It makes me think of my Cleo. As a baby he was the sweetest, most loving of them all. But as soon as he could walk, Themistocles decided he needed to learn how to be a real man. So there was Cleo, barely two years old, stark naked, beating his chest and howling like some wild animal. Hopefully, when he begins to grow fuzz on his face, he'll revert to the gentle soul I birthed. But you never know."

"It's going to be a long road, isn't it?"

"A lifetime long. But . . ." Archippe frowns lightly as she changes the topic. "We need to finish yesterday's talk."

"Oh?" Lela peers into her friend's face.

"Yes." Archippe pauses. "Before we go to the agora today, we need to talk about Magacles. About who, or what, he really is."

"Wait, what was that?" interrupts Lela. She jumps up and quickly walks out of the room, returning a moment later. "I know I heard something. I thought it was your boys returning but there was nothing there. Strange."

"Are you all right?"

"I think so." Lela shakes her head. "It was the same feeling I had when Alyssa was sleeping in your bedroom. Anyway, you were saying?"

As Lela walks back to sit down, two apparitions step aside to make way for her. The apparitions and the women look similar—or would, if the apparitions allowed themselves to be seen. Demeter, the Goddess of Fertility, seems much the same age and the same ripe beauty as Archippe, and Demeter's daughter, Persephone, seems like a nubile eighteen-year-old girl, a slightly younger version of Lela. Now, on this warm summer morning, the two goddesses stand close together as they silently watch and listen to the women speak.

"I've been thinking about what we're getting ourselves into," says Archippe. "Last night was not a good one for sleep, so let me just say it and get it behind me. After we met with Magacles yesterday, I made light of the conversation and how you talked to him, and I said we should hurry back so we could check on the children. But that wasn't the real reason I wanted to leave. I was becoming frightened. It surprised me. I didn't want you to see it. That man terrifies . . ."

Lela interrupts her. "If we were children, Archi, you might have been able to fool me." Her voice softens. "But I wasn't fooled yesterday. I could see you were worried. After all, we're almost like sisters."

The two women look at each other for a long silence that Archippe is the first to break. "You give me such comfort, but we must finish talking about Magacles."

Lela shakes her head in disgust.

"I fully understand your feelings," says Archippe. "But you also must understand that Magacles is more than just a crude man without scruples. Themistocles made it clear to me that he also is very shrewd and dangerous, and my husband detests him almost as much as he detests Hippias. Is the picture clear enough?"

"More than enough. How can such a man be held in any esteem or given any respect?"

"He doesn't really have either," says Archippe. "He has influence mainly because of his family. A long history of aristocrats and wealth. He's from the same tribe as Cleisthenes, who created our new way of governing. The aristocrats still hold sway over many citizens. As far as Themistocles is concerned, all the wealthy aristocrats receive far more deference than they deserve. Actually, he thinks they deserve no deference at all."

"It seems to me Magacles should be banished from the city! Can't the citizens see what a danger he is for all of us?"

"As I said, Magacles is shrewd," replies Archippe. "And when people want to shut their eyes and ears to facts or suspicions they don't want to know or believe, they find ways to do so and justify their folly to themselves. That is just the way it is and probably always will be."

Archippe pauses to let Lela respond, but Lela just looks at her, so she continues.

"That is what I was thinking about after we met with Magacles yesterday and most of last night when I couldn't sleep. And the longer I struggled with what was going through my mind, the more my worry turned into fear. I'm beginning to have second thoughts. I'm not sure the risk is worth it."

"Now you tell me, Archi!"

Taken aback, Archippe studies her young friend's face.

"You're a little late." Lela goes on. "Is the risk worth saving our city from a fate worse than the terrors of death? We *have* to do this, Archi, for our families, our friends, for everyone we love in the city."

Lela's beautiful lips curve into a smirk, then a smile full of gleaming teeth, until she gives in to a loud laugh. "Besides, if the bastard likes my looks better than yours, so be it."

Now it's Archippe's turn to laugh. "Last night, when my mind was bouncing around, I thought of a good line to use when you talk to Magacles."

"Really?" says Lela. "I thought of one, too. What's yours?"

"Tell him you never met a man like him."

After another laugh, Lela says, "My line is, 'I never knew *anything* like *you.*'"

~

A short while later, Lela is walking through the agora about twenty paces in front of Archippe, the farthest apart they can be and still see each other in all the congestion. After checking all the gaming areas, they head once again for the cockfights. The crowds thin a bit so Archippe drops farther back. As Lela nears the cockfight area, she puts her hand on the back of her head as a signal, then glances over her shoulder to see Archippe turn and walk away. Lela suddenly feels very alone, even though there are still lots of people around. She walks on and, a moment later, Magacles sees her. She gives him a discreet wave and he does not hesitate. His first few steps are quick and sprightly, but then he remembers to limp.

"Well, well, quite a coincidence," says Magacles as he approaches. "I've been thinking about you quite a lot, actually. What brings you back to these nasty cockfights? And alone."

"The truth is I love them," Lela lies, with a broad smile frozen on her face.

"Really! Most women hate them."

"They thrill me. They have ever since I was a child."

"Oh, that's right. You were born in Persia. That's where cockfighting comes from, you know."

"So that explains why I get so excited at them; it must be my Persian blood. I never thought of that before." Lela gives him an enigmatic look.

Pausing just long enough to figure out what this desirable young slave means, Magacles says, "Yes, of course, your Persian blood, that's why you . . . why you get so excited."

"Maybe that's one reason they say we Persians have hot blood."

Without pausing this time, Magacles responds, "That is definitely one reason they say so. Come sit with me, and we can watch the cockfights together. We can speak of many things while we watch."

"I'd love to do that," says Lela, "to sit with you. But I'm sorry I can't now. I have to get back before my absence is noticed. Next time I'll plan on staying longer, but now I just want to talk about something briefly, if that's all right."

"Of course, I understand, that's certainly all right," says Magacles, guiding her to a quiet corner away from the shouting in the bloody arena. "So, Lela, what is it you want to talk to me about?"

Lela is silent a moment, with her head lowered.

"Well, to be completely frank with you, I'm afraid."

"Afraid of what? Of the invasion?"

She looks up at him with all the vulnerability she can put into her face.

"Yes."

"We're all worried," says Magacles. "And our protection is our hoplites at Marathon."

"Yes, but . . ."

"But what? You're afraid because you're Persian?"

"Well, yes." Lela thinks carefully before continuing. "What if the Persians succeed?"

"What if the Persians succeed? But they cannot succeed, not against Greeks," Magacles says.

Knowing his words are bluster, Lela continues, "But there is no certainty in fortune." She treads as cautiously as she dares while staring into Magacles' eyes. "Even the gods are ruled by fate. And fate is known to be . . ."

"Treacherous?"

"I was going to say 'fickle.'"

"Yes," Magacles says, staring into Lela's deep dark eyes. "Fate can be very fickle."

Before Lela can respond, the crowd around the arena lets out an enormous roar. Magacles and Lela turn and look into the cockfighting pit. Magacles smiles at the blood still being splattered in the air and on the ground. Lela exhales with relief tinged with nausea; the brief reprieve gives her a little time to gather her thoughts. She swallows before continuing.

"I would find a way to thank you if you could help me."

Magacles says nothing at first, then asks "But what if there is nothing I can do?" The tip of his tongue slowly moves back and forth over his lips. His lust is obvious.

Lela knows the time has come to use an uncommon ability she discovered long ago—she can shimmer her eyes so they give off an alluring sparkle, even when she is at her most serious. Her mind flashes to the first time she knowingly did this. She was lying on top of Sicinnus, and they were gazing at each other with their faces so close their noses almost touched.

Conveying one emotion to Magacles with her eyes, another with her words, Lela says, "I have a friend who lives in the city. He's a few years older than I am. My husband doesn't know about him. He's close to one of the city's wealthy citizens, an aristocrat. My friend is very discreet, but he told me something. He said if I think the Persians will take the city, I should talk to you, you might know someone who could protect me. When I told you my husband wanted me to meet you, I lied. It was my friend. I don't quite trust Sicinnus. He's too close to his master."

"I'm not sure I understand." Magacles leans back, suspicious. "Why did your friend tell you to seek my help?"

"He didn't tell me. He just said to talk to you. He wouldn't tell me more. So I can't answer your question."

"And your friend's name?"

"Glaucon." Lela gives her imaginary lover an innocuous, common enough Athenian name. "He's at Marathon with the other hoplites."

"And the aristocrat your friend is close to?" asks Magacles.

"Miltiades," says Lela, which is the name Archippe suggested she use if Magacles inquired; the name of a man renowned for successful acts of duplicity against Persians—and Greeks.

Magacles stares at her with popping eyes, then bursts into laughter. He bends over and when he stands up again, Lela sees he is laughing so hard he is crying.

"Oh my poor dear!" Magacles gasps. "Miltiades! You have been had! Oh dear. My poor, gullible dear!"

Lela stares at him, genuinely terrified that she has made a dreadful mistake.

At last Magacles settles down, wiping the tears from his eyes.

"My poor lamb, you have been made a *very* pretty fool of. But I can see how frightened you are. Fear not, dear Lela! I will protect you! You need have no fear when the Persians come. Or, I should say," he quickly corrects himself, "*if* they come."

"Thank you, thank you," Lela says, almost weeping with genuine relief.

"Yes, very well," says Magacles, suddenly calm. "We understand each other then." He takes her by the shoulders and forces her to look straight at him. "Don't we, my dear little Persian?"

Lela nods solemnly, writhing inside.

"We will meet again," says Magacles, reluctantly letting her go. "Soon."

Lela whispers, "Soon." She turns and walks away, singing a victory song in her soul while her body tries not to shudder.

It isn't long before she spots Archippe who, seeing her, turns away and starts walking slowly. Lela catches up and, without looking at each other, they begin talking softly.

Archippe asks, "Did you get him to reveal himself?"

"The hook is set."

"You think he plans to betray the city?"

"I am sure of it. He said he would help me. Then he made a little mistake—he said *when* the Persians come."

"*When.*"

"He quickly corrected himself to '*if* they come.' But 'when' was the truer word. He knows."

"If we're going to figure out his plan," says Archippe, increasing her pace, "we don't have much time."

Archippe and Lela are about to leave the agora when they notice two beggars sitting beside the path. One is an old hag wearing a black robe. Her face is pocked with open sores. The other beggar is much younger, perhaps a granddaughter who looks to be in her late teens. No one walking around pays any attention to them, as if the beggars are invisible. But both Archippe and Lela feel drawn to them.

They walk over. Archippe reaches into her leather bag and gives the young beggar a coin. Then she reaches back into her bag, takes out all the coins she has, and hands them to the young woman. Lela sees none of this because she is transfixed by the old woman's eyes. Lela reaches into her bag, grasps all of her coins, and gives them to the hag.

"May you be blessed by the gods," says the young woman to Archippe.

"May a goddess keep you and your family," says the hag to Lela.

Lela gazes at the hag and Archippe stares at the girl. Mesmerized by the beggars' faces, Archippe and Lela fail to notice the slow, slithering shadows circling behind them. Finally, without saying anything, Archippe and Lela turn and walk away.

After a few steps, Archippe says, "That was strange. I just gave that girl all my coins. I've never done anything like that in my life."

"It was more than strange. I did the same thing. All of my coins. Did you see the old woman's eyes?"

"No, I didn't really look at her. I couldn't take my eyes off the girl. Did you see her face?"

"No, I was like you. I couldn't stop staring at the old woman."

"You should have looked at the girl," says Archippe. "It was like looking at a younger sister of yours. More than that, she looked like your twin from a few years past. I felt I was looking at you."

"I've never seen anything like the old woman's eyes. Young eyes. Bright and intense. The most penetrating eyes I have ever seen. Then, when she spoke . . ."

"And I still don't believe what I just did; I gave the girl every coin in my bag!" Archippe interjects. She starts to hold out her bag to show Lela, but stops. Archippe hefts her bag then jerks it open. Raising her eyes to Lela, Archippe whispers, "Did you see me give all my coins to the girl?"

"No, I was staring at the old woman and giving her my coins."

Archippe narrows her eyes and says, "Look in your bag."

Lela does as she is told, then reaches for Archippe's bag, pulls it open, and peers in. Both women turn to look back at the two beggars, who have disappeared.

After a moment, Lela says, "Our coins are still here. What do you make of it?"

"I don't think our coins just stayed in our bags. We gave them away, then they were returned."

"This is absolutely crazy. We can't both have had the same daydream at the exact same time."

"It's some sort of sign."

"Or test."

The two women walk the rest of the way home in silence. When they arrive, they touch each other's arms, and then separate to go into their homes. They are unaware that a man has been following them since Lela left Magacles. The man watches Lela enter her home. When he can no longer see her, he turns and runs back to his master.

CHAPTER THIRTY

A DANGEROUS MISSION

A field of tall mignonettes envelops the two of them, its perfume the sweet seductive scent of herbal ambrosia.

He sees her face in shadow against the sun; she is on top of him. That is always their way. They wrestle, and she ends on top, holding his arms down with her knees. He can throw her off, of course. They both know that. But he seldom does. He likes to hear her laugh because she is the conqueror. He pretends to struggle while listening to the joyful sound—music he cherishes and wants to hear forever.

This time is different. She is laughing as she always does; he listens and feels himself grinning. But she is holding down his arms with her hands, not her knees, and staring into his eyes. She started it. But he wanted it. She pulled his tunic up and over one shoulder, then the other, and then her chiton was in his hand.

After a long look into each other's eyes, she stops laughing but her smile persists. She leans down and rubs his nose with hers, back and forth. She straightens up while watching him watch her. Spontaneously, she kisses him. She pulls her head up and then comes down again, kissing him a second time, passionately. She pulls her head up yet again. He raises his head and they kiss a third time. His kiss is even more eager.

Their mouths separate but their eyes do not.

As Sicinnus looks at Lela, he is fascinated by something he never saw before—her eyes are shimmering. They scintillate and titillate. He is staring into the eyes of desire.

Slowly he begins to raise an arm and turn his body. She pushes down as hard as she can and starts laughing again. In slow motion he continues to steadily raise his arm and turn. She is forced to lean over more and more—until he gently topples her. She expects him to throw his leg over and get on top, but he does not.

More than three feet high, the elegant stalks of mignonette and their flowing masses of yellow and white flowers perfectly hide the young lovers' nakedness. This is the first time for both of them, and they are unsure of themselves. Lela lowers her eyes and visually caresses Sicinnus' body as far down as she can see.

She reaches over with her bare arm and uses her fingers and thumb to encircle the soft profusion. Then she slides her grip up to the very top, where she uncoils her fingers, glides them in tiny circles around the tip, and snaps off a little mignonette flower from its cluster. She brings the yellow blossom to his face and tickles him with it under his nose. He breathes in the spicy fragrance and looks up as the warm breeze makes more flowers sway above them. He looks higher toward the estival sun and then closes his eyes, delirious with pleasure.

Opening his eyes a moment later, he sees the mignonettes waving slowly. He looks back at Lela and knows she never took her eyes off him. Gently he pushes her shoulder and she rolls on her back. Now it is his turn to pick flowers. Clutching a handful of tiny blossoms, he carefully places them on her erect nipples. She watches him arrange the little bouquets. She turns her head to look into his eyes again, but he is not watching her face. His eyes meander down to the small oasis where her thighs meet. His hand briefly hovers, and then he slowly lowers it to barely touch her softness. His eyes wander up her torso, pausing to study the rhythmic undulations of her breathing before continuing to her breasts. He brings his hand over to lightly caress one of them, and then the other.

"Your breasts," he whispers. "Do you realize how wonderful they are?"

Her knowing smile is instinctive and belies her inexperience. She pushes Sicinnus' shoulder more firmly than he pushed hers. He rolls on his back, and she reaches up and grabs a handful of flowers and sprinkles them all over his loins. Her mouth is on his nipple, kissing and licking. Her moist tongue runs down below his chest. She pushes her tongue into his navel. Her head moves in small circles as the tip of her tongue orbits and examines his firm skin. Her mouth moves lower and he feels her teeth. She pretends to bite him. Her hand squeezes his pulsating hardness. Her tongue runs back up his entire torso but her hand stays low, gripping him. Their tongues meet and go deep, twisting, turning, each feeling the inside of the other's mouth. She is stroking him down below. He wants to be on top of her. Her grip is firm. He puts his hand on her forehead and smooths her hair back. The stroking is harder. Faster. She puts her hand behind his head and pulls up. She puts another hand on his shoulder and grips him. She murmurs his name. Her mouth is moist. Her hand below. Faster. Her hand under his head pulling up. Her hand clutching his shoulder. He hears a moan and then a gasp. He is warm and wet.

His unfocused eyes open slightly. Her hand is still down below. Her hand is behind his head. Her hand is gripping his shoulder—gripping it hard—too hard. Three hands. She calls his name, "Sicinnus, Sicinnus!" Through the haze he sees she has a beard.

Sicinnus snaps his eyes all the way open. Themistocles takes his hand off his shoulder.

"Pleasant dreams?"

Sicinnus looks up at his master's smile, but does not respond.

"I think the fancy talkers call that a rhetorical question," says Themistocles. "No need to answer. I'm sort of envious. Haven't had that kind of fun for a long time. I like to think you were dreaming about Lela, but who knows what a man's fantasies are?"

"Lela is my fantasy," says Sicinnus.

"Glad to hear it. You're a fortunate man. But I'm not here to talk about dreams. Come with me; we need to see the warleader."

A short time later, Themistocles and Sicinnus walk toward a fire where Callimachus sits by himself. Sicinnus is surprised to see him alone. Darkness encloses the fire like a shell; cicadas hum in the olive trees. The men can barely hear the distant sound of the shore under the shrilling of the insects. Fires farther off are surrounded by hoplites waiting for sleep and uneasy dreams. It is very late.

The warleader looks even more imposing than usual. At first, Sicinnus thinks the way the flickering fire reflects off Callimachus' face accounts for his grave expression. But the slave quickly realizes something else is afoot.

"How much did you tell him?" asks Callimachus.

"Nothing, I'll leave it to you," answers Themistocles.

Callimachus turns to the young Persian. "Sicinnus, I'll speak to you as if you were already a free man, which you will be when we finish at Marathon. I'm going to ask you to make a decision. Your decision will not affect the freedom you'll be offered. Is that clear?"

"It is clear, Polemarch."

"Good. I am about to ask you to volunteer for a very dangerous mission. If you accept the assignment, the possibility of death is great. I believe Themistocles has something to say."

"Sicinnus," Themistocles begins. He stops, clears his throat, and begins again. "Sicinnus, my friend . . ." Again he stops. The others wait as if nothing untoward was happening, as if for a master to call his slave his friend was the most common thing in the world.

Themistocles continues, "If you volunteer for this mission and do not survive, Lela and Alyssa will be under my protection." He pauses again. "They shall want for nothing—except you."

"And on behalf of myself and the city," Callimachus says, taking up Themistocles' avowal, "your wife and child also shall be under my protection and the protection of Athens. This I swear. Do you follow our words thus far?"

"Yes, Polemarch, I follow your words," Sicinnus answers, his mouth suddenly dry.

"Fine," says Callimachus. "And henceforth, you may continue to use my formal title of Polemarch, if you wish. But you also may address me as 'warleader' or use my surname if you care to. My only request is that, when you use less flattering words to describe me as so many of our hoplites like to do, you do it beyond my hearing. Agreed?"

"Agreed, warleader."

"Listen carefully. A short distance from here we have a captured Persian spy under guard. We caught him in our camp an hour ago, talking to one of our own. It did not take long for us to persuade the Persian to reveal that he came to deliver a message to an apparent traitor among us. The message comes from the Persian commander, Datis, and the purpose is a proposed secret meeting with Datis and Hippias. So, we are dealing with the top of their command. The spy now thinks he awaits death, hopefully without further suffering. Instead, I want to shock him with something he doesn't expect. If you volunteer for the mission I will explain, you will be sparing the spy's life. Do you continue to follow my words?"

"Yes, warleader, I follow most of what you are saying," says Sicinnus. "I understand enough to anticipate where this is heading. I suspect my fluency with the Persian language will be helpful."

"It is one reason we've chosen you," says Callimachus, then turning to Themistocles, "as well as being quick, confident, and modest."

He turns back to Sicinnus. "If you volunteer for the mission you will go with the spy. You will present yourself to the spy and to the Persians as Themistocles' slave, and you will speak in Greek. The spy speaks good Greek and there will be other enemies who can do the same. You will not switch to Persian unless they decide to torture or kill you. Changing languages and explaining that you are from Persia should give them pause and perhaps cause second thoughts. It might save your life, but you will keep it in reserve until you need it. Again, do you follow me?"

"I follow every word, warleader."

"Good. Now hear the message you will carry to the Persians."

As the warleader tells Sicinnus in detail what he is to say to the Persian leader, Sicinnus listens intently, showing no shock or surprise, though he glances more than once at Themistocles. Themistocles watches his young friend's face.

"You now know your mission and your message," Callimachus says. "Your decision?"

"I accept, warleader. I volunteer for the mission."

Callimachus nods. "Spoken without even taking a breath. Do you have any questions?"

"Yes, what about the Greek in our camp who the Persian spy was talking to? When I encounter Datis and Hippias, they surely will want to know what happened to him."

"Tell them the truth."

"But I don't know."

"That's the point," says Callimachus. "You should not know what you do not need to know. You might find yourself under torture. The less you can reveal, the better—both for you and for us. Follow?"

"Yes, warleader, I follow. I expect the same explanation applies when they ask for more details about my message."

"Correct," says Callimachus. "Tell them what you know, which will be nothing beyond what I just told you. When they interrogate you, fall back on the fact you are just a slave conveying a message. Any more questions, Sicinnus?"

"I don't think so, warleader . . . actually, one final question. When do I depart?"

"Now is a good time. I trust you had enough sleep before Themistocles woke you?"

"I'm sure he did," interjects Themistocles. "I could tell he was just about to wake when I roused him."

"Well then, are you ready?"

"I will be in a few moments, after I relieve myself."

"Good idea," says Themistocles. "It's best to empty yourself before you encounter the Persians. That way you will keep your tunic clean."

Themistocles and Callimachus laugh and Sicinnus manages to smile.

Looking at Sicinnus, the warleader says, "No need to discuss it now, but after your return I hope to talk with you about both valor and glory. Until then, I will pray to the gods for your safe return."

"You do me honor, Callimachus."

~

A half hour later, Themistocles and Sicinnus are walking toward the captured spy.

"I know what you're thinking," says Themistocles. "Most men would be thinking about torture and death. Instead, I'll bet you're thinking about the irony of it all. That's what intellectual men do—think about life's ironies. Your certain freedom and possible death coming at the same time."

"I think it's a big coincidence and a small irony," says Sicinnus. "But right now I'm actually thinking about two goddesses—Demeter and her daughter with two names, Persephone and Kore. They help steady my nerves."

"You're starting to sound like Archi. She talks in circles sometimes. Impossible to figure out what she's trying to say. I often wonder if she does it intentionally just to irritate me. But circle-talking is strange, coming from you."

"I hope to explain myself after we get back to Athens. I'm dealing with a family secret and will tell you about it right after I tell Lela."

"A family secret you need to tell Lela about?"

"Yes, a secret I have with my daughter."

"I see. A secret between you and baby Alyssa that you need to explain to your wife and her mother."

"Yes."

"Glad to have that all cleared up," says Themistocles. "I look forward to your explanation. But we're almost within hearing distance of our captured spy. You can do the talking. I want to watch his face when he learns his imminent death is being postponed indefinitely. So," he says, giving Sicinnus a serious look, "to treachery."

Sicinnus looks back at him keenly. "To treachery."

A short while later, three figures move through the darkness, with the Persian spy in the lead. The spy appears to be in his late twenties with a small, sinewy frame. He not only speaks Greek well, he looks Greek. Sicinnus wonders if his personal history might somehow be the reverse of his own—born and raised Greek, then, for whatever reason—a raid? a lost battle? a shipwreck?—ending up a slave of the Persians.

The three men are nearing the edge of the terrain controlled by the Greeks when Themistocles softly says, "Hold."

Looking at Sicinnus, he says, "Time for me to turn around. I expect to see you again either tomorrow or the next day."

"Probably tomorrow."

"Spoken with confidence."

"I speak with confidence because I have it."

Themistocles' jaw muscles tighten, and he says, "Tomorrow then."

He turns to the spy and puts his hand on the man's shoulder. "I can tell that you are a good and brave man. I don't know if you are married and now is not the time to discuss it, but if you have a wife she is a very fortunate woman. I look forward to the time we meet again, as I know we will."

Sicinnus realizes Themistocles is manipulating the spy to leave a favorable impression. Themistocles turns away without looking back and disappears into the darkness.

Sicinnus and the Persian spy press on. The spy is in the lead by three steps; they move quickly and quietly. They are going downhill, paralleling the river Charadra as it heads toward the Great Marsh and the Persian camp. The terrain is perfect for an ambush in the darkness, with tall fennel and grass everywhere, intermingled with large bushes and olive trees. They walk carefully through the dark undergrowth.

The spy abruptly stops. Sicinnus sees nothing out of the ordinary in the moonlight, but he can tell the spy is listening. The spy moves forward, but more slowly. Another few steps and the spy stops again. Then he cautiously, warily continues.

"Hold." The menacing voice is a short distance in front of them. "Who goes there?"

Sicinnus and the spy freeze. The voice is speaking Greek. The spy says nothing. Sicinnus responds, "I am the slave of Themistocles who sent me here. I have no arms."

"Step forward," commands the voice. "If you run you die."

Sicinnus and the spy follow the voice's orders. Four men appear and surround Sicinnus and the spy. They are Persian. Sicinnus holds his arms out from his sides to show he has no weapon. In response, the Persians point their spears straight at him.

In front of Sicinnus and the spy, a man steps forward and says, "How was my Greek? I am told I speak it well."

"What you are told is true," says Sicinnus. "Very well, although I knew you were not Greek."

"That is good for both of us," says the voice. "A good compliment for me. And for you, I am told a man should say something good just before he dies."

The Persian gives his command with a savage, "Hut!"

In unison, all four Persians jerk their spear-throwing arms up high and step forward with one foot, positioned for the next order.

In a desperate effort to save himself, Sicinnus opens his mouth to scream in Persian.

CHAPTER THIRTY-ONE

NEWS FROM PERSIAN SPIES

An instant before Sicinnus can shout at the spear-throwers, the spy starts yelling in Persian and waving his arms.

The leader of the spear-throwers takes a step forward and signals for the spy to approach. They confer in Persian, assuming Sicinnus does not understand them. He soon learns the spy has saved his life, or at least delayed his death. The soldiers have decided to take him to Datis and let the commander decide what to do with their captive.

With Sicinnus surrounded, the soldiers lead him down through the brush and wooded area toward the beach. The Persian spy follows behind.

∼

Datis stands by himself near the Persian warships and barges moored off Marathon's beach. It is dark except for a few torches thrust into the beach sand, so there is little to see except for the outlines of the boats. He listens to the water slosh against the vessels. The sound is rhythmic and calming. He takes a deep breath, but the air is far less pleasant than the sound of the water. It has taken only a few days for the occasional hint of raw sewage to become a pervasive stench.

Several long days and nights have passed since the Persians landed. This stalemate must come to an end, but the solution is far from obvious— attack from a poor position, or wait for an unexpected opening, a miracle.

He hears footsteps running toward him on the sand and turns to see a guard approach.

"Commander, two of our spies are here," says the guard. "One from afar, to the south, the other from the hills above the Greek camp."

Datis considers briefly. "Bring me the spy from the south."

The spy arrives a moment later. His clothes are dark gray to make him difficult to spot from a distance. Without preamble, he says, "Commander, I have a report the Spartans will be at Marathon in three days."

Datis freezes. "From what source do you know this?"

"A runner from Corinth. He received it this morning by flashing shields from our informants in Sparta."

"It took them long enough to get the news to us."

Datis is perturbed that such important information did not reach him sooner. He knows the Great King has spies everywhere—using traders, slaves, migrant Persians, disgruntled natives turned traitors. But he understands that Sparta was difficult to infiltrate until the Persians realized what their one great weakness was—the helots. Many a bitter Messenian was willing to risk torture and death to betray their autocratic masters.

"You are excused for now," Datis says, "but stay close by."

The spy backs off into the darkness, and Datis motions to the guard to send him the spy from the hills above the Greek camp.

"Yes?" Datis demands when the second spy arrives.

"Commander, I am here with more information about the Greek games I reported on earlier."

"Well?"

"There were changes in the main game I described before." The spy hesitates. "During my earlier report, your Greek advisor, Hippias, was here. Do you want him to be present this time, too?"

"No," replies Datis. "Proceed."

"The main change to their strange game was that they added more men—many more. They made their lines of men longer. They increased the men in each line from one hundred to two hundred, then again to three."

"So the foolish games are more complicated. Anything else?"

"They added more rows of men, from two to five, and now have eight rows in each game." The spy pauses.

"And?"

"They keep repeating this same game over and over, and the more they play it, the straighter their lines become. I cannot fathom the rules of the game, but Hippias had answers when I gave you my earlier report. It might make sense to him."

"Hippias said the game was strange, but he thought it was a variation of an earlier game." Datis stops and scratches his chin, pondering. "More lines, more men in each line, all armed, held straight as they move . . . it makes me wonder."

Another guard runs up and stops just beyond the torch light. He looks unusually excited.

"What is it?" Datis asks.

"Some of our soldiers have just arrived and they captured a Greek under strange circumstances," says the guard.

Datis waves the back of his hand at the spy from the hills, "Return to your post above the Greek camp. Dismissed."

The spy rushes off as Datis motions to the guard to come forward.

"Tell me about this Greek our soldiers captured."

"He claims to be a slave of one of the leaders of the Greeks named Themistocles and says he has a message from him to you."

"I know that name," says Datis, instantly gripped by curiosity, suspicion, and a strange sensation, as though he has just felt the touch of his God, Ahura Mazda. Maybe, just maybe, this is what he has been waiting for. "Go find Hippias and bring him to me now."

A short time later, as the guard and Hippias arrive, Datis turns to Hippias and says, "The Spartans will be here in three days. We will discuss that later. Right now we have a more pressing matter."

To the guard, Datis says, "Bring me the Greek slave."

Turning back to Hippias, he continues, "We captured a Greek who claims to be a slave of Themistocles and says he bears a message from him to me." Hippias stiffens; he knows that name far better than Datis. He also knows they may be able to catch one of the Greeks' biggest fish—a renowned general.

"Before we interrogate the slave," says Datis, "I want you to tell me everything you know about his master. After we interrogate him, we will see what more he can tell us about the Greeks, especially any of their weaknesses."

"By what means?" asks Hippias.

"The usual ones."

"And after that?"

"Then, of course," says Datis with a shrug, "we will kill him."

Datis and Hippias are still deep in conversation when Sicinnus approaches, surrounded by soldiers and followed by the Persian spy who accompanied him. The soldiers and their prisoner stop a short distance from Datis, who promptly gestures to the slave to come forward.

Sicinnus carefully studies the Persian commander's expression and subtle body movements. They leave no doubt—he is a dead man.

Speaking in Greek, Datis says, "I am Commander Datis. You have a message for me. Is the message written or will it be spoken?"

"Commander Datis, the message is in my mind and will be spoken."

"Speak."

"My master, Themistocles, wishes to abandon the Greeks and serve the Great King of Persia."

Datis raises an eyebrow and looks over at Hippias, who is listening intently. Then he crosses his arms and looks back at the slave. "More?"

"My master has a plan to ensure the Persians will defeat the Greeks."

"A plan to guarantee victory for the Persians," Datis muses. Then, speaking directly to Sicinnus, he says, "Exactly what is this plan?"

"I know nothing of it. I am only a slave. The message from my master is that if you, as the Persian commander, agree to grant my master's requests, and swear on behalf of Darius the Great as well as Persia's supreme god—I think my master called him Ahu Mada—then my master will fully explain his plan."

"Ahura Mazda, the only God." Datis scowls. "So your master wants assurances."

Sicinnus thinks, *What a stupid comment. Of course he wants assurances.*

"What assurances?" continues Datis.

"Safety and wealth. Also, my master wants to be second-in-command of all the military forces throughout the land of the Greeks."

"Second-in-command," blurts Hippias. "Second to me?"

Datis looks at Hippias and, with a derisive smile, says, "He could have asked for more." Turning back to the slave, Datis continues, "And how does your master expect me to convey those assurances to him?"

"Through me," replies Sicinnus. "Pledge your word, and I will take your message to my master. Then he will tell me his plan and I will bring it back to you."

Datis strokes his beard and rubs his fingers back and forth across his lips. Then he abruptly walks past Sicinnus. He approaches the soldiers who seized the slave along with the Persian spy who was with him.

Looking at the spy and speaking Persian, thinking Sicinnus does not understand, Datis says, "You heard what the slave said. Did you detect any falsehood in his words or something that might not make sense?"

"No, Commander, nothing. I think it likely the slave speaks the truth. I cannot be certain, of course, but I think Themistocles wants to join you. My sense of him is that he is a man of his word."

"When you infiltrated the Greek camp, your mission was to find a man called Eury. Did you?"

"Yes, Commander. I was just beginning to talk to him when some other Greeks approached and asked him to go with them. Shortly after that, more Greeks came and took me prisoner."

"Was there violence?" asks Datis.

"There did not seem to be any problem when Eury left with them. But after that, when the Greeks came up to me, I knew there was a big problem."

"What happened to Eury?"

"I do not know, Commander. I never saw him again."

Datis turns on his heel to face Sicinnus. "The Greek called Eury, what happened to him?"

"I do not know the name, Commander."

"When I put you under torture, perhaps you will remember."

"If you torture me, I expect I will tell you whatever I think you want to hear. But that will not change the fact that I have never heard of the man."

Datis motions to the solders and commands, "Take the slave away but hold him in my sight."

After they depart, Datis turns to Hippias and says, "There's something strange about that slave. He's smart."

"Many slaves are smart."

Glaring at Hippias, Datis sarcastically growls, "Once again, you helpfully state the obvious. Do you have anything better to offer?"

"Torture him."

"Not much better. Torture does not work on that type of man. There really are only two questions."

"And they are?" asks Hippias.

"Do we kill him or use him?"

CHAPTER THIRTY-TWO

THE GREAT KING EXPLAINS

G reat King Darius returned to the city of Susa a few days ago. He is sequestered in the grand palace and not attending public events, which is most unusual. Rumors are starting to swirl. Perhaps the Great King is sick. Perhaps on his deathbed. Apparently, there has been shouting in the grand palace for the last two days. But the women are not wailing, so the Great King must still be alive.

Phar decides to get some answers. As he approaches the palace, he is once again awed by its grandeur. The palace complex is built on Susa's northern terrace, with an impressive view of the city. The complex covers more than twelve acres. Great towers of yellow stone rise above the walls against an intense blue sky, throwing shadows over northern sections of the city. Sculpted lions rage in silence at the flanks of each gate.

Just as the Egyptian arrives at the palace, the entrance gates swing open and Xerxes storms out. Seeing Phar, Xerxes stops and stares at him. "What are you doing here?"

"I came to ask permission to see the Great King."

"The answer is no."

Phar pauses and thinks about taking a step backward but decides against it. Speaking firmly, he says, "The permission I seek should be granted or denied by the Great King and only the Great King."

"I said the answer is no. I do not intend to repeat myself again."

Looking coolly at Xerxes, Phar responds, "With respect, no one speaks for the Great King unless he grants that authority. The Great King does not know I am here, so no authority has been granted."

The Persian prince glares contemptuously at the Egyptian, then marches past him and walks away.

Phar makes his request to a palace guard, and moments later the guard returns and gestures to Phar to enter. As Phar is escorted through an unfamiliar part of the vast palace complex, he is amazed by what he sees. Extravagances from throughout the empire are everywhere: cedar timbers and other exotic woods in a range of shades from nearly white to ebony, and with grains from the finest to coarsest he has ever seen; tall polished and engraved rock columns; precious stones including bright blue lapis lazuli, deep red carnelian, and glossy turquoise; small and delicately etched ivory ornaments as well as entire tusks carved with intricate designs. And most impressive of all are the flashes of light everywhere Phar looks—shining from the ever-present gold and silver.

Phar reaches two gigantic golden doors. They appear too heavy to move, but his escort easily opens them, waves Phar through, and shuts them behind him. Phar is alone with Great King Darius, who sits on a golden throne at the far end of the room. Phar bows.

"Arise and approach," commands Darius.

When Phar is near him, Darius says, "He called me an old man."

"Great King?"

"You can't understand. A man hates to be called an old man, especially when it is true."

"Xerxes?"

"Who else?"

"Yes, of course, Great King. There could be no one else."

"Phar, I want you to do something you have not done before," says Darius. He stands and steps down from his throne and approaches the young Egyptian. "For the rest of this conversation, let's just talk as if we are . . . no titles, for once. Later you shall return to the proper way of addressing me. Do you understand?"

"Yes, Grea—yes, I understand."

"You asked permission to see me. Why?"

"I had a question about rumors going around the city. But before I ask about that, I have a question about what you just said."

"Proceed."

"My question is about Xerxes." Phar hesitates. Darius stands before him, expressionless.

"Why is he your favored son? I assume that means he will be the next Great King after you. Why him?"

"Why do I exist, Phar?" Darius asks in a quiet, almost intimate voice.

"I don't understand."

"I exist for the empire. To preserve it and to expand it."

"Yes, I believe I understand. But Xerxes, I still don't understand why you want him to be the next Great King. After all, he is not your oldest son."

"No," Darius sighs, "he is not. But of all my sons, Xerxes will be best to preserve and expand the empire. He has his weaknesses—no one is more aware of them than I. But in spite of them, he has skill and he has determination and courage."

Darius pauses before continuing coolly. "There is another matter. He is ambitious—and ruthless. Indeed, if another of my sons became the Great King, Xerxes would have him killed. I am not sure he even realizes this. But I do. The only way I could designate another son king would be to tell him to kill Xerxes. Immediately. And that I will not do."

Stunned by Darius' words, Phar falls silent, and then decides to ask a different question. "Why does Xerxes hate me?"

"Hate is a strong word but accurate. His hatred toward you is not personal."

"With respect, hatred is always personal for the person hated. I sense that Xerxes would gladly kill me if he had the chance. I think he hated me the first time he saw me."

"That is my son; he must have someone to be the focus of his dark mind. Just before you arrived in Persia, the man he most hated died, leaving an emptiness Xerxes needed to fill. You can call it chance or luck or fate, but it is not personal. At least, not entirely."

Phar is again shocked into silence. He knows that people and families can be very strange, but he never contemplated anything like this.

Changing the subject again, Phar says, "I asked permission to see you because of the rumors going around the city. No one seems to know exactly what is happening, but there is concern for you. The people want to see you and be assured you are fit. I am here to find out what is going on. Is there a problem?"

"The answer is that I have received no word from Datis for two days."

"Two days late. What does that mean?"

"Something has gone seriously wrong at that place with the absurd Greek name."

"But there might be other explanations: a storm, a flood, another lame horse."

"That is almost exactly what Xerxes said before he called me an old man."

Darius and Phar stare at each other in silence. Finally, Darius says, "There is another reason Xerxes hates you. He is envious. Earlier I told you how Great Kings should conquer enemies—find traitors among the enemy and use treachery. I also said Great Kings need a good advisor. Cyrus had his Chief Counselor, Croesus. I do not have anyone like Croesus. Xerxes wants to play that role. That cannot be, and he knows it. He thinks I am grooming you to be my Croesus."

"Are you?"

"No longer."

"No longer?"

"You have excellent instincts," says Darius. "But it is too dangerous here because of Xerxes, and you have a character flaw."

"A character flaw?"

"Your heart is pure. Like Croesus, an advisor to the Great King should have a good heart, but not pure. Your heart must have a dark streak."

"Are you saying I am too good a person to be a good advisor?"

"Yes, Phar, that is what I am saying. And tomorrow you will leave me and begin your journey home to the land of the pyramids."

"But you will still be without a good advisor."

"As I have been for a long time. But I have the One True God, Ahura Mazda, who listens to my prayers."

Darius raises his head and intones, "Ahura Mazda, the Wise Lord, the Uncreated Creator. Ahura Mazda, who demands Truth and Good Works and, in return, gives us Order out of Chaos. Ahura Mazda, who uses Fire to banish Darkness. Ahura Mazda brought me help, and by the favor of Ahura Mazda I rule as your Great King, King of kings, King of the Empire of the Persians, King of all countries. Ahura Mazda listens to the Great King's prayers."

Phar realizes the conversation is finished. He bows deeply.

"Arise," commands Darius.

"Great King, I am your servant."

In a voice seemingly devoid of emotion, Darius says, "Dismissed."

As Phar departs, he thinks he hears Darius softly say, "Farewell."

Phar wonders about the future. He also wonders about Ahura Mazda. Does the One True God of Persia really listen to the Great King's prayers?

CHAPTER THIRTY-THREE

ANOTHER PERILOUS MISSION

It is midday and Themistocles is alone with his thoughts.

If Sicinnus dies, it will be an act of valor. But not enough for glory; not enough to be remembered forever.

He shakes his head and looks down.

He'll be remembered by me. And not only by me.

He puts a hand over his eyes.

I'll provide for Lela and little Alyssa, but what's the worth of that compared to a man who's gone forever? This happens all the time, but that's no answer.

Themistocles runs both hands through his hair.

If Sicinnus dies, what will be the justification? A young man with a wife and baby, but he'll have no glory. It's not right. Still, it's what he must do. What we all must do.

He hears a hoplite walk up behind him and announce, "The Polemarch wants you to come to him. We just got word that Sicinnus is back, and he has been ordered to report to the Polemarch."

"Where is Callimachus?"

"Outside his tent."

Themistocles sets off running.

～

Callimachus and Sicinnus are conferring by themselves when Themistocles arrives, winded. Themistocles looks Sicinnus up and down, then gives him a hard slap on his upper arm.

"He just started his story," says Callimachus. "Tell Themistocles about your two close calls."

Sicinnus recounts how he was almost run through by the spear-throwers, and then he turns to his encounter with Datis and Hippias.

"When they brought me to the commander, I could see my death in his eyes. He and the old Greek, Hippias, interrogated me. Then Datis sent me away. Later he brought me back and said I would be allowed to live. He gave me a message to deliver to you, Themistocles."

"And that is?"

"He wants me to return tonight with you."

Themistocles looks at Callimachus. The warleader shrugs.

"Not a surprise," says Themistocles. "They want exactly what the warleader and I would want if we were them."

"We tested their stupidity and they passed our test," says Callimachus. "Now we have to make a decision about our plan—do we change it?"

"I have something else to report," says Sicinnus.

"Yes?" asks Callimachus.

"The Persians know the Spartans are coming to help us," says Sicinnus. "And they know when the Spartans should arrive—in three days."

"Well!" exclaims Themistocles, with a look at Callimachus. "We knew they had spies all around here, apparently even in Sparta."

"I never spoke Persian the whole time," Sicinnus continues. "Almost, but I didn't need to, and I did what you said. The Persians around me assumed I was Greek and didn't understand their language, so they talked more freely than they should have. The coming of the Spartans was whispered among several of them. I suspect they just recently learned about it."

"Well, it's very helpful to know what they know," says Themistocles. "And knowing that makes it easier to respond to their invitation for another meeting."

"One of these days you're going to really surprise me and fail to read my mind," Callimachus says to his cunning general. "So tonight, we'll increase our offer to the Persians. Instead of giving them the chance to kill one of our best men, now we'll offer two. And when you meet them, don't forget the most dangerous man who'll be there."

"I won't," replies Themistocles.

Seeing Sicinnus' confused expression, Themistocles says, "The old Greek, Hippias. The threat of Hippias is as great as the threat of all Persia."

~

After the sun's faint glow disappears, Sicinnus retraces the path toward the Persians with Themistocles three paces behind him. Sicinnus suspects there are some Greek hoplites silently tracking them, but he is not sure; he had no reason to know so he was not told. The two of them pass through most of no-man's land and are approaching terrain controlled by the Persians. Just as before when Sicinnus was with the Persian spy, they go downhill, paralleling the small, increasingly malodorous river as it flows toward the Persian camp. And once again, the surrounding shrubs and stubby trees provide excellent cover for an ambush. The darkness is intimidating. The cicadas continue their shrill whirr.

"Hold, who goes there?" The voice ahead of them is speaking Greek just as it did two nights earlier.

Sicinnus quickly replies, "Sicinnus, on the orders of Commander Datis. And Themistocles, also on orders of Datis."

A Persian soldier appears out of the darkness and says, "Follow."

The Persian leads them toward a heavily wooded area with tall trees, and a short time later the three men walk into a clearing. There is a small fire with one man close to it and another just outside the light.

"Well, I see the slave's word is good," says Datis, speaking in Greek. "And his companion must be Themistocles, yes?"

"Yes," says Themistocles. "And I expect I am speaking to Commander Datis?"

Datis nods brusquely.

Themistocles says, "You appear to be alone except for your companion just beyond the light of the fire."

"As I suspect you are alone, except for your slave," says Datis with barely concealed skepticism.

Themistocles nods. "The difference is you had plenty of time to prepare for my arrival."

"Which means if I intend you harm, the sooner I act, the better."

"If that is your plan." Themistocles' assertive response is almost challenging. He is staring down death because he is sure unseen Persian soldiers are watching and waiting in the darkness for Datis' signal.

Another pair of penetrating eyes is also watching them. High up in a tree, the large eyes of a golden owl are concentrating on five Persian archers hidden in the night. The owl knows it will be best if Themistocles is persuasive enough to talk himself out of danger. But she lusts for carnage. In her heart, the Goddess of War wants Persian blood. She repeatedly flexes her talons.

Datis says to Themistocles, "But killing you would be a mistake if the message your slave delivered is true."

Themistocles speaks with confidence, "Exactly what I was about to say, and I am here to prove it."

"So prove it," says Datis. "And I think you should get reacquainted with the man who will soon be Great King Darius' satrap of all the lands of the Greeks."

Datis motions and Hippias steps forward into the firelight.

"I remember you, Hippias," says Themistocles.

"And now I'm back."

"Twenty years is a long time. I was a young man about to enter military training."

"And now you are a general," says Hippias dryly. "Further, you say you want to follow my footsteps and serve Persia's Great King. What do you offer?"

"You have friends in Athens," says Themistocles. "I have friends there as well. Your friends, by themselves, may have a fair chance of helping your cause. But combined with mine, their success is certain."

Datis smiles grimly.

"I have confidence in my friends by themselves," replies Hippias.

"And what I offer should increase your confidence. It will also increase the likelihood that the Persians can take Athens with little bloodshed. I prefer that, though naturally you don't care what I prefer. However, I am told the Great King also prefers it. I am told the Great King is most generous to commanders who accomplish their victories through guile rather than battle."

Though focused on Hippias, Themistocles sees Datis slightly nodding.

"I'm not impressed," says Hippias. "What else do you offer?"

"A plan for the Persians to take Athens while the Greek hoplites are still at Marathon," says Themistocles. "To send a small but sufficient number of Persians to capture Athens while the bulk of your troops remain here."

Datis spits and snorts, "Hah. I thought you were one of the Greeks' generals. Don't you think we have already thought of that?"

"I expect you have, but I also expect you have not thought it through my way."

"Perhaps," says Hippias. "Continue."

"Before I continue, we should talk about my requests for being of service to the Great King."

Datis steps forward and says, "It is not yet time to discuss your requests, and it won't be unless your service to the Great King is deemed worthy by his representative—me. What I grant you now is safe passage back to the Greeks. On that, you have my word, but nothing more yet."

"And safe passage for my slave."

Datis pauses and then asks, "After I said 'nothing more' you want to negotiate over the life of a slave?"

"This slave is young and strong," says Themistocles. "He is a valuable possession."

Datis nods and says, "Safe passage for you and the slave—my word on it."

"My plan will work, but its different parts must fit together securely," says Themistocles. "And that begins with using my friends, in addition to the friends of Hippias, to increase the chances that the right gate into Athens can be opened exactly when we want. And it will take about a thousand of your men to be shifted down to Athens."

Hippias shakes his head. "I doubt a thousand men will do it. Anyway, that many men cannot be moved in secret. The Greeks will respond."

"If your men put out to sea at night and sail far enough away from the coast, their movements will be secret until they arrive."

"Even if I agree with that, your phantom men will land at the port of Phalerum, which is the only logical place," says Hippias. "The distance between Phalerum and Athens is more than three miles. Before those men start to disembark, the alarm will be raised, signal fires will relay the warning, and hoplites will be sent back from Marathon. The Persians can get to Athens before the hoplites, and we should still be able to get past the gates, especially with our friends combined, but there won't be enough time to subdue the city. Too few Persians and too much distance between Phalerum and Athens."

"Men on horses can get from Phalerum to Athens in no time," says Themistocles. "And men fighting on horses are worth at least four times as many fighters on the ground. Men on horses can subdue Athens quickly, then close the gates and hold the women and children as hostages."

"Horses!" exclaims Datis, who takes another step closer to Themistocles. "Are you saying we should move the horses to Athens from

Marathon?"

"The different parts of my plan must work together, and horses are the linchpin."

"Our cavalry is here to do battle along with all our other troops. Dividing military resources almost never makes sense."

Datis turns his head sideways to study the Greek general from the corner of his eye. "Why would you make such a proposal? Stupidity or insanity might explain it. But far more likely is that you are a bold liar."

"You fail to mention the other possibility," says Themistocles, having anticipated this response.

The Persian stares hard at the Greek. "And that is?"

"That what I say is the truth. Normally, I would agree with you; dividing fighting resources usually is a mistake. But all great military men understand there are exceptions to every rule. And if you knew what I know, you would agree that now is one of those rare exceptions."

"What do you know?"

"I know the Greeks' abilities," says Themistocles, "and I can see yours. The number of Persian fighters is far beyond anything the Greeks have ever confronted. So lopsided, it's absurd. And your archers, how they start shooting high, then lower their aim with each round; by the time they level their arrows there will be few hoplites left. Why do you think I'm here? My point is simple; your horses are unnecessary. They can be put to much better use taking Athens."

Datis takes this in while continuing to stare directly into the Athenian's eyes. Themistocles does not look away.

Finally, the Persian commander asks, "Why not just make a frontal assault against your Greeks in the hills? With all the Persian advantages you rightly describe, I wonder why you don't suggest a straightforward approach. Bloody, perhaps, but effective. Or don't you agree?"

"No, I do not agree. And I suspect you don't agree either, or you would not have risen to the rank you hold." Themistocles goes on without hesitating. "If a frontal assault was your intention, you would already have done it, and if you're contemplating the thought, you would not tell me. You know exactly what I know; unless your warhorses can fly like Pegasus, they'll be worthless in the hills. And the Greeks waiting in ambush will kill most of your archers before they shoot their first arrow. So you would end up with a great number of Persian soldiers stumbling around trying to find hidden Greeks who know every rock and crevice on those hills."

Datis takes a step back from Themistocles and folds his arms.

"What else do you have to offer?" he asks.

"I told you what I would do if I were in your place," says Themistocles. "What I haven't said is when I would do it. When and why."

"Proceed," says Datis.

"Before I continue, I will tell you my requests to the Great King. You said if my advice is worthy, my requests will be considered. I take you at your word, and you should at least know my requests."

"Continue."

"I have two requests," says the Athenian. "First, life and luxury for my family and me as well as life for my slaves. Second, I want to be second-in-command to the Great King's satrap over the land of the Greeks."

Hippias makes a deep guttural noise and spits a large glob of gunk near Themistocles' feet.

Datis says, "The Great King will decide as he will, and my recommendation to him will have influence. The Great King can be most generous to those he favors. You speak of luxury. Might a large enhancement of luxury create some flexibility in your requests?"

"Not with respect to the lives of my family and me."

"Understandable. No matter the amount of your future wealth, you and your family must be secure to enjoy it. But if the Great King granted wealth beyond your imagination, might you have less interest in becoming second-in-command to Hippias?"

"I might," replies Themistocles.

"And might you have less interest in the welfare of your slaves?"

"I might," repeats Themistocles.

"I see," says Datis with a glance at Sicinnus. "And no more requests?"

"No more requests."

"I understand your requests, and I'm beginning to understand you," says Datis. "You were talking about the when and why of your plan."

"You should load up your warhorses and embark from Marathon tomorrow night. Row straight out to sea, beyond the sight of land, then down the coast during the day, and wait until nightfall to disembark at Phalerum."

"Now the why," says Datis. "Your plan has our cavalry attack Athens two days hence. Why is that a special time?"

"Because the Spartans will arrive at Marathon on the following day."

Themistocles watches their eyes closely, waiting for a glance between them. No glance. Themistocles silently compliments them.

"Are you certain?" asks Datis.

"Absolutely, unless the Spartans are liars; they are a lot of things, but not liars. The Athenians are desperate for their arrival in three days."

"Any more offerings?"

"No, I trust my offerings will be favorably received by the Great King when he hears them, and I trust my offerings are received favorably by you, now."

Hippias steps up very close to Themistocles and puts his face right in front of him.

"Listening to you tonight, I am reminded of myself when I was younger. You are more like me than you realize. I am confident of that."

Hippias starts to turn away but then turns back and says, "One more thing. A question about Athens' current system of rule, which will of course be abolished when the Great King becomes your ruler and you become his obedient slave, as we all are. I don't need to tell you what I think of democracy and my banishment by Cleisthenes and the Spartans. But some time ago, when I first began to hear how popular you are in the Assembly, I wondered what I would do in your situation. What I would do after democracy was created and became available for my use, and it turned out I was good at using it. Those thoughts say something about a man—who and what he is. How much do you like your democracy, really?"

Although surprised by the question, Themistocles relies on his instincts to quickly respond, "You already answered your own question, Hippias. You said I am like you. If you receive a gift that gives you power, who cares whether the gift is beautiful or ugly? What you care about is power, so you use the gift, regardless of what you think about it."

Hippias nods his head.

Looking at a guard, Datis says, "Ensure their safety through no-man's land."

⁓

Later, when Themistocles and Sicinnus are by themselves back inside Greek-controlled territory, Sicinnus breaks their silence. "Brilliant, that's the word for it. I've seen you in fine form many times before, but that was your best. You didn't tell them a thing they didn't already know, and I think you lured them to do what you want. You almost convinced me, and I knew everything you said was total rubbish."

Themistocles does not reply.

Sicinnus looks at him and says, "What's the matter with you? We are back and alive, and you just put on the performance of a lifetime. And not just for you—for all of us, for the entire city."

"He said I was just like him, a younger him," mulls Themistocles. "Hippias was confident of that."

"And your response was superb. You pretended to agree with him, and your words sounded as if you were speaking the absolute truth."

Seeming not to listen, Themistocles repeats himself, "He said I was just like him."

Sicinnus slaps a hand on his forehead and exclaims, "I hope the gods aren't listening. You need a good night's sleep. You're talking about Hippias. He's a decrepit old tyrant. A traitor. All Athens detests him, except for a few rich aristocrats. Why could you possibly care what he thinks?"

Themistocles exhales loudly but does not speak. Sicinnus is elated with the success of their mission, but he sees that Themistocles is severely troubled.

Themistocles silently repeats three words to himself: *Tyrant. Traitor. Never.*

CHAPTER THIRTY-FOUR

TAKING A RISK

Lela is walking rapidly through the agora in the shadow of the tall slave. He had come to her house to tell her Magacles needed to see her right away. He said it was urgent, that her safety was at risk, and that Magacles could save her if she reached him in time. Archippe was not around, so Lela had handed her small daughter to the old woman. Lela also told her who she was seeing, where she was going, and when she would return—within three hours, no matter what. The sun was still high; she would be back well before dark.

The entire time Lela was preparing to leave, the little dog, Argos, kept barking and growling at Magacles' slave. Lela thought the puppy was trying out the role of household watchdog, and she approved of its instinct to keep anyone associated with Magacles at bay. She was uneasy too, but meeting Magacles at the cockfights could not be terribly dangerous with so many people around. And if she had refused to go, that might have invited disaster.

Lela focuses on keeping up with Magacles' slave as they hurry through the agora.

When they arrive at the cockfights, the slave looks around. He tells Lela to wait, then moves into the crowd to continue his search. Shortly afterward he returns.

"The meeting must have already started," the slave says. "We'll need to go straight there."

"What meeting? You didn't say anything about a meeting."

"I was leaving that to my master. It's the meeting he wanted you to attend. He was going to take you there."

"You didn't say anything about any of this. I was supposed to meet Magacles here. Where all these people are."

"And then he was going to escort you to the meeting. But obviously the meeting started earlier than I expected, so now I'll escort you. The meeting is just a little way from here."

"This isn't right," says Lela, adamantly. "I am a woman alone. That's uncommon enough out in the open, away from the house. Being told to come here and then being surprised and told to go there, wherever there is; it's not right."

"There's nothing uncommon here, because you are *not* alone. You're being escorted by a trusted servant of Magacles," the slave says, clearly offended. "My reputation is flawless; you can ask anyone here."

The two slaves stand face to face, staring at each other. There is a shout from the cockfight arena.

"This meeting you are talking about," says Lela. "Who else will be there?"

"Several other citizens of the city. But I'm not allowed to name them or their wives."

"Their wives!"

"Yes, they usually attend these meetings."

"Women attending a meeting of citizens? That's even stranger than a woman wandering through Athens alone."

"It's not a slave's role to question who participates in meetings his master attends," the slave says wryly.

Lela, too anxious to notice the allusion to her own status, looks around her, desperately hunting for someone she knows, someone trustworthy she can leave a message with. No one.

"Where did you say this meeting is?"

Pointing over his shoulder, the slave says, "Just a short walk. You can almost see it from here, except it's around a bend in the path."

"Show me."

After walking longer than she expected, Lela stops and stamps her foot, saying, "Your time is up."

"Over there, you can see where we're going, the large building on the left; that's where they're meeting."

Lela looks around. They are well away from the agora and in an area Lela does not know. There are only a few people in the vicinity.

Reluctantly, she says, "Continue."

When they arrive at the building she stands outside, studying it. There is a small window. She looks through it and sees a silent, nearly empty room, with a small statue of Hermes in a shadowy corner, facing her with his hand raised. In salutation? In warning? She shakes off the thought.

"The meeting will be in the back," says the slave.

Lela considers this. "Ask Magacles to come to me."

"Gods on high, I can't do that," says the slave, impatiently. "A slave doesn't interrupt a meeting of citizens."

He waits for Lela's reaction.

"I at least need to know how many people are there."

"Very well," replies the slave. "I'll go find out."

The slave enters the building and returns a few moments later.

"Four citizens in addition to my master," says the slave. "Their wives are there, too. I was able to briefly whisper to my master. He said he cannot leave, but you should come in now because they're just about to discuss what's going to happen that will affect you."

"Lead the way."

When they enter the building, Lela immediately sees a long hallway and, at the far end, she can see Magacles' profile. He sits, gesturing as if talking to a group of people to his left, out of Lela's line of sight. She follows the slave down the hall. The building is well lit, with the sun's rays coming through several small windows. And the place smells clean. The light and odor give her comfort.

Just outside the room where Magacles sits, the slave stops and motions Lela forward. Magacles continues to gesture and now Lela can hear him talking. But his voice is soft so she cannot make out his words. He glances at her, smiles, and motions to her to enter. She moves past the slave and steps into the room. She looks to her left. The room is empty; she is facing a blank wall.

At the edge of her vision, she sees a fist coming toward the side of her face and everything slows down. Her eyes turn back to Magacles. His smile widens. She sees his teeth, then the clenched fist next to her head. She can almost count the hairs on the fingers but the fingers blur into . . . flashing pain. And something else. More smiles, two this time. No, not smiles. She studies the emerging faces, and it is very clear they are not smiling. The faces materialize and begin to float away. They become two beings holding hands. Sicinnus and Alyssa, waving to her. Waving very slowly. How wrong she was to think they were both smiling. They are crying. Their bodies are becoming misty. They are gone.

CHAPTER THIRTY-FIVE

THE PERSIAN PLAN CHANGES

"Did you find the maps useful?" asks Hippias. It is the morning after the night meeting with Themistocles.

"Indeed." Datis turns toward him. "I've already had several bands of soldiers sent off. They'll skirt the hills to the east of the plain beyond the Great Marsh, and then turn inland so the Greeks will see nothing. Then, with the help of your maps, the men will circle back to Athens. The Greeks will be completely unaware."

"It will certainly surprise Themistocles, if he was lying to us. How many men?"

"Six groups traveling separately, ten men in each. They speak good Greek and are dressed like Greek shepherds and farmers, unarmed except for knives. That's more men than we need, but the countryside may have been alerted; with luck, most of them will make it."

"When did they leave?"

"Well before dawn."

"Did you send shield signals to Athens?"

"Of course. Early this morning. We received the return signals a short time ago."

"So tonight a gate opens for a few dozen Persians disguised as Greeks, who will be armed by traitors in the city and hidden until they're needed," says Hippias. "Then of course you're sending cavalry by ship to follow up, and we'll have no need for Themistocles' friends."

Datis does not respond, so Hippias continues, "Magacles is going to open a gate for us. A good man. He should be my second-in-command."

"Not Themistocles?" asks Datis with a sinister smirk.

Hippias harrumphs. "Absolutely not. He is a dangerous man."

"Yes, but it's not clear if he is a threat to us or the Greeks."

"So the horses are away tonight?" asks Hippias.

"I haven't decided yet."

"You just sent sixty men to Athens! They are supposed to make sure a gate will open for the cavalry. If you don't send the horses, why send the men at all?"

"I like to have options. Hiding our fighters inside Athens gives me an option that can be useful for many purposes."

"Your Great King—our Great King—prefers to conquer by treachery, not battle. You have said the same thing hundreds of times. This is your opportunity, and you need the cavalry in Athens to make it happen."

"I do not need lectures about the Great King. The cavalry is a difficult decision. I don't like to divide my forces."

"You don't need the cavalry here. You have forty thousand fighters. The Greek reinforcements won't have a tenth of that. Even with them, how many soldiers will be in the whole Greek army?" Hippias spits and points to the splotch in the dirt. "That many."

"True enough. But you've been away from your homeland too long. You're forgetting something important that you should remember from your days as the Tyrant of Athens."

"And what is that?"

Datis looks coolly at the impatient Greek. "Their reinforcements are Spartans."

Hippias scowls and thinks: *The Persian bastard is right. The very thought of the Spartans will put the fear of the gods into the Persian troops. And when they see them marching as one machine of bronze, in cloaks the color of blood . . .*

"So what *is* your plan?" he says gruffly.

Sparing Datis the need to answer, a Persian herald walks up and waits to be acknowledged.

"You have a report?"

"Yes, Commander. The problems are increasing and have begun to affect the horses."

Datis looks at him. "The same symptoms?"

"Yes, Commander. Vomiting and diarrhea."

"How many horses are affected?"

"More than twenty, Commander."

Turning to Hippias, Datis says, "Sick men can be made to fight; I'll put them in the front ranks. But we can't allow an epidemic among the horses."

"Perhaps your God, Ahura Mazda, is sending you a message that the horses should depart."

"Perhaps Ahura Mazda is telling us that landing at Marathon as you suggested was a mistake," Datis replies.

Undeterred, Hippias responds, "Perhaps Ahura Mazda is saying we stayed on this beach too long and should already be in Athens."

Datis turns on his heels and walks away.

CHAPTER THIRTY-SIX

WOMEN'S VALOR

The sun is going down. Archippe sits anxiously beside the old woman who is holding Lela's daughter on her lap. The old woman's face shows her fear. The toddler also seems to sense trouble, but she has no idea what is happening. All Alyssa knows is that she wants her mother.

Archippe hears the door open behind her. She stands, hopeful, but it is not Lela. She gestures to the slave to stop and then, passing him, steps outside. He follows.

"Anything?" she asks.

"Nothing. No one has seen her, and no one knows where Magacles is."

"Did you talk to anyone you thought might be lying? Anyone who might know something but won't tell you."

"No, I got no sense of that."

Archippe pauses to consider before continuing.

"Find all the household slaves," she says in a cool, clipped voice. "Do it fast. Everyone who can walk. No children. Have them gather here in front of my house, right where we're standing. And tell them to remain quiet. We don't want to frighten the toddler. And here, take this."

Archippe hands the slave a small piece of goatskin covered with writing. He looks at the list—eighteen names, all women.

"You will recognize most of these women. They all live close by. Find them. Tell them Archippe, wife of Themistocles, touches their knees and pleads for their help. Tell them to come immediately to the front of my house. Tell them each to bring a knife, the largest they can handle and hide under their tunics. Make sure you tell them about the knives. And when you look for them, run as if Hades is chasing you. Now go!"

As the slave races away, Arch walks up behind his mother. He had just finished telling his two younger brothers the story of the boy who slew a fierce giant with a sling and stone, and was showing them how to throw a rock with a sling when he saw his mother giving instructions to the slave.

"Mother, what were you saying about knives?"

His mother turns to the twelve-year-old.

"Arch, you shouldn't listen to words not meant for you," she says, a little flustered and afraid of how much he might have heard. "But, well, we have a problem I need to fix. Now, I want you and your brothers to go inside and get your sister, and then the four of you go to the old woman and Alyssa, in our house. Stay with them until I come for you."

"I want to help," says the boy. "I can use a knife."

Archippe's voice turns harsh, "No, Arch. Your father told you many times you are never to point a knife or sword at anyone until you receive proper military training, and that won't happen for several more years. Do as I say. And do it now."

Archippe watches her boys go into the house. Then she takes a few deep breaths and enters.

Speaking to the old woman in a slow, soft voice, she says, "There is no doubt anymore. Lela is overdue too long. Take Alyssa to the back of the house. Keep her occupied and away from the activity here and in front of the house. Stay as calm as possible. And pray in silence."

Fortunately, Alyssa does not see the tears running down the old woman's cheeks. "I knew it was wrong," the old woman says. "The way Argos acted when that man was here. I've never seen the puppy act that way, baring his teeth and growling like a full-grown watchdog. I knew Lela shouldn't go with him, but there was nothing I could do to stop her."

Archippe shakes her head and says "Enough. Do as I said. Please."

As the old woman starts walking toward the back of the house, she hears Archippe quietly say to herself, "How can the gods allow this?

How did I let this happen?"

⁓

Lela's first sense is sound. Men's voices in the distance. Then she realizes the voices are actually close to her. Her next sensation is pain on the right side of her head and jaw. And the throbbing inside her head.

"She's a slut."

Lela tastes blood. She realizes she is breathing through her nose. She cannot take a breath through her mouth. She moves her tongue around and starts to carefully stick her tongue out, but it is blocked. The cloth covering her mouth is tight.

"She's cuckolding her husband with some hoplite associated with Miltiades." There is a laugh. "Can you imagine, Miltiades of all people? The stupid bitch. If her husband knew, he'd thank me."

Lela smells sweat. Her own.

"After the Persians finish with her, she'll never cuckold anybody again."

Lela sees a blur as she opens her eyes just a slit. She is looking at her armpit. She wants to move her head, but something tells her not to. Something tells her not to move at all.

"Sixty?"

A different voice. The slave who led Lela to Magacles.

"That's what we were told. I want you to keep count as they take her. It'll be interesting to see how long she lasts. And then how many more Persians want her when she's dead."

Lela realizes it is Magacles speaking, talking to his slave.

"What's her husband's name?" asks the slave.

"I don't remember," Magacles says contemptuously.

Lela can tell she's on her stomach. Her eyes are barely open, but she knows she is lying on straw that feels like a thousand bristly twigs. Her face is turned to the right, so her right eye can see best, but the room is dim. What little she can see is by torchlight and small oil lamps. How long has the sun been down?

"She'll deserve what she gets," says Magacles. "She's bad luck."

"Bad luck?"

"My Big Red! I should be the richest man in Athens, but when I encountered this slut, he ended up dead. The finest fighting cock in the land until she came along. Big Red will have his revenge."

The slave is silent.

"I'm about to leave," says Magacles. "Don't untie her for any reason and clean her up while I'm gone. I'll have her twice before I introduce her to our Persian guests."

Lela doesn't dare pull on her arms, but she can feel the straps around her wrists. She wonders about her feet. She can't feel any straps down there.

"How long will you be gone?" asks the slave.

"Two hours, no more than three," says Magacles. "We'll open the north gate in a little over an hour and we have to get the Persians—hah, I mean the Greek country folk—inside and back here. That will take some time. We need to be slow and casual. Everything has to look normal, unrushed."

Lela can hear Magacles' voice move around as he talks. His movement has a pattern, back and forth. He is pacing. She can see her bare arm. She can feel air pass over her body. She knows she is naked.

Lela wonders what else they did to her when they took her clothes off and tied her up. Her head, arms, and shoulders hurt. But those pains can be explained by the slave's fist and the tight straps stretching her arms. She feels no other injuries, but she cannot be sure because she has not tried to move.

"You're certain about the regular guards who were at the gate?" asks the slave.

"Small bribes work wonders," replies Magacles. "And it helped to tell the guards a stupid story they wanted to believe so they could have a break from the tedium of an all-night watch. I was very convincing when I said my friends wanted to relive their youth and guard the gate until dawn."

"You're going to be busy for the next few hours."

"Then I'll be back for my reward. Two rewards. Look at those cheeks, where they come together. Makes me drool. I hope I can control myself."

"Control yourself?"

"Not that way," says Magacles. "No controlling that. I mean resist the thrill of snapping her neck. After raping her, to twist her neck as far as it'll go and watch her eyes—then jerk. That's the thrill—the sound of the snap and the look of the eyes when they stop blinking—a dessert almost as tasty as the main course. Too bad I've decided to entertain the Persians, but we'll see. You know sometimes I just can't control myself."

The slave says nothing.

Magacles continues, "I'm leaving, so remember what I said. Clean her up before I get back."

A moment later Lela hears the door open and close. Then the light from the torch moves around the area, dims, and disappears. Lela realizes the slave has walked away with the torch. She moves her feet back and forth just enough to be certain they are not tied down. She hears the slave returning. The area around her now is lit by only two small oil lamps. She hears him blow one of them out.

"'Clean her up,'" he mutters. "That's what you non-humans do—clean her up. I am Magacles, an aristocrat, and I'm not like you, nothing like a worthless slave; I'm a *real* human. Poor garbage like you can count how many Persians have her while she's still alive. Then count how many want her when she's dead."

The slave walks around Lela and keeps talking to himself.

"I don't think so. Not this time. This time it's my turn. It'll be better for her, too. She won't suffer nearly as much. Suffocation won't take long. Easy to explain. She just stopped breathing. What could I do? And I'll clean her up just the way I was told. She won't tell Magacles anything. Can't let her tell Magacles about the fun we have—well, that *I* have. He might send me to work to death in the mines at Laurium."

The slave moves to Lela's left, and behind her. It sounds like he is kneeling down; she hears the straw crunch. She opens her eyes wide, seeing the faint light of the oil lamp against a wall. His breathing grows louder. She feels his hand on her back. The hand glides down and his fingers slide between her buttocks. It is awful. His fingers go deeper. His hand moves on to the inside of her left leg. He stops. He lets go and stands up.

Lela hears him begin to disrobe. She slowly takes the deepest breath she can. Just as slowly, she exhales. Again, the deepest breath, carefully, in and out. Then once more, filling her lungs with all the air she can inhale. The fear is inside her, but for now she has it under control. Sicinnus and Alyssa flash through her mind and she immediately banishes them. This is not their time. They cannot save her. Fury is what will save her, if she can be saved. Fury and valor.

He is naked now. She cannot see him, but she knows he is about to climb onto her. She clenches her jaw and takes another silent, deep breath. He is in for a rougher ride than he expects.

~◦

After leaving Lela and his slave, Magacles walks through Athens and arrives at the north gate. He climbs the steps to the top of the wall and walks over to his cousin Callixenus, another wealthy aristocrat who preferred Hippias to the unpredictable democracy their uncle Cleisthenes established in the tyrant's place.

"See anything?" asks Magacles.

"Nothing so far," answers Callixenus.

"Shouldn't be long."

"Any problem with the guards?"

"No. They'll return an hour before dawn, long after we finish the job."

"What about the Persian girl you told me about? Everything ready after we're done here?"

⁓

Lela hears the straw crunch again behind her. The slave is kneeling. All of her senses are heightened; she focuses on the sound of the straw crunching beside her left shoulder. It's his hand. She takes one more deep breath. A piece of straw drops on her thigh just below her left buttock. She cannot see any of this, but she knows the man must be swinging his right leg over her, momentarily balanced on his left arm.

This is her chance. This is when she must break the strap on her right wrist. This is when she will save herself or die.

Lela blasts out her breath like an animal, muffled but fierce, from deep within her body.

Her timing is perfect. The slave's right leg is above Lela's body as her right foot passes just beneath it. She is blindly aiming for his groin. She almost finds her mark, although the blow is not a direct hit. A tangential strike to his right testicle and a hard hit to his upper left thigh. He grunts, falls back, and hits the ground to her left. She wrenches the strap on her right wrist but fails to break it, excruciatingly tearing her shoulder muscle instead. She wastes no time thinking about it. Her chances are down to one—break the strap on the other wrist, or die.

She turns her head to the left, shifts her hips, and strikes at the slave's head with her left foot. A good hit. She sees blood spout from his mouth. She swipes again but misses. He falls backward, out of range.

Lela's gag stifles her cry as she yanks her left hand with all her might to break the strap.

Failure.

The slave is up with one hand on his mouth and the other hand on his groin. He glares at her and then steps toward her feet, out of sight.

Lela feels a strap coiling around her left ankle, the pulling of the leather stretching her whole body, the pounding of the stake into the ground. Then the same for her right ankle.

A moment later his face is an inch away from hers. She hears his guttural growl, "This time I won't be nice."

Lela hears his words but cannot comprehend their meaning. Her brain is frozen. She is overwhelmed by terror.

~~~

At the north gate, after Callixenus asks his question, Magacles sneers but does not answer. So Callixenus repeats himself, "What about the Persian girl?"

This time Magacles responds. "Yes, yes, everything will be ready. But you'll have to wait in line."

"What?"

"After me," Magacles says, with a leer. "Look, this is what we'll do. I want the first go, then you can take a turn, or we can have her together, whatever we want. After that I have something special planned. I promised her to the Persians."

Callixenus gives Magacles a disbelieving look. "Sixty?"

"Consider it entertainment for our guests."

"Entertainment!" Callixenus takes a step back and frowns. "That's insane. They'll tear her apart."

"So?"

"So? You're talking about . . ." Callixenus shakes his head. "I thought I knew you better."

Magacles snarls, "Since when did you become so pure?"

"Being pure has nothing to do with this." Callixenus shakes his head again. "You know I've had my share of . . . but never torture and murder. Sixty men! That's beyond brutal. Beyond anything." He looks Magacles up and down as if he were a stranger. "I'd heard rumors, but . . . you're inviting trouble. If our other men find out . . ."

"By the time they hear of it, if they ever do, it will be over. And, my dear cousin, isn't going 'beyond anything' the whole point?"

Callixenus does not respond, but his expression is clear. Once they've opened the gate, he wants nothing to do with the rest of Magacles' plan.

⁓

The slave shoves his hand underneath Lela's left breast. He squeezes. He means to inflict pain, but only partly succeeds because she is nearly catatonic. He pulls his hand away and, just as before, he swings his right leg over her and now his knees are straddling her upper thighs. He puts the palms of both hands on her shoulder blades and leans forward. This time the pain in her right shoulder is so extreme that her brain unfreezes, and she shrieks into the gag over her mouth.

The slave laughs and says, "Ah, I have your attention. Are you ready? Here I come, bitch."

The slave lets go of her shoulders. The pain eases a little but her mind stays clear. She knows exactly what is going on. She closes her eyes and waits.

"What's happening?" asks the slave.

She opens her eyes.

"What's happening?" he repeats.

She feels him lift his left leg and get off her to the right. She cannot see what he is doing.

"What's happening?" he asks a third time.

His voice is changing—it sounds higher and bewildered. She hears him walking toward her feet and then around to her left side. His stride is hurried and different, as if he is shuffling. *No*, she thinks, *more of a scuttle, a scurry.*

"What's happening?" he asks again. "You're bigger. You're growing. Everything is growing; everything is getting bigger!"

He comes into view, and she immediately sees he is shorter than before. His face is changing and he is shrinking. Forgetting her pain, she is amazed. His nose is growing larger. No, not just his nose, his whole face is elongating. And his head is flattening.

Panicking now, he screams "What's happening? What's happening? Everything is huge!"

His mouth is wrapping itself around the edge of his entire stretched-out face, and it is no longer human; it is reptilian.

He continues to shrink before her eyes. She sees him raise both arms. They are grotesque; thin as twigs with claws instead of hands—long, slender, and sharp.

"What's happeneeeee! Eeeee!"

She hears "Eeeee!" again when his rear end begins to change. Like his face, it is elongating. But this is more; something new is forming. He is growing a tail.

She knows what she is seeing is impossible. This is madness. She has gone crazy. That means the slave must still be on top of her. The images she thinks she sees must be false. She has lost her mind. She shuts her eyes and tries to lock her mind again. Everything will be over soon.

But an instant later her eyes flash open. Her shout is muffled but her eyes are fierce, "No, not yet! I am not done yet. For Alyssa and Sicinnus, I am not finished!"

She blinks, shakes her head, and looks again. The slave has become a lizard. She sees the panic in his eyes. He looks straight at her and squeaks, "Eeeee!"

Something is happening to her right wrist. No one is there, but she feels strange movements. Then a soft sound—a whisper. Someone is there. *How?* The whisper is a wordless murmur—a soothing humming. A lullaby. The voice sounds like her own. But not quite. Now the sensation at her wrist is more distinct. It is as if many sleek cords are twisting and turning around her hand, manipulating the knot in the strap. Then a similar sensation around her right ankle. She realizes her right arm and leg are free. The little lizard skitters out of sight.

She rolls to her left and, even though it hurts mightily, quickly unties her left wrist and leg. She sits up and rips the cloth away from her mouth. She wonders again if this is all a delusion. *Am I out of my mind?* She looks around the room and sees what seems to be a vague apparition of a young woman floating away from her and passing through the doorway to the next room. There she sees still more insanity.

The floor just beyond the doorway appears to be rippling like water. In the dim light she cannot make out exactly what is happening, but the lizard is terrified. Squeaking its high, shrill "Eeeee!" over and over, it races back and forth across the floor behind her. The mysterious movements in the next room are blocking its only way out.

She concentrates and opens her eyes wide. All the small undulations suggest she is looking at water, but the continual twisting and turning hint at something else. She catches her breath when she realizes what she is seeing. She has always been terrified of snakes, and the other room is full of them. She remembers when she and Sicinnus were young and he wiggled a live snake in her face. She stopped breathing until she fainted. He never did that again. But now everything is different. She is not afraid. There are hundreds of snakes in the next room, and the door is wide open. And she is not afraid.

Lela looks up from the writhing floor. The apparition of the young woman is clearer now. She stands fully materialized among the snakes. The mysterious figure is holding dozens of snakes in her arms, stroking them as they slide over and under one another.

The apparition looks down at the floor, so Lela also looks down, and her amazement gives way to awe. An enormous snake is slowly appearing. The snake's head is huge, and its body is as thick as a large log. Lela looks up to see the image of the young woman fading. The other snakes are also fading. Soon the apparition and all the smaller snakes are gone, or at least Lela can no longer see them. But the gigantic snake is there and coming closer. Lela feels completely alert, but calm. Fascinated. And her fascination with this great snake gives her a peculiar pleasure.

The panicking lizard tries to scamper up the wall but falls back to the ground. Another desperate effort, and it gets a little farther up this time. It stops and takes one slow and careful step, then another, and then it falls.

Lela watches the snake watch the lizard. She cannot be sure, but she thinks the snake is smiling. The snake slithers over to a different wall and easily climbs it. Then it pauses, its head against the ceiling with several feet of its tail still on the floor. It turns around and just as easily descends to the ground. Both she and the snake look to the lizard. It is frozen in terror. Lela smiles.

"Eeeee!" squeaks the lizard.

"Sssss," hisses the snake.

The lizard runs over and presses against Lela's right thigh. Her first thought is that just a moment ago this slave-lizard dared to terrify her. Now it is her turn. But she cannot make a fist with her right hand.

She looks at the snake inching toward them. The snake is looking directly at her. Its eyes are perfectly round. The black pupils are thin vertical slits surrounded by glossy green irises. Reptilian eyes, but she detects something more. *Those eyes; I know them. Where have I seen them before? When? Whose?*

She snaps out of her thoughts and nods at the snake.

Neither she nor the lizard sees the quick movement. She only feels it as the snake streaks along the outside of her leg. Then it raises its head to the level of Lela's face. Only a few inches separate them. Again, she is entranced by the snake's huge eyes. Then she sees the thing wiggling frantically in its mouth.

It is the lizard, thrashing. The snake has partly swallowed the creature head first, leaving its legs and tail exposed. With a shake of the snake's head, the lizard's legs also disappear. The only thing left is its whirling tail.

Lela and the great snake study each other's faces. The snake is definitely smiling, she is sure of it; she smiles back. The snake's head stays motionless as the little tail spins. The snake is waiting for her. She nods her head again. The lizard's tail splats onto the ground next to the young Persian. Gore from the tail spreads over the floor.

She looks back up, but the snake is already gone. She jumps up to her left, using her left side because of the pain in her right shoulder. She also wants to avoid stepping on the oozing, still-wiggling tail. She moves around the dim room and finds what she is after—the tunic Magacles and the slave stripped off her. She also had sandals but does not want to take the time to find them.

She starts for the door, then stops. She does not want to do it, but she cannot resist. She turns around. The lizard and snake—it is just not possible. She thinks, *Am I still in a dream, even now? Maybe still unconscious? Dead? Is this what happens when you're dead? Or maybe dying? That might explain it. Dying—it seems like a long time but perhaps it's just an instant.* She looks at the gooey blob on the ground. The lizard's tail is still there. She cautiously walks over to it. She will not touch it, but she wants to examine it carefully. She squats down for a good close look. The tail jerks violently. Lela jumps up so quickly, she nearly falls.

Enough. She does not care if she is in a dream, or unconscious, or dead. She has to get out of here. She is through the door and racing as fast as she can, holding her right arm next to her body. Nothing will slow her down now. No power on earth will stop her.

She is halfway home when the realization hits her. The snake's eyes—intense and beautiful. The eyes of the old hag who was begging with the girl. The beggars she and Archi gave all their money to when they were leaving the agora. The snake's eyes were the hag's eyes.

⁓

Magacles is pacing the top of the wall near the north gate. The moon has begun to set, and it is time for the Persians to show themselves; he wants to be conspicuous to anyone who might be watching outside. He walks over to Callixenus and, in silence, they scan the deepening darkness. Moments later, just as the moon vanishes behind the western hills, they see it—a little flame moving in the shape of a triangle. Callixenus reaches down to a small metal box holding hot coals and inserts a bundle of twigs and straw, then, using a leather strap attached to the box, lifts it over the wall. The coals soon ignite the bundle and Callixenus makes a triangular motion with the lamp. Callixenus and Magacles see another triangle of flame answer them in the distance.

Magacles leans over to Callixenus and whispers, "I'm going down. Signal me when they're at the gate."

Magacles goes down the steps to the ground and quietly tells four men to stand by. He moves far enough away from the gate to have a good view of Callixenus and waits, expecting the signal. Then, out of the corner of his eye he detects movement. He turns and sees someone running toward him. There is more movement behind the runner—more runners. *Betrayal!* Then he realizes the first runner is a woman; they are all women. Now he sees the first woman clearly. The mistress of the Persian slave he plans to rape.

She stops in front of him, panting and glaring. She stands between Magacles and the wall. The other women quickly arrive, and they all take up positions behind Archippe with their backs to the wall.

"Archippe, what can you all possibly be doing here? Women of repute, out late at night, alone! What will your husbands think when they hear?"

"We don't care what they think! We care about the gate! Where are the guards?"

"They are taking a little break from the tedium of the watch. Surely you cannot resent them for that. My friends and I are fully capable of watching it for a while."

"Since when do guards take a break from their assigned posts?" Archippe's voice is quivering, which she hopes sounds more like anger than the dread she feels.

"There's nothing to fear." Magacles' voice is oily and smooth. He is used to dealing with frightened women. "I take full responsibility. I told them to take a break. My friends and I will watch the gate until they return."

"On whose authority?"

"My own!" Magacles straightens up and sets his shoulders back. "Everyone in Athens knows and honors Magacles and the Alcmaeonid family. So the answer to your question is that I, on my own authority, allowed the guards to take a break from their assigned duties. No other authority is needed."

Archippe's mind is shouting at her. *He lies! He's bluffing.* She gathers her strength to speak with conviction despite her fear of him. "In that case," gesturing to the women gathered behind her, "we will help you watch the gate."

"You should all be home with your children, where you belong. Watching the gate is men's work. Your services are not needed here."

"No, it is *your* services that are not needed. We will watch the gate until the real guards return. You and your men are dismissed. Tell them to leave!"

Archippe knows she is speaking too quickly, too shrilly; she must find some way to govern her fear.

Magacles looks at the top of the wall and sees Callixenus watching them. He was probably ready to give Magacles the signal, but now realizes there is a problem.

Magacles' voice turns menacing, "Archippe, you are playing a dangerous game."

"You're half wrong and half right," says Archippe, slowing her voice and speaking with great emphasis; miraculously, this seems to stifle at least some of her terror, "We're not playing a game, but what we are doing is dangerous, very dangerous, for you and for me."

"I suggest you think again. The danger is yours; there's no danger for me."

"This time you're entirely wrong. There is danger for you. Great danger!"

Magacles leans toward her until his face is so close she can smell his breath. "I do not take kindly to insults, especially from women. Archippe, I am tiring of this. You have one last chance before I give my men their orders. Depart now."

"We will not!" Archippe shouts. "What are you going to do, order your men to kill us? Even men with morals like yours will hesitate before slaughtering the city's women!"

"How dare you! You're out of your mind. If we have to, we will remove you by force. We'll try not to hurt you, of course, but you will be removed."

"I count you and your men at six! I brought more than a dozen women with me, and others are coming. We have more than twice your number. And we have something else."

Archippe pulls a long knife out from beneath her tunic and raises it high above her head. Then she lowers it and points it at Magacles' throat. Leveling the weapon at her enemy, and seeing him flinch as she does so, she realizes she is changing. She feels powerful.

Almost as one, the other women take out their knives as well.

"All of us are armed!" she says loudly. Her words come clearly now. "Unlike the women you have ruined—and worse. We can and *will* defend ourselves."

Magacles takes a deep breath and pretends to ignore the knife. "You're forcing me into a corner. That's a mistake."

"The mistake is yours. You put yourself into that corner. What I'm doing is giving you a way to save yourself. Get out of here with your men. If not, go ahead and give your order. But before you do, one of us has something to tell you—*and your men*."

Gesturing toward her right with the knife, Archippe says, "Over there."

Magacles looks over as Lela steps forward. Her arm is in an improvised sling.

"How—?" sputters Magacles.

"I'll let your slave answer that, if you can find him," Lela answers. "But if you find him, you should be very careful."

"I have no idea what you're talking about," Magacles says, barely managing a contemptuous look.

"So you say," Archippe retorts. "But now Lela has something to announce. I'm sure your men will be interested. It's one thing to hear rumors about what you do to women. It's another to hear the facts from the woman herself. How will your friends react when they hear what you do to women *after* you assault them? When they realize how evil you truly are?"

"What's happening?" The loud voice startles Archippe, but she never takes her eyes from Magacles.

It is Callixenus, who has come down from the top of the wall and is walking toward them, past the other women. On seeing Archippe's knife, he stops.

"I've heard that question many times tonight," says Lela. "The answer is something very strange."

"You don't belong here." says Callixenus, "Your husbands won't approve."

"Our husbands are at Marathon, where you would be too, if you were worth anything," Archippe says. Her voice becomes calmer, harder, even taunting. "Magacles, a moment ago you talked about playing games. This is becoming a game, and it's time to end it one way or another. Be gone from here or Lela will tell her story."

"Who is Lela?" asks Callixenus.

"Magacles will explain later if you're all still alive."

"Still *alive*?" asks Callixenus.

Archippe turns to Lela and calls out, "Enough! Lela—speak."

"Wait!" shouts Magacles.

Magacles and Archippe stare at each other across Archippe's knife.

"Very well," says Magacles. "We will leave."

"What?" exclaims Callixenus. "But the plan . . . out there . . ." Callixenus catches himself too late.

"Out *there*!" Archippe shouts in triumph. "Traitors! The gods condemn you."

"Callixenus," Magacles says, his mind working rapidly, "I'm leaving and . . ." He stops when he spots a rapid movement off to the side. Archippe looks over and gasps. Her oldest son is running headlong toward them.

"Arch, what are you doing here?" Archippe cries, her fear returning in a sudden flood.

The boy appears to be racing toward her, but he swerves instead toward Magacles and, swinging something over his head, brings his arm down and around in a whirling circle until a heavy object at the end of his sling slams into Magacles' groin.

With a grunting gasp, Magacles' body rises into the air and then collapses onto the ground.

"Arch, what are you doing?" Archippe cries out again.

The boy runs up to his mother and grasps her tunic.

She hugs her son to her, suddenly feeling weak, and looks down at Magacles, who is on his knees and bent over with his head in the dirt. He is gagging and convulsing.

"Is it all right, Mother?" Arch asks. "I heard everything Lela told you; I was there when she got back to our house. Will Father be proud? He never said anything about not using a rock."

Arch seems suddenly afraid he has done something terribly wrong.

Lela walks up to Archippe and her son.

"Do you want my knife?" Archippe asks her, gesturing toward the groaning traitor.

The young woman looks at Magacles and watches as he starts vomiting over and over. She says, "Look underneath him."

Archippe and Callixenus both see the spreading pool of blood flowing from Magacles' groin.

"Even if he survives, he's ruined for life," says Lela.

"We must steady ourselves," says Archippe, still holding her son. "We are here to protect the gates. There are at least four other men besides Callixenus. They may be stunned right now, but we don't want to deal with them even if we can defeat them. We need them to leave."

Without being asked, Lela takes Arch by the hand and steps back. Archippe turns and smiles at her son, and then at Lela. Both mothers sense the depth of their alliance and the strength of their determination.

Archippe turns back to Callixenus, who is standing as still as a corpse, and raises her gleaming knife. "Now it's your turn." The threat in her voice is unmistakable. "Either haul this monster away from here or there'll be another mess on the ground between us, and you know where it will come from."

Magacles lets out a burbling whine. With his head still in the dirt, he reaches out a hand toward Callixenus, who hesitates, then hoists him to his feet moaning in pain. The two of them start hobbling away.

As they depart, Archippe shouts, "Our women will be watching every gate in the walls. If any of your men are foolish enough to try to open one to our enemies, we'll kill them. Do not doubt us."

With young Arch still holding Lela's hand, the two women turn and stare at each other. Lela's face radiates confidence because of what the women just accomplished. But Archippe looks worried. Her thoughts have already leapt ahead to Marathon and what may be happening there.

Her son looks up at her, doubt still on his face. She remembers she never answered his question. "Yes, Arch, it's all right," she says, suddenly exhausted after the drama of the night. "You were brave. Your father will be proud."

Looking deep into her son's eyes, Archippe reaches out and firmly puts both hands on his shoulders. "And I am very proud."

She does not want to say more; she does not want to let go. But steadying herself so her voice will neither waver nor crack, she says, "Arch, you are becoming a man."

CHAPTER THIRTY-SEVEN

FIRE WITHOUT SMOKE

Themistocles' fire is roaring hot. He likes them that way. A fire too intense for other men is just right for him.

The sun is long down, and several men stand around the blaze at a fair distance from its scorching heat. On one side Miltiades and Aristides are talking with Callimachus. On the other, Aeschylus, Kye, Arrichion, and Phidippides confer quietly behind Themistocles, who stares into the flames, deep in thought.

A silent figure appears out of the darkness. He walks up behind his master and softly says, "I need to speak with you."

Themistocles knows the voice well and turns to tell Sicinnus he can speak now. But seeing his man's expression, Themistocles changes his mind and walks with him away from the fire.

While they are gone, Callimachus growls to Miltiades and Aristides, "Damn their horses. The Persians didn't take the bait."

"The day after tomorrow the Spartans should be here," says Aristides.

"A help," replies Callimachus. "But not enough."

"You're not thinking about retreating to Athens?" Miltiades blurts out.

The warleader avoids looking at him when he answers, "I will not let our hoplites be slaughtered without any chance of victory." Miltiades glances at Aristides, but says nothing.

With a loud whoop, Themistocles returns with Sicinnus right behind him. Themistocles approaches the fire and starts throwing handfuls of straw on the flames. He does the same with some twigs, then more kindling, and finally larger sticks of wood. Next, he grabs a long piece that is sticking out of the fire and points its flaming end to the black sky, like a torch. He plunges the burning end back into the fire and stirs and pokes it around so vigorously that the other men begin to wonder whether his mind has snapped.

"That's the way I like it!" he shouts. "Really hot! No smoke—none at all. Red hot! Then orange! Then, if it has enough character, blue within white. And no smoke! As hot as you can make it!"

Just as Callimachus is about to walk over and try to bring the little drama to a conclusion, Themistocles turns toward him. Still grasping the flaming stick, he announces, "Fellow hoplites! I just received news from a worthy hoplite who will be with us in the phalanx. He gave me the news so I could have the honor of informing our Polemarch."

Pointing the torch at Callimachus, Themistocles continues, "But I would prefer to hear the news-bearer make the announcement himself." Moving the torch in a quick half-circle that leaves a trail of sparks in the darkness, he points to Sicinnus and shouts, "Your announcement, hoplite!"

Taking a step toward Callimachus, Sicinnus says in a strong voice, "Polemarch, the horses are away."

All of the men start to speak but the warleader raises his hands, for quiet.

"You are certain?" he asks.

"I am certain," Sicinnus replies.

"All the horses?" asks Callimachus.

"When our spies left their view of the Persians' loading area, three barges with horses had already embarked, and two more were loaded and ready to leave," says Sicinnus. "All the other horses were waiting in the area. And many of the riders were boarding. Their total count was about a thousand horses."

"Sounds like every single one," says Themistocles. "One thousand is a nice round number."

Callimachus snorts and says, "You count your numbers and I pray to the gods—both worthy pursuits."

Callimachus takes a few steps back so he can see and speak to everyone. "The Persians have just made the mistake we've been waiting for. You know what we face when we go to battle, so I will be brief. Without the cavalry, the Persians still have two big advantages. Their archers. We have a surprise for them, but how well our surprise will work remains to be seen. And the number of their fighters. For that we have no surprise, except that we will actually attack. Many Persians will be stunned by our sheer folly. But their shock will last less time than it takes a spark from Themistocles' fire to go out. Their advantage in numbers has been described more than once as 'absurd' and that description is accurate.

"We have our advantages: our bronze armor and our phalanx. In the same way we have never confronted anything like these Persian hordes, they have never confronted our phalanx. And finally, our greatest advantage—our valor."

Callimachus pauses and slowly turns to each man, one after the other. Then he peers into the fire and says, with his voice raised, "We assemble on the plain at dawn."

He turns and starts to walk away, then stops, turns back to Sicinnus, and asks, "What is the Persian word for 'fire'?"

Surprised by the question, Sicinnus answers, "Atar. Atar comes from the Prophet Zoroaster and it means Holy Fire used for the worship of their God."

"Holy Fire," repeats Callimachus. "I like that."

"Anyone who doesn't speak Greek," Themistocles interjects, with a smirk, "is a barbarian."

"We all have some barbarian inside us," the warleader adds. "Some of us more than others."

Callimachus turns again and walks off. The other men glance at one another, wondering what Callimachus and Themistocles were talking about. Finally, everyone goes their separate ways.

A few moments later Themistocles and Sicinnus are walking together. Sicinnus considers asking Themistocles why Callimachus wanted to know the Persian word for fire, but decides to skip the question and instead says, "Thank you. As you said, it was an honor to inform the warleader. Now, when the other men tell their stories, they will mention my name."

"No need to thank me," says Themistocles. "Just consider it an early bribe."

"Bribe?"

"Yes, you know the meaning."

"Oh, I see; we're playing hide the ball. Will it speed things along if I drop to my knees and beg?"

"Look," says Themistocles, "I want you to be free, but I don't want you to leave us either. Archi will be miserable if you all leave. I'm trying to protect myself. You know as well as I do there's nothing worse for a man than a miserable wife."

"Well, I can tell you this. If I told Lela we'd leave you and Archi, I think she might castrate me in my sleep."

"Oh, that's good to hear," laughs Themistocles. "Talk about motivation. That's better than any bribe I can think of."

Sicinnus comes to an abrupt halt, so Themistocles also stops.

"I want to tell you something," says Sicinnus.

"I'm listening."

"I recently mentioned a family secret I wanted to tell Lela before I told you."

"Yes. I remember."

"I want to tell you the secret now. There's no reason I can't tell you first. It doesn't break any oath. I just wanted to tell Lela first, but now I want to tell you."

"Why me first, now?"

"Because of tomorrow. We may not both survive."

Themistocles asks, "So if you die and I survive, you want me to tell Lela the secret?"

Sicinnus smiles. "I believe I will survive tomorrow, but I want you to know the secret now."

"All right. You have my attention."

"Almost two years ago, Lela was in danger of dying from the birth of Alyssa."

"I remember."

"You held my hand."

"I trust you honored my request and told no one about that?"

Sicinnus smiles again. "Your understandable and silly request continues to be honored."

"Thank the gods," says Themistocles, wryly. "The silliest requests are the ones most important to honor. You were saying about your secret?"

"I prayed a lot when everyone thought Lela was dying. I prayed to every god and goddess I could think of. If I lost Lela I was going to be lost myself, and what would happen to the baby? I was shattering like an imperfect bowl tossed out by a potter."

"I was there. I saw it."

"Then the goddess Demeter came to me. She made a promise to me and then made the strangest requests—more than requests, they were demands."

"Strange demands from gods and goddesses are normal, or so I'm told."

"I know your attitude toward religion. All I can do is tell you what Demeter said, and I believe it is true."

"I am listening. And I'm not making light of what you say."

"Demeter promised a long life for Lela. And the same for the baby and me. And the happiness in our lives would exceed the sadness. Demeter then made three demands for her promise to be fulfilled. The strangest demand was that our baby's first word must be the name of Demeter's daughter."

"Persephone?"

Sicinnus smiles and says, "That's exactly what I assumed. Demeter didn't actually say her daughter's name. She just told me to softly and continually repeat her daughter's name in Alyssa's ear. So, based on my assumption, I constantly whispered 'Persephone' to Alyssa, especially when she was about to drift off to sleep."

"Demeter's other two demands?"

"The second was that Demeter's promise and demands must be kept secret, even from Lela, until Alyssa says her first word. Finally, I must remain faithful to Lela but not make love with her until our child spoke her first word."

"So it's been over a year?" Themistocles looks stunned.

"Almost two. Lela and I stopped when her pregnancy became troubled before Alyssa was born. But now, when Phidippides arrived here a few days ago, he brought news that our daughter had said her first word."

"Well, that must be a joy for you. And you must be anxious, very anxious, to get back to Athens."

Sicinnus laughs softly as Themistocles continues. "Persephone—quite a mouthful for a baby's first word."

Sicinnus' laugh becomes louder and he says, "That's exactly what I thought from the beginning. It was a real worry. How is a baby going to learn to pronounce such a word? It seemed impossible. And all that time I failed to remember your constant refrain about assumptions."

"That they are the mothers of mistakes," says Themistocles.

"Exactly," says Sicinnus. "Alyssa's first word was 'Kore.'"

Themistocles is silent, taking this in. Finally, he says, "You spend well over a year whispering the word 'Persephone' into Alyssa's ear and when she finally speaks her first word is 'Kore'—the ancient name for Persephone?"

"Gods and goddesses do act in strange ways."

"So most everyone says," says Themistocles. "But what few people talk about is that all gods and goddesses—all of them—are jealous;

they demand to be worshiped and want to be worshiped in their own special way."

"What you're saying is Demeter's demands of me were the ways she wanted to be worshiped?"

"How she wanted to be worshiped and how she wanted you to prove your devotion. Once Demeter was satisfied, she solved the impossible problem in a way gods and goddesses supposedly can. She helped Alyssa say a word a toddler can pronounce—a word with a meaning identical to your mistaken assumption."

Sicinnus nods. "It's indeed strange."

"And this is one of those times when the strangeness is favorable. Demeter seems to be pleased with you. That might be helpful tomorrow. Stay close to me in the phalanx. I won't mind if a little of the favor rubs off on me; I could use the protection."

Sicinnus smiles, shaking his head in pity. "I'm afraid my master is going soft."

The two friends laugh like a pair of young boys.

CHAPTER THIRTY-EIGHT

THE CHARGE

A man's inner preparation for battle begins around age three. A little boy sees and hears stories. The seeing comes first because he does not comprehend the words. He sees his father and other men talking, sometimes raising their voices and waving their arms. He sees their eyes brighten, their gestures quicken. Even when they shout, the boy can tell they are holding something back; he can sense their restrained excitement. They seem to want to yell at the top of their lungs. They keep using a word he does not yet understand—valor. The men seem to have so much fun and the boy wants to be part of it.

But sometimes the men seem sad when they talk. Their sadness confuses him. How can such fun ever be sad? The boy also is confused by his mother's behavior. When the men talk at home, they are in his mother's domain. She ought to join the men's talk, but she seldom does. In fact, when the men start shouting and shaking their fists, his mother usually leaves the room. The boy does not understand her. Perhaps she does not understand the men.

As the years pass, the men's words take on meaning, but a boy's path can be long and challenging. To truly understand valor is not easy. Eventually, the boy reaches the age to start military training—eighteen, when he becomes an ephebe. Two years later he is ready to join the phalanx as a hoplite—to fight in unison, shoulder-to-shoulder, in a formation so tight that the men's overlapping shields protect one another while their spears do their deadly work.

After the first phalanx battle, some of the young men realize that when they were boys, their mothers understood something they did not. War is more than excitement, much more, and valor can invite vainglory. After more battles, more young men come to appreciate their mothers' wisdom. Some men die before they ever understand. Some grow old without learning anything, so they still know nothing when death finally claims them.

The men who survive their early years in the phalanx discover what it really takes to fight a battle. Some are thinkers, some are not. But in the phalanx, intellectual prowess is not what counts. In the phalanx, what matters most is each man's commitment to hold his ground. That is the imperative. Simple to say, not at all simple to do. Greek men who live long enough understand that imperative better than men anywhere else on earth.

⁓

It is an hour before dawn. Kye and Arrichion are helping each other put on their heavy armor. When a man dresses himself he often thinks nothing about it. But consciously or unconsciously, dressing for battle can profoundly affect him, especially when his armor and weapons have a combined weight of almost half his body. The sweaty effort makes him grit his teeth. As he struggles with the straps and fittings, he gets irritable and swears. But when he finishes the work, he changes again. He cannot see himself, but he sees his fellow hoplites. They are frightening, every one of them, so he smiles, knowing he looks just like them.

Unlike most other hoplites, neither Kye nor Arrichion are drinking wine as they dress. Kye would like a hefty swig or two but he is too worried about his partner. This is Arrichion's first battle, and Kye plans to keep a close eye on him so he needs to stay as lucid as possible. He will wait until after the battle, and then he will have his share of wine and more.

Also unlike some other hoplites, their sets of arms—panoplies—are complete and well made. Every hoplite must provide his own panoply, and

Kye's and Arrichion's families can afford the full array, including heavy bronze Corinthian helmets, cuirasses to cover their torsos, and greaves to wrap their shins from knee to ankle. Each of them also has a spear, a short sword to strap to their hips, and a thick wooden shield coated with bronze.

The partners are at odds. Kye says, "Don't just do something because I do it; it doesn't always make sense. You need to wear the greaves. They provide important protection against hits and slashes to the legs. Most of the hoplites will be wearing them. But some of us can't run in them. We learned that in our drills. The greaves hurt too much for some of us. It's how our legs are shaped. They hurt me, but they don't hurt you."

"But I don't want to be treated like I'm afraid, as if I need someone to constantly watch over me."

"Arrichion, stop it. Aeschylus, Themistocles, Callimachus—they'd all say the same thing I am. This has nothing to do with valor. It has to do with using your head. It's ridiculous. Stop it."

"All right, I'll wear the damn greaves."

"You're really stubborn!"

"Just like you!"

"Whatever you say. Now strap them around your shins. Put them on first because after you put on the cuirass, it'll be hard to bend over."

Arrichion does as he is told, then reaches over to pick up the four pieces of Kye's bronze cuirass. At twenty-five pounds, this is the heaviest part of the panoply. It consists of a breastplate, a cover to protect the back, and two side plates, all held together with hinges.

"Let's see how you look in this," says Arrichion.

After putting on his cuirass and attaching the hinges, Kye flexes his shoulders to make the plates as comfortable as possible.

"Your turn," says Kye.

Kye studies Arrichion's face as they work on the second cuirass. Kye sees what he expects but decides to wait for the right moment. Both men pick up their helmets and look at the oval eye-openings with their malevolent, otherworldly appearance. Based on appearance alone, Greek hoplites are the most terrifying warriors in the world. Encountering a hoplite is like confronting a monstrous creature with a metal head, straight from the Underworld.

They run their hands over the stiff horsehair crests on top of the helmets. Straight up and barely flexible, the narrow crests run from front to back. Most Greeks are shorter than five and a half feet, and they know the taller a man appears, the more fearsome he seems.

Seeing Arrichion still stroking his helmet's red crest, Kye decides to say his piece. "Remember when we were about to start the quick march from Athens and you met Themistocles for the first time?"

"Of course," his friend answers without looking up.

"And when he asked you what you would do in the phalanx when the man in front of you shits?"

"I remember."

"It reminded me of something Aeschylus told me several years ago. We were helping each other with our armor, just like now. Aeschylus started talking about fear. It was my first time in the phalanx."

Arrichion stops stroking his helmet's crest and looks up at Kye.

"Aeschylus also talked about shitting in battle, just as Themistocles did," Kye continues. "He laughed, sort of, but I knew what he was saying was more than a joke. We don't learn about it when we train as an ephebe. And not in our practice drills. But in battle, it's all over the place. And a man doesn't know he's going to do it until it happens."

"Why are you telling me this?" asks Arrichion.

"Because there's something I want you to know. I shat myself once, in the phalanx."

"Oh!" exclaims his friend. "You never told me."

"It's not something I go around talking to everyone about."

"I'm not everyone."

"Of course you're not. And I'm telling you now. What's more, it didn't happen my first time. It was my second time in the phalanx. Aeschylus laughed his head off. Then he stopped laughing and got serious. He told me to shake it off. Shitting means nothing. What counts is holding your ground and the line. Shitting has nothing to do with valor. He said he himself shat more than once over the years. He said he expects he'll do it again; he just doesn't know when."

"Aeschylus!" exclaims Arrichion.

"My big, brave brother. But don't tell him I told you."

"Are you saying he's afraid?"

"Yes. He has it well under control, I'm sure, but the fear is there."

"Themistocles?" asks Arrichion after considering.

"The same as Aeschylus."

"Callimachus?"

Kye pauses to think and then says, "Aeschylus says the fear is always there in the phalanx. All normal men feel it. But when you ask about Callimachus, you're asking about a man who is not normal."

"He's our Polemarch."

"I know, and I mean no disrespect. He has my highest admiration. All I'm saying is that you don't become the warleader by being normal. Among all of us, the strangest man I know is Themistocles. His mind is a wonder. Not as smart as Aeschylus, but far more mysterious. However, when it comes to war, Callimachus is even stranger than Themistocles."

"I'm beginning to realize all of us are pretty strange," says Arrichion.

"My brother would agree with that," says Kye. "Themistocles too, I'm sure. But enough talk about shitting in the phalanx."

"That's not what we're really talking about, is it?"

"No, it's not," says Kye. "Still, we've talked enough. As Aeschylus says, it's time for both of us to shake it off."

"One more thought. Last night your brother said you're a good judge of character. I trust he knows the same is true about me."

"He knows."

Kye pauses and takes a deep breath. They look at each other in silence for a long moment.

"If we go down this path I'm going to start blubbering," says Kye. "Let's wait till tonight when we'll get really drunk."

"Yes, tonight will come soon enough," says Arrichion. "Besides, I want to see what you look like in your full panoply. Grab your shield, spear, and sword."

"You too."

As they pick up their broad shields, Kye says, "Light as a feather, only fifteen pounds."

"Yet when they're lined up in the phalanx," says Arrichion, thoughtfully, "with their edges almost touching, they make us invincible."

"Almost. As invincible as men can be. Now let's see how you look. Sheathe your sword and stick the spike end of your spear in the ground so the tip points to the sky."

Kye circles and inspects Arrichion.

"Speaking of men, I think you're no longer one of us," says Kye. "You're a god."

"Hah, which one?"

"Which one do you think? A frightening god—Ares, the God of War."

"And you too look like a god. Apollo."

The two men stand silent, face to face, shield to shield, in their terrifying war gear, their spears aloft, like creatures risen from the deepest depths of the earth to do battle under an alien sky.

Kye grins at his friend and says, "Let's go!"

⁓

As the sun begins to rise, the Greeks are streaming from the hills down onto the plain. The men all know their positions in the phalanx, and the right flank starts to take shape near the sea.

The Persian camp comes alive. A soldier reports to Datis as Hippias rapidly walks up.

"Commander, it looks like all ten thousand Greeks are coming down from the hills," says the soldier.

"You know what to do," replies Datis. "Form up the archers and assemble the men. Left flank near the water."

"What do you make of it?" Hippias asks.

"I don't know yet. One thing is certain; it would be madness for them to attack. We can't take any chances, but I don't think they're that crazy or stupid."

"And if you're wrong?"

"If they really are out of their minds, they'll die," Datis says with a shrug. "All of them. No exceptions, no mercy."

The Greek phalanx quickly begins to form up, stretching from the sea, eight lines deep, each line more than half a mile long and holding more than twelve hundred men. After forming up, they reorganize; the hoplites in the center of the last four rows do an about-face and walk farther to the rear. Once there, this group splits into two sections, half moving left, the rest right. The maneuvers cause a cloud of sand, dirt, and dust to be kicked up, so they are largely invisible to the Persians a mile away.

At the orders of their commander, the Persian forces bunch together in typical fashion—archers in front with the greatest mass of men in the center behind the bowmen. Toward the left and right flanks, the number decreases. But even to the far left and right, the thinnest depths of the Persian ranks are deeper than anything the Greeks can muster.

If the Athenians attack, Datis will be immediately behind the archers in the center of the line and in front of most of his men.

The Persians' typical formations are well known to Miltiades, which means Callimachus knows them, too. On the Greek side, there are only four rows in the center now instead of the usual eight, with twelve rows in the flanks. Callimachus has arranged the hoplites so the weaker center of the phalanx will face the Persians' greatest strength. For a normal man, this tactic would be illogical. But Callimachus is not a normal man.

As the hoplites finish forming up, most of the men strike similar poses. Kye and Arrichion put the bottom edge of their shields on the ground and lean them against their legs. They stick their spears in the ground, butt-spikes downward and tips toward the sky, and tilt their helmets back atop their heads.

The two partners look at each other and nod, trying not to show how anxious they feel. They have been taught that this is the time to focus on valor and glory. But right now, each is more concerned for the other.

Callimachus marches out in front of the phalanx. He will offer no speeches; those were made earlier by the leaders of the ten tribes. His purpose here is to be seen. His sure stride shows fierce conviction. His chin juts forward.

The Polemarch turns toward the men and looks up and down the lines three times. Then he walks forward to approach the center of the front line. Waiting there side by side are Themistocles and Aristides, the leaders of the two tribes designated to hold the center of the phalanx. Behind Themistocles and Aristides stand three more rows of hoplites. Only three.

Callimachus says, "Today your tribes have the highest honor, and the two of you will fight in the phalanx in positions of greatest valor."

Aristides responds, "You honor us, but we all know I speak the truth when I say you, Polemarch, will hold the position of greatest valor."

"Aristides speaks the truth, as always," says Themistocles.

"You know the plan," says Callimachus. "When the Persians release their arrows and we make our move, our shields must stay together and our lines must stay straight. When we clash and go hand to hand, even men of your quality will find it hard—very hard—to do what I have asked of you. All your instincts will urge you to do the opposite. You and your tribes will be in an impossible position. You will not be able to hold your ground, and you *must* step back. That is the only way to save yourselves, your tribes and, ultimately, Athens. When the time comes, remember that. Resist the enemy as valiantly as you always do, but accept the inevitable. You must step back and endure. Listen for the trumpet's double-blasts on my orders. We will be coming for you. Keep your tribes together and stay alive until the double-blasts."

Themistocles' reply is firm. "Today is our day and your instructions will be followed without exception."

"Both of you know that danger and valor grab hold of each other," says Callimachus. "If the grip is firm enough, perhaps glory follows. I don't expect to see either of you in the Underworld anytime soon."

Callimachus abruptly turns around and walks out in front of the men again. Then he turns to march toward his position at the far right of the front line, near the water's edge. Themistocles and Aristides look at each other but say nothing about the warleader's words.

~&

While Callimachus is marching, far from Marathon another proud being is strutting in his banquet hall. Atop Mount Olympus, Zeus walks heavily among the assembled gods and goddesses, who are stuffing themselves with ambrosia and drinking nectar to excess, as always. Hebe, the cupbearer to the gods and goddesses, is even busier than usual.

Hera sits at the side of the hall, angrily watching her husband; how many of her favorite Greeks must go to Hades this day to keep her thunder god amused?

Zeus slams his foot down and announces, "Gods and goddesses, our entertainment today will be better than usual. Watch and enjoy."

~&

Callimachus takes his position in the phalanx. He looks down the long line of hoplites to his left, and then turns to look straight toward the enemy. His mind flies to his wife as it always does just before he gives the order. He has never told anyone this—about how present she becomes at such moments—including her. And just as quickly and inevitably, she vanishes. He is ready.

He looks across the plain toward the huge army of Persians a mile away, and past the Persians to the lush greenery of the Great Marsh and the beach where the moored ships wait. He curls his upper lip into a strange smile, then opens his mouth as wide as it will stretch and bellows like an enraged bull. The trumpet next to him blasts once. Ten thousand hoplites step forward as one, and begin to march.

Datis turns to Hippias and snaps, "Old man, get on a boat; this is no place for you. We have killing to tend to and you'll be in the way. The Greeks are out of their minds. In two hours they'll all be dead. Today, the Great King's empire expands west."

As Hippias turns toward a ship and begins to walk away, he mutters, "For once Datis is totally correct. This is no place for me, and the Greeks are mad."

The Greek phalanx moves forward, and all the hoplites' spears point up. They are ten feet long with an iron spearhead, counterbalanced at the opposite end by a bronze butt-spike. The butt-spike is called the lizard killer, but today it will serve a more important purpose as a backup weapon if the spear shaft breaks. The butt-spike also finishes off fallen enemies. A short downward thrust does the job.

As the hoplites march, they await the trumpet's next blast.

~⌒

Looking down from Mount Olympus, the gods and goddesses consider the armies on Marathon's plain. They compare the Greek and

Persian formations. From on high, the most dramatic difference between the opposing sides is obvious—the vast Persian horde makes the Greek phalanx look almost insignificant.

The other clear difference is their apparel. The Greeks' bronze armor is formidable, but it looks modest compared to the flamboyance of the Persians—a bright menagerie of fighters made up of different peoples and races from throughout the Great King's empire.

The Ethiopians wear lion and leopard skins and cover their heads with the scalps of horses. The men paint themselves red and white and carry long bows very different from the short recursive bows the Scythians carry. Then there are the Phoenicians in garments of Tyrian purple, the most expensive color in the world.

From the heart of the empire, the Medes are adorned with gold that flashes in the sunrise. They also favor purples and yellows and an abundance of reds and blues, both in their clothing and in the vivid designs on their rectangular wicker shields. Indeed, the gods and goddesses can see every imaginable color somewhere in Datis' army.

For headgear, some of the Persians wear thick cloth or felt caps that hang down their backs and the sides of their heads. The fabric splits at the shoulders to keep their arms unencumbered. Others wear turbans with long cloth tails to wrap around their faces, covering everything but the eyes, nose, and mouth. Long shirts hang down almost to the knees, over cloth pants. And underneath the shirts—scale armor, made of hundreds of linked ringlets.

From his majestic banquet hall, Zeus smiles at this particular contrast between the Greek and Persian forces. Compared to a Greek's solid bronze cuirass, a Persian's scale armor is comfortable, flexible, and light. But the cuirass has one advantage—strength. A spear thrust against solid bronze might dent the armor and break the spear. But a spear thrust into scale armor can drive the broken scales right through a man's guts and out his back.

～◗

As the Greek phalanx advances, its pace is deliberate and unhurried. Phidippides is in the fourth row, toward the right flank. If a man in front of him falls, he will step forward and join the first three killing rows. That time may come soon enough.

Phidippides' mind goes back to when he left Sparta and ran past the Spartan phalanx. When he imagined himself as one of them, he was awestruck by the music of the double aulos. His body absorbed the sounds, and the phalanx absorbed him. The noises from the Athenian phalanx are so different: hard breathing, stomping, grunting, growling, cursing. All in unison as part of the constant beat. With each step, the hoplites are speaking to one another without words. No words are needed because the message is clear: I fight for you, you fight for me. Phidippides understands now that despite the differences, the Spartan and Athenian sounds have the same effect—to show the men they are there for each other, and to help them merge with the phalanx until the entire phalanx is one.

The marching Greeks are only a thousand feet from the front of the Persian line. Keeping his gaze forward, Themistocles shouts to Aristides, "Almost time."

An instant later the trumpeter next to Callimachus blows hard again. All ten thousand hoplites pull down their helmets. The men in the first three rows level their spears. The men farther back prepare to push forward with their shields when the collision comes. And they all await the next blast of the trumpet.

～◗

In Zeus' great hall, more gods and goddesses rise from their seats in anticipation. Some of their voices rise also. Many of them love the supreme sport of war. But not all. One goddess in particular has little taste for violence—delicate Aphrodite, Goddess of Love and Beauty. She has a well-deserved reputation for conniving, but when savagery is afoot, she usually averts her eyes.

She is ignoring the battlefield to pretend to listen to her unattractive husband, Hephaestus, the lame God of Metalworking and Fire. Hephaestus is talking at great length about the latest creation he is hammering out on his anvil. And, as usual in these exchanges, Aphrodite is bored almost to tears.

Two other gods are not paying attention to Marathon either. Instead, they are whispering and chortling like schoolboys between glances at the odd pair sitting across from them.

"I wonder if Hephaestus *knows*...?"

"Whether his wife is faithful? A better question is does *Aphrodite* know..."

"Oh, that's a good one!" the God of Wine interrupts, nearly choking on his ambrosia.

"...how he *really* became lame?" asks Hermes, the God of Cunning and messenger for Zeus.

"Worst kept secret on the mountain. But I bet she doesn't. Beautiful but a bit dim; she isn't called 'cow-eyed' for nothing! Anyway, *he* always claimed he was born that way."

"And Athena gives him cover. She mightily dislikes the story; the image certainly doesn't suit her."

Dionysus stifles a laugh and says, "Wish I'd been there to see it. The story *I* heard is she'd just finished bathing and was bending over to retrieve her garments when he ran up behind her and tried to stick it in—but missed! Can you imagine? Splattered his seed all over her thigh. What a mess! Athena whirled around to kick him in the groin, missed too, and smashed *his* thigh instead. He's been lame ever since."

Hermes clasps both hands over his mouth to muffle a guffaw. He chokes, spitting out half the nectar he'd been drinking, "A thigh for a thigh. Now *that's* what I call rough justice!"

~~~

Datis waits in the center of the Persian lines, immediately behind the archers and in front of his massed troops. Although he clearly sees the Greeks steadily advancing, he cannot quite believe it. His fleeting thought is that the Greeks will abruptly halt and ask to parley. Datis will refuse. But the thought is a fantasy anyway; he knows that. The Greeks are off their heads, so he is left with only one option—kill them all.

He gives the signal. The Persian trumpet blows. The archers reach for their quivers and nock arrows to their bowstrings.

The phalanx nears eight hundred feet.

The Persian trumpet blasts again, and the archers raise their bows to an angle of forty-five degrees—maximum range. The archers wait for the next signal to draw their bows.

At sixty, Callimachus' eyesight is still as good as ever. He watches and waits as the phalanx continues to close the distance. Seven hundred feet.

The Persian archers should be looking up along the line of their arrows. But many have their eyes on the oncoming phalanx. Some of the archers wet themselves.

The phalanx nears six hundred feet. The time has come. Another blast from the Persian trumpet and the archers draw their bows.

Now a different trumpet's shattering burst. The loudest Marathon has ever heard. The Polemarch smiles when he gives the order and breaks into a run. Callimachus glances to his left to see the entire phalanx keeping pace with him. The lines are straight. Ten thousand sprinting hoplites and their lines are straight. Callimachus feels twenty again. He has just finished training as an ephebe. His time is finally here. The time has arrived for Athens, for the Greeks. Valor and glory for them all—or enslavement and death.

The Persian trumpet blares and the archers launch their arrows; the Greeks raise their shields and tilt them over their heads, without slowing their pace. Metal covers to ward off raining arrows. Kye and Arrichion quickly glance at each other, eyes open wide. They let loose a screaming roar while thousands of men around them do the same. The horrific noise rolls toward the waiting Persians.

The archers grab another arrow from their quivers. As they nock their second arrows, their eyes bug out at the oncoming Greeks. They are supposed to launch at least ten arrows each at their onrushing enemy, but that is no longer possible—not even close. Some archers' arms are shaking. Other archers are hopelessly vomiting, shitting, or both. They are all waiting for the next signal to fire.

From a Persian boat, Hippias watches the Greeks charge. He and Datis have the same thought: *This is the strange game our spy described, but it's no game.* Hippias looks down and shakes his head. He remembers the omen that came to him during his fit on the beach when they first landed—the omen he had said nothing about and hoped he had misunderstood. He looks back up and watches the Greeks running, now only four hundred feet from the Persian line.

The Persian trumpet blares again and a second volley of arrows is away.

For the Persians, the frightening effect of the speed of the approaching phalanx is compounded by the terrifying noise. The Persians know war cries well, but not the unified, rhythmic screaming that is blasting them now. Although the sound originates from individual men, what the Persians hear is the single merged noise of ten thousand screams reverberating, echoing, and amplified by the hoplites' helmets. It is the sound of a continuously bellowing monster and it is getting louder. With every passing second, louder and louder.

The phalanx's other sound is something the Persians have never heard before—the clanking, rattling, grating racket of a gigantic machine grinding its way forward, bronze striking and scraping against bronze. The hoplites are running in close formation, so their shields and shoulders repeatedly strike the men to their left and right, mixing the rhythm of metal with the hoplites' shouts.

The vulnerable archers start to look over their shoulders at the Persian soldiers standing behind them. For an archer, the penalty for looking away from the enemy is death. But fear is overcoming them.

Datis, however, is confident—surprised by the Greek charge but self-assured. He knows his numbers. Forty thousand Persians against only ten thousand lowly Greeks. Nothing can stand against such lopsided numbers. He smiles at the thought of his imminent victory. The Great King will be pleased.

Datis nods and the Persian trumpet blares once again; a third volley of arrows flies. The closing speed of the hoplites is impressive. Datis estimates the time; only one more volley is possible. He understands the importance of momentum and knows he must not delay his counter-move.

The Persian trumpet blares and the final volley of arrows is in the air. The trumpet immediately blasts again, with a different sound. Datis shouts to the sky and charges past the archers, followed by the Persian horde.

CHAPTER THIRTY-NINE

THE BATTLE BEGINS

Athena and Ares are standing next to each other on Mount Olympus to watch the Battle of Marathon begin. They make an intriguing pair—the Goddess of War and the God of War. Her specialties are tactics and strategy. His is ruthless brutality. Athena's arms are crossed, and her face is serious and calm as she assesses nuances and calculates probabilities. Ares' face strains with excitement like a spectator at a fierce competition. He keeps clenching and unclenching his fists.

Athena is not only the patron of her namesake city, but also of its shrewdest man. And right now she must devote her full attention to the battle that will decide both their fates.

After evaluating the unfolding scene, she says to Ares, "Look at those Persian floppy hats. I wonder how they'll look when a Greek sword splits them in two."

"I was wondering when you'd compliment the Persians on their pretty clothes."

Turning to him with her intense gray eyes, she says, "Your words are always so charming! How can anyone resist you? How can I resist you? How can I *stand* you?"

"So why, oh wise one, *do* you tolerate me?"

Facing him now, Athena answers, "Because I respect you. Not during times of peace. But when killing time comes, you are necessary—and necessity justifies respect."

"I'm not sure I follow you."

"What a surprise."

"And what does that mean?"

"Following my words is not one of the essential services you provide. Your ferocity is your claim on my respect, not your intelligence."

Ares shrugs and looks back at Marathon. "Hard to see how the Greeks will hold on against all those Persians."

"Keep your eyes on the Greek flanks."

Ares turns back to ask her why, but she is gone.

—◦—

For the Persians, the horrible metallic crunching of the collision tells them they are up against a rolling wave of bronze. For the Greeks, who are used to fighting other Greeks, phalanx against phalanx, metal against metal, the sound of bronze smashing against weak wicker shields is something new. With both armies running, the sheer momentum of the clash shatters hundreds of Persian shields. Persian fighters fall next. It is difficult to hear anything clearly inside a Greek helmet, but the sounds of breaking bones and tearing flesh are unmistakable.

Mere moments after the first collision, sounds of death take over—the primeval cacophony of slaughter, man against man. Groans, snarls, shrieks, screams.

On the Greeks' left flank, farthest away from the water, a tall Persian and a stocky young Greek are the first to engage. That flank is the responsibility of the thousand hoplites from the small city-state of Plataea who have come to the Athenians' aid, so the high respect accorded to the first Greek death goes to a Plataean.

His death comes with an adroit maneuver by the Persian warrior— a lightning shift to an underhand grip on his spear while bringing the weapon from above his head down to his knees. Once there, he thrusts the point through a gap along the left edge of the Greek's shield. The spearhead pierces the Greek's side just below his cuirass, slicing through his torso, glancing off his right pelvis, and exiting below the ribs. The Greek drops his own spear, bends forward, then starts to fall back. The Persian yanks out his spear, pulling the Greek upright. The hoplite opens his mouth wide, looks at his destroyer, and drops on his haunches as urine and excrement spout from the two spear holes in his gut as if he were a human fountain.

Back in the center of the phalanx, Themistocles strikes his first blow. With his spear he hooks a Persian under the chin, hoisting him up like a gaffed fish flipping and flopping. The doomed man goes limp as he arcs over Themistocles and smashes headfirst to the ground. Themistocles steps on the man's neck and jerks hard to free his spear, yanking out the Persian's jaw. Broken teeth fly in all directions.

Themistocles controls his exhilaration as he thrusts himself back into the ranks and realigns his shield to protect himself and the hoplite to his left. He can tell this first clash has gone well for the Greeks, but he is worried—very worried. The forward momentum of their center has already stopped. The pressures from front and back are not right. The force of the Persians attacking is greater than the forward push of the hoplites in the few rows behind him. He understands the danger in the lopsided strain.

An owl begins to fly over the battle. She sees Themistocles with Aristides at his right, fighting in the center of the Greek front line. She also sees the bulk of the Persian army straight ahead of them. Thousands of hoplites stab and slice away; the Persians fall one after another, but she knows none of that matters. She can see the imbalance Themistocles can feel; the number of Persians is far too great. Fresh Persian fighters continue to swarm forward, trampling their fallen comrades, and vast numbers wait in reserve. She knows the Greek hoplites in the center are already tiring. The center of the phalanx cannot hold for long.

Themistocles is the first to step back. Only half a step, taken with courage and conviction, because a half step is all that the pushing from the rear will allow. Sicinnus is directly behind Themistocles, his spear leveled just above his master's shoulder. He realizes what is happening and also takes a half step back.

Athena concentrates. This is a dangerous moment. If the front lines falter, the entire phalanx feels it, and that can invite a rout. Athena knows all the hoplites have their instructions. She stood invisibly among them earlier when Themistocles, Aristides, and the other leaders of their tribes conveyed the warleader's orders. But hearing orders is not the same as following them on the battlefield. The men in the center must control themselves despite the Persian onslaught or all will be lost.

The fighting on the flanks is just as fierce. Callimachus is beset by spears and slashing swords. All the Persian fighters know Datis has promised vast riches to any man who strikes the Greek warleader with a fatal blow. The assaults keep coming and Callimachus revels in the challenge. This is how a man of sixty should feel—alive. For an instant, he even believes he will live forever.

Callimachus shoves his spear into the throat of an oncoming Persian. He tries to avoid running his spear all the way through and out the back of the neck, so it will be easier to pull the weapon out. But the Persian's rush is too fast, so now both the spear and Callimachus are slathered with bright blood gushing from the Persian's mouth and throat. The dead man stands while his body quivers, and his hands grip the spear as if trying to throttle it, though it has already killed him.

As Callimachus starts to lift his leg and push the Persian off his spear, a sword slashes down at him from the left. It misses but cuts his spear in half. He flips the shaft to reverse it, and the remnant is just long enough to do its job. Callimachus rams the butt-spike into the second Persian's face and drives it deep enough to burst the man's brainstem.

Another sword comes at Callimachus from his right through a spray of surf. This is where he is most vulnerable—where there is no other hoplite to help protect him, only the sea. But Callimachus has been warleader for a long time. He crouches and shifts his shield to the right just far enough to make the attacker's sword, gleaming and wet, glance harmlessly off the shield's bronze bowl. The warleader's own sword is anything but harmless. Still crouching and leaning back, Callimachus looks ready to throw a discus, but the only thing he plans to send flying is the Persian's head. The maneuver kills his attacker but the sword lands high. It severs the Persian's head just above his ears; the top of the head flies off and rolls away, leaving a trail of ooze like a giant slug on the wet sand. When the man topples over, the rest of his brain plops out next to his body.

Yet again a sword comes at Callimachus, this time from his left. Another shift of his shield, another deflection off the shield's outer bowl. Now it is Callimachus' turn and he wants to aim better this time. His swinging blade is perfectly aligned with the enemy's neck. The Persian raises his wicker shield, but he is not skillful enough. The sword skims over the shield with the warleader's full strength behind it and strikes high once again. The motion also twists Callimachus' sword so its flat side slams into the Persian's head like a hammer. Just before impact the Persian instinctively turns his face away, so the sword bashes the back of his head behind the ear. The skull splinters deep into the brain and his left eye leaps from its socket to dangle down his face. The Persian falls, stiff as a tree in the forest.

Callimachus looks around for his next victim but for now, no one is close; he takes advantage of the chance to catch his breath, satisfied with four kills in less than thirty seconds. He can remember doing better, but he was younger then.

Floating above them all, Athena is still worried. She keeps assessing the Greeks' offense and defense. Right now, defense is most important. There must be no rout in the center of the phalanx. So far, the center is holding together while it slowly backs up. But she also sees Themistocles doing something that alarms her. Just before the two armies collided, he saw Datis a short distance to his left, and he has been repeatedly glancing in that direction, hoping to somehow work his way over to kill the Persian commander. He cannot make that happen as long as the phalanx maintains its tight cohesion. Athena scowls; even quick glances mean distraction, and this is no time for any diversion from the essential action.

The timing of Themistocles' next attempt to catch sight of Datis could not be worse. He risks it because he sees no immediate threat in front of him, but when he looks back a Persian sword in mid-arc is coming straight for the left side of his neck. He and Aristides both see the impending blow, but there is no time. As the sword slashes down toward its target, the Persian blinks and fails to see the golden owl's sudden shadow. He is stunned. Perplexed. His sword has somehow shifted from his right hand to his left and is still above him. He is ambidextrous, but he cannot believe he made such a shift just now. Yet there it is; the sword is in his left hand and poised above his head, aimed this time for the right side of Themistocles' neck. Aristides' spear slashes through the Persian's armpit, out the top of his shoulder, and straight into his ear. The Persian is stunned a second time and releases his sword, which scrapes Themistocles' greave as it falls to the bloody sand. Using both arms to hold up the shaft of his spear, Aristides momentarily displays his victim, who hangs as if half-crucified with his left arm still above his head.

Athena returns to observing the battle from above. She hopes Themistocles has learned his lesson.

Flying higher, she sees the center of the Greek phalanx is moving backward faster now. That can only mean their time is running out.

She grimaces when she looks along the Greeks' front line and sees Miltiades trying to help a general from Athens who has shattered his spear. The general reaches for the sword on his hip; too quickly a Persian fighter lunges forward with his own sword. Miltiades' spear is intact, but he is too far away to get to his colleague in time. Instead, he avenges his death. The brief, bloody encounter leaves Miltiades looking down at both bodies— the general and his killer.

Athena begins to fly at random around the battlefield, almost as if she is disoriented. She is the Goddess of Wisdom as well as War, but she can tell her divine intelligence is failing her, at least for now. What is happening here is beyond even her ability to fully comprehend.

At this critical stage of the battle, Athena knows the key to victory or defeat remains the solidarity of the Greek phalanx. But she still cannot answer the crucial question: Will the center hold together and resist the weight of the Persians long enough? She knows the logical answer is no but refuses to accept it. She knows also that she can only do so much. She can help her favorite, Themistocles, but she cannot save them all. The outcome of the battle is up to them and them alone.

She looks down and sees the start of what she has been dreading. A small crack has opened in the center of the phalanx. Its tight formation is beginning to fail.

Down on the ground, the Greeks cannot see the looming disaster, but they feel it in the confusing melee. Persians are no longer just in front of them, but on all sides now, and the hoplites are getting separated so their shields no longer overlap enough to protect each other.

Stabbing and slashing in all directions, Themistocles is being pushed to his right. He sees Aristides now on his left. Everyone is being shoved. Then the shock—Aristides goes down. Themistocles lets out a horrific howl. Six Greek and Persian fighters are jammed between him and his lifelong friend, and more men are pushing their way in. Aristides just saved his life, but Themistocles cannot get to him when Aristides' need is critical. In the chaos he can no longer even see him.

Themistocles' fury immediately overtakes his grief, and he yells, "Back up faster! Do not turn. Back up faster!"

Few hoplites can make out the words echoing from inside Themistocles' helmet, but they understand. They have understood since they were trained as ephebes. When the worst happens, reverse your steps but never turn your back to the enemy. The worst is happening now. Their disciplined retreat is being overwhelmed. The center of the phalanx is collapsing.

CHAPTER FORTY

SHE SOARS

The ways of gods and goddesses can be hard to fathom. As the battle rages and the phalanx collapses, Athena disappears from Marathon. And she soars.

She soars to Helios, the sun, and circumvents his intense flames.

She soars higher, to the stars and beyond. All the way to the edge of infinity and back again.

She circles the earth, around and around. She dreads what may be about to happen, and everywhere she looks she senses the concern of mortals for their own unknown futures.

She sees Phar in a caravan traveling south toward the pyramids. She sees his future. Three years hence, he will struggle to convince his people to avoid an appalling mistake. He will cajole and plead, scream and cry. Finally, he will invoke all the gods of the Nile Valley. His people will not listen, nor will their gods, and Egypt will revolt against Persia. The resulting battles will end with the slaughter of countless Egyptians. And the difficult campaign will hasten the Great King's death.

Phar will grieve when news reaches him that Darius is no more. His eyes will narrow into slits as he listens to the proclamation that all honor and reverence shall be rendered to the Persian Empire's new sovereign, the supreme ruler of almost half the world's population, Xerxes the Great.

Athena knows Phar's future thoughts. After he is rejected by his people and their gods, Phar will remember what Darius said before he returned to Egypt: Phar is too good to be a good advisor. His heart lacks a necessary dark streak. Phar will wonder if that is why his people did not listen to him.

Could that also be why the gods of Egypt paid him no heed? Did he fail to understand both the nature of humans and what the gods truly want? Perhaps they want goodness but not purity. Phar will examine his life and grow in wisdom.

Athena shakes her bewildered head. How can she see Phar's future so clearly but not know the final outcome and lasting effect of the furious Battle of Marathon?

She soars north and then west across the sea she loves. Above her namesake city she looks down upon Archippe and Lela with their children. Athena feels their fear. The women seem to know the battle is boiling over at this very moment. Lela's right arm is limp, but she holds little Alyssa tightly with her left. Worry haunts everyone in the household except for Archippe's son, Arch. He is the man of the house now and knows he must be brave. His father taught him well. He tries to gently lift Alyssa and relieve her exhausted mother. The toddler tightens her grip on Lela and looks defiantly at Arch. One more move and she will scream. With a slow shake of her head, Lela smiles faintly at the young man's kindness.

And Athena soars.

High over Marathon, she looks up at Helios. Just for an instant, she thinks of herself. She so wants Themistocles' love. Seven centuries ago, Odysseus showed his love through thoughts and, especially, prayers. He worshiped her above all other gods and goddesses. He knew she was his patron. But today Themistocles cannot even conceive of a divine patron. If he eventually comes to love her, the choice must be his and his alone. She cannot compel him. Her yearning fuels her belief that he will choose her one day. But to do so, he must live.

She turns her head and looks down. The Battle of Marathon is just as it was when she left. She has been gone for less than the blink of an eye.

CHAPTER FORTY-ONE

THE BATTLE ENDS

As the center of the phalanx collapses, something else begins to take shape. The outer edges of the phalanx start slowly but steadily moving forward beyond the center. Athena nods. From the clouds, the Greek phalanx appears to be forming a half-ellipse.

The first sign of what the goddess has been watching for appears on the Greeks' left flank; they pick up speed. Then a mirror image on the right flank near the water, where Callimachus leads an even swifter push forward. A few moments later, the Greek left flank overwhelms the Persian right. These Persians are the farthest from the safety of their all-important ships. Their sanctuary. Their only way home. If they cannot reach the ships, they die. Unlike the disciplined hoplites, the Persians begin to turn and run.

The Persian left flank near the water starts to disintegrate in a second rout as the Persians there also turn to run for the ships.

The Greeks in the center know nothing about what is happening on the flanks. All they can be sure of is that they are rapidly retreating and being pursued, and that death must be close.

Back-to-back trumpet blasts from the far right, near Callimachus, shatter the air. The center of the phalanx erupts with the shouts of men instantly reinvigorated by hope. The Persians in the center hear the roar and see the hoplites' bodies harden with new strength.

Callimachus is furious. The trumpet's double blasts signal the left flank to turn toward the right and the right flank to turn left, to keep herding the advancing Persians toward the center. But as more Persians turn their backs on the main battle and run for the beach, the hoplites are pursuing them. Callimachus understands the impulse, but that is no excuse. Disobeying orders cannot be tolerated. And he rightly senses the danger facing the Greeks in the center of the phalanx. He signals another round of double blasts from the trumpet. The disobedient hoplites come to their senses and retake their positions. Together the Greek flanks curve and slam, stab, and slash into the Persian center.

The Greeks are attacking from both sides now. Sicinnus is in the thick of it. He cannot see his master, but off to the right he spots a Persian with his sword raised, taking a final step toward Phidippides. Sicinnus charges but knows there is not enough time. However, the Persian inexplicably freezes with his sword still high and his eyes and mouth wide open. Phidippides also seems frozen; he stands motionless and shocked as he looks high above his Persian attacker.

Leaning forward with his full weight as he charges, Sicinnus drives his spear through the Persian's solar plexus and far out his back. Sicinnus ends up face to face with the Persian only inches away.

Staring at Sicinnus, the dying man wheezes, "Tell Afari . . . and our baby girl . . . Tell them I . . . very much . . ."

The Persian vomits a wide stream of bright blood straight into Sicinnus' face. Sicinnus lets go of his spear, the Persian falls forward, and Sicinnus barely has the presence of mind to grab the spear shaft behind the Persian's back and pull it out. He looks at Phidippides.

"Did you see that?" gasps Phidippides.

"What?"

"The giant. He stepped between the Persian and me. It was Pan. I saw his horns and hooves. He was huge."

"You're saying the god Pan saved you?"

"No, you saved me. But Pan gave you time to do it. He told me on my run to Sparta he would be here. And he is."

In the distance, Sicinnus hears Callimachus shout, "Atar!" Then, much closer, he hears Themistocles. "Atar!"

Last night, when Callimachus asked him the Persian word for fire, Callimachus did not explain because Sicinnus did not need to know. But now he understands. Sicinnus knows Homer. Everyone knows Homer. Marathon is another Troy. The Trojans sowed panic when they called for fire in an attempt to burn the Greek ships and destroy the only way the Greeks could return home, so now Callimachus is calling for holy fire to burn the Persian ships. Sicinnus leaves Phidippides and forces his way toward the beach. The whole time, he alternates between Persian and Greek to shout, "Atar, Fire, Atar, Fire!"

Callimachus is once again beset by Persians all around him. He dispatches the first three attackers but more keep coming. Miltiades sees the assault. He tries to work his way toward the warleader, but the brawling battle around the Persian ships makes for slow going. Miltiades screams when he sees four simultaneous spear thrusts at Callimachus. The warleader knocks two away but the other two find their mark, one in his lower left back and the other in front, straight into the liver through the gap under his cuirass. Instead of trying to yank out their spears, both Persians let go, draw their swords, and jump on the ship next to Callimachus.

Within seconds, four more Persians spear Callimachus, two in the lower back and two in the groin, and these Persians also leave their spears and scramble onto the ship. Finally, Miltiades arrives with two other hoplites to protect the warleader's body from further insult.

From a short distance inland, Datis sees Callimachus die. The commander's laugh is loud and mocking. On a nearby ship, Hippias watches the same scene and sneers.

Another free-for-all is underway next to a different ship. Aeschylus, Kye, and Arrichion are in a group of hoplites trying to board the ship and take control or demolish what they can. The stern is toward the beach. Kye slashes with his sword in his right hand and grabs hold of the stern with his left. Aeschylus and Arrichion watch the next scene as if in slow motion. As Kye hangs from the stern, a Persian sword cuts though his left forearm, severing his hand and wrist. Kye drops back to the beach and, deranged with fury, throws down his sword and jumps back up to grab the stern with his right hand. The same Persian slashes at Kye again as both Aeschylus and Arrichion throw their spears. The Persian's sword cuts off Kye's right arm just below the elbow. Kye falls again. So does the Persian, with one spear through his neck and a second through his stomach.

Kye lies next to the water, between two ships that provide a brief escape from the raging battle. Aeschylus and Arrichion are on their knees beside the dying man.

Looking at Arrichion, Kye says, "Your helmet. I want to see your face one more time."

Arrichion grabs his helmet and lifts it off. His face is soaked with tears and sweat. He begins to moan.

"So handsome . . ." says Kye. "Remember me."

Arrichion slowly shakes his head and is only able to say, "Remember."

Kye looks over to Aeschylus and whispers, "I don't see . . ." He pauses, as though waiting for something. "No . . ." he finally says, ". . . nothing."

His eyes close. Then his muscles tighten and his breathing goes shallow and rapid.

Aeschylus shuts his own eyes and says, softly, "He's gone."

"But he's still breathing!" exclaims Arrichion.

"His body is breathing; his spirit is gone," says Aeschylus. "And his breath will go swiftly. Now put your helmet on and protect yourself. Kye wants you to live to remember him."

"What was Kye saying to you?" Arrichion asks. "What didn't he see?"

"It was a long time ago," says Aeschylus. "We were children. We made a pact and promised to tell each other what we saw when we were dying, if we were together, whichever one of us went first. We were convinced we would see something when Hades came for our soul. We didn't know what, but we were sure we would see something."

Aeschylus and Arrichion both stand up when they hear the tremendous heaving of the ship next to them. The Persians are starting to row it off the beach and out to sea. Looking around, the two Athenians realize this is the first ship to escape. They both know the battle for the ships is far from over. What they do not know is that the entire battle on the plain and the beach is about to take another threatening turn.

The Persians farthest away from the water are desperately fighting their way toward the ships. When they hear the welcome news of Callimachus' death, they assume the Greeks are demoralized and seriously vulnerable, so their leaders consider three choices: They can press on toward the ships and struggle through all the congestion of fleeing Persians on the narrow beach, or try a shortcut to the ships across the deadly marsh, or return to the battle on the plain. If they return, they can attack the Greek flanks that are moving in to encircle the Persians who are still savagely pursuing the retreating center of the phalanx.

Certain the Greeks will weaken without their warleader, the Persians turn away from their ships to renew their assault. But their assumption is wrong. Greeks respect their leaders, but they do not revere them. Greeks do not fight for their leaders; they fight for their comrades and the chance to show valor. The Greeks are not demoralized. If anything, they are emboldened by the desire for vengeance.

When the Persians from the right flank resume their attack, the Greeks are ready for the challenge. At the same time, the mass of Persians in the center of the battle remains encircled by Greek maneuvers that keep closing in. Beset in front and back, the trapped Persians are being slaughtered. So many are falling that the Greeks are constantly flipping their spears to use the butt-spikes to finish off the wounded. Persian dead cover the ground.

Although the Persian right flank cannot clearly see the massacre in the center, its men can see something else that fills them with terror: More ships are abandoning Marathon. A moment ago, they thought they had three ways to save themselves, but now they only have one: crossing the Great Marsh is their only chance of reaching a ship in time. Thousands of Persians turn and wade into the treacherous sludge.

The Greeks pursuing them do not venture into the swamp, partly because of their heavy bronze armor and partly because they do not need to. The muck forces the Persians to advance so slowly that the Greek spears have plenty of time to reach them. And uncountable numbers simply sink until the inescapable slime silences their screams.

By the time the marsh takes its victims, all but seven of the Persian ships have launched and headed out to sea. The remaining seven have either been captured or set on fire. The battle is coming to an end.

Themistocles stands near the water's edge. Around him, the deafening tumult has given way to an eerie quiet, broken only by the sounds of the dying. Thousands of Persians litter the ground; an unknown number lie submerged in the marsh. But fewer than two hundred Greeks are dead or dying. Themistocles is well-known for his indifference to all talk of gods and goddesses, but he cannot shake a sense of reverence as he realizes what he has just been part of. For the Greeks, this is a victory beyond any conceivable expectation. Themistocles prides himself on his cunning and skepticism. But this must be a gift from the gods.

He walks up to Aeschylus and Arrichion, who are standing above a motionless figure between gullies of sand carved by the Persian ships' hulls. He tilts his helmet back to reveal his sweaty and exhausted face, then looks down at Kye, who has stopped breathing.

"He will be buried here with the other fallen hoplites—a high honor never to be forgotten," says Themistocles. "He will be remembered."

"Yes," Arrichion says quietly, "he will be remembered."

Themistocles turns and looks out to sea. He steps away from

Aeschylus and Arrichion and stands alone, concentrating on the departing ships and assessing their movements. As he continues to stare, he rubs his fingers back and forth across his downturned lips. He looks puzzled at first. Then alarmed.

He jerks his hands up to his face, cups them around his mouth, and starts shouting as loudly as he can, "Where is the warleader? . . . Where is the warleader?"

CHAPTER FORTY-TWO

THE RUN

As Themistocles shouts for the warleader, a hoplite points up the beach to where Miltiades and Callimachus appear to be standing together. Themistocles starts walking toward them, breaks into a run, and stops next to Miltiades. The dead warleader is still propped up by six Persian spears stuck deep in the sand.

"Did he speak?"

"Yes. He asked me to tell his wife his last thought was of her. He closed his eyes and then opened them. He said maybe I shouldn't tell her; it would make her sad. Then he closed his eyes again and that was the end."

"Not of glory," Themistocles says softly.

"No. He was a strange man."

They fall quiet until Themistocles finally says, "I don't know what you should say to her, but that must be for later. You are the warleader now. We have no time for an election. Look at the Persian warships."

Miltiades looks around and uneasily scans the sea. Even though most of the Persian ships are not yet in deep water, their direction is already clear. They are heading south, toward Athens.

"Those warships are their fastest," says Miltiades.

"They'll go to Phalerum. Probably arrive about the same time as the horse barges that left last night."

Miltiades looks at the sun. "Late this afternoon."

Hurrying away from Themistocles, Miltiades starts shouting, "Form up, form up!" He turns back toward Themistocles and, looking past him, yells, "Aristides, I need you."

Themistocles wheels around to see his friend trotting toward them. He runs to him and embraces him in a powerful hug. Stepping back, he barely manages to stifle a sob long enough to get the words out. "You went down and I wasn't there and . . ."

Feigning aloofness to mask his own relief and joy that they are both alive, Aristides says, "Correct on both counts, so I had to get back up by myself. That's harder than you might imagine. You owe me one."

Miltiades shouts, "Aristides, help spread the word to all the tribes' leaders. Form up! Form up!"

The hoplites are utterly exhausted but also exhilarated, and they move as quickly as possible to follow the orders. Nine other generals gather with Miltiades. The only one missing is the man Miltiades saw fall—an astonishing survival rate given that all the generals, as leaders of their tribes, were in the front line.

"Listen," says Miltiades. "Look out to sea. Those Persian warships will reach Phalerum before the sun is down. Their entire cavalry will also be there. Today we killed thousands, but they still vastly outnumber us. They could be inside the walls of Athens an hour after they land. Do you know what that means? They will have our women and children. If that happens, we're lost. Half an hour from now, we march. Our fastest march ever. Half an hour. Rest while you can. Any questions?"

Miltiades pauses and then shouts again, "Convey the orders to your tribes. Begin by telling them to look at the Persian ships. Dismissed."

Except for Themistocles and Aristides, the generals leave to rejoin their tribes.

Miltiades says, "Aristides, you and your tribe will remain here to begin burying the dead and protect what the Persians left behind." He gestures toward the huge abandoned encampment. Parts of it are already on fire.

Aristides responds, "Miltiades . . . warleader . . . my tribe and I would rather join you."

"I realize that," says Miltiades. "But my order stands. Your tribe has proven its valor. Your tribe lost more men than any other. And you are an honorable man. This place must be protected; the land is now sacred. Marathon's earth must welcome the bodies of our men. I know you will show them proper respect."

Turning to Themistocles, Miltiades says, "I need a runner."

Themistocles walks quickly to where the phalanx is already separating into tribes to prepare for the quick march. He sees Sicinnus and beckons him forward.

"Find Phidippides and bring him to me," Themistocles says.

Themistocles turns to walk back but Sicinnus grabs his arm.

"I'm not sure of your plans, but don't make Phidippides run to Athens," says Sicinnus.

"I won't make Phidippides do anything. It will be his choice. Find him."

"Themistocles, you should not give him the choice. He has endured too much already, and I don't mean the battle here today. All the running—from Athens to Sparta to here. No human can keep doing it. There are other runners. I can do it if you want—just not Phidippides."

"I told you, it's not my decision. It's up to him. Now let go of my arm and find him. Don't make me change my request to a command."

Sicinnus lets go and walks back to the phalanx. Themistocles returns to Miltiades.

A short time later Sicinnus and Phidippides approach to find Themistocles and Miltiades engaged in heavy conversation. Themistocles is waving his hands in the air.

Miltiades steps forward and says, "Phidippides, because of your valor, I feel obliged to allow you to decide if you want to run and carry a message to Athens instead of joining our march. Themistocles and I prefer that you stay with us. We have other runners. But both of us will defer to your decision. What is your answer?"

Phidippides immediately responds, "I will run."

Miltiades and Themistocles watch Sicinnus lower his head.

"So be it," says Miltiades. "You will carry two messages to the city. The first message is that the goddess Nike has granted us victory. The second message is that we are on a quick march and will arrive soon. Tell them also they must prepare for the impending arrival of the Persians and their cavalry. We're in a race against the Persian ships, and we want the city to hold strong until we arrive. Do you follow?"

"I follow," says Phidippides.

"Any questions?"

"No questions, but I have something to say."

"Say it."

"Sicinnus saved my life today. I know that is common among hoplites, but the way he saved me was not common. Pan intervened and halted the death-blow aimed at me so Sicinnus had time to kill my attacker. I expect the god helped save other hoplites, although they may not know it. Days ago, I encountered Pan in the middle of the night during my run to Sparta. He said he is a friend of Athens, but we do not show him the respect he deserves. We do not worship him properly. He wants Athens to build him a temple."

Miltiades looks over to Themistocles, then looks back at Phidippides and says, loudly, "Know this, Phidippides—and Pan, great God of the Wild, if you are listening—Athens will build and dedicate a temple to Pan, and henceforth the city will ensure that his worship is proper."

"The God of the Wild will be pleased," says Phidippides.

"How soon will you be ready to start your run?"

"Now is a good time." Phidippides laughs. "It's only twenty-six miles."

"The gods be with you."

Phidippides starts to walk away but stops when Sicinnus puts a hand on his shoulder.

"Pace yourself," says Sicinnus. "You will be far ahead of the quick march and the Persian fleet. Keep your wits about you."

"You're a good friend, Sicinnus; I will always remember you."

"We will always remember each other."

Phidippides walks off in search of water pouches for his run.

Themistocles steps over to Sicinnus and says, "He had to make his own decision."

"I know, and he chose glory."

"Yes, he wants to be remembered."

Sicinnus snaps, "It's all based on nothing. Nothing at all."

Themistocles is taken aback. "Are you talking about Phidippides?"

"I'm talking about all of us."

Themistocles stares at Sicinnus and then says, "I don't follow."

"What we remember is what we wish to remember—nothing more."

Themistocles is silent for a moment, then says, "We can talk about this later. We need to get back to our tribe so the men can make ready to leave."

Nearly a half hour later, the hoplites have assembled and are awaiting the order to march. Miltiades stands near Themistocles.

"Your man Sicinnus is a different sort, isn't he?"

"Yes. Very smart. Thoughtful and perceptive."

"Perceptive?"

"Sensitive. The most sensitive man I've ever known."

Miltiades briefly crosses his arms, considering. "This is a hard day for such a man." Turning toward the hoplites, he gives the signal to begin the quick march to Athens.

It is not long before the hoplites are breathing hard. They are separated into two contingents. The first is a flying column of nine hundred, made up of the youngest strong hoplites from each tribe, including Sicinnus. They lead the advance. Behind them, Miltiades leads the rest.

~

Barely three hours after leaving Marathon, Phidippides is nearing the end of his run. He can see the outskirts of Athens now and is surprised by how good he feels, almost euphoric. He seems to be floating. He knows he is running fast, but the speed is not bothering him. *The joy of victory,* he thinks, then gives his head a quick shake. Maybe he is feeling too good. *Concentrate. Watch the ground. This is no time for a fall. This is the time for glory. I will be remembered. I will be remembered forever.*

He sprints toward the city walls with both hands high above his head. The air is heavy now, redolent of crowded people and city life—of home— and he loves it. This is the air he wants to breathe forever.

A guard on top of the north wall is the first to see him and shouts, "Runner approaching fast! He is coming from the direction of Marathon!"

Word passes quickly and a crowd begins to congregate near the gate. Women, children, and old men, many of whom fled from Attica to Athens in fear of the Persians, start filling the area—a space crammed, like many of the city's streets, with hastily thrown up shelters for these refugees. It smells of fear and a population held for too long in a place too small. The air is alive with rumors; uncertainty has haunted all of Athens for many days. Even the children, many of them holding tight to their weary mothers, look dazed and afraid.

Faintly at first, they hear a new sound, a voice repeating something.

The guard shouts, "The runner is alone. Open the gate!"

The runner's chant grows louder and the people stop talking among themselves to listen closely. The sound is the same word, over and over, and now it is clear.

"Victory! . . . Victory! . . . Victory!"

The people look at one another, not daring at first to believe.

The gate opens; the runner comes into view beyond it. The crowd stares, amazed. Even from this distance the runner looks pale as death.

An old veteran limps forward from the crowd. Leaning on a gnarled cane, he walks out through the gate. He will be the first to welcome the runner home.

Arms still held high, Phidippides keeps shouting, "Victory!"

When the runner is close, the old man drops his cane to raise both hands above his shoulders. The runner stops with his hands still high, as if frozen there. His face is confused and questioning.

The old man walks toward him and says, "Phidippides, welcome back to Athens. You are home."

The runner tries to shout one more time, remembering there is more to say, but first his voice fails him, and then his heart. His spirit goes out like a snuffed candle. The old man catches him as he falls and lays him carefully on the ground. Other men rush up to help.

"Pick him up gently," the old man says.

The men do so, and together they carry Phidippides' spent body into the city.

CHAPTER FORTY-THREE

THE RACE

Two hours after Phidippides' arrival, the flying column of nine hundred hoplites approaches Athens. Guards atop the city walls watch, surprised, as the men quick-march past the city instead of entering it. The marchers do not even acknowledge the greetings and questions the guards shout down to them. The flying column has maintained an exceptional pace from Marathon without stopping once, and they have only a few miles to go to reach Phalerum. They may have enough energy to fight the Persians there if they do not waste any of it now.

They cover the last few miles in less than half an hour. The hoplites see the Persian barges with the cavalry anchored offshore and, in the distance, the Persian fleet coming in fast. The trumpet blares and all nine hundred men move down to the beach to spread out. Once in place, a few dozen men break away to find wood and anything else that will burn. The sun will be down in a little more than an hour and the fires must be ready.

As the Greeks rush to prepare, some are too exhausted to help. Sicinnus is one of them, but his problem is not physical. There is still strength in his body, but he just sits and stares. If the men around him looked at his eyes they would see only blankness.

Out at sea, Datis and Hippias stand together on the Persian flagship as it heads for the horse barges. They see the hoplites swarming the beach like a mass of hungry crabs.

"The Greeks must be exhausted," Datis says, "and our soldiers are rested. We can hold them off while we unload the horses."

"You aren't thinking straight. You're assuming the Greeks on the beach are from Marathon. They could be from the city, fresh for battle."

"I thought the only men left in Athens were old and decrepit."

"Don't count on it." Hippias continues, "Even if that beach is filled with nothing but old men, they'll put up a fight you won't easily forget. They have nothing to lose but their honor. I'd rather face a young Persian in battle than . . ." he pauses before adding wryly, ". . . *another* old Greek."

Datis snarls, "So what's your advice, *old* man, accept defeat?"

"I offer no advice. It's a waste of time because you won't listen. Instead, I follow the omen I received. Two omens, in fact. The first was good, or so I thought. The second was unquestionably bad. The omens say we're finished here."

Datis is so furious that at first, he cannot speak. Then he asks in a barely controlled voice, "Are you talking about the dream you had, where you were in your mother's lap?"

"That was the first omen I told you. I interpreted it to mean I was returning to my motherland and would reclaim Athens and the surrounding land."

"Yes, yes, I remember," says Datis impatiently. "And the other?"

"It was on the beach after we landed. I had a sneezing and coughing fit. The worst one I ever had. I blew out a tooth. I dug in the sand everywhere but couldn't find it. I realized I was receiving a second omen. My claim on my motherland had been fulfilled. My tooth possessed all the land I was going to get. I didn't want to believe it, so I told no one."

His face flushed, Datis stays silent for a long breath, and then says, "You are a fortunate old man. Fortunate that I do not believe in your Greek omens. Otherwise, I would throw you overboard with a heavy anchor tied around your neck."

Datis walks away to resume studying the beach. His flagship is coming alongside the horse barges. The smell of manure sharpens the air.

~⁓

A half hour later, the main body of hoplites passes the city and the guards solemnly salute them as they pass.

"We may have done it," Themistocles says between huffs as he marches. "No Persians in sight so far."

"I want to see it with my own eyes," Miltiades responds.

In another half hour they see the water. The entire Persian fleet is still anchored offshore. Miltiades gives the signal and the trumpet blares. The hoplites pour onto the beach and join their comrades. The sun is setting. Fires flare up all along the sand. The hoplites raise their fists in the air and shout at the top of their lungs. The shouting becomes a roar loud enough to reach the Persians.

"See?" Hippias turns to Datis. He feels an odd surge of pride in his fellow Greeks, even though this proof of their fortitude means the end for him.

"Yes." After that blunt reply, Datis turns to make what he knows will be one of his last commands. As soon as his orders reach the ships, the Persians weigh anchor and head back to the open sea. The Greeks' cacophony turns into shouts of joy.

But Themistocles is not shouting. He is hunting for Sicinnus, and Sicinnus is nowhere to be found.

CHAPTER FORTY-FOUR

FREEDOM

Themistocles works his way among the hoplites, constantly asking if they know Sicinnus and where he might be. One man points east along the beach. Themistocles presses on as the number of hoplites thins. Another hoplite points inland toward some woods. Themistocles reaches a secluded patch of ground thick with trees and brush. The foliage and darkening surroundings have an eerie, almost ominous, quality. Night is closing in but there is still enough light for him to search by. He finds what he is after. Sicinnus is sitting on a log, alone.

Themistocles walks toward him, "Sicinnus . . ."

Sicinnus leaps up and screams, "Get away from me!"

Shocked, Themistocles steps back, instinctively bracing for an attack. After a pause, he asks, "Can we speak?"

"No!"

The young man crouches down hard and lowers his face to his knees. He covers his ears with his hands. After standing and looking down at his friend, Themistocles quietly sits at the far end of the log and looks straight ahead. The shadows deepen as the night gathers around them.

A few moments later, without looking up, Sicinnus says in a muted voice, "I asked you to go away. Please."

Also in a quiet voice, Themistocles responds, "Sicinnus, whether or not we talk is up to you. But I'm not going anywhere."

Sicinnus lowers his hands and crosses them over his knees, but continues to stay bent low, staring at the ground. After a short time, he looks over toward his friend. Themistocles keeps looking straight ahead.

The young Persian abruptly stands up, so Themistocles follows suit and turns to face him. Sicinnus snaps his arm up and points a finger at Themistocles who does not move. Studying Sicinnus' expression, he realizes his troubled friend is pointing past him. He turns and sees a man approaching.

The moon rising in the east is softly illuminating the grove. By its dim light, Themistocles recognizes Miltiades and quickly walks over to stop him.

Miltiades says, "A couple of men said you came this way. Is that Sicinnus behind you?"

"Yes."

"How bad?" asks the warleader, lowering his voice.

"Right now, very bad. We need to give him time. I'll stay with him."

"Most of the men are returning to the city," says Miltiades.

"And you?"

"Yes," says the warleader. "We will have lookouts posted just in case. But I'm sure the Persians are gone and won't return."

"When you get inside the walls, find Archippe. I expect Lela will be with my wife. Tell them Sicinnus and I are alive and well. Tell them we'll see them tomorrow."

"They'll want to know more than that."

"Tell them we're too exhausted to return just now," says Themistocles. "No, they won't believe that. Tell them we volunteered to stand guard so others can go back to the city. Tell them whatever you think they'll believe. If necessary, say I command them ... no, not that. Say I ask them to respect my request that they stay in Athens and wait for us tomorrow."

"I will."

He walks off and Themistocles turns back to Sicinnus, who is sitting on the log with his head bowed. At least he is not gripping his head in anguish any more.

Without looking up, Sicinnus asks, "What did he want?"

"Miltiades said most of our men are returning to the city."

"I'm not going."

"That's what I told him. I asked him to tell Archippe and Lela we'll go back tomorrow."

"I won't be ready."

Themistocles is tempted to snap at him, to tell him to come to his senses. But he has tried that in the past with other men, and it was the wrong approach. Themistocles knows many good men are ruined after a battle. Some recover, some do not. He has learned to listen and to be very careful with what he says.

"I think you will be ready tomorrow," says Themistocles. "Lela and Alyssa . . ."

Sicinnus shouts, "Don't use them against me!"

Barely controlling his anger, Themistocles replies, "Use them against you? Lela, the woman you told me a few nights ago is your fantasy. And your child, Alyssa. I'm not using them against you, so don't say I am."

"Leave me alone."

After another pause Themistocles cannot keep himself from saying, "They need you. That is a fact, and stating a fact is not using them against you. You're smart enough to know the difference between what is true and what is false."

Straightening his back and looking through the darkness at Themistocles, Sicinnus says, "Yes, I can tell the difference between what is true and what is false."

Themistocles is glad Sicinnus' voice is steady and controlled. But even in the dark, he can see that Sicinnus' eyes are not right. They are blazing, unnaturally iridescent in the moonlight as if lit from within.

Sicinnus continues, "And I can tell the difference between what is worthy and what is not. Valor is worthy. We should respect courage. But not the desire to be recognized and remembered at any cost. Glory is not worthy; it's based on an illusion! We want to think of ourselves as gods, and we want everyone else to recognize and remember us as if we deserve to be thought of as gods! How are we, how is anyone, justified in thinking such nonsense?"

"You came close to saying that earlier today, after Phidippides decided to run. You said the desire for glory—to be remembered—is based on nothing because what we remember is what we wish to remember."

"That's right," says Sicinnus. "When Phidippides decided to kill himself."

"Why do you say that?"

"I know it; I can feel it. I knew it would happen when he decided to make that run. He knew it too. Insane, after what he did over the last few days. He is not a god, and no amount of glory will change that!"

Sicinnus stares into the moonlit shadows. "He and I . . . we had a special bond. We ran together, swift as birds."

He looks up to the dark sky and says softly, "Yes, like birds, ascending, floating, together."

Closing his eyes, he goes on. "When we marched back from Marathon, I felt the knife in my gut. He's dead. I am sure of it."

"If you're right, he will have glory," says Themistocles. "Glory is what he wanted."

"Yes, that is what he wanted," says Sicinnus, with a rasp of bitterness. "He was my good friend and he was a fool. He was a ridiculous fool, and so are we—so are all of us."

The young man's eyes seem to blaze even brighter. Themistocles falls silent and sits down on the log. The two of them stay there for a long time, saying nothing.

Eventually, Themistocles stands back up and says, "So you reject glory, something we Greeks strive for, and many of us die for. I won't argue with you. I don't understand, but I won't argue.

"However, when you talk about illusions and nonsense and ridiculous fools—when you talk about nothingness—you go too far. You sound as if our lives have no meaning. So why are we here? Why did we fight at Marathon? The answer is more than valor and glory. The answer is something you should understand better than most, including me. You are a free man now, but you spent much of your life as a slave. Does freedom mean nothing?"

Themistocles pauses for a reaction, but Sicinnus stays quiet.

"My question deserves an answer," Themistocles says. "We overthrew Hippias twenty years ago, and we now rule ourselves based on freedom, not the dictates of a tyrant. These last few days, Hippias threatened us once again, and once again we—and our freedom—defeated him and the freedom-fearing Persians. What we just did was worthy. I hope to hear you say it is so."

Themistocles pauses again and this time he detects a change in Sicinnus' expression. His friend is actually listening to him, perhaps for the first time tonight. And Themistocles realizes that Sicinnus is not the only one listening—Themistocles is absorbing his own words in a way he never considered before.

"Sicinnus, you know I speak the truth as I see it. I would not lie to you, even now. I said I don't understand your thinking, but perhaps there is something . . . perhaps our times are changing and I don't fully understand; perhaps none of us understands. The old way, back to the Trojan War and before that, was to demonstrate valor and strive for glory. But today we're also fighting for something newer, something different. For the right to govern ourselves according to our intelligence, our skill, our sense of good and evil, of right and wrong—our right to have no masters, whether from Persia or even Olympus, but ourselves. We are living, and fighting, for our freedom. You should acknowledge this, as I now do."

Themistocles tilts his head back as if he is about to make a speech to a throng of Athenians in the agora. But his audience is limited to Sicinnus—and himself.

"Forget about glory. You acknowledge valor as worthy. Valor demands that you act on what you believe. Freedom is exactly the same. It's not given to you by some passive magic. Freedom is earned, and to earn it you must show valor to ensure your liberty is respected and no tyrant or Great King can dictate your thoughts or choices. You are fully capable of doing what you must, and I now ask you to acknowledge your duty on behalf of yourself, your family, and all Athens."

Hesitating only briefly, Themistocles finishes with a quiet word, "Please." Then he adds, "My best friend."

Sicinnus stands up as if to respond, but before he can speak both men hear a noise near the spot where Themistocles met Miltiades. Themistocles turns and stares into the shadows. Miltiades is back, and he steps into a slant of moonlight.

Walking quickly over to him, Themistocles is about to speak when Miltiades gestures for silence.

Miltiades whispers, "Archippe and Lela are a short distance behind me. On my way back to Athens I found them walking fast toward us. I told them your reasons for them to go back to Athens and wait, but they would have none of it. At least I persuaded them to give me a moment now before they come forward. They are hardheaded. I don't think Zeus in all his might could have stopped them."

"I understand," says Themistocles. "I'm married to one of them. Stay here with Sicinnus. I'll talk to them."

When Themistocles finds them standing in a small meadow bathed in moonlight, he catches his breath and embraces his wife. After the exhaustions and traumas of the day, and seeing her now kissed by the moon's radiance, she has never looked more beautiful to him or felt more real.

Stepping back and pulling himself together, Themistocles says, "You both are making a mistake; please return to the city. We need some time to recover. Sicinnus and I will be with you tomorrow. Give us some time, please."

Lela steps forward and says, "No. What is going on is not about you.

It's about Sicinnus. I know it. I can feel it. Themistocles, Sicinnus and I admire and respect you. I never imagined a time we would not defer to you. But that time is now. Sicinnus is your friend, but my love. I must go to him."

Without saying another word, Themistocles steps aside and points in the direction where Sicinnus stands out of sight among the trees' shadows. Lela walks into the darkness. Themistocles embraces Archippe a second time, and they hold each other tightly.

Miltiades walks out from the woods and asks, "Shall I stay?"

Releasing Archippe, Themistocles says, "No, there's nothing more for you to do. You should return to your wife and family."

For an instant, Themistocles' thoughts shift to himself. All his life it has been difficult for him to say "thank you" to anyone for anything. He sometimes wonders why this is part of his nature; more often he avoids thinking about it. Now, looking hard into Miltiades' eyes, Themistocles slowly nods but says nothing.

Miltiades understands and returns the nod, saying only, "Tomorrow."

After Miltiades leaves, Themistocles speaks softly to Archippe, "There's nothing for Miltiades to do, and I don't know if we can help, either."

Archippe nods toward something behind Themistocles' shoulder. He hears rustling and turns around to see a young woman stepping out from the darkness.

"Lela seems to be coming without Sicinnus," he says, uncertainly.

Archippe shakes her head. "That isn't Lela."

As the woman approaches, she says, "Greetings. Mother asked me to tend to Sicinnus."

Archippe stares hard at the young woman, barely visible in the dim moonlight. Then she gasps.

"The beggar girl! Even in the darkness I know those eyes."

"So my apparition did not fool you?"

"It did then, but not now. You're not an apparition now. You're real."

Themistocles looks back at his wife. "What are you talking about?"

"I . . . it's a long story."

"Yes, you both have long stories to tell," says the young woman. "I bring you two messages, and then I will leave you to your stories. The first message is that Sicinnus will recover, but it will take time."

"How long?" Themistocles asks.

"That will depend on Lela and little Alyssa as well as you and Archippe. Mother has promised Sicinnus that he and his family will have happiness. But that does not mean their lives will always be easy. Nor does it mean that his mortal friends are of no importance in helping him attain that happiness. Gods and goddesses can do only so much. Do you follow my words, Themistocles?"

Themistocles gasps and says, "You are Persephone—Kore."

"Yes, I am Persephone to Sicinnus, Kore to little Alyssa. Mother was amused by the confusion."

Themistocles slowly shakes his head. "This is all hard to believe."

"We tolerate the doubts of some mortals," says the young goddess. "You are wise enough to refrain from disparaging the divinities. Your doubts do not cross over into disrespect. You do not take our names in vain, so your doubts are tolerated and largely ignored. However, there is one very special exception. She believes in you; she is your patron."

"What?" Themistocles is amazed.

"She asked me to convey the second message. It is that your time has not yet come, but it will. You have the ability to look into the future and see what others fail to see. The battle at Marathon is over but the war between your civilizations is not. Your patron wants to assure you that when your time comes, she will be there."

"But who is she? Don't go before you've told me."

"Failing to understand what you should already know—a mortal trait that repeats itself so often. Open your eyes and look up to the dark night and the shadowy trees. Look at the trees that are hardest to see. Look within those trees to where it is even darker. You love your hot smokeless fires with their bright flames, but your patron loves the dark nights. Look into the darkness and open your mind."

Peering up into the trees around them, Themistocles draws a sharp breath and murmurs a name.

Archippe leans close to him and whispers, "What do you see? What did you say? What is she saying about the future?"

"A long story ahead for you and me. And for our people." He takes another breath before continuing. "And for our progeny—forever."

Both Themistocles and Archippe turn to look at the young goddess in the moonlight, but she is gone.

Themistocles looks back up into the darkness. He studies a tree with strong boughs near its top. One of those limbs is vibrating; a powerful night bird has just left. Above the tree, a moonbeam catches a fleeting glint of gold.

EPILOGUE

Ten years after the Battle of Marathon, the Persians return to finish the job. They come from throughout the empire, and Persia's fourth Great King, Xerxes, leads them. His massive army marches north around the Aegean Sea and turns south toward Athens. Herodotus, the "Father of History," says the Persian soldiers are one million seven hundred thousand strong with a cavalry of eighty thousand. So many men and horses and beasts of burden that they drink the rivers dry. Still more Persians come by ship across the Aegean. Herodotus says the Persian fleet numbers over four thousand vessels, ten times the number of Greek ships.

In northern Greece, far from home, Spartan King Leonidas makes his stand at Thermopylae. The Persians shoot enough arrows to blot out the sun. Leonidas laughs and shouts at the darkened sky, knowing he and his three hundred Spartans will fight in the shade and die for glory.

The Persians burn Athens to the ground and slaughter everyone they find, which is not many, because the Spartans' bravery gives the Athenians time to abandon their city. Much of the population retreats across a narrow waterway to the island of Salamis.

On the shore of Salamis, Themistocles, now leader of Athens and still the most cunning man alive, watches smoke rising from his city. Beside him stands Sicinnus, his closest friend. As the two men survey the destruction, they hear rumbling to the north. The noise grows louder until it thunders directly overhead.

Themistocles and Sicinnus listen intently. They know this sound and they have the same question: *What is Zeus thinking?*

Neither of them realizes that three other divinities also are watching and considering the Greeks' fate. Demeter, the Goddess of Fertility, her daughter, Persephone, and Athena, the Goddess of Wisdom and War, will each play a role in what is to come.

Themistocles and Sicinnus will also play theirs. Themistocles still desires glory. Sicinnus still believes glory has no worth. But those differences will matter little when they confront the coming challenge that will be even greater than the Battle of Marathon. What will matter is the commitment they share. Their commitment to freedom.

MYSTERIES OF MARATHON

When a novel involves historical events, we are always confronted with questions of accuracy: What is fact and what is fiction? Are the purported facts thoroughly researched and carefully assessed? To briefly address these questions as they pertain to *Race to Marathon*, the notion of "history" can be divided between the "broad sweep" of events (what basically happened and what are the lasting implications) and the "details" (who did exactly what, when, and where).

The Battle of Marathon's broad sweep is fairly straightforward—the Greeks won an astonishing victory over the Persians in a battle that is widely considered to be among the most significant in all of human history. If the Persians had won, the world's first system of self-rule that we now call democracy would have been crushed in its infancy. Likewise, and even more importantly, the "classical" period of Greece—an extraordinary flowering of arts and learning that, together with democracy, made Athens the cradle of Western civilization—would have ended just as it was beginning. Think of our society without the inspirations of Socrates, Plato, Aristotle, Aeschylus, Sophocles, Euripides, and many, many more.

Although the outcome and implications of the battle are reasonably clear, the details of how events unfolded are not. This is no surprise. The details of historical events are often muddled, and the further back in time we go, the likelier it is that details are lost, confused, or contested. Given that the Battle of Marathon occurred more than 2,500 years ago in 490 BC, it is remarkable that we know as much about it as we do.

So what is fact and what is fiction in *Race to Marathon*? The novel has been extensively researched (so extensively, in fact, the unpleasant term *ad nauseam* applies). Nevertheless, the book is, first and foremost, a work of fiction replete with imagined details. For example, while the great majority of the novel's characters are true historical figures, I invented a few, including Lela and Phar. Most of the dialogue is necessarily fictional, although I gave careful consideration to conversations in order to conform characters' words to their probable personalities and the historical setting. The important storyline about the women of valor in Athens is fictional but based on two historical realities—the high probability that traitors within Athens intended to help the Persians capture the city, and the fact that, with most Athenian men away at Marathon, Athens' defense against such treachery would have depended on vigilant women.

A final and critical point to clarify is that scholars and historians disagree over several key events about the battle. Let's call these unresolved issues "Mysteries of Marathon." These mysteries force a storyteller to make choices. Before we look at some major choices that shaped *Race to Marathon*, it's important to recognize the ancient sources of our knowledge about the battle.

Fifty years after the Battle of Marathon, Herodotus produced *The Histories,* which describes the Greco-Persian Wars (starting with the Battle of Marathon) and their antecedents. Another ancient commentator was Plutarch, a first-century AD Greek who wrote *The Lives of the Noble Grecians and Romans.* A third eminent historian was Pausanias, a second-century AD Greek traveler and geographer who wrote a ten-volume description of Greece. Among these and a few other pundits from antiquity, Herodotus stands, without question, as our most authoritative source for what happened before, during, and after the battle. He fully deserves his "Father of History" appellation, although scholars broadly acknowledge that Herodotus' standards for accuracy fall short of modern norms. He tended to exaggerate here and embellish there.

And, as we'll see, sometimes he was simply wrong.

~◦

How were the opposing armies lined up on the battlefield?

Two very different battlefield orientations are used to explain how the Greek and Persian armies lined up and faced each other. One places the Persians with their backs to the sea (the Bay of Marathon). The other approach shifts the orientation ninety degrees so the Persians' backs were to the Great Marsh, with the Persian left flank and the Greek right flank near the sea. *Race to Marathon* uses this second approach for two reasons. (See the map of Marathon near the beginning of the novel.)

First, lining up with their backs to the sea would have made the Persians unnecessarily vulnerable. If forced backward, they would have found themselves in the water. Granted, the Persians would have been supremely confident because of their overwhelming numbers, but no commander worth his salt would have casually positioned his troops in a weakened position. And while it is also true that the Great Marsh would be dangerous if the Persians were forced into it, the clear threat of the sea would have been far more obvious and ominous.

Second, Pausanias tells us that a multitude of Persians died in the Great Marsh. After reviewing the map of Marathon (including the location of the Great Marsh, the moored Persian ships, and the narrow beach leading to the ships), it is difficult to make sense of Pausanias' observation if the Persians lined up with their backs to the sea, but his statement makes perfect sense if the Persians had their backs to the Great Marsh.

Who was the leader of the Greeks?

Herodotus says that Miltiades led the Greeks at Marathon. But Herodotus also acknowledges that Callimachus was the "warleader"

(Polemarch). These seemingly conflicting observations are not easily resolved.

During this time, the command structure of the Greek military was not rigidly hierarchical. On the battlefield, some decisions were the responsibility of ten generals plus the warleader. Nevertheless, the warleader was more than just "the first among equals." He had a potent direct and indirect influence on battlefield decisions, although that influence was not always clearly defined (nor easily understood today).

The many experts who argue that Miltiades was the "real" leader frequently base their contention on a simple fact—Herodotus said so. And the issue here is not one of exaggeration or embellishment. Either Herodotus was right or he was wrong. Supporters of Miltiades as the leader also contend that the role of the warleader was primarily ceremonial and emphasized religious sacrifices and interpretations of omens more than military leadership.

However, there are compelling counterarguments. Those who say Callimachus was the leader contend that the transition of the warleader's role to more symbolic functions began *after* this battle. Thus, they argue, Callimachus' position as warleader at Marathon meant he was, in effect, the commander-in-chief.

Supporters of Callimachus also make other persuasive arguments. Callimachus was killed at Marathon, and his death left a void that Miltiades might have filled fairly easily, in light of the vagaries of Greek military leadership and especially if Miltiades had been second-in-command (as postulated in *Race to Marathon*). Also, prior to the battle, Miltiades had only recently returned from a long stay in foreign lands where, for some years, he was aligned with the Great King of Persia, which helped establish Miltiades' reputation for duplicity. This would make him a questionable candidate for leading the Greeks in a life-and-death struggle against the very same Great King. And because of the severity of their situation, the Greeks would have wanted to be sure their leader was unquestionably qualified, experienced, and highly regarded. Such a man would have been Callimachus, not Miltiades.

But if the Greek leader at Marathon was Callimachus, why would Herodotus say it was Miltiades? Perhaps because of the political environment in Athens when Herodotus was producing *The Histories*, some fifty years after the battle. He would have presented his works as oral history, and presumably their popularity, and in turn, his own, would have been important to him for all the normal reasons, including the potential for financial gain. That popularity would have been influenced by the powerbrokers of Athens. One of the most formidable leaders was none other than the son of the late Miltiades—Cimon (also Kimon, ca. 510–450 BC). Cimon was engaged in a strenuous effort to rehabilitate his father's reputation. There would have been no better way to win favor with Cimon than to help persuade the people of Athens that Miltiades had led the Greeks to their glorious victory at Marathon.

What happened to the Persian warhorses?

Ancient sources as well as modern historians have proposed wide-ranging estimates of the number of Persian warriors at the Battle of Marathon, from a low of around twenty thousand to well over half a million. (*Race to Marathon* postulates that the Persian fighters totaled forty thousand—a reasonably conservative estimate.) As for the Persian cavalry, most modern historians put the number of warhorses in the neighborhood of one thousand. (During this period, the Greeks made very little use of cavalry, in part because so much of their land was too rugged to be suitable for horses. The flat plain and beach of Marathon, however, were perfect for them.)

It's hard to overstate the significance of the Persian cavalry. The warhorses could race back and forth along the adversaries' flanks while the riders shot lethal arrows one after another, all while staying beyond the range of enemy spears. The Persian cavalry could seriously weaken and sometimes even devastate an enemy before their infantries clashed.

If the Greeks had faced the Persian cavalry, they might well have lost. But the Persians did not use their warhorses at Marathon. It's as if the horses, one of the Persians' greatest fighting strengths, somehow disappeared.

What happened to them? The best answer, arguably, is revealed in Chapters 33 and 37.

Did the Greeks really charge the Persian army at a full sprint?

"The Charge," described in Chapter 38, is the last mystery we'll consider. Scholars have sometimes twisted themselves into knots trying to explain it. Herodotus says that, on the battlefield, the Greeks sprinted one mile before they clashed with the Persians. Herodotus, the "Father of History," was wrong.

Herodotus' claim has been tested and proven impossible. University professors used their best male student athletes to reenact "The Charge" wearing seventy pounds of bronze armor or equivalent weight (which actually would have been less burdensome for most modern-day male athletes than for ancient Greek men who, on average, weighed only one hundred and fifty pounds). Many of the college athletes could not complete the run. Of the men who did finish, most could barely remain standing, much less fight for their lives. Keep in mind that the majority of Greeks were farmers by trade; they were tough as nails, to be sure, but they were not trained runners or military professionals. (Sparta was the only Greek city-state with large numbers of military professionals, but the Spartans were not at Marathon.)

Some experts say that perhaps the Greeks' charge never happened. But this argument confronts two serious problems. First, would Herodotus simply have created such a significant event out of thin air? Possible, but not probable. Second, there is archeological evidence showing that Greek hoplites (soldiers) in their phalanx formations did, in fact, run. Vase paintings created around the time of Marathon unambiguously display such scenes.

Some others who support Herodotus' claim suggest that the Greeks' armor and weapons (their panoply) may have been lighter than the generally accepted estimate of seventy pounds (an estimate based on panoplies recovered from Greek archeological sites). However, to make a real difference in the Greeks' ability to run a mile in battle-dress, their armor and weapons that day would have had to be substantially lighter. Light armor would have provided far less protection against the enemy's spears and swords. Given how obvious the lopsided odds against the Greeks were before the battle, it is difficult to imagine that they would have chosen lighter armor and, in effect, given up one of their most important assets.

So what actually happened? The most likely answer is that the Greeks did, indeed, make a running charge, but did not run as far as Herodotus said. In other words, this is an example of Herodotus' tendency to exaggerate.

How far did the Greeks actually run? The Greek leaders were no fools. They and their men would have run for a reason, and the distance would have been carefully considered. Well before the battle, all ten thousand Greeks would have streamed down from the hills and formed up as the Persians watched and prepared, so the element of surprise would not have been a factor and running a full mile would have accomplished nothing. Good answers to why and how far the Greeks charged must be tightly linked, as envisioned in Chapters 26, 31, and 38, plus the Glossary entry for "hoplitodromos."

The story of *Race to Marathon* is built from certain choices among these mysteries, as well as detailed research. Perhaps your choices would differ. But we do know the outcome, and a conclusion worth considering is that this particular victory against overwhelming odds did more than save the ancient Greeks. Their triumph made possible everything that has happened since.

Jay Greenwood, 2018

GODDESSES, GODS, MORTALS, PLACES, AND TERMS

Unless specifically identified here as fictional, all of the characters and references (except for nicknames) are based on historical records or recognized myths. However, we know little about many of the characters' actual personalities. Dates, including years of birth and death, may be approximate.

Achilles. Mythological hero in Homer's *Iliad*. Achilles is portrayed as the greatest Greek warrior of the Trojan War, whose wrath was matched by no other man.

acropolis. Literally, "upper city." A settlement built atop a hill in the middle of a city-state, it often served as a showcase for monuments and, when necessary, a citadel. The most famous acropolis was in Athens, site of the Parthenon. (The Parthenon was built during the classical period of Greece, after the Battle of Marathon. The classical period is commonly considered to have extended either from the beginning of democracy in Athens in 508–507 BC, or from the Battle of Marathon in 490 BC, until the death of Alexander the Great in 323 BC.)

Aegean Sea. An arm of the eastern Mediterranean Sea that separates the Greek mainland from the western edge of the former Persian Empire, modern-day Turkey.

Aeschylus (525–456 BC). Known as the "Father of Tragedy," he was the first of the renowned trio of ancient Greek tragic playwrights, which also included Sophocles and Euripides. Many literary scholars say the quality of these tragedians' work was unrivaled until Shakespeare began to write. Aeschylus fought at Marathon. Although his literary accomplishments brought fame during his lifetime, his epitaph, which he likely wrote himself, reveals other priorities and provides insight into the ancient Greeks' minds:

> *Beneath this stone lies Aeschylus, the Athenian, son of Euphorion,*
> *Who died in Gala's wheat-growing land.*
> *His glorious valor the hallowed Plain of Marathon can tell,*
> *And the long-haired Persians know it well.*

Also see arete (valor) and kleos (glory).

agora (AG-er-uh). The "gathering place" of a Greek city-state, which served as the marketplace for merchants and the center of commercial and (in Athens) political life. According to Herodotus, when Cyrus the Great, founder of the Persian Empire, first heard of the agora, he dismissed the Greeks, saying he had nothing to fear from a people who set aside a special place to "tell lies and cheat one another."

Ahura Mazda. The Wise Lord of one of the world's oldest religions, Zoroastrianism. Ahura Mazda is associated with the cult of Holy Fire, Atar, which symbolizes the victory of Truth over Evil. See also Atar, Magi, Zoroaster, and Zoroastrianism.

Ajax. Mythical Greek warrior in Homer's *Iliad*; his fighting prowess was second only to that of Achilles.

Alcmaeonid (alk-ME-ah-nid). The Alcmaeonids were an influential noble family in Athens. Cleisthenes (6th century BC), the founder of democracy, was an Alcmaeonid.

Alyssa. Fictional daughter of Sicinnus and Lela.

amphora (AM-for-ah). A two-handled jug with a narrow neck, used to carry wine or oil.

Aphrodite. Greek Goddess of Love and Beauty. Known to the Romans as Venus.

Apollo. Greek God of Prophecy, Medicine, Music, and Poetry. Associated with truth and other noble attributes. Twin brother of Artemis, Goddess of the Hunt. Because of his moral nature, complexity, and diverse patronage, Apollo is considered the "classic" Greek god. He is the only member of the twelve Olympians whose name the Romans did not change when they adopted the Greek pantheon of gods and goddesses as their own.

Arcadia. A region in the central Peloponnesus (southern Greece). Arcadia was the realm of Pan, God of the Wild Woods. South of Corinth and north of Sparta, Arcadia was relatively isolated and a forested, pastoral wilderness.

Archeptolis (Arch) (ar-KEP-tol-us) (ark). Son of Themistocles and Archippe.

Archippe (Archi) (AR-kih-pee) (ARK-ee). Wife of Themistocles. Aside from the fact that Archippe had several sons and daughters by Themistocles, we know next to nothing about her. According to Plutarch (1st century AD), Archippe was the daughter of Lysander of the deme (subdivision) Alopece, which was part of Athens. It is unlikely that Archippe came from a family of significant influence. (Neither did Themistocles).

Ares. Greek God of War. Ares was associated with the violent aspects of war, whereas Athena, the Goddess of War, was associated with strategic acumen. Ares was known to the Romans as Mars.

arete (AR-eh-tay). The complex Greek word for valor. It had multiple connotations in addition to bravery or courage, including moral virtue, excellence, and fulfillment of purpose. From the time of Homer or before, arete applied to women as well as to men—a view held by the Greeks that existed nowhere else in the ancient world.

Aristides (AR-ih-STIDE-eez) (530–468 BC). Renowned for his honesty and referred to as "Aristides the Just." Herodotus described him as the most honorable man in Athens. Aristides fought at Marathon as the military leader of his Antiochis tribe (see tribes of Athens). Aristides and Themistocles were lifelong friends and rivals. The relationship of these two powerful and influential Athenians must have been complex. Their friendship and mutual respect appear to have been genuine, but their rivalries seemed to intensify as they got older and eventually posed serious threats to each other.

Arrichion (the Elder) (uh-REE-kyun) (died 564 BC). Three-time champion of the Olympian Games in the always dangerous and sometimes deadly sport of pankration that included boxing, wrestling, kicking, strangling, and breaking of bones. Arrichion was victorious in the 52nd (572 BC), the 53rd (568 BC), and the 54th (564 BC) Olympian Games. In his final victory, Arrichion died in the ring an instant after his opponent conceded defeat.

Arrichion (the Younger) (uh-REE-kyun). Fictional great-grandson of Arrichion the Elder, and Kye's partner in the story.

Artemis (ARE-tah-mis). Greek virgin Goddess of the Hunt. Associated with wild lands and animals and the moon. Twin sister of the god Apollo. Artemis was known to the Romans as Diana.

Atar (AH-tar). The Holy Fire of one of the world's oldest religions, Zoroastrianism. Atar plays a complex role in Zoroastrianism. Perhaps most significantly, Atar represents the nature of the Wise Lord, Ahura Mazda, who gave humans his flaming fire of pure and good thought. Atar further symbolizes Truth and Light that will dominate over Evil and Darkness. See also Ahura Mazda, Magi, Zoroaster, and Zoroastrianism.

Athena. Greek virgin Goddess of Wisdom and War. At birth, Athena emerged from the head of Zeus fully grown and wearing a complete set of armor. During war, Athena was renowned for calm strategy as opposed to Ares, the God of War, who represented the brutality of battle. Athena was the patron of Athens. Known to the Romans as Minerva.

Attica. An area of Greece that included Athens and a large swath of land primarily to the north and dominated by the city. While not synonymous, Attica and Athens were closely associated with each other.

Babylon. Based on its political influence, its physical grandeur, and its history of more than 4,000 years, Babylon was arguably the greatest city of the ancient world. Babylon was located in Mesopotamia next to the Euphrates River (in present-day Iraq). For centuries Babylon was assumed to be impregnable, with defensive walls over 300 feet high and 80 feet thick. In 539 BC, the founder of the Persian Empire, Cyrus the Great, proved that assumption wrong when he conquered the city. Exactly how Cyrus defeated Babylon is uncertain, but the diversion of the Euphrates (as described in our story) is a likely explanation.

barbarian. To ancient Greeks a barbarian was anyone who did not speak Greek; instead they spoke an unintelligible "bar-bar-bar." To the Greek ear, a speaker of any non-Greek language seemed to be stammering or babbling.

Battle of Marathon. Fought in 490 BC, sometime between mid-August and mid-September. Considered by historians to be one of history's most important battles; if the Greeks had lost, the classical period of Greece almost certainly would have been stifled at birth. The Battle of Marathon was the first Persian assault on the Greeks. The Athenians, supported by a small contingent of hoplites (soldiers) from the city-state of Plataea, were heavily outnumbered, and appeared to have no chance of victory. Phidippides' celebrated 26-mile run from the battlefield to Athens to announce the Greek victory is the basis for marathon races of today. The second assault of the Greco-Persian Wars began 10 years later and, after a series of major battles, ended in 479 BC.

Belshazzar (bel-SHAZ-ar). Probably died 539 BC. Belshazzar was the son of the last king of Babylon, Nabonidus. Belshazzar ruled Babylon for many years while his father lived in the distant oasis of Taymar. Belshazzar witnessed "writing on the wall" by a disembodied hand that, according to the Old Testament, Daniel interpreted as the judgment and prediction of Yahweh (the God of the Hebrews) that the fall of Babylon was imminent. Cyrus the Great of Persia conquered Babylon shortly thereafter. See also Nabonidus.

Callimachus (ka-LIM-ah-kus) (died 490 BC). The warleader (Polemarch) of the Athenians at the Battle of Marathon. Scholars disagree over the identity of the true leader of the Athenians at Marathon—whether it was Callimachus or Miltiades. Our story posits that Callimachus was the true leader (or the "first among equals," along with ten other Athenian generals) and Miltiades was second-in-command.

Callixenus (ka-lik-ZEN-us). Ostracized (banished) from Athens after the Battle of Marathon, as was Magacles. Historians believe but are not certain that both men were traitors who supported the former Tyrant of Athens, Hippias.

Cambyses (cam-BYE-seez) (died 522 BC). The second Great King of the Persian Empire and son of the empire's founder, Cyrus the Great. Cambyses extended the empire to include Egypt and the Nile Valley.

Carnea (CAR-nyuh). A religious festival in honor of Apollo and the most important annual festival of Sparta, a city-state renowned for its conservatism and religiosity as well as its militaristic social organization.

Caspian Sea. The world's largest lake, located in the north-central portion of the Persian Empire (currently surrounded by Azerbaijan, Iran, Kazakhstan, Russia, and Turkmenistan). The Caspian Sea is east of the Black Sea and west of the Aral Sea. All of these major bodies of water (along with the Indian Ocean and Persian Gulf to the south and the Mediterranean Sea and Red Sea to the west) abutted the vast Persian Empire.

cave of Eleusis (e-LOO-sis). A mysterious cave in the sanctuary of Eleusis, fourteen miles west of Athens. Many ancient Greeks believed this cave provided an entryway to the Underworld ruled by Hades. See also Eleusis.

Charadra River (cha-RAD-rah). A main source of fresh water for the plain of Marathon and the Great Marsh.

Chersonese (KUR-sah-neeze). A peninsula in southern Thrace far to the northeast of Athens, close to the western edge of the Persian Empire. Long before the Battle of Marathon, the Chersonese was an Athenian colony ruled by the family of Miltiades. A few years before the Battle of Marathon, the Persian king Darius the Great advanced on the Chersonese. After a period of allegiance to Darius, Miltiades returned to Athens. See also Hellespont.

city-state. An ancient Greek city and its surrounding territories, combining the concepts of city and country. Each city-state was independent of other city-states. Individuals did not consider themselves residents of "Greece" because Greece as a single political unit or country did not yet exist. Individuals were residents of a particular city-state or a city-state's nearby territory. Instead of nationhood, the unifiers for ancient Greeks were language, customs (such as the Olympian Games), and religion.

Cleisthenes (KLISE-theh-neez) (born ca. 570 BC; date and manner of death unknown). Cleisthenes was a member of the powerful Alcmaeonid family in Athens. He served as the archon (highest magistrate) of Athens in 525–524 BC. Supported by Sparta, in 510 BC he led a successful revolt to overthrow Hippias, the last Tyrant of Athens. Shortly thereafter, Cleisthenes instigated reforms in Athens that created the world's first democracy.

Cleo. Nickname used in the story for Cleophantus (KLEE-uf-an-tis), a son of Themistocles and Archippe. According to Plato, when Cleo grew up he became an excellent horseman but accomplished little else.

Cleomenes (clee-OM-eh-neez) (died 489 BC). A king of Sparta and brother of Leonidas, who succeeded him as king. Cleomenes had an aggressive foreign policy that included helping the Athenian Cleisthenes overthrow Hippias, the last Tyrant of Athens. Cleomenes later died under mysterious circumstances, perhaps suicide caused by madness.

Code (or Laws) of Hammurabi. The ancient code of 282 laws attributed to the Babylonian king Hammurabi, ca. 1754 BC. The laws were inscribed on an upright stone pillar or stela over seven feet tall, and several copies were produced. Many themes of justice in the Code of Hammurabi are similar to those in the Old Testament, especially the notion of "an eye for an eye."

Corinth. Located on the Gulf of Corinth at the isthmus that connected central and southern Greece, the city-state of Corinth was about 60 miles west-southwest of Athens and 90 miles northeast of Sparta (measured over very rugged terrain). During Homeric times (9th century BC), Corinth was a wealthy maritime power. Even with the subsequent dominance of Athens in central Greece and Sparta in the south (Peloponnesus), Corinth remained one of the most influential city-states.

Corinthian helmet. Named after the city-state, the Corinthian helmet was popular among Greek hoplites (soldiers) during the time of the Battle of Marathon. Made of thick, solid bronze, the helmet weighed up to eight pounds. Although it was stifling to wear and severely obstructed a man's vision and hearing, the helmet provided superb protection for the head and neck. Stiff horsehair crests dyed red and other colors were often mounted atop the helmets to make hoplites look taller and to help deflect blows. With its oval eye-slits and masking of the wearer's face, the Corinthian helmet was intimidating.

Croesus (KREE-sus) (6th century BC). The last king of the land of Lydia (in today's western Turkey), reputed to be the richest man in the world at that time. The phrase "rich as Croesus" memorializes him. Croesus was defeated by the founder of the Persian Empire, Cyrus the Great.

Cynegirus (Kye) (ky-NEG-ih-rus) (died 490 BC). Younger brother of Aeschylus. As depicted in our story, Kye's exploits and death at Marathon are based on Herodotus, but his relationship with Arrichion (the Younger) is fictional.

Cyrus (SIE-rus) (died 530 BC). Cyrus II, commonly known as Cyrus the Great, was the founder and first Great King of the Persian Empire. One of history's greatest military leaders, Cyrus preferred to conquer his enemies through deceit and treachery rather than bloodshed, although he was fully capable of engaging in brutal warfare. Cyrus also was an enlightened ruler of his vast domain and tolerant of his subjects' wide variety of religions and customs.

Darius (duh-RIE-us) (550–486 BC). The third Great King of the Persian Empire. Although Darius I was not a blood relation to the first two Great Kings (Darius usurped the throne after Cyrus and Cambyses), he and Cyrus had similar crucial attributes. Like Cyrus, Darius had superb military abilities and preferred to conquer through treachery and deceit, although he was proficient at using bloodshed to get his way. He too was an enlightened ruler and tolerant of his subjects' religions and customs. He ruled when the empire was at the apex of its size and grandeur. Darius started the Greco-Persian Wars by sending his soldiers and sailors across the Aegean Sea to Marathon in 490 BC.

Datis (DAT-us). A high-ranking general who served Darius the Great as commander of the Persians during the Battle of Marathon. The time and manner of Datis' death are unknown, although Herodotus says Datis survived the battle.

Delphi (DEL-fie). A small city-state located approximately 120 miles west of Athens. Delphi was the ancient world's most renowned religious site and sanctuary. See also oracle, Oracle of Delphi.

Demeter (dih-ME-ter). Greek Goddess of Fertility and the Harvest. Mother of Persephone (Kore). Archeological evidence suggests that in very early times Demeter may have been the Goddess of Snakes. Demeter was known to the Romans as Ceres.

democracy. The world's first known democracy was established in Athens shortly after the Athenian, Cleisthenes, led the successful overthrow of the last Tyrant of Athens, Hippias, in 510 BC. By the time of the Battle of Marathon, Athenians had lived under self-rule for fewer than 20 years. Athenian democracy was "direct," unlike almost all modern democracies, which are "representative." That is, Athenians employed a one-step process to make governing decisions. Thousands of male citizens gathered at least once a month to hear speeches and cast votes, which determined the decision. (The votes of ancient Athenians were secret. Athenian voters dropped pebbles or small pieces of broken ceramic [shards] into urns to designate their votes.) Today, democracies usually employ a two-step process by first electing representatives who then vote on behalf of those they represent to make decisions. The voters of ancient Athens were restricted to citizens, and citizenship was usually restricted to free adult males born in Athens. Women, slaves, and free men not born in the city were not citizens and therefore had no voting rights. These restrictions usually applied to slaves who became free men—citizenship did not automatically follow, although occasionally dispensations were permitted. See also Cleisthenes.

Dionysus (die-uh-NIE-sus). Greek God of Wine. Associated with orgiastic rituals and religious madness. Known to the Romans as Bacchus.

Ecbatana (ek-BAT-ah-na). One of the oldest cities in the world,

Ecbatana was conquered by Persia's first Great King, Cyrus, in 549 BC, and absorbed into the central part of the Persian Empire. Today, the site is the city of Hamadan in western Iran.

Eleusis (e-LOO-sis). A community and shrine located 14 miles west of Athens. Eleusis is famous as the location for the celebration of the ancient world's greatest mystery religion—the Eleusinian mysteries—with rituals that were observed for 2,000 years until they were stamped out in the 4th century AD by early Christianity. The Eleusinian mysteries primarily celebrated the goddesses Demeter and Persephone and secondarily celebrated the god Dionysus. See also cave of Eleusis.

ephebe (eh-FEEB). In ancient Greece, a male youth from 18 to 20 years old. During these years the adolescent prepared to assume the responsibilities of citizenship. In Athens and most other city-states, this preparation included vigorous training to become soldiers (hoplites). However, in Sparta, military training began at ages six or seven.

ephor (ef-OR). One of five elected "overseers" of Sparta. Sparta was ruled by a combination of two kings (from different royal families) and the five ephors. As a general rule, votes of the five ephors determined policy, which the kings then implemented. But the theory of multiple rulers (oligarchy) tended to be confounded by intrigue and internal conflicts.

Eretria (ehr-eh-TREE-uh). A Greek city-state on the southern coast of the island of Euboea off the Greek mainland. When Datis and the Persians crossed the Aegean Sea, they attacked Eretria before proceeding to Marathon. Datis conquered Eretria and killed or enslaved the entire population.

Euboea (yoo-BEE-uh). An elongated island in the Aegean Sea that parallels the nearby east coast of the Greek mainland.

Euphrates River. One of the two major rivers of ancient Mesopotamia. The Euphrates flows southeast from today's Turkey through Syria and Iraq and empties into the Persian Gulf near the junction of Iraq, Kuwait, and Iran. Babylon was founded on the banks of the Euphrates. The Euphrates runs largely parallel to and southwest of the Tigris River.

Euryptolemus (Eury) (yoo-rip-TOLL-eh-mus). Historical son of Magacles. (The nickname "Eury" is fictional.)

Fravartish (frah-VAR-tish) (6th century BC). A ruler of the land of Media, subjugated by the Persian Empire. He rebelled against Darius the Great. After Fravartish's second defeat, his punishment (as described in this novel, based on historical records) was gruesome. Darius was known to be tolerant toward newly conquered subjects who respectfully submitted to his rule, but his "enlightenment" did not extend to subjects who resisted him, and especially to previously conquered subjects who rebelled.

glory. See kleos.

Great King. The most common of many titles given the rulers of the Persian Empire. Cyrus II (died 530 BC), founder of the empire, was the first Great King.

Greece. The concept of Greece as a country did not exist at the time of the Battle of Marathon. Rather, Greeks associated themselves with a particular city-state or its nearby territories. The unifiers for Greeks as a people were language, certain traditions (such as the Olympian Games), and religion. See also Olympian Games.

Hades. Brother of Zeus and Poseidon, Hades was the Greek God of the Underworld. In Greek mythology, the word "Hades" was used for the name of the Underworld as well as for its ruler. Upon death, a person's soul was transformed into an image of the person when alive and then transported to the entrance of the Underworld to be ferried across the river Styx. The Underworld was a place of shadows without physical pain. However, there was emotional pain, or at least depression, caused by the feeling of weakness and separation from life and the living.

Hammurabi (HAM-uh-RAH-be) (died 1750 BC). Sixth king of the First Babylonian Dynasty. Most famous for the Code (or Laws) of Hammurabi. See also Code (or Laws) of Hammurabi.

Hanging Gardens. One of the Seven Wonders of the Ancient World. Probably constructed by King Nebuchadnezzar of Babylon around 600 BC, the Hanging Gardens looked like a lush green mountain with ascending terraces made of mud-dried bricks overflowing with gardens and flowers. The "mountain" may have been a lavish ziggurat or step pyramid. The irrigation system alone was a remarkable feat of engineering. It used a system of buckets attached to screw elevators to draw water from a neighboring river and raise the water up the manmade hill. Until recently there was consensus that the Hanging Gardens were in Babylon, but some scholars now argue that Nebuchadnezzar had the Gardens constructed elsewhere.

Hebe (HEE-bee). Greek Goddess of Youth and cupbearer who served ambrosia and nectar to the Olympian gods and goddesses to keep them eternally youthful. Hebe was known to the Romans as Juventas.

Hecuba (HECK-you-buh). As portrayed in Homer's *Iliad*, Hecuba was the Queen of Troy during the Trojan War, married to King Priam, and mother of Hector, Paris, and Cassandra.

Helios (HE-lee-oss). Greek Titan God of the Sun. Helios is credited with being "all-seeing" (though not "all-knowing" or omniscient). Helios was known to the Romans as Sol.

Hellespont (HELL-ess-pont). A strait connecting the northeastern Aegean Sea with the Sea of Marmara, which in turn connects with the Black Sea farther to the northeast, by way of the Bosphorus (also Bosporus). The ancient city of Troy was located near the entrance to the Hellespont. Today the Hellespont is known as the Dardanelles. See also Chersonese.

helot (HEL-ut). Helots were Greeks of Messenia, an area subjugated by nearby Sparta. While helots were not technically slaves, they were treated like them. Helots could have families (to produce more helots as serfs for the Spartans), but, with few and sometimes no restrictions, a helot could be murdered at a Spartan's whim. The helots of Messenia were the only Greeks subjugated for centuries by other Greeks.

Hephaestus (hee-FES-tus). Greek God of Fire, Metalworking, and Volcanoes. Hephaestus was lame but that did not restrict his abilities as an artisan and metalworker. He was highly regarded, especially by Athenians, because of the practical skills he imparted to working men. Hephaestus was married to Aphrodite, Goddess of Love and Beauty. Known to the Romans as Vulcan.

Hera (HERE-uh). Greek Goddess of Women, Marriage, and Childbirth. As the wife of Zeus, Hera was the Queen of the gods. Well aware of Zeus' constant philandering, Hera was extremely jealous and knew how to make her husband miserable. Hera was known as Juno to the Romans.

Hermes. Greek God of Cunning. Also served as the messenger for other gods, especially Zeus. A bust of Hermes was often displayed on a pillar as a greeting near the entrances to residences and other buildings. These pillars also frequently depicted male genitals. Hermes was known as Mercury to the Romans.

Herodotus (heh-ROD-uh-tus) (484–426 BC). The "Father of History." Barely a generation after the Battle of Marathon, Herodotus wrote *The Histories,* focused on the Greco-Persian Wars and their antecedents. Herodotus is the authoritative source of what we know about that period of Greek history, but scholars agree that he sometimes embellished and exaggerated events he described.

Hippias (HIP-ee-us). The last Tyrant of Athens, who ruled from 527 to 510 BC, when he was overthrown and exiled.

Homer (ca. 850 BC). The first Western poet and creator of two renowned epic poems—the *Iliad* and the *Odyssey*—that are among the greatest and most influential works of Western literature.

hoplite (HOP-lite). Heavily-armed ancient Greek soldier. "Hoplite" is derived from "hoplon," the massive shield a hoplite carried.

hoplitodromos (HOP-lit-oh-DROME-ohs). Literal meaning: race of hoplites (soldiers). A competitive running sport introduced into the Olympian Games in 520 BC, ten years before the last Tyrant of Athens, Hippias, was overthrown and exiled. Olympic sports were usually conducted in the nude, but in the hoplitodromos, contestants wore most of the heavy bronze armor used on the battlefield, except for the cuirass around the torso, and they carried shields, for a combined weight of about 50 pounds. (With the cuirass, a full armor panoply weighed 70 pounds.)

There was no standard distance for the hoplitodromos. The length of the run was usually at least one stade (about 600 feet), which approximated the maximum range of an arrow shot from a Persian bow. The most common length for the race was two stadia, but longer races also took place. See also stade.

hoplon. The shield (aspis) carried by a hoplite (Greek soldier). The hoplon was round (circular) and deeply dished with a convex outer side (to ward off blows from arrows, spears, and swords), and a concave inner side with a hooked rim that allowed the hoplon's upper edge to rest on a soldier's shoulder when it was not in use. The hoplon was three feet in diameter, one to one-and-a-half inches thick, and weighed about 16 pounds. It was made of hardwood and often coated with a layer of bronze on the outside.

Isaiah (the Second). Modern scholars attribute the Book of Isaiah in the Hebrew Bible to three different "Isaiahs." The actual names of the Second and Third "Isaiahs" are unknown. The Second Isaiah likely was a contemporary of Persia's Cyrus the Great; he repeatedly referred to Cyrus as the Hebrews' "messiah" ("anointed one") because Cyrus released the Hebrews from the "Babylonian Captivity" when he conquered Babylon in 539 BC. Their captivity had begun in 597 BC after Babylonian King Nebuchadnezzar conquered the Hebrews. Cyrus' religion was Zoroastrianism, and he was not in the bloodline of the House of David, which was a requirement to be considered a "messiah."

Ishtar (ISH-tar). Mesopotamian Goddess of Sex and Warfare and the most widely worshipped goddess in Babylon. Her primary symbol was the lion.

Ishtar Gate. Dedicated to the Goddess of Sex and Warfare, the Ishtar Gate was constructed ca. 575 BC, on the orders of Nebuchadnezzar, as the main entrance to Babylon. A spectacular sight, the Ishtar Gate is made with bricks glazed deep blue and decorated with bas-relief sculptures of lions, bulls and mythical animals. The gate is huge, about 50 feet high and 100 feet wide. Excavated in the early 20th century, the Ishtar Gate is on display in the Pergamon Museum in Berlin.

kleos (KLEE-ohs). The Greek word for "glory," sometimes translated as "renown." Kleos was the ultimate goal in the life of an ancient Greek man. Kleos meant being recognized, respected, and remembered, hopefully forever. This goal could be attained by demonstrating arete (valor), particularly in war. See also arete.

knucklebones. An ancient game played by children and adults, precursor to the modern game of jacks. The game pieces were made from the knuckles of sheep and goats. Children used five bones and, throwing them into the air, attempted to catch as many as possible on the back of a hand. Adults used four bones and threw them on the ground. Each side of these latter game pieces had a different value and, after a round of 35 throws, the total value of the sides facing the ground was tallied to determine the winner.

Kore (KOR-ee). Kore is an alternative and less common name for Persephone, daughter of Demeter, Goddess of Fertility and the Harvest. "Kore," or "the maiden," emphasizes her persona as a child goddess of vegetation while "Persephone" emphasizes her role as the Goddess and Queen of the Underworld after her abduction by Hades, God of the Underworld.

krater (or crater). A wide, two-handled ceramic bowl used for mixing wine and water.

Laurium (LORE-ee-um) (also Lavrion). A small seaport about 30 miles southeast of Athens. Laurium was famous for its silver mines, which were operating before 1500 BC. Slaves dreaded being sent to work in the mines because of the awful conditions and likelihood of death. In approximately 483 BC (seven years after the Battle of Marathon) a major vein of silver was discovered there, and Themistocles convinced the Athenians to use the riches to finance the construction of two hundred triremes (warships) that became critical three years later when the Persians returned to seek revenge for their defeat at Marathon. See also triremes.

Lela. Fictional wife of Sicinnus.

Leonidas (lee-oh-NIE-dus) (died 480 BC). King of Sparta who, along with 300 Spartans and other Greek contingents, fought and died at Thermopylae when the Persians, led by Great King Xerxes, returned to the land of the Greeks to avenge their loss at Marathon.

Lydia. An ancient realm in today's western Turkey. Renowned for its wealth, Lydia may have been where minted coins were first used (7th century BC). Croesus (6th century BC) was the last king of Lydia. Croesus was defeated by Cyrus the Great and Lydia was absorbed into the Persian Empire. See also Croesus.

Macaria Springs (mah-kah-REE-uh). A source of fresh water for the plain of Marathon and the Great Marsh.

Magacles (mah-GAK-leez). Ostracized (banished) from Athens after the Battle of Marathon, as was Callixenus. Both men may have supported Hippias, the former Tyrant of Athens.

Magi (MAY-jie). Plural of magus. Magi were members of the priestly caste of Zoroastrianism. The Magi are best known in the West from the New Testament's Gospel of Matthew and its description of the Three Wise

Men of the East who, guided by a star, visited the Christ child. The visit and veneration by these three Magi are now celebrated by the Christian holiday of the Epiphany. See also Ahura Mazda, Atar, Zoroaster and Zoroastrianism.

Marathon. Derived from the Greek word for the herb fennel. (1) A coastal plain, including a small settlement, 26 miles northeast of Athens, and site of the Battle of Marathon in 490 BC. Today, the site of the battle retains the original burial mound (called the "Soros") for the 192 Athenians who died there. (2) The 26-mile marathon run, performed as an annual race in many countries. It commemorates the run from Marathon to Athens to announce "Nike" (victory) after the Athenians defeated the Persians at the Battle of Marathon. The identity of the original runner is uncertain, although Phidippides is often cited. See also Phidippides.

Marduk (MAR-dook). Mesopotamian God of Water and Judgement and patron deity of the city of Babylon.

Medes. An ancient people who lived in Media (located in today's northwestern Iran). Herodotus says the equipment and dress of the Medes and Persians were virtually identical. In fact, the two cultures were so intertwined and similar, the Greeks did not distinguish between them. When Cyrus the Great of Persia came to power, the Persians were subjects of the Median Kingdom. Later, Cyrus revolted and defeated the Medes in 550 BC, which was the beginning of the Persian Empire.

Messenia (meh-SEE-nee-uh). An area of southern Greece (Peloponnesus) subjugated by nearby Sparta. The Greeks of Messenia became serfs (helots) who labored for the Spartans. See also helots.

messiah. In the Hebrew Bible, the messiah is anointed by God (Yahweh) as the true king of the land of the Hebrews—the Kingdom of Judah. See also Isaiah (the Second).

mignonette. An intensely fragrant flower that grew widely throughout the Mediterranean region.

Miltiades (mill-TIE-uh-DEEZ) (550–489 BC). Born into a prominent Athenian family, Miltiades spent much of his adult life ruling a far-off Athenian colony in southern Thrace (the Chersonese). Known for his survival instincts and duplicity, Miltiades aligned himself with the Persians but then changed allegiances and eventually returned to Athens before the Battle of Marathon. Herodotus says Miltiades was the main leader of the Greeks at Marathon, but some scholars persuasively argue that Miltiades was more likely the second-in-command to Callimachus, the warleader or Polemarch.

Mount Olympus. See Olympus.

Nabonidus (NAB-ah-NIE-dus). Last king of Babylon, who reigned from 556 to 539 BC. For many years Nabonidus effectively abandoned Babylon to live in the distant oasis of Tayma while leaving his son, Belshazzar, to rule Babylon. The reason Nabonidus left Babylon is unknown, but it may have been due to his worship of the moon-god, Sin. Such worship would have been vehemently opposed by the priests and worshipers of Marduk, the longstanding patron god of Babylon. Nabonidus returned to Babylon sometime before 539 BC when Cyrus the Great of Persia conquered Babylon. The fate of Nabonidus is unknown. See also Belshazzar.

naiad. A nymph of a river or spring. See also nymph.

Nebuchadnezzar (NEB-uh-kad-NEZ-er) (died 562 BC). Babylonian

King Nebuchadnezzar II constructed a large number of extraordinary edifices in and near Babylon, including the Hanging Gardens, the Ishtar Gate, a third high defensive wall around the entire city, and another key defensive barrier known as the Median Wall that stretched between the Tigris and Euphrates rivers north of the city. In addition, he reconstructed the Temple of Marduk (also known as the Esagila), dedicated to the supreme god and patron of Babylon. Nebuchadnezzar conquered Jerusalem in 586 BC and destroyed the First Temple of Jerusalem, which, according to the Old Testament, was constructed by King Solomon in 957 BC. The Temple was an extremely holy site where Hebrews could properly sacrifice to their God, Yahweh. Nebuchadnezzar also enslaved large numbers of Hebrews and deported them in bondage to Babylon, an event that became known as the "Babylonian Captivity." See also Hanging Gardens, Ishtar Gate, Temple of Jerusalem, Temple of Marduk.

Nike (NIE-kee). Greek winged Goddess of Victory. The words "Nike" and "victory" often are used interchangeably. Nike was known to the Romans as Victoria.

nymph. In Greek mythology, a young and enticing female deity associated with nature, including the fresh and pure water of springs and rivers (fresh water nymphs are called naiads), the sea (dryads), and flowers, trees, lakes, and mountains.

Odysseus. Mythical protagonist of Homer's *Odyssey*. After spending 10 years as one of the Greek leaders fighting in the Trojan War (described in Homer's *Iliad*), Odysseus spent another 10 years struggling to return home to Ithaca (the subject of the *Odyssey*). See also Homer, Trojan War.

Olympia. Olympia is the home of the Olympian Games, in southern Greece (Peloponnesus), not to be confused with Olympus, home of the gods and goddesses, in northern Greece. See also Olympian Games.

Olympian Games. The Olympian Games were Pan-Hellenic (involving all Greeks) athletic games and contests of choral poetry and dance. The games were held every four years at Olympia in southern Greece (Peloponnesus), in honor of Zeus. The games began in 776 BC and ended in AD 393 when they were banned as "pagan" by Theodosius the First, a Roman Emperor renowned for his devotion to Christianity and disregard for the pre-Christian heritage of Greece.

Olympians or Olympian gods. The ancient Greek religion was polytheistic and the full pantheon consisted of well over one hundred gods and goddesses. Twelve of these divinities were supreme and closely associated with Zeus, who ruled the universe from Mount Olympus in northern Greece. (The Olympians' rule had limits. The gods and goddesses had to respect the dictates of the Fates—three white-robed female beings who controlled everyone's destiny. Even mighty Zeus had to defer to the Fates.) The twelve supreme Olympians were, in alphabetical order (the names in parentheses are Roman equivalents): Aphrodite (Venus), Apollo (Apollo), Ares (Mars), Artemis (Diana), Athena (Minerva), Demeter (Ceres), Dionysus (Bacchus), Hephaestus (Vulcan), Hera (Juno), Hermes (Mercury), Poseidon (Neptune), and Zeus (Jupiter). For non-Olympian divinities in the story who have different Roman names, see Hebe, Helios, Pan, and Persephone. See also Aphrodite, Apollo, Ares, Artemis, Athena, Demeter, Dionysus, Hephaestus, Hera, Hermes, Poseidon and Zeus.

Olympus or Mount Olympus. Olympus, home of the Greek gods and goddesses, is a 9,570-foot mountain near the northeast coast of Greece and the Aegean Sea. It is not to be confused with Olympia, home of the Olympian Games, in southern Greece.

oracle. (1) A prophecy or prediction, often a vague, enigmatic response to a question that is easily misinterpreted. (2) A person, often a priestess, who gives the enigmatic response. (3) A sacred place or shrine where the priestess makes her prophecy. See also Delphi, Oracle of Delphi.

Oracle of Delphi. Located 120 miles west of Athens, the Oracle of Delphi was the principal shrine of Apollo and one of the ancient world's most renowned religious sites. Because it was visited by notables from so many locales, it was also a center of great political influence. The oracles or prophecies were made by an entranced and smoke-shrouded priestess known as the Pythia. Her predictions were often vague and difficult to decipher, and were sometimes misinterpreted with profound consequences, including a misinterpretation by Croesus, King of Lydia, which led to his defeat by Cyrus the Great of Persia. See also Apollo, Delphi, oracle.

paean (PEE-un). A song or chant of praise, triumph and invocation, often dedicated to Apollo. The paean was usually performed by a chorus but might also have been sung by Greek soldiers (hoplites) as they marched in their phalanx toward the enemy. See also Apollo.

Pan. Greek God of the Wild Woods. Pan was a joyful god with a goat's horns, ears, rear legs, and cloven hooves. He was famous for his ugliness and amorous pursuits. Pan was known to the Romans as Faunus.

pankration (pan-KRAY-shun). Also pancratium. A dangerous and sometimes deadly sport, a no-holds-barred combination of boxing, wrestling, kicking and strangling. Breaking an opponent's bones was a common tactic, usually starting with the fingers. Pankration was introduced into the Olympian Games in 648 BC. The rules for the Games prohibited only biting and eye-gouging. Spartans, however, objected to these two restrictions and refused to participate in the sport during the Games. The most famous pankrationist was Arrichion, a three-time champion of the Olympian Games, who died in the ring at the 54th Games in 564 BC. See also Arrichion (the Elder).

panoply. Each hoplite's full array of Greek arms and armor at the Battle of Marathon consisted of: (1) a round shield (called a hoplon), three feet in diameter, made of thick hardwood and often coated with bronze on the outside; (2) a spear with a wooden shaft, eight to ten feet long, with a sharp, leaf-shaped metal tip at one end and a metal butt-spike (the "lizard killer") at the opposite end; (3) a short double-edged sword about two feet long, made of iron or bronze and carried at the waist as a backup weapon; (4) a bronze helmet in one of several different styles, most commonly the Corinthian style; (5) a bronze bell cuirass, which was a breastplate that surrounded the entire torso; and (6) bronze greaves that covered the legs from knee to ankle. Greek citizen-soldiers (hoplites) were required to pay for and furnish their own equipment, so their panoplies were not uniform and were often incomplete. A complete panoply weighed about 70 pounds, which was almost half the body weight of an average Greek man. See also Corinthian helmet, hoplite, hoplon.

Parthenium (par-THEE-nee-um). A mountain between Athens and Sparta near the settlement of Tegea in the region of Arcadia. According to Herodotus, when Phidippides ran from Athens to Sparta to seek aid against the Persians, he encountered Pan, God of the Wild Woods, on Mount Parthenium.

Pegasus. The winged stallion of Greek mythology. Usually depicted as pure white, Pegasus sprang from the head of the snake-haired Medusa as she was dying.

Peloponnesus (PELL-uh-pa-NEE-sus). Also Peloponnese. A peninsula forming the southern half of Greece, south of the city of Corinth and the Gulf of Corinth.

Pentelicon (pen-teh-LIE-kon) (also Pentelikon, Pentelicus, Brilissos, Brilittos and Penteli). A 3,638-foot mountain situated between Athens and Marathon. At the time of the Battle of Marathon, there were two routes between Athens and Marathon. The main route circumvented Mount Pentelicon to the south. A slightly shorter and much rougher path circumvented the mountain to the north. Mount Pentelicon was renowned for its beautiful marble, which was used at numerous sites in Athens, including the Parthenon on the acropolis after the Persians destroyed the older city ten years after the Battle of Marathon.

Persephone (per-SEF-eh-nee). Mythological daughter of Demeter, Goddess of Fertility, and Zeus, God of the Sky and Thunder. Persephone was abducted by Hades, whereby she became Queen of the Underworld. The four seasons were created to accommodate Hades' demand that Persephone spend every winter with him in the Underworld, as a condition for allowing her to spend the other nine months of spring, summer, and autumn with her mother. (There is scholarly debate over whether she spent three or four months in Hades every year.) Persephone was known to the Romans as Proserpina. See also Kore.

Persian Empire. At the time of the Battle of Marathon, the Persian Empire contained approximately 44 percent of the earth's population. In terms of today's countries, the heart of the Persian Empire was Iran and Iraq. At its zenith during the reign of the third Great King, Darius the Great (550–485 BC), the Persian Empire included all or parts of the following modern-day countries: Afghanistan, Armenia, Azerbaijan, Bahrain, Bulgaria, China, Egypt, Georgia, India, Israel, Jordan, Kazakhstan, Kuwait, Kyrgyzstan, Lebanon, Libya, Macedonia, Pakistan, Palestine,

Qatar, Romania, Russia, Saudi Arabia, Syria, Tajikistan, Turkey, Turkmenistan, United Arab Emirates, and Uzbekistan.

petteia (pah-TEE-ah). A very ancient game with similarities to a combination of chess and checkers. The game was most often played on a board with a total of 64 squares (the board had eight rows consisting of eight squares within each row, like modern checker and chess boards). Each of the two opponents started with eight flat stones. The objective was to eliminate all of the opponent's stones by sandwiching them between one's own. The complicated game could last for hours and require intense concentration. Homer wrote that the Greek warriors Achilles and Ajax became so engrossed in a game of petteia during the Trojan War that they failed to notice a furious battle swirling around them.

phalanx (FAY-lanks). A compact fighting formation of Greek soldiers (hoplites) in which each man's shield protected his left side while overlapping and protecting the right side of the man on his left. A phalanx usually had eight rows of hoplites, but that changed as needed to match the length of the enemy's lines. The men in the first three rows fought with their spears and, when necessary, swords. The men behind them wedged their shields into the backs of the men in front and pushed. When a man fell, he was replaced by the man behind him. If a fallen hoplite did not die of his wounds, he could be trampled to death. The phalanx formation was the key innovation that made the Greeks during the time of the Battle of Marathon the most fearsome fighting force on earth.

Phalerum (PHALE-er-um). Located on a bay of the Saronic Gulf approximately three miles southwest of Athens, Phalerum was the city's main port during the time of the Battle of Marathon. A few years later, at the instigation of Themistocles, Piraeus replaced Phalerum as Athens' main port. Piraeus, seven miles southwest of Athens, remains the city's main port today and is one of the largest ports in the world.

Phar (far). Nickname for the fictional son of Pharandates the First.

Pharandates (the First) (far-un-DAY-teez) (6th century BC). The Persian Empire's satrap of Egypt during the reign of Darius the Great. See also satrap.

Pharandates (the Second) (Phar). See Phar.

Phidippides (fih-DIP-ih-deez) (also Pheidippides). Perhaps the greatest long-distance runner of all time. According to Herodotus, as the Athenians were preparing to fight the Persians at Marathon, Phidippides ran from Athens to Sparta (about 152 miles over rugged terrain) to beseech the Spartans to come to the aid of Athens. Then, with barely two days' rest, he made a return run to Marathon (about 178 miles) to convey the Spartans' answer. Many historians also believe it was Phidippides who, a few days later, ran the 26 miles from Marathon to Athens, announcing "Nike" or "victory" of the Greeks over the Persians. This final run (that, according to legend, killed him) was the originator of the marathon race. See also Marathon.

Phigalia (fi-GAA-lee-uh). A small city-state in southern Greece (Peloponnesus), northwest of Sparta and southeast of Olympia. Arrichion (the Elder), the three-time champion of pankration at the Olympian Games during the 6th century BC, was from Phigalia.

Phoenicia (feh-NEESH-yuh). A very ancient territory and culture located primarily in today's Lebanon and Syria. Tyre and Sidon were Phoenicia's main cities. The Phoenicians were the dominant seafaring navigators and traders by the time of the Trojan War (ca. 1270 BC). Their most lasting gift was the alphabet, which eventually replaced cuneiform and hieroglyphics.

Pisistratus (pie-SIS-trah-tis) (also Peisistratus or Peisistratid). Both a family name and individual name of several Athenian tyrants during the 7th and 6th centuries B.C. The last Tyrant of Athens, Hippias, ousted in 510 BC, was a member of the Pisistratus family. His father, Pisistratus, was renowned for establishing the Panathenaea, the most important cultural and religious festival in Athens.

Plataea (pla-TEE-uh). A small city-state near the north shore of the Gulf of Corinth about 40 miles northwest of Athens. The Plataeans sent 1,000 soldiers (hoplites) to help the 9,000 Athenians at the Battle of Marathon, and were the only non-Athenian hoplites to fight there against the Persians. Also, the last land battle of the Greco-Persian Wars was fought near Plataea in 479 BC.

Polemarch (POLE-march). The "warleader" of a Greek city-state. At the Battle of Marathon, Callimachus was the Polemarch for Athens.

Poseidon. Greek God of the Waters and Earthquakes. Brother of Zeus and Hades and uncle of Athena. His primary realm was the ocean, and he is often depicted with his three-pronged spear, the trident. Known to the Romans as Neptune.

Purple People. The Phoenicians who, among other accomplishments, were renowned for producing the most expensive and beautiful color in the ancient world—Tyrian purple. (Tyre was a major city in Phoenicia—today's Lebanon). See also Phoenicia, Tyre.

Sardis (SAR-dis). The ancient capital of the realm of Lydia (in today's western Turkey). In 547/546 BC, the King of Lydia, Croesus, was defeated at Sardis by Cyrus the Great, and Sardis (along with the land of Lydia) became part of the western edge of the Persian Empire. The 1,700-mile-long Royal Road of Persia stretched from Sardis in the west to the city of Susa in the central part of the empire. Sardis was located at today's village of Sart, Turkey.

satrap (SAY-trap). A provincial governor or local ruler in the Persian Empire.

Scythia (SITH-ee-uh). A large, ancient realm of semi-nomadic peoples, Scythia was north of the Persian Empire (predominantly in today's Ukraine and southern Russia around the Black Sea and Caspian Sea). Darius the Great invaded Scythia ca. 513 BC but did not entirely conquer the area.

Sicinnus (suh-KIN-nis). Slave of the Athenian leader, Themistocles. Sicinnus probably was of Persian heritage and was the teacher of the children of Themistocles and Archippe. We know of Sicinnus because of brief references by Herodotus that identified him as a messenger and negotiator sent from Themistocles to Xerxes during the second assault of the Persian Empire against Greece in 480 BC (10 years after the Battle of Marathon). Remarkably, Sicinnus successfully deceived the Great King twice, which included luring Xerxes and his triremes (warships) into a deadly trap set by Themistocles. Our story's placement of Sicinnus at the Battle of Marathon is certainly conceivable but not based on known history.

Sidon (SIDE-un). A major city of ancient Phoenicia located in today's Lebanon and, during the time of the Battle of Marathon, part of the Persian Empire.

Sin. The God of the Moon in Mesopotamian mythology. See also

Nabonidus.

Siren. One of several sea nymphs who used seductive songs to lure mariners off course to their destruction on rocks near their legendary island. The Sirens were the subject of a famous episode in the Odyssey.

Solon (ca. 638–558 BC). Athenian "lawgiver," statesman, and poet. As a leader of Athens, Solon instituted sweeping political, economic, and social reforms. His laws were substantially more humane than the previous harsh laws of Draco (7th century BC). From "Solon" we derive "solon" meaning legislator, and from "Draco" we derive "draconian" meaning harsh, severe, or excessively stern.

stade. An ancient Greek unit of measurement related to the length of a "stadium" and based on the length of a pace, which varied in different parts of Greece. The most common length of a stade was just over 600 feet.

stoa (STOW-uh). An ancient Greek covered walkway with a roof held up by columns.

Susa (SUE-sah). Among the many capital cities of the Persian Empire, Susa was one of the most important. It was located in the heart of the empire (at the site of today's town of Shush in western Iran). Susa was absorbed into the empire ca. 540/539 BC by Cyrus the Great. The 1,700-mile-long Royal Road of Persia stretched from Susa in the central part of the empire to the city of Sardis in the far west.

symposium. A wine-drinking party involving several men, usually in a private home. Women were excluded except for cultured "companions" (hetaira) and flute girls who provided entertainment. Topics of discussion typically included politics, current events, and philosophy. (One of

Plato's most important dialogues is called *The Symposium*.) Symposiums were usually highly sophisticated, but they sometimes degenerated into raucous affairs. Ancient Greek wine was notoriously strong and almost always diluted with various proportions of water. The amount of dilution was determined by the symposium's leader and, if he miscalculated, the participants' heads and reputations suffered the consequences.

Tegea (TEE-gee-uh). A settlement in the Peloponnesus (southern Greece) in the region of Arcadia, north of Sparta.

Temple of Jerusalem. According to the Old Testament, the First Temple of Jerusalem was built by King Solomon in 957 BC and destroyed by the Babylonians in 586 BC. The Second Temple was authorized and financially supported, beginning in 538 BC, by Cyrus the Great of Persia after he conquered Babylon and released the Hebrews from their "Babylonian Captivity." The Second Temple was destroyed by the Romans in AD 70. The Temple of Jerusalem was a very holy site where Hebrews could properly sacrifice to their God, Yahweh.

Temple of Marduk (MAR-dook). Also known as the Esagila, the Temple of Marduk was completed in its final form by Babylonian King Nebuchadnezzar II, although the temple's origins would have been much older. According to Babylonian belief, the temple was inhabited by Marduk, God of Water and Judgment, the supreme god in the Babylonian religion and the patron divinity of Babylon. A huge complex near the Euphrates River, the Temple of Marduk was considered the heart of Babylon. See also Nebuchadnezzar.

Themistocles (theh-MISS-tah-kleez) (524–459 BC). Renowned for his cunning, political savvy, and legendary military leadership. He seems to have been extraordinarily skilled at the art of persuasion and, when it suited his purposes, deception. He was particularly effective in using the new tools of democracy created after the fall of Hippias, the last Tyrant of Athens, in 510 BC. Themistocles was elected archon (chief magistrate) of Athens in 493 BC. He fought in the Battle of Marathon in 490 BC as the military leader of his Leontis tribe. Ten years later he gained everlasting glory as the leader of all Athens during the Battle of Salamis, which was the decisive struggle between the Persian Empire and the cradle of Western civilization. Themistocles was particularly admired as a hero and exemplar by President Dwight D. Eisenhower. Evan Thomas, in his book, *Ike's Bluff: President Eisenhower's Secret Battle to Save the World,* notes that Eisenhower admired Themistocles' ability to employ his image as a man of the people to overcome the prejudice of aristocrats. This became especially impressive a few years after the Battle of Marathon as the Athenians increasingly transitioned to a seafaring city-state and tens of thousands of commoners (relatively poor citizens, though they could vote) became sailors who rowed the triremes (warships); during this time Themistocles assumed the role of admiral and commander of the fleet. Eisenhower most respected Themistocles' clever manipulations of the enemy, with no reservations about duplicity. Themistocles was a master at lulling the Persians into underestimating the Greeks. Eisenhower believed that Themistocles' insights were every bit as appropriate for modern as for ancient times. See also tribes of Athens.

Thrace. An ancient region located in today's southern Bulgaria and the far northwestern portion of today's Turkey. On a peninsula in southern Thrace known as the Chersonese, the Athenian Miltiades ruled a Greek colony that was eventually absorbed into the Persian Empire. Today, the Chersonese is known as Gallipoli. See also Chersonese, Miltiades.

Tigris River. One of the two major rivers of ancient Mesopotamia. The Tigris flows southeast from today's Turkey through Iraq and empties into the Persian Gulf near the junction of Iraq, Kuwait, and Iran. The Tigris runs largely parallel to and northeast of the Euphrates River.

Titan. In Greek mythology, a member of the primordial family of divine giants who ruled the universe until they were overthrown by Zeus and the other Olympian gods and goddesses.

Tower of Babel. There is considerable scholarly disagreement about the Tower of Babel, including its location, although Babylon often is cited. The Old Testament Book of Genesis mentions the Tower of Babel in the context of the Hebrew God, Yahweh, scattering the survivors of the Great Flood around the world and confounding their speech, thus explaining why different cultures have different languages. While many modern scholars argue that the Tower of Babel was mythical, some scholars believe the tower was a ziggurat associated with or perhaps a predecessor of the Temple of Marduk in Babylon. See also Temple of Marduk, ziggurat.

tribes of Athens. After the exile of the last Tyrant of Athens, Hippias, in 510 BC, the new leader of Athens, Cleisthenes, enacted sweeping economic and political reforms, including the creation of the world's first democracy. To weaken entrenched clan loyalties that invited constant intrigue and power struggles interfering with the proper functioning of democracy and other reforms, Cleisthenes devised several methods to disrupt the status quo, including the creation of numerous "demes" (geographical districts or subdivisions) and ten "tribes" (groups of individuals) to which every Athenian belonged.

trireme (TRY-reme). An ancient warship with three tiers of oars on each side used throughout the Mediterranean. The Greek trireme normally had a crew of about 200 men: 170 rowers/sailors and 30 soldiers/marines. The trireme was agile and fast, capable of sustained speeds of more than seven knots, which allowed a trireme to easily cover more than 60 miles a day and, weather permitting, more than double that distance when necessary. Throughout the Greco-Persian Wars, triremes played critical roles for both the Greeks and the Persians.

Trojan Horse. According to Homer's *Odyssey* and Virgil's *Aeneid*, after 10 years of fighting in the Trojan War, the Greeks sailed away and appeared to abandon their siege of the city of Troy. When the Trojans' investigated, they discovered a huge wooden horse. Believing the horse was a gift from the gods, the Trojans pulled the enormous statue past Troy's defensive wall and into the middle of the city where everyone could celebrate their apparent salvation. Late that night, 30 Greeks led by Odysseus crawled out of the hollow horse and opened the city gate. The other Greeks, who had sailed back to Troy under cover of darkness, entered through the open gate and sacked and burned the city. The expression "Beware of Greeks bearing gifts" is a legacy of this deception.

Trojan War. According to Homer's *Iliad*, the Trojan War lasted 10 years until the city of Troy fell to the Greeks (Mycenaeans); this is believed by most scholars to have happened ca. 1270 BC. The Trojan War supposedly began with the abduction (or, more likely, the willing choice) of Helen, wife of Sparta's king, Menelaus, who was taken to Troy by Paris, a Trojan prince. The Greeks went to retrieve the woman now known as Helen of Troy, about whom the English playwright, Christopher Marlowe, wrote in *Doctor Faustus:*
> So this was the face that launched a thousand ships
> And burnt the topless towers of Ilium.

Troy. Site of the Trojan War (ca. 1270 BC) made famous by the *Iliad* of Homer (ca. 850 BC). The city of Troy was located at the modern-day site of Hisarlik, Turkey, close to where the ancient Hellespont (today's

Dardanelles) joins the Aegean Sea. For many centuries after the Trojan War, the city of Troy was lost to history and believed to be mythical, along with the war itself. Then, in the 1860s, English archaeologist Frank Calvert and German archaeologist Heinrich Schliemann excavated a hill at Hisarlik and discovered a series of settlements built on top of one another beginning as far back as 3000 BC. These settlements are now widely accepted as different "Troys" built and rebuilt over time. The settlement designated as "Troy VII (a)" is deemed most likely to be the Homeric Troy. See also Trojan War.

tyrant. In ancient Athens, the era of tyrants immediately preceded the era of democracy. Hippias was the last Tyrant of Athens, and shortly after he was ousted and exiled in 510 BC, democracy began. In ancient Greece, the word "tyrant" did not necessarily have the connotations of cruelty and oppression that we think of today. A tyrant was simply an absolute and authoritarian ruler who was not constrained by dismissible matters such as laws. The term itself implied nothing about the tyrant's character or quality. As time passed, and as the mentality of democracy took hold, the term "tyrant" took on a more judgmental and negative connotation.

Tyre (tire). A major city of ancient Phoenicia located in today's Lebanon and, at the time of the Battle of Marathon, part of the Persian Empire. See also Phoenicia.

Tyrian purple (TERE-ee-un). Tyrian purple was antiquity's most expensive and, according to the ancients, the world's most beautiful dye. A rich and vibrant shade of purple that the people of the Phoenician city of Tyre produced from sea mollusks from the Mediterranean Sea. When squeezed, each mollusk produced barely a drop of the liquid needed. Thus, it took hundreds of thousands of mollusks to produce enough Tyrian purple to dye the garments most often worn by royalty. See also Tyre.

Underworld. See Hades.

valor. See arete.

wine-dark sea. A Homeric epithet describing the Aegean Sea (and perhaps the Mediterranean Sea). Such epithets are common in the *Iliad* and *Odyssey*. Others include "the rosy-fingered dawn" and "Odysseus, the man of twists and turns."

Xerxes (ZURK-seez) (519–466 BC). The fourth Great King of the Persian Empire and son of Darius the Great. Ten years after the Battle of Marathon, Xerxes personally led the Persians back to Greece to seek revenge for the earlier defeat. Xerxes marshalled forces from throughout the empire and, according to Herodotus, the onslaught included 1,700,000 soldiers, 80,000 warhorses, and 4,000 sea vessels. Herodotus said the Persian soldiers "drank the rivers dry" as they marched toward Athens. Xerxes was perhaps the most confident man on earth before he came face to face with cunning Themistocles.

Yahweh. God of the Hebrews. In Hebrew tradition, the name "Yahweh" was considered too sacred to be said out loud.

Zeus. Greek God of the Sky and Thunder. Zeus was the dominant god of the Greek pantheon. He was the "father" of the Greek gods and goddesses, both figuratively and, in many cases, actually. Zeus feared no mortal or divinity, with one exception—his wife, the goddess Hera (although Zeus' wariness of Hera did not stop his incessant philandering). Zeus was known to the Romans as Jupiter and also Jove. See also Hera.

ziggurat (ZIG-uh-rat). A pyramid-like structure with a flat top where in most cases a shrine stood. Ziggurats originated about five thousand years ago in Mesopotamia. A ziggurat often had terraced levels, and the biblical description of the Tower of Babel may have been an example of a ziggurat.

Zoroaster (ZOR-oh-AS-ter) (also Zarathustra) (6th century BC). The Persian prophet who founded one of the world's oldest major religions, Zoroastrianism. Zoroaster consolidated and modified numerous preexisting tenets and beliefs in early Persia to create a religion that still exists today. Zoroaster was a contemporary of Cyrus the Great, founder of the Persian Empire. See also Ahura Mazda, Atar, Magi, Zoroastrianism.

Zoroastrianism (ZOR-oh-AS-tree-uh-niz-um). One of the oldest religions in the historical record. Zoroastrianism was founded by the Persian prophet Zoroaster in the 6th century BC, with roots that predated Zoroaster by 1,000 or more years. Zoroastrianism divides humanity and the cosmos into two opposing groups—the followers of truth, who worship the Wise Lord, Ahura Mazda, and practice the ritual of his cult of Holy Fire (Atar), versus the followers of evil. Zoroastrianism is usually viewed as monotheistic, although its roots prior to the prophet Zoroaster were polytheistic. There is little doubt that Zoroastrianism influenced the Abrahamic religions (Judaism and, later, Christianity and Islam), although the nature and extent of that influence remain the subject of scholarly debate. Today there are an estimated 200,000 Zoroastrians around the world, primarily in India, the United States, Iran, and Iraq. The largest current population of Zoroastrians is in India, especially the city of Mumbai, and members are known as Parsi (or Parsee). See also Ahura Mazda, Atar, Magi, Zoroaster.

ACKNOWLEDGEMENTS

This book is the creation of many people, and a few of them are identified below. Any effort to prioritize their handiwork would be folly, so they are listed according to the alphabet—a script given to us by the ancient Phoenicians well before the Battle of Marathon.

Ann Amberg, provider of webinars and workshops on transformational ecology and producer of terrific book designs; **Christopher Bernard**, erudite editor, author of several novels (e.g., *Voyage to a Phantom City; A Spy in the Ruins*), and founding editor of the webzine Caveat Lector; **John and Nancy Bither**, primal friends and early reviewers whose recommendations were invariably rock solid; **Anne Dubuisson**, top-notch publishing consultant and wonderful editor whose heavy influence felt like a light touch; **Alison Greenwood,** whose role as "project manager" meant she juggled so many balls they blurred, and who supported her wide-ranging insights with a thorough knowledge of social media; **Anna Greenwood,** who offered wise suggestions, including how (and how not) to portray the special emotion of desire; **Deb Greenwood**, the first and last reviewer whose discerning thoughts and sharp eyes made profound differences from beginning to end; **Ryan Lewis**, designer who produced all of the book's striking cover illustrations as well as the interior images and meticulous maps; **Sherry Sherry,** whose admonition "butt-in-chair is how you do it" served as an ongoing reminder that grit makes all the difference; **Holly Thomas**, poet, writer, and fantastic, eagle-eyed editor, who applied her wordsmithing mastery with a surgeon's precision and a poet's insight; **Tom Trimbath**, author of numerous non-fiction books (e.g., *Just Keep Pedaling*) and nature essays, as well as a superb provider of creative consulting services.

Finally, a special acknowledgement goes to **Donnie Garibaldi Jauregui** and **Taylor Greenwood Jauregui**. Children offer us an abundance of inspiration and the highest reasons to think about the future.

ABOUT THE AUTHOR

Jay Greenwood has served as Chief Consultant in the California State Legislature for many years. His professional career has been devoted to writing about complex political issues, including extensive studies of the role of money in election campaigns as well as analyses of legislation dealing with wide ranging subjects. His work has resulted in numerous publications by the State of California over the last three decades. Jay is a veteran of the Vietnam War and, among other awards, he received the Vietnamese Medal of Honor. He has an undergraduate degree in English and a graduate degree in Political Science.